MAYHEM AND THE MARQUESS

EVERNIGHT PUBLISHING ®

www.evernightpublishing.com

MAYHEM AND THE MARQUESS

DEDICATION

To Robert and Valerie—the kind of love that lasts a lifetime is often seen between the pages of books, but the truest incarnation I have seen is between the two of you. I am so very fortunate to have begun my story as part of yours.

MAYHEM AND THE MARQUESS

MAYHEM AND THE MARQUESS

Lords of Havoc, 1

Win Hollows

Copyright © 2019

Chapter One

Leeds, Yorkshire
December 28th, 1840

"Why won't you just go away?" Asher whispered, teeth squeaking from the force of his clenched jaw.

No one answered. That's what usually happens when one talks to oneself, he had found. Twasn't a socially acceptable habit, and a fat lot of good it did him anyways. He should probably stop.

The smokestacks of Leeds on the brightening horizon outside his room's window evoked a more visceral reaction in the Marquess of Blackbourne than most would say was warranted. It was that time of morning when the sky blushed a surreal cast of tangerine over the face of all things. The vast majority would consider it lovely, if one was impressed by the sort of tenacious urbane beauty to be found in moments like these.

He wasn't one of them.

"Your attention is woefully divided of late. Come back to bed," the blonde woman complained from atop his bed's counterpane where she lay in deliberately tempting dishabille.

His heart beat a panicked tattoo under the lawn shirt he hadn't bothered to change from the night before. He always dreaded this part, knowing he would have to obey her command eventually.

Asher smiled briefly at her and looked back at the sharply interrupted sky which both repulsed and kept him rapt.

It had begun again already, more quickly this time than last. Geometric shapes within the outlines of buildings formed in front of his eyes, numbers appearing soon thereafter. Lines were drawn, and equations melted into one another in succession. All angles and patterns were laid bare, and he connected the information into a supposition concerning Leeds's geo-industrial development on the East Bank in recent years. This all occurred in the time it took lightning to complete an arc in the sky.

After his mind had examined and discarded those thoughts, it moved on to calculating the speed of the carriage trundling down the street below, taking into account the measurements between landmarks, the curve of the street, and time it took between those measurements. Just for fun, he threw in the number of times the carriage wheel rotated per second.

He closed his eyes, willing the flashes of thoughts to stop. Sometimes this worked. This time, it did not.

Tendrils of pain began to worm their way through his head and dissolve as quadratics danced behind his eyes.

Shame washed through him. He would not let it win.

A memory seethed to the surface. He had been nineteen years old the last time it had won.

Upon his parents' death in a house fire, solicitors had come to Cambridge for the reading of the will and to bestow upon him his birthright as their only child. But instead of being able to concentrate on the words spoken, his mind had raced behind and ahead, calculating how long it would have taken his family's manor home to burn, solicitor's fees, funeral costs, the time it took to die from smoke inhalation, staff change pensions, the temperature of melting skin, estate management records, and a thousand other things he knew he was now responsible for.

The pain, sudden and sharp, had pierced his mind like an arrow. He had cried out and doubled over, clutching his head and pulling at his hair. Unresponsive to touch or sound, his mind had trapped him in a place where only agony existed, only trains of numbers rushing in, pits of hypotheses and cages comprised of innumerable matrices.

He had been told later that those in the room thought it might be a reaction to the sudden and terrible news. However, it soon became clear that it wasn't grief affecting him, but something else entirely.

Shocked, the solicitors had called for a doctor and a mental competency hearing. His mind had been declared sound but unstable, and so every few months since, eager men in suits would appear to assess his faculties and suitability in governing the Marquessate.

He could not afford to ever let it win.

"Take off your clothes," he said to the woman

through gritted teeth.

An opera singer, she was. He remembered her name—he remembered every name he'd ever heard. Yet he didn't use it.

"Already done, Lord Blackbourne," she informed him in calculated tones.

He turned and opened his eyes, taking in her form. The equations disappeared, obliterated by simple need. He went to her swiftly and laid her back on the bed. She squealed in high-pitched giggles and drew him down. The pain receded as his hands smoothed over her hips, and he pushed aside any guilt he had over the use of her body. She didn't mind, and as long as his head was filled with her heady perfume and tangled limbs, he welcomed the oblivion her lust invoked. For now, he only had to tire himself to exhaustion in her arms to earn a few more hours of blessedly blank sleep.

And tonight, he would start the search for another diversion again after he attended his Society's monthly lecture series. Maybe a brunette next time, to keep his mind busy with the novelty. He made sure they never cared, he reminded himself, sinking into the insensibility of skin and heat...

****

Ivette stopped to rest in the alleyway. She put the handles of the cart down and wiped the droplets of sweat from her brow. Though the night was frigid, she could feel perspiration trickling down her neck and chest. Her small, wheeled handcart of porcelain vases seemed to become heavier by the minute, siphoning the vestiges of her energy more quickly than she could recover.

It was only a little further to go, however, so she took a deep breath and mustered her remaining stores of willpower for the last stretch of the journey to Merchant Fabrice's townhome. He would be waiting for this special delivery, hopefully with a contract soon to follow.

"Chin up, Ivy," she murmured to herself. "You are no withering vine." She snorted at her jest and then sighed as she grabbed the handles of the cart and began pushing it once more.

The darkness of the night didn't frighten her. It hadn't for a long time. Despite her slight stature, her awareness of the city's underworld and the knife stashed between her corset strings quelled any concern she might have had about being accosted in this area.

In fact, it was safer to travel at night in this case. Pickpockets and traffic were much more likely to disrupt her cart during the day, and she couldn't let that happen.

This was going to be her saving grace. After almost two years working at a paper mill in the bustling city of Leeds to survive, she had finally caught her break. When the dye merchant Fabrice Rouleau had seen a painting of a vase she had given to the miller's wife as a wedding gift, he had informed her that she could make them both wealthy with her talent.

"I have connections to the manufacturing designers for Josiah Wedgwood and Sons, and they often contract design work to artists they deemed worthy. I have represented two other artists to them in the past."

Ivette's eyes had grown round as paint pots. "You truly think I could paint for Wedgwood?"

Fabrice had chuckled. "I assure you, if you can design a showcase as good as this painting that meets with approval at Wedgwood, I will offer you a contract. You will be paid handsomely on a regular basis for your work."

Ever since, she had been laboring round the clock after her shifts at the mill to complete designs on the six large vases that now sat in her rented handcart.

"However," Fabrice had warned her, "If the showcase isn't ready on time, there won't be another chance. I cannot waste time or money purchasing more porcelain for you to work with. I need a business partner, understand?"

Ivette had smiled. She understood, all right, and Hell would freeze over before she let this opportunity pass her by. Nothing else was more important than this showcase.

Pulling the cart down the empty cobblestone street, she looked at the numbers on the low stone wall passing by. 2224 Corsair Place, 2226 Corsair Place...

Finally. There it was, right on the corner. 2228 Corsair Place. Mr. Fabrice Rouleau lived here while looking in on his factories.

She would not miss the long days of working the paper press, pulling the large steam-powered stamps up and down and up and down, marking the newly mulched paper with the different stationary designs required for each order. Though she also designed the expensive stationary watermarks that were now associated with the Mill's brand, it was mostly tedious, sweat-drenched days that often turned into nights.

Yet lately, even when she worked more hours than anyone else, she didn't have enough to pay for her boardinghouse rent or enough food to eat. Rents had been climbing steadily since other factories for wool, printing, and iron had been built nearby. Now there were too many people wanting rooms near the industrial center, and she knew that it wouldn't be long before she could not afford to keep her closet-sized room and communal privy. If something didn't change, she would be back on the streets in the middle of winter, a situation she knew from experience could be fatal.

Her neighbor down the hall, Priscilla, said she

should start accepting late-night customers to make rent as she did. The young redhead had told her that, with her abundance of chocolate-colored hair and large blue eyes, men would line up to take her to bed. But the thought of that made her stomach clench. It just wasn't for her. No matter how many times she had to forgo a meal or steal an item of clothing from the morgue's refuse bin, she couldn't bring herself to do it.

Sometimes, she lied in bed and wished there was a man there to just hold her. To keep her warm and tell her that he would make sure everything was all right. The sort of men that liked to visit Priscilla, however, weren't the type that stayed. They never did, no matter how prettily Priscilla spoke to them and did their bidding.

Besides, she couldn't allow herself to be intimate with anyone. Her tainted family blood had eliminated that possibility before she'd ever had a chance to make the decision for herself. Who her father was would forever determine her future.

Tears of relief welled in her eyes. A life of worrying about keeping a roof over her head would soon be over. Each vase had taken her many hours, and she knew the work she had done on them was immaculate. Fabrice would be impressed, she was sure. She turned to maneuver her cart to the side of the walkway, and then swiveled backwards to drag the cart up the white steps of the immense home, anxious to see the man who would ensure her future.

As she turned to face the gate, a large mass rammed into her shoulder, shoving her slight body into the cart at her right and sending it toppling over on its side. As if it took an hour instead of a second, her breath caught, and she watched as the contents of the cart crashed to the ground and shattered.

"No!" she cried, falling to her knees to examining

the shards of pottery. Not one vase had been left intact. She felt her future slipping away as flakes of snow already began to scatter over the intricate designs.

"What have you done?" Ivette sobbed, gathering the broken pieces towards her. Why, she didn't know. They were useless now. She looked up to see a tall, elderly man with a gray beard and glasses standing over her.

"I'm sorry, madam," He squinted at her in puzzlement. "Didn't see you there. Came around the corner too fast, I think," the man said, itching his head.

As if speaking too loudly would summon more doom upon her, she whispered, "You've ruined everything. My life." She indicated the pieces scattered across the damp cobblestones. Ivette looked up at the man who had just quite literally broken her future irreparably.

"I'll pay for it all, never worry. Reginald Morganstern pays his debts," he guaranteed, giving her shoulder an awkward pat.

She met his eyes and frowned. One bushy eyebrow was coming off of his face. She narrowed her gaze on his skin—his remarkably young skin. "Are you—are you wearing a false beard? And a wig?"
****

Asher's hands immediately went to his face. The long gray beard was still intact, as was his matching wig.

"Erm... No, of course not. That would be ridiculous." He chuckled in his best old-man rasp.

"All right," she answered. "But I think you should know your eyebrow is falling off."

"Wha-?" He reached for his eyebrows and found she was right. The left one was dangling with no hope of being put back without more glue. He sighed and took it off the rest of the way.

In his usual dry tones, he asked, "I don't suppose you'll forget you ever saw me?"

She pursed her lips, looking as if she was going to cry. "Not likely, seeing as you have ruined my chance of paying my board and having food to eat and ... and," she waved her hand in a wide arc, tears beginning to fall. "...and not accepting night visitors who won't stay, and I'll probably be cold forever now," she wept, curling into a defeated heap on the walk, one shard of what looked like white and blue pottery grasped in the palm of her small hand.

Asher had no idea what she was talking about, but it was clear he had done something which had grave consequences for her. However, he couldn't be caught dawdling out here any longer. Someone from the British Association for the Advancement of Science lecture might see him, and that wouldn't be good at all.

He had already been questioned about his background last time, and he had made the mistake of making up a family, complete with a deceased wife and younger siblings who also took an interest in science. Now all the patrons wanted him to bring some of his family to the next soiree, and they wouldn't be put off again. He couldn't afford to have any more mysteries attached to his name in the Association.

He crouched down next to her and gently took the piece of pottery from her open hand as she sniffled. "Madam, you'll cut yourself if you continue to handle those shards. Will you come with me to the inn, and we'll sort all this out?" he asked, putting a hand on her shoulder.

She flinched, and her eyes grew wide with panic. "Don't touch me!"

Ash drew his hand back quickly. "I'm sorry. I meant no harm, madam. I truly want to help. Tis only right, wouldn't you say?"

She paused, and he could see she was weighing her options. In the end, her entire being seemed to let go of some invisible string holding it up, and she shrugged dejectedly, which he figured was as good a response as he was likely to get. He put his hands around her slim shoulders and pulled her up, escorting her to his carriage, which was parked only a few dozen yards away. She kept her head down, not seeming to care where she was going.

He positioned himself across from her in the carriage, wondering what he was going to do with her. He couldn't tell much about her from her appearance. Her face was obscured by a mass of tangled hair, and the rest of her was wrapped in a nondescript cloak that had seen better days. No sounds emitted from her now, no movements, as if she'd decided to decline to participate in reacting to the debacle now that it was done.

His stomach churned with guilt as he eyed her huddled form. Asher knew he could easily repay whatever the pottery had cost, and they had looked to be high quality. Being a Marquess with a well-endowed set of estates had its advantages, and one was the luxury of not worrying about paltry sums that might have crippled another man. Offering her a comparable amount should suffice to satisfy her apparent desolation and send her on her way to whatever she had planned.

When they reached the inn, he shuffled her out of the coach and straight up the back stairs to his room, not wanting to embarrass her by having any locals note her presence in his company. Women tended to be put into a certain category after they were seen with a man at an inn, and he didn't want to further destroy her plans, whatever they may be. She didn't protest, letting him push her along docilely till they were safely in the privacy of his rooms and the door locked behind them.

He sighed, watching her still, silent form stand in the center of the sitting area. It was one large room that included a bed on one end and a divan, two chairs, and an already blazing fireplace on the other. The best available, he'd been assured. Still, she looked dwarfed by the surroundings, small as she was.

He realized then that he didn't know her age, her marital status, not even her name. Tugging the wig from his head and running a hand through his dark gold locks, he blew out a stream of air. Time to resolve this matter and get back to business.

He came up behind her and put a hand gently on her shoulder, directing her to a chair near the fire. "Please sit, madam. Would you like me to send for some tea?" He tried to get a look at her face through the matted strings of hair, but couldn't discern anything telling of her features other than that she had them.

She shook her head, keeping her face downturned.

"I would like to see to your comfort while we figure this out, as a gentleman," he insisted.

"None of that matters now," she said quietly, hands curled in her lap.

He cocked his head. "You must care a little bit to risk coming with a stranger to a private room. You aren't afraid of me?"

She did not look up, but spoke to her knees. "No. I long ago learned what sort of man I have need to fear. You aren't him."

Interesting.

"Plus," she added flatly, "If you do try anything, you'll learn quickly I am as skilled with a blade as you are with your silver tongue."

He raised his brows. Now *that* was even more interesting.

He wasn't used to women responding this way towards him. It might have something to do with the fact that he'd supposedly ruined her life, and he looked like a deranged old man at the moment.

Taking the other chair, he carefully peeled off his false beard and remaining eyebrow, setting the accoutrements on the round table betwixt them. Asher rubbed his jawline, making sure no vestiges of glue remained. His outdated jacket came off next, and then his padded waistcoat, freedom from the suffocating clothing causing him to sigh in relief as he draped them over the arm of the chair.

The woman's sharp intake of breath made him glance up.

Ah, yes. There was the reaction he usually evoked in the fairer sex. *Awareness.*

In his disguise, he could be Reginald Morganstern, free from the trappings of his rank, reputation, responsibilities, the ability to use his mind in ways he could never show to his peers...

But as himself, there was always this.

Except, this time, it was he who couldn't look away. Her hair was still covering most of her face, but one and a half vivid blue eyes were riveted on him, wide open and surrounded by dark sable lashes that swept down once she realized she was staring. He couldn't help the primitive reaction of looking into eyes that had more blue depths and shades than his own, which he understood without conceit had considerable draw.

The cacophony of noise in his head quieted for the first time in what felt like years. No numbers, no equations, no diagrams whirled in frenzied loops. Just an ever-changing blue that enveloped and took up all of his concentration.

She recovered quickly. "Who are you?"

He quirked the corner of his lips into a smile. "Why, it's me, Reginald Morganstern," he said gruffly, adopting his alter ego's voice.

"Never heard of him."

He chuckled, mentally calculating the odds of this turning out in his favor. They weren't good.

Even knowing it was unwise, he felt a keen desire to tell her. He had never told anyone this, and yet, for reasons he couldn't fathom, he wanted to tell this woman with the blue eyes the truth. Mayhap it was precisely because they didn't know each other, and they were unlikely to ever meet again. She clearly didn't have contact with anyone in his social circles, so the danger might be somewhat mitigated.

Clearing his throat, he sealed his fate. "Perhaps you've heard of my better-known title—the Marquess of Blackbourne?"

****

Ivette saw him studying her reaction as her eyes widened, and she leaned back in the wing-backed chair. "Sweet Lord Almighty."

"No, just a Marquess," he corrected wryly.

His now clean-shaven face was devastating. Strong and defined as his bone structure appeared, there was a sense of mischief that lit his angular features. His real hair, now that she could see it, was dark gold with a distinct wave to its texture, and his skin glowed with a golden warmth as well, though it was the dead of winter. The paunch around his middle was gone to reveal an impressively fit physique, clearly born out of regular intense physical exertion. Dressed as he was now in only a white shirt and loose black pants that had matched his ratty old man's coat, the lines of his lithe, muscular body were all too clear. No wonder he went about town with a gray beard. If he didn't, he'd leave a trail of swooned women in his wake.

She gulped. What had she gotten herself into? All she had wanted was to make a better life for herself. And when that had gone awry, she hadn't known what to do. All of her work, gone. The merchant wouldn't care about seeing fragments and dust and excuses. Up until the moment she had seen his face, she had been numb, putting one foot in front of the other, not clear what she was supposed to do. She had been almost glad to let him whisk her away in a cushioned carriage and offer to repay her. But now...

"I haven't... I mean, I should go," Ivette said, rising. "I don't belong here."

He caught her by the sleeve of her cloak and rose to tower above her. Now that she was aware of his true appearance, his height just seemed unfair.

"Wait." He looked into her eyes and slid his hand down to embrace hers. "I meant what I said. I would like to compensate you for the contents of your cart."

She could barely think straight with him being so close. Such men weren't even meant to be looked upon by women like her. She decided honesty was the fastest way to leave this place. "You can't. Second chances cannot be paid for sometimes."

"You'd be surprised what money can buy. All sorts of things that aren't normally for sale," he told her, raising a brow.

Ivette's heart sputtered. What he suggesting what she thought he was suggesting? She took her hand from his and backed away. "I'm not that kind of woman," she said firmly.

"What? No, no, you misunderstand," he stepped closer. "I wasn't ... goodness, you must really think me a cad, don't you? I suppose I did knock over your cart and give you a false name, but I can promise that all I want to do is help you." He held out his hands.

She was suspicious by nature, but Ivette really didn't know what to make of him. He was a Marquess, for heaven's sake. She'd never even been within a hundred feet of an aristocrat in all her adult life, much less held hands and spoken to one in their private chambers. What did a man like this want with helping her? He couldn't feel that burdened by her plight, could he?

"If you are indeed genuine, then I appreciate your offer. However, I wouldn't be able to tell you the value of the vases even if I wanted to, my lord. I'm afraid I don't know."

He smiled, and Ivette's knees about gave out. She was out of her depth with this man.

"That's no matter. I've already figured it out," he said matter-of-factly.

"How could you have possibly done so? You don't even know what sort of vases they were or how many they numbered." She didn't mean to sound disrespectful, but her tone was incredulous.

He smirked. "Simple calculation of the average size of the shards, reassembled in appropriate geometric patterns, and the area of the cart, coupled with the knowledge of how much such vases are worth, according to my estate records, and ... approximately four thousand, one hundred and twenty one pounds. But I thought I'd add on a hundred pounds for all the trouble I've put you through tonight." After he'd finished, he blinked and then suddenly blushed, as though he'd admitted to stealing pastries from the bakery counter. "Or something like that," he mumbled, waving his hand to indicate the inconsequentiality of his previous statement.

Ivette stared, her mouth hanging open. Just what sort of man was this? He was turning red over computing sums in his head. How strange. But the biggest question she had was, "Are you offering me four thousand pounds?"

He shrugged. "Yes."

Ivette sat down on the divan and put her hand to her chest to calm her heart. "Four thousand pounds," she breathed, not quite ready to believe it. With four thousand pounds, she could open her own gallery. With four thousand pounds, she would never have to worry about boarding costs or food or clothes again. This could not be real.

"But I must ask for something in return," the Marquess said, sitting down next to her.

Here it came. Ivette stiffened, steeling herself to make the decision that Priscilla had made years ago—her pride or her survival.

She looked straight ahead, not wanting to be affected by the way his cheekbones sloped down to disappear into a chiseled jaw that looked like it was carved from marble. His scent, a subtle blend of tangy pine and amber, wrapped around her senses. She supposed there were certainly worse men to have to give up one's morals for.

She heard him take a deep breath. "I must ask that you never tell anyone that Reginald Morganstern and I are the same man."

Ivette's dark brows drew together, and she shook her head. "That's it?" She turned toward him, unsettled by how near he was.

He frowned in confusion. "Yes, that's it. I can't be having it bandied about that the Marquess of Blackbourne roams England as a batty old mathematician when it suits him."

"And why, precisely, would you do such a thing to begin with?" She was genuinely curious. Men such as he had no need to sneak about town as someone else. They could do whatever they wanted and people leapt to accommodate them.

Blackbourne shifted and looked away, rubbing his palms on his thighs. "It's complicated."

"I gathered." She raised her own brow.

He seemed to like her expression because he smiled a wide, white-toothed grin that caused funny little swoops in her stomach. He dodged the question, leaning back and crossing his arms behind his head, seemingly perfectly at ease again. "I'd rather know about you instead, Miss...?"

Her heart ticked faster. Knowledge was power to this man, and she didn't want to give him any more over her than necessary, although there was a part of her that thought it might be nice to unburden herself to him. "I don't see what that has to do with anything."

"Well, for one thing, I can't even address you as it is. And for another, how am I supposed to direct my solicitors to draft you a bank note if I don't know who you are or what address to have it delivered to?"

This was all becoming too real. He was speaking of actually drafting her a bank note!

Her stomach twisted in guilt. There was no way Merchant Fabrice would have given her even a fraction of that amount for her designs. The vases hadn't been actual Wedgewoods to begin with. She wasn't sure what the right thing to do was, but she would never know if her life could be different if she didn't take what was offered.

Still, there were other considerations. Her identity was tricky in itself. She supposed she did have to give him her name, though doing so would surely change his relaxed attitude towards her. She swallowed, looked straight ahead, and prepared for his censure. "Ivette. My name is Ivette Wollard of the Brandsby Wollards."

The Marquess paused, taking it in. He was silent for a long while, and then said solemnly, "A pleasure, Miss Wollard."

Ivette released the breath she was holding and looked to where he sat in repose. "You don't want to rescind your offer? I wouldn't blame you if you did," she said quietly.

He considered this. "Did you, as a small child, help plan your father's deeds, Miss Wollard?"

A strange lump welled in her throat. "No," she whispered.

"Then I think it would be rather obtuse to blame a person's offspring for someone's actions, don't you?"

A tear escaped, which she swiftly wiped away, hoping he wouldn't notice. "You would be surprised at what people will blame a person for," she echoed his earlier statement.

"They are fools," Blackbourne declared, coming forward to take the edges of her hood and draw it back.

Suppressing a gasp, she met his blue eyes, which were several shades lighter than her own. Touching her hair, she cringed, knowing her appearance did not fit into his world of perfumed and powdered ladies who had maids to brush and twist their hair into beautiful creations. She knew what he saw—matted hair, a dirty face streaked with sweat, and a second-hand cloak that hid any shape beneath. She could barely afford to use soap once every few weeks, she and Priscilla sharing a heated basin of water purchased from the boarding house proprietor when they had extra money.

"Do you want to know what I see?" he asked in a low voice, pinning her with his gaze.

There was no denying she was firmly under his spell as she answered, "What?"

"I see a young woman who has probably been snubbed, mistreated, and rejected by the very people who should have taken care of her when such a thing happens."

She looked down, conflicted by his words. At first, she had thought the same thing. When her father had been arrested and taken to London to be sentenced, not one person of her acquaintance or extended family had offered to take fourteen-year-old Ivette in, and that was especially true of anyone on her deceased mother's side. Not one person had offered food or even scraps to get her by. The local vicar had offered prayers for her soul, but naught else. When she had tried to become employed at the local shops earning any sort of money, no one would let her in the door.

Without resources, she had soon made the decision to sell the run-down cottage left to her and move to the city, hoping her name would not be the deterrent it was in the village. After many months and failures, depleting her meager funds and being told she could not afford to be associated with, the paper miller had overhead her pleading for a position at a seamstress shop, and took pity on her. Ever since, she had worked as hard as possible at the mill, knowing she might never be able to find work elsewhere.

Now, at age twenty-one, she understood reality. Her blood was tainted with evil and decent folk couldn't be expected to treat her with kindness or respect knowing the same madness might one day manifest itself in her. She was a danger to everyone around her, an unpredictable powder keg whose fuse might or might not be lit.

It was why she would never have a family of her own. She couldn't risk others being in harm's way if she did contain the essence of her father's violent desires inside her. No one would be in danger from her if she didn't let them close enough.

Ivette's mouth twisted. "You can say it, you know. I'm the daughter of a murderer. It's not just "such a thing." It's horrific. Believe me, I am reminded of it often enough."

A small indentation appeared on his forehead. "I just think of it as meeting a celebrity of sorts," he said jovially.

She shook her head. "No, please don't say that either. There are people who write letters of admiration to him, letters describing unthinkable things..." She constantly tried to wash away the words she had read, scrubbing her mind clean of the contents of those missives, but the disgusting images painted by their words persisted.

"I am not an admirer," he assured her, covering her hand with his. "I just want to make it clear that I, for one, do not hold you accountable for someone else's crimes."

The warm pressure of his hand on hers was almost too much. No one had touched her in any manner in so long that the sensation felt forbidden. His touch burned with a heat that had nothing to do with warmth.

She slid her hand from beneath his and tucked it into the folds of her cloak. "I am not deserving of your esteem, my lord," she said honestly. She had never done anything for anyone else whilst trying to survive and hadn't gone to Sunday services since the vicar had told her she was unclean. She lived next to a prostitute and rarely bathed, much less used the arts of ladyship she had been taught by her tutor growing up.

He studied her, his eyes roaming her features. He couldn't possibly see anything of worth, yet somehow, a tiny part of her had burst into hope at his earlier words.

She both wanted him to see something in her that was deserving and wanted to shrink away back into the darkness in which she had existed for so long.

Finally, his face bore the barest hint of a smile, as if he'd reached a satisfactory conclusion. "Whoever did something to you to make you believe that you aren't someone of worth should be wiped clean from the slate of humanity and never allowed to speak such blasphemies again," he said softly. Then his tone changed, and he said briskly, "I only hope that, from now on, you will begin to see yourself differently. It's clear that your situation is not ideal for a woman of your standing. Your father was a Squire, was he not? I remember reading about his history in the papers." He leapt from the couch and began to pace in front of the fireplace, the light from behind him outlining his broad shoulders and slim waist.

"Er … yes," she replied, struggling to keep up with his logic and not notice his form through the white starched shirt he wore.

"And so you were raised to be a lady, I assume?"

"I was, until…" she trailed off.

"Yes, yes, of course," he waved her unspoken statement aside, still pacing.

"You'll need a bath," he said absently.

"Excuse me?" she squeaked, shrinking into the cushions of the divan.

"And a wardrobe. Everything, really, if we're to pull this off."

Ivette's heart pounded. "What are you talking about?"

Blackbourne stopped pacing and faced her, looking like a fallen angel rimmed in the light of the fire. "I've decided something, Miss Wollard. You don't need four thousand pounds."

She blinked. This wasn't good. "I don't?"

"No. What you need is a job," he declared proudly.

"I have one of those," she informed him, feeling her pride pricked. She crossed her arms, eyes narrowed.

"I'm sure you do. However ... how do I put this delicately?" he ruminated, scratching his chin. "Your current state of dress and hygiene suggest that your employment situation is not meeting your needs. So I suggest an alternative."

"I was on my way to an alternative when you knocked my cart over," she reminded him acerbically. The nerve of the man! As if she couldn't provide for herself. As if she didn't know her situation wasn't "ideal." It must be nice being a Marquess whose every aspect of life was ideal.

"My apologies. You were selling the vases, I take it?" He didn't wait for a response, continuing his manic speed of spewing words. "Were they family heirlooms? And if they were, why haven't you sold them off long before now? I can't see you having stolen them, to be honest, but one never knows. The fact that you were transporting them at night is a bit suspicious, but also reasonable if you stop to consider the rate of crime in what surely has to be a poor neighborhood at your point of origin. Leeds hasn't been very proactive in protecting their citizens of late, according to the annual reports published by the Home Office. At this juncture, whether they were stolen or not doesn't really signify because they're gone, so it follows that your anticipated income is gone as well, leaving you in dire need of assistance. Hence, my alternative."

Ivette quickly shut her mouth, which had been hanging slack as his train of thought bore out. This man was either mad or brilliant. Perhaps both.

"So what do you say?" he spread his arms wide. "Would you like to go on an adventure, Miss Wollard?"

****

Asher might have come on a bit too quickly. It was odd. He never behaved like this, speaking as fast as his mind worked and proposing ridiculous schemes to women he barely knew. But there was something about this one... Something that made his chest burgeon with a sort of giddy freedom.

She already knew his biggest secret. Well, maybe not all of it, but he'd never had anyone with whom he could share things like this. He could be both Morganstern and Blackbourne at once—minus the beard, of course. It was a risk, he knew that, but he was inordinately glad that the choice had already been made. She had seen through his disguise immediately, and he couldn't have just left her there with her cart of broken pottery. Now that she knew his identity, he could only hope she didn't blackmail him at some point in the future. However, he intended to pay her handsomely for her time in the scheme he'd been developing in the last several minutes, so he trusted she wouldn't need to.

"Miss Wollard?" he repeated after a moment of stunned silence in which Ivette Wollard merely stared at him with saucer-like pools of blue.

She shook herself and pursed her lips. "I think I'd rather have the four thousand pounds, please," she stated.

He came towards her and knelt beside the arm of the divan. "No, no, no, Miss Wollard. If you agree to participate in this endeavor, you would earn much more than that over time."

She threw her hands up, sending particles of filth into the recesses of the divan. "I don't even know what this endeavor is! Your mind is a spinning wheel of death. Do you know that?"

"You have no idea," he admitted gravely. "But I shall tell you that the plan involves pretty dresses, balls, and all the hot baths you want." He winked for good measure—the wink always softened them up.

Her eyes narrowed. "You are awfully sure I need a bath, aren't you?" she spat.

Asher froze. He wasn't used to this level of scrutiny or resistance. Was she one of those women who didn't like men? He supposed it was understandable that she wouldn't trust his gender, given who her father was. But he knew she was affected by him from the shaking of her hands to the blush that flamed beneath the layer of grime on her face. "Not at all," he recovered, knowing there was most definitely a wrong answer to that question. "I just know that women like baths and doing their hair and such," he shrugged.

"I'll bet you do," she said airily, tipping up her nose.

This was going to be more difficult than he thought. And things were rarely that.

A strange euphoria came over him. He had encountered women who needed more persuasion to come to his bed than usual, and it was always a relief. His concentration on them sharpened, and his calculations switched from formulas to human chemistry—the science of seduction. The challenge plucked him from the mire of ever-present numbers and words marching across his mind's eye and let him live for the moment with other people.

He wasn't trying to land Ivette in his bed, but her defiance struck the same chord in him. This called for some unique tactics. Money seemed to be the most persuasive factor in her decision-making thus far. As far as her demeanor, she was an interesting dichotomy of timidity and pluck, so he calculated that playing to her insecurities might just work.

"Miss Wollard, I know that few people have given you the benefit of the doubt, and that it has been hard to hold your head high in light of what people think. Yet the benefit of the doubt and the opportunity to waltz through a ballroom on a cloud of diamonds far above anyone's reproach is precisely what I want to give you."

Ivette's eyes lit up at the picture he painted. Her haughty posture left her, and she slumped down on the cushion. "I don't understand. In what circumstance could I possibly do those things?"

He smiled. "Let me explain," he started, clearing his throat. He rose from his perch near the arm of the sofa and sat in the chair she had recently occupied. "I need a sister. More accurately, Sir Reginald Morganstern needs a sister."

Ivette's face scrunched. "That doesn't explain anything."

He cleared his throat. "I am a member of the British Association for the Advancement of Science."

"That's nice," she commented, patting him on the knee the way one would reassure a child they weren't in trouble.

"However, I must only be known in those circles as Sir Reginald Morganstern. And Reginald Morganstern might have let slip that he has a sister who is a naturalist, so now my colleagues want to meet her. In fact, it was made clear that my standing is now dependent on whether I can recruit the first female member if she is qualified."

"And you want me to pose as your sister at these functions?" she asked with raised brows.

"Exactly!" Now she was getting it.

She laughed, a rather beguiling sound, if he was honest. No mere engineered chuckle for Ivette, but a full-bodied bubbling of pitches that made him want to make her do it over and over until she was breathless with it.

Only, she was laughing at his proposal just now, which confused him. He had reasoned that his offer would be both advantageous and pleasant for her. What did she have to lose, exactly? What was holding her back?

"That is the most ridiculous thing I've ever heard," she stated baldly.

"I don't see how," he replied, folding his arms sullenly. He really never had this much trouble convincing women to go along with his whims.

"I can't pretend to be your sister! Or a scientist!" she declared. "It would be ... it would be..." She gestured, making swirls through the air with her small hands trying to find the words.

"It would be great fun," he interjected, leaning forward. "All I'm asking is that you dress nicely, mingle at a few social gatherings, and attend a few lectures. You barely have to do anything except eat, drink, dance, and nod."

"Sounds terrible," she spouted.

He continued. "And I will give you fifty pounds for each event you attend with me."

Asher watched as she narrowed her eyes, calculating.

"I would, of course, also offer you lodgings, staff, and a wardrobe as needed. And you would earn over five hundred pounds a year if you attend the monthly lecture series and the occasional social engagement." He waited expectantly for her to catch up.

"I know what it amounts to," she said defiantly, her nose in the air again, but Asher grinned.

He had her now. He could sense it. It was the same feeling he got when a woman was about to leave with him for the night after he had expended energy persuading her to do so.

Asher shoved those thoughts away. This woman was not for tupping, challenging blue eyes or not. It wasn't as though he was attracted to her anyways. She was more like a lost puppy—one that might prove useful as an employee. Not as a dog, of course. He pictured her on all fours, wagging a non-existent tail, his mind beginning to calculate how her small proportions might translate into a canine bone structure. Asher shook his head. That image wasn't helping anything.

"Do you know you get this far-off look sometimes like your thoughts exist in another realm altogether?" Ivette said softly, her eyes on his face.

Asher's eyes snapped back to hers, and he stared. She was eerily perceptive, although he figured she wouldn't have appreciated the comparison he had just been thinking of. Then he grinned, partly because of the puppy image, and partly to throw her off of her train of thought. His smile tended to do that to people. "I was just thinking of the piles of money you'd have if you agreed," he said with a wistful look. He added a sigh for effect. This had been a proven tactic in the past as a final ploy, but it usually went something like, "I was just thinking of all the fun you'd have sharing my bed tonight…" And then the sigh. Worked every time.

What he wasn't prepared for was Ivette's non-plussed response of, "You might be just a little bit insane."

"Excuse me?" His perfected beatific expression disappeared. His heart raced, her accusation dredging up the part of him that was always on guard against such perceptions.

She sat rigidly straight on the sofa, her hands folded neatly in her lap as if to keep them from giving her emotions away. "Isn't there someone—anyone—else that you could hire to do something of this nature? An actress, perhaps? Why me?" Suspicion seemed to be this woman's primary functionality.

Asher sighed, for real this time. He slumped back into the chair. "I might be ... shall we say, well-known to the actresses of London. To be truthful, I hadn't had time to think through the possibilities before you were thrown into my path quite literally."

"Imagine that. You, not thinking quickly enough." There was humor in the slant of her lips, which he just now realized were quite full.

She had caught him off-guard again. He couldn't help the upturn of his lips in response. "Believe it or not, I don't always think before I speak," he admitted. "I hadn't anticipated my colleagues in the Association taking such an interest in meeting my fictional sister. Could have something to do with the fact that there aren't any women currently admitted into the society. I don't think some of those men have spoken to a woman in decades."

She didn't seem fazed or insulted by his revelations. "So you want to throw me to the wolves while you prance about doing whatever it is you do at these things in order for no suspicion to arise about your identity?"

Asher shifted in his seat, her lack of prevarication making him uneasy. "Not in so many words, but yes. Hopefully for a long time, if we can manage it."

She nodded slowly. "And what if I choose to take my four thousand pounds now and leave?"

He looked her in the eyes. "Then I will honor what I said, and draft a note to my solicitors here and now." He waited, praying she wouldn't choose that option. For some inexplicable reason he didn't care to examine at the moment, he wanted her near him. He wanted to see what she would say or do next, since it was never what he expected.

As he watched her muddied face, he could almost see the cogs of her mind working to come to a decision. She seemed to be truly struggling, though with what factors she was assessing the situation, he couldn't fathom. Ivette Wollard was an assessor, that much he knew. She was sharp, and she was interesting. Perhaps her mind didn't work as his did, but it was a rare person who made him work to keep up with their cognitive processes. When she let out a breath of finality, he drew in one and held it, waiting for her to speak.

"If we are to do this, we must have some rules, Lord Blackbourne," she announced decisively.

He exhaled, trying not to show his relief. "Of course, Miss Wollard," he agreed readily, keeping his facial muscles stiff to hold back a grin.

She held up a hand and began to tick off requirements. "I would like to be paid in pound notes once a month, I require at least two acceptable dresses and pairs of shoes, and my lodgings must have at least a slipper tub that I am allowed to use regularly." She looked at him wide-eyed after this recitation, as if she knew she had gone too far and was now expecting to be booted from the premises.

Asher bit his lip harder to stave off an uncontrollable smile, thinking of the expression on her face when she realized he would be gladly providing far more than her meager list of demands. By the time he was done with her, she would feel like a princess, if he had anything to say about it.

"Done.

Chapter Two

Somewhere in Southeast England
December 28th, 1840

The straps were all wrong.

Claymore unhooked the leather harness from the back of the wooden board. He punched an additional hole in the neck strap and reattached it further up.

This project has taken him months to design and build himself. Thanks to the brilliant minds of medieval torturers, there had been a plethora of ideas and more primitive designs from which to base his device.

The platform was plain enough, just a wall of wooden boards attached to a heavy base, like an upside down T. But the modifications were what made it a striking piece for its intended purpose. Straps of deep brown leather protruded from several places on the wall, one for each foot spread shoulder width apart, and one for the wrists high above, designed like the "Come-along" cuffs Scotland Yard sometimes used. The hands were chained and the "T" bolt turned until the chains were tightened sufficiently to the size of the wrists.

Really, that was the concept of the entire device as the neck strap also operated in a similar manner. The neck cuff came from below where the wrists would be and was connected to a round hand crank that, when twisted, drew the leather straps through the chair and tightened the circumference of the cuff. He had made sure that the metal crank came around to the front of the chair so he could operate it while watching his subject. There was no point if he couldn't watch.

Pulling at the buckle completing the circle of

leather, he smiled.

Perfect.

His breath quickened picturing someone secured to the wall. Man or woman would do, but it was always a woman when he imagined it. The gasping sounds she would make, the look of panic in her eyes as she realized her lungs could not draw in air...

Claymore shivered, enjoying the rush of energy flowing through him. He turned away from it to stay the temptation to delve further into the fantasy. He would enjoy it later.

Of course, this was all for a higher purpose. The pursuit of death was a calling that only a select few were capable of fulfilling. If he could observe life leaving the body, then that energy could be mastered. Life and death could be harnessed—given or taken away. All was within his grasp with the proper study.

His pleasure in taking life was a gift in order to bear out his mission. Ever since he had begun to indulge the idea of others' deaths, he had begun to realize that he was no ordinary man. He must obey his true calling.

It was time to share his accomplishment with his predecessor. The man who now unjustly sat behind bars for carrying out the art of death would be pleased to know of his progress. He sat at the small escritoire in the corner of his shop and began to write.

Dear Mr. Wollard...

****

Ivette felt like a pack mule.

A very confused, overwhelmed pack mule who must have taken a wrong turn somewhere. Lord Blackbourne had left her in the entry hall carrying all of her belongings (which, to be fair, only consisted of a single battered valise) of what had to be the largest home she'd ever set foot in. Her father having been a Squire, they had been invited to various events at surrounding homes of the local gentry, but nothing as grand as this.

Gleaming oak paneling met the eye everywhere one looked, and crystals shone from chandeliers throughout the space. Polished columns lined the entry, and a marble bust of what was clearly Lord Blackbourne himself graced an alcove to her left, the artist managing to capture his perpetual look of mischief with a quirk of the lips.

Her mind was a bit fuzzy since she had slept almost the entire way from Leeds to London, spending hours staring out at the passing countryside between naps, waking to change horses, and use the necessary at various stops. Lord Blackbourne had ridden beside the carriage most of the journey, taking a turn sleeping on the bench on the other side of the carriage for a few hours during the night. She had tried not to think about the fact that she was sleeping in a carriage with a peer of the realm as her stomach was already easily upset at coach travel.

When they had finally arrived in London, Blackbourne had woken her and deposited her in the foyer, informing her he would be back soon. How long "soon" was, she didn't know. He had murmured instructions to his housekeeper, a large woman with thick eyebrows, and then promptly left without another word.

A nauseous feeling crept through her.

She had probably made a huge mistake by coming here. She should have stayed where at least she knew she had employment, albeit employment that didn't seem to feed her or bathe her or keep her warm. She had slipped a note under the proprietress' door informing her that she would no longer be needing her room and to please tell Priscilla goodbye for her. She would have left a note for Priscilla as well, except Priscilla couldn't read.

Ivette already missed her box of a room, with its drafts and straw mattress and her things strewn around it. She felt tears in her eyes, willing them to not fall. She did not belong here.

"This way, miss," the housekeeper ordered when the door had shut behind Blackbourne. "I'm Mrs. Rushkova. You will take the blue suite, His Lordship says." Her accent was blunt and round. Ivette had never heard anything like it before. She turned abruptly and went to the stairs, which, unsurprisingly, were made of more polished oak. The round woman seemed to expect Ivette to follow, so she did, lugging her valise up the center runner of the stairs so she wouldn't slip.

Ivette tried to take in everything she could as she went, but there was simply too much of the place to observe properly all at once. Generations of Marquesses and their families had added to the splendor that was now amassed here in this house.

Was this truly to be her home for the foreseeable future? It was too much.

"Master Blackbourne said you would prefer a bath, miss. I will have the maids bring water straight away," she announced, opening a door and indicating that Ivette go through it before her.

She did so, drawing in a breath. "Is this…? Am I to sleep here?" she asked, afraid of the answer.

The housekeeper looked confused. "Yes. Do you not approve?"

Ivette took in the bedchamber suite that was more spacious than an entire floor of her boardinghouse. Plush royal blue carpets, a bed of the same color piled high with pillows, and thick tasseled curtains gave the room its name. It was such a rich color that Ivette had the absurd urge to lick a dollop of it, to possess it, to paint with it. Such a color was expensive to purchase in the smallest amounts of paint, so she understood that just the dyed materials in this room alone were worth a fortune.

There was a separate sitting area with chairs, a settee, and a massive fireplace set into the wall. But Ivette's gaze was drawn to an open door to her right, and she drifted towards the small room set off from the sitting area. Her breath escaped all at once at the sight of the bathing chamber with its pristine white and blue tiling, and an armoire featuring glass-paned doors through which she could see towels and various bottles. The tub in the center of the chamber was large enough to fit three of her and long enough for her to be able to lay down in the length of it completely.

"Miss Wollard, are you all right?" Mrs. Rushkova asked hesitantly.

Ivette wiped away the tear that had made its way down her face and smiled tremulously. "Yes. I believe I am."

****

Asher had commissioned a Bond Street dressmaker to visit his residence that day, paying an exorbitant amount of money to ensure her immediate and exclusive services, as well as her discretion regarding Ivette. Madame Chelfore had assured him that she would have a ready-made dress modified for Ivette today and then a dozen more gowns ready in a week's time. Undergarments, sleeping clothes, stockings, gloves, shoes, hats, and the like would be delivered as well. Because he understood the power of his very deep pocketbook, he was certain Ivette would be well taken care of by the modiste.

In the meantime, he had work to do.

Ash had been working on a project based on a conversation he'd had with a scientist who had recently attended an Association lecture series. The young university student from France, Pasteur, had been spouting the most fascinating theories about invisible flying organisms that could invade one's body and then transfer itself from person to person with a single breath or touch.

He and Pasteur had ruminated on the ramifications of such a theory, Ash mentioning Europe's decimation from the Black Plague in the 14th century. If the man's theory didn't turn out to be a wild goose chase, then it could explain how such a sickness could have ravaged the population so quickly and thoroughly.

Ash had rented a flat located a stone's throw from the National Archives building, where all of the census records from England's parishes were housed. By looking at the records from 1348 and extrapolating an estimate of the population of England's shires from that point, he hoped to use data from Pasteur's working theory to develop a mathematical model of how the plague would have spread in such circumstances from human contact. With any luck, Morganstern and Pasteur would be able to present their findings at the next Annual Meeting of the British Association for the Advancement of Science.

The project engaged the majority of his mind while sorting through ancient documents, calculating populations, mapping those populations' interactions, and so forth. It ate up his time and energy to the point that he didn't spend his every waking hour computing data, but could enjoy his meals and other activities in peace. Punishing rides on his horse became bearable without having to calculate the speed, how long it would take to reach a certain point, the height of the hedge being jumped... He was even able to take pleasure in evenings at White's just sitting and chatting with his friends on occasion since he'd begun working on the project two weeks ago.

He knew that, eventually, the effects of the project would wear off. His mind would become bored, and he would need to go searching for other outlets, but for now, it was engrossing enough to provide him some peace.

Then her letter arrived on the fifth day, piercing his concentration.

Lord Blackbourne,

I would like to thank you for the accommodations and clothing you have provided. I must say, I was not expecting such treatment and am quite happily surprised. Your staff is excellent and has taken extra pains to ensure my comfort. I hope you do not mind me using your upstairs drawing room as an art studio on occasion, as no one else seemed to be using it for its intended purpose. I didn't realize you possessed such a large inventory of blank stretched canvas and painting supplies in your attic, but was assured by Mrs. Rushkova that they were available for my use.

While I appreciate the leisurely pace of the assignment you have given me, I am not sure that I am fulfilling the duties of my position in such a way that merits the luxury and pay offered. I will be honest with you and state that I am rudderless without a defined purpose. Having not heard from you in several days, I didn't want to take advantage of your hospitality or underperform in some way.

Your butler, who insists on being called simply Milton, gave me your direction to be able to inquire after your guidance. Is soaking in the bath, reading, and painting what I am supposed to be doing with my time in your home? Mind you, I'm not objecting. I simply seek to be deemed a worthwhile employee.

Please Advise-

Ivette Wollard
P.S. I feel as if I must have gained a stone since being introduced to your cook's food. Hoping this is also not an issue, as I know that dresses and such are being commissioned.

****

Dear Miss Wollard,
While I appreciate your integrity in this matter, you may abandon all such concerns. Take as many baths as you wish and paint as many paintings as your heart desires. Your worth to me will not diminish with the number of wrinkles you accrue while soaking or squinting at your canvas. In fact, developing such attributes may very well help in convincing my colleagues of your interest in the sciences, as members of the Association generally squint often and have an abundance of wrinkles.

I must confess, I had no idea I possessed such an array of artistic supplies either, but this does make sense, as my mother was an avid painter. She was rubbish, to be quite honest, but never gave up the pastime. I am glad to know someone is going to benefit from their use, but I plan on judging your talent with a critical eye, regardless of your frail sensibilities.

Milton insists on Milton for two reasons, Miss Wollard. One is that it is the tradition of butlers everywhere in England to be referred to simply by their last name, the other being that his first name is even more uninspiring than his last. Out of respect for the poor soul, I will not reveal it to you.

Please be advised that I expect you to be ready to attend a soiree hosted by one of the Association's members Wednesday next. You should have your choice of dresses by then, including all the fripperies associated with them, and I have just now realized as I write this that I neglected to ask you if you know how to dance. If you do not, please send word, and a dancing master will be sent posthaste. Although there might not be dancing at this particular gathering, I would not want it said that Reginald Morganstern's sister is lacking in social graces.

Ever Your Advisor,
Asher Montague Blackbourne,
Marquess of Blackbourne and Forsythe, etc.

P.S. Although I would never presume to comment on a lady's figure, I believe yours will not be detracted from with some meat on your bones. The dresses will no doubt fit you splendidly.

P.P.S. You have excellent penmanship, Miss Wollard, as well as a superb grasp of the English language in written form. This bodes well, indeed.
****

Dear Lord Blackbourne,

You might want to clear some wall space in your gallery near the Renaissance section in the East Wing. I might have become a bit obsessed lately with imitating the masters since you have some excellent examples of their work, and I may have created some hang-able pieces. I assume you are aware of the Raphael forgery that hangs in the largest grouping as the brush strokes are obviously incongruous with his other work. I hope you did not pay overly much for it. If you'd like, I would be happy to repaint the piece with the quality expected of such a famous artist, although I can tell I would need at least two more paint pots to achieve the colors in the original.

I'm quite certain I shouldn't be discussing baths with you, but I assumed you'd want to be apprised of the fact that, although I have done my utmost, it appears the wrinkles developed in the tub will not be permanent. We will have to convince them some other way that I am your spinster naturalist sister.

As for the dancing—shame on you. If course I can dance. I was raised as a lady, Sir, and, although I have not danced in public due to the possibility of my coming out being rather abruptly severed, I still retain my skills in the feminine arts, including dancing (I love dancing), needlepoint (I hate needlepoint), watercolors (watercolors are child's play), singing (in the tub, mostly, since I have been here), household management (of two servants), social etiquette (I won't eat with my hands or send my fan flying across the room at someone's head, even yours), and last but not least, excellent penmanship and a superb grasp of the English language. Please note the rolling of my eyes at this juncture.

I received the packet of papers outlining the purpose and hierarchy of the British Association for the Advancement of Science, and will study it diligently so as not to seem ignorant at the soiree. I admit I am quite nervous and excited for this event. Is there anything else I should know before stepping into the role of—what's my name supposed to be?

Your "Something-"
Ivy Wollard

****

My Dear "Something,"
The Raphael is a forgery?!

I cannot fathom this. It has been in the family for five generations, and it was a particular point of pride to my parents. Please purchase whatever products necessary to create an acceptable replacement on my line of credit, although I think the principle of the matter might be past redemption. I will be hunting down the purveyor of the piece, if he is still alive, and ~~strangling~~

maiming him, so please burn this letter after reading it.

It is heartening to know that you possess the requisite skills to pass as Reginald Morganstern's sister, who, by the way, is named Corrine Morganstern. Corrine hails from Leicestershire, where she grew up admiring her much older brother, Reginald, and so followed in his footsteps in her interest in science. She has never married due to her deformity, which she hides well, but will never allow her to pursue marriage. You can feign any number of things regarding this, I'm sure. She is fond of Reginald and keen to find acceptance in scientific circles, though she knows her gender is not conducive to such things. Also, she enjoys croquet and croissants. These characteristics are non-negotiable, as I've already had occasion to mention them when referencing you in conversation with my colleagues.

I find myself now curious about often you actually bathe, my male instincts for these things tending toward picturing the baths themselves instead of establishing a guess at a reasonable amount. Which reminds me, I am not altogether certain what you look like now that you have been properly outfitted as a lady of your station should be. I do remember your eyes, however, which were a remarkable shade of blue, if I may say so.

-Blackbourne

****

Dear Blackbourne,

What do you mean, a deformity? I am not deformed as far as I know, and would hesitate to guess at what you mean by such a thing. The dresses, which arrived today, do not leave much room for imagination.

I will not be a hunchback. I refuse.

As for my appearance, I have all of the usual features—a nose, eyes (blue, as you say), mouth, and anything else necessary to function as a human being. I hope you find my appearance pleasing, as I wouldn't want to embarrass Reginald Morganstern in front of his friends. I warn you, I might have trouble feigning fondness for you, so I hope Reginald's personality is discernably different than your true identity's and evokes feelings of affection.

I usually bathe once a day now, in the evenings. I cannot express how wonderful it feels to soak in a hot tub with a novel while the fire crackles nearby. I have grown attached to the rose and vanilla-scented oil in the cabinet and am trusting you don't have an aversion to it.

I have begun working on the Raphael, but it is slow-going since he used a layering technique that requires time to achieve. I want to thank you for the supplies. It has been a long time since I have been able to use quality paints without financial ruin looming.

Your staff is marvelous. I'm sure I have been nothing but a bother, but they have welcomed me with open arms. I don't believe I have ever been so fussed over in my life. Please consider giving them a bonus out of my first month's wages.

Yours,
Ivy

****

My Dear Ivy,
I am happy to be of service to your artistic whims, and even more pleased that you are rectifying the Raphael situation. Are you really that good at imitating artistic style, I wonder? I mean no offense, but there is a reason they are called the "Masters."

Please be assured that my staff are very well-compensated for their time and efforts, including anything you need from them. You do not have to sacrifice your pay to feel you have thanked them. Indeed, if you wish to show them your appreciation, you are welcome to purchase anything you deem appropriate in my name at the shops on Bond Street. Have Herbert, my driver, take you. I have established a line of credit for you in your name (That is, Corrine Morganstern) at all of the major shops.

I'd like you to be aware that I will be attending the soiree as myself (Blackbourne) for the first little while, as the Royal Society has asked me to act as a liaison (more like spy) to the BAAS. Although it might prove tricky to make the switch, I've done it once before without issue. I will need you to come up with a viable excuse as to why Reginald Morganstern is running late and field any questions before he "arrives." As this is a social engagement held at a family home and not an official function, there could be other ladies present with which you can associate until Reginald shows up, at which time I'll introduce you to my colleagues properly.

You should know that there is a fierce rivalry between the BAAS and the Royal Society stemming from their differing approaches to membership. The Royal Society, which I am a member of as Lord Blackbourne, only accepts the peerage into its ranks, regardless of any scientific credibility, whereas the BAAS includes anyone who has an interest in serious scientific pursuit. Acceptance in the BAAS is predicated more so on scientific achievement than rank. However, the Royal Society is the most well-respected scientific governing body in Britain, and any technological progress made in this country has been through their influence. The subject might arise during conversation, and members of both organizations usually have strong feelings, Reginald included.

Your revelations about your bathing habits are ... intriguing. There are a multitude of questions I would like to ask, but I wouldn't want to overstep my bounds, so

I will refrain. For now. Suffice to say that your scent will not produce an aversion—quite the opposite, in fact, although "brotherly" affection might prove a challenge.

Yours,

Ash

P.S. What is so wrong with my personality that is isn't deserving of sisterly affection?

P.P.S. I just have one question. What novel are you reading while bathing?

****

Dear Lord Asher,

I fear any respect you have for me would diminish if I told you the book in which I have been indulging. To be perfectly honest, I haven't read a book in ages. They were simply an unattainable commodity until now.

Oh, all right—since you've twisted my arm—The Mystery of Mooreshead Manor. It's a gothic murder tale. I know, I know. It's not what a woman of science should be reading, but I promise I'll be in character as Corrine and not breathe a word of it to anyone. And I know what you're thinking—why would the daughter of a murderer want to read about such a thing? Well ... I don't really know. I think it's the mystery of it. Putting together the pieces and understanding the motivations. Perhaps it's because my father is who he is that I can't help wanting to understand these things. I hope this revelation does not lower me in your sight, seeing as it has been inordinately pleasant to be considered sane and respectable by someone again.

Your plan for the soiree sounds fraught with possible mishaps. I do hope we can pull this off without anyone making a connection between Blackbourne and Morganstern. I will do my utmost to make sure your identities are never questioned and will try to contain my excitement at wearing such lovely clothes. I hope there will be food at this event. I have grown used to eating regular meals the past several days, but will forego it if necessary. Or perhaps I'll stuff a few of cook's pasties in my reticule, just in case.

Yours,

Ivy

P.S. Make sure your eyebrows are firmly attached.

Chapter Three

Ash arrived at the Honorable Percival Finchley's home right on time. He couldn't afford to be late if he was to spend half the night as himself and half as Morganstern. He meandered through the brightly-lit rooms, nodding to familiar faces here and there, careful to remember those who he knew as himself rather than his alter ego. If he didn't have prefect memory recall as he did, he would have flubbed this up long ago.

Grabbing a glass of champagne from the punch table, he scanned those assembled in the large drawing room, which had been rearranged for the occasion with enough room for a few couples to dance if they so chose. It was often this way with these sorts of homes, having larger public rooms instead of a full-blown ballroom.

Ash looked over the faces of the women in the room, trying to ascertain if Ivy was there yet.

Ivy.

He had begun to think of her that way over the past two weeks. He would have to remind himself to call her Miss Morganstern while being himself, and Corrine as her brother, Reginald.

His mind latched onto the pocket watch that Squire Philby was twirling from where he stood talking with another BAAS member. The circular device went round and round, filling his head with diameters, radials, speeds, and force calculations.

Taking a sip of the champagne to bring himself back to the present, he looked over the women again, ruling them out one by one. Of the two brunettes, one was much too tall to be Ivy, and the other too sophisticated. The woman's hands were animated, and she was laughing at something one of the two gentlemen speaking to her had said. Combine that with the way she held herself, and it had to be some pampered debutante, no doubt a family member of one of the attendees. So she must not be here yet. One of the men bent down to brush a kiss across the woman's gloved knuckles, and he saw her face.

Now that was intriguing.

His blood immediately began to gravitate away from his brain, the familiar sensation a relief. She smiled down at the man kissing her hand with wide, seashell-pink lips and then slowly raised dark lashes that rimmed her striking eyes. Her cheekbones were wide and delicate tapering to a pixie of a chin, giving her face an elfin beauty that was complemented by the shining mass of chocolate-colored hair gathered high with one long coil left to lay over her shoulder. A thick side sweep of hair angled over her pale forehead and was tucked back with a sapphire comb to contrast with the cream of her skin.

Ash looked downwards to where her shoulders were exposed, her milky chest straining against the lace-edged bodice of her dress. A rich shade of royal blue silk that seemed to shimmer as she moved, her dress spread from her nipped waist in layers that ruched daringly in front to show a layer of tantalizing cream lace petticoat beneath. She was petite, but delightfully curved in all the right places.

Exactly the type of woman he enjoyed becoming distracted with.

As if she could sense his perusal, she glanced between the men facing her and met his eyes. Her pale cheeks colored a charming shade of peach as he grinned and lifted a brow.

She gulped.

Good.

He didn't bother to hide his thorough inspection of her person, but blatantly looked her up and down as he knew she watched. His eyes blazed back up to her chest to see her suck in a breath.

With a wink, he deliberately turned away from her to amble over to a group of BAAS members, slapping one on the back as he approached.

This should be fun.

It was a calculated move he'd learned long ago. Show interest and then move on, inevitably causing the woman to want to regain that interest.

Half an hour later, however, it was clear that the lady wasn't going to be a fawning participant in his game. She hadn't attempted to make her way over to him at all, staying on the far side of the room, usually being fawned over by others. Her mannerisms were vivacious, but reserved, as if she held secrets she would love to reveal with the proper temptation.

If that's what was required to get under her skin, he would gladly provide it.

He needed to make his move quickly, however, if he was going to be able to plan an assignation by the time he needed to become Morganstern.

As he was planning his introduction to her in his mind, the host, Finchley, announced that a special musical performance by a visiting musician would begin momentarily. He had booked a cellist from Spain to give a rendition of his latest compositions, gaining a chorus of interested murmurs from the guests.

The assembled audience drew away from the center of the room to give the musician space for his large instrument. Ash subtly made his way towards her so that, by the time everyone had settled on furniture or against the walls, he was directly behind her as she stood near the back wall listening to the heavily accented cellist introduce his first piece.

She shifted from one foot to the other as the first notes swelled into the room, the blue silk flowing over her lithe curves like a liquid metal melted down specifically for her. He watched as the hairs on the back of her nape rose with the haunting notes of the cello, her soft sigh barely reaching his ears.

A music lover, then? He could work with that.

Ash took a step forward and leaned down to murmur in her ear. "Did you know that plants grow more healthily with music?"

He saw her tense and then turn her head to face him. She was surprised by his proximity, but maintained her outward composure. "Is that so?" she replied, her low tones sending rivulets of sensation straight downward.

He was finally able to gaze straight into her eyes, which reflected the lamplight in the wall sconce nearest them. They were an infinite blue rimmed with the deepest violet he'd ever seen, and something about them shot through his mental somersaults to cause him momentary blankness.

The welling strains of the Spaniard's instrument rose around them like a cocoon, creating a space that was both safe and intimately frightening, as if the piece had been written for this exact moment in time to heighten the awareness that flowed through his veins at her nearness.

And suddenly, his mind wasn't blank any longer. It was an overwhelming maelstrom of images flowing across his mind's eye with every stroke of the cellos bow. It was the two of them tangled up and laughing beneath satin sheets. It was moonlight and fingertips caressing her white limbs as she writhed in pleasure at his touch. It was burying himself in her so deeply that nothing in either the outside world or his own traitorous mind could ever reach him again. It was time, every moment of the rest of his life spent lost in the mystery that was her, knowing her so intimately she wouldn't dare keep secrets from him.

Vaguely, he knew he was just staring at her like an imbecile, which was quite uncharacteristic for him, but she seemed to be under a similar influence, her generous lips parted in breathlessness as she waited for some unspoken thing.

And then he realized that the unspoken thing was his—he hadn't replied to her in quite some time now, although it didn't seem to bother her in the least. He cleared his throat, the music around them masking his words from anyone else. "Yes," he replied, adding huskily, "You seem to have grown up quite nicely under its influence, judging by your enjoyment of it." He reached up and gently stroked the downy petal of her earlobe between his thumb and forefinger.

Her gasp caused his blood to burn as he watched her eyelashes swoosh down taking in the sensation.

Ash watched her catch her lower lip with her teeth, and he longed to do so himself. Watching her eyelids flutter as his fingertips skimmed down her neck was like drinking a fine wine full of sweetness and hidden depths.

He was an expert at seduction. He had honed it to a science, as he was wont to do with every aspect of his life, but the times interactions surpassed his ability to analyze them were what kept him sane. Literally.

This was one of those times.

"Do you feel that?" he rumbled, placing his fingers against the throbbing heartbeat in her throat. He smiled as it sped up just slightly. "That's music."

"It's been a long time since I've enjoyed music like this," she whispered, her voice barely discernable above the music around them.

He dipped his head towards her. "Would you like me to give you more? I could play you like a sonata, all the movements a beautiful escape."

She didn't answer, but met his eyes with a wide, questioning look.

"Why have I never seen you before?" he murmured, racking his brain for a remembrance. If he had ever met her, he would remember it perfectly.

"I don't think you were really looking the last time," she replied, her lips quirking. "Men like you only see what glitters at first glance."

Ash's heart constricted. There was a last time?

She was more than likely right about him. If she hadn't been wearing such an alluring dress or sapphires in her hair or been smiling like a beacon, he would have passed her over in favor of more obvious game. The women he usually pursued knew how to show themselves off to the best advantage. Low-cut gowns, kohl-lined eyes, and flashing jewels dripping down into powdered cleavage were all expected. They wielded fans like weapons with perfected come-hither glances, understanding that they were being chased just as he intended for them to. The game wasn't fun unless everyone knew they were playing.

At least that's what he'd always believed.

Yet this woman didn't contain such artifice. Even though he was sure he would have remembered her face had he stumbled across her before, he could tell she wasn't one who traversed the circles to which he gravitated. Namely women who understood the ramifications of what he wanted from them.

The cellist executed a tense vibrato drawn out over a long moment, everyone's attention riveted on the musician's poignant melody. Everyone's except Ash's.

"You may be right. But I'll never forget you now," he told her. It was true, whether or not he had perfect recall.

"I would hope not, if this is going to work," she laughed softly, eyes dancing.

He grinned. "And what is it we should work on?" he asked, innuendo coloring his tones.

"I think convincing everyone we aren't what we seem is a good start," she said wryly.

"What do we seem like?" Conversation with her was captivating, which was exactly the kind of woman he needed.

She frowned. "I'm not sure. You are you, and I..." she trailed off.

"What are you?" Her answer seemed to be of the utmost importance to him in this moment.

"I don't know. What do you think I am?" Her wide, dark blue eyes searched his for the answer.

He blinked, unprepared for once, to give a response. He'd had women ask similar things, but it was always with the shared knowledge that they were seeking a compliment to heighten his pursuit. But she wasn't asking for that, he sensed. What was he to say? He didn't even know her name.

"I think you might be my cure," he said baldly.

Her gaze probed his, expression unmoving. "Cure for what?" she asked seriously.

Asher grinned and eventually shrugged. "Everything."

She didn't laugh. His answer could have been taken as simply a tacky line meant for a willing woman, but she didn't treat it as such. For that, he was glad because it truly wasn't. It was meant for her and her alone, although he did want her willing. He wanted her so willing, she'd let him do anything to her, all the things his mind had already shown him were possible.

She was so small, the top of her head only reaching his chin... He wanted to envelop her in his arms and overwhelm her slight body with his. Hiding the hunger in his eyes was nearly impossible.

Finally, she smiled, her small, pearly teeth showing in the lamplight. The shine of her dark hair caught his eye as she said, "Perhaps you ruining all my plans might turn out all right after all."

Ash's eyes smoldered and he leaned closer. "I have plenty of other plans for you."

"I'm sure you do," she responded pertly, raising a brow.

Damn his alter ego. He had to have her now. "Will you leave with me?" he asked, risking her rejection and hoping it wasn't too soon to ask her such a thing, hoping the moment had affected her as much as it had him. She had to have felt it, hadn't she?

At this, she looked up at him again and blinked, cocking her head to this side. "I thought that was the plan all along."

Her words snaked through him, hardening his growing need for her. "Yes," he replied simply, excitement at her words tightening in his chest. "It was," he smiled.

Victory soared through his veins. Tonight, no equations or complications would get in the way of his claiming her. What if she was the answer to the question he'd had his entire life? What if he didn't want just one night or one week with her like all the others?

The music continued to flow around them like silk over skin, but if he wanted to have her this night, he needed to shake himself from the spell weaving around them and make preparations. "I need to have a word with the host, and I'll be right back. You'll wait for me?" he asked, trying not to sound as desperate as he felt.

He was never desperate. He was the conqueror, not the beggar, and he could only hope she couldn't hear his heart thumping over the deep tones of the cello.

"Of course, Lord Blackbourne." She smiled knowingly.

Ah, so she did know who he was. Perhaps his reputation had preceded him. It wouldn't be the first time a woman had decided she would have him before even speaking to him.

"I believe you have me at a disadvantage, Miss—?" he hinted expectantly.

She laughed quietly, her small snort charming him. "Your sense of humor is appalling," she informed him.

He tilted his head. She wasn't going to make this easy, was she?

"I'll pretend that was a compliment and not a mortal wound to my ego." He winked.

"I have a feeling your ego could take the insult," she replied saucily.

Ash smiled. She wasn't wrong. "Stay right where you are, sweetheart." He leaned in to gently kiss her cheek, and her beguiling scent wafted up to his nose as he pressed his lips slowly against her velvety skin.

What was that scent? Vanilla and … roses, he thought. Intoxicating.

What did that remind him of?

Words tugged at the edges of his memory, and because his wretched mind wouldn't let him forget even one thing he'd ever seen, a line prettily written in feminine script rose in his mind's eye.

I have grown attached to the rose and vanilla-scented oil in the cabinet and am trusting you don't have an aversion to it.

He froze, his lips stilling on her cheek.

All the thoughts he'd had in the past few minutes in her presence flashed across his mind with painful clarity, momentarily blinding him to anything around him. His muscles wouldn't move, shock coursing through him.

He closed his eyes and swallowed. Cold waves of realization washed over his senses as he thought back to her responses.

Ash pulled back the barest of inches. "Ivy?" he whispered, the word strangled.

"Yes, my lord?" Her voice was as hushed as his was, but puzzled.

He let out the breath he'd been holding.

Bollocks.

****

Lord Blackbourne was acting in the strangest manner.

Had he actually said bollocks in her ear just now?

She had thought they were having a grand time, secretly joking about the unconventional circumstances in which they found themselves. He was treating her as if he enjoyed her company—like she was any other lady he had a rapport with, and it had felt wonderful to be treated like a normal human being.

Well, a human being whose knees were about to collapse from his glances.

When he spoke, when he looked at her … it was shattering. Did he realize he was even doing it? Perhaps he was so used to speaking to women with that husky tone and intense stare that it wasn't deliberate.

Either way, she suspected she would have to make a valiant effort every time she was this close to him to not fall at his feet in a heap of overstimulated nerves.

As soon as he had kissed her cheek, he had acted

as if he'd had a bucket of water poured over his head. He'd straightened and stepped back, staring at her and tugging at his cravat as if he were suffocating.

Ivy reached for his arm. "Are you all right?" she asked, sparing a glance for the rest of the room. No one had noticed their exchange or his current state, the cellist still holding everyone rapt.

But as the cellist ended his composition with a series of fierce, short strokes of the bow, he stumbled back at her touch like she'd scorched him. "I-I have to go," he mumbled, still gaping at her like she had sprouted wings and started clucking like a chicken.

"Yes, I would think you'd want to give someone else a chance to be here," she said pointedly, the clapping of the guests covering her words.

"Right. Yes, of course. I-I'll be back shortly." Before giving her a chance to respond, he turned away and shoved his way past several people on his way to the drawing room door.

He was so odd. She had even thought for a moment that he might have been flirting with her…

No. That couldn't be, could it?

He was a peer of the realm, and, according to the gossip she'd overheard from his own staff, quite the libertine, flitting from one beautiful woman to the next because he could.

Yet he had leaned so close, whispering in her ear, touching her. Perhaps he did that to all women, but to Ivy, it had felt like all of his considerable charm had been focused on making her bones melt.

And, the scary thing was, it had been working. She would have to be careful not to accidentally fall for this man. Priscilla had made the mistake of becoming too attached to some of the men that frequented her at night, and she remembered the tear-filled shouting that always ended in the woman coming to Ivy's room for consolation and the stuffing of precious tea biscuits into her trembling mouth for hours afterwards.

At least she had made a good impression on his colleagues so far. After a few conversations with various men and their companions or family members associated with the BAAS, she had established a believable identity as Reginald Morganstern's sister from the country. Once Morganstern himself showed up, she assumed he would help her to fill in the gaps and introduce her to more of his friends.

After a period of fifteen minutes or so, Morganstern showed up looking the complete opposite of Lord Blackbourne. Walking stiffly, he shuffled into the room in a dull black suit of clothes, leaning heavily on a lion-headed cane. His hair was an iron gray, beard, wig, and eyebrows in place. The only vestige of Asher Blackbourne that remained were his flashing blue eyes that took in the room with crinkled enjoyment.

Ivy watched as he was greeted by several men and included in their enthusiastic discussions. After a moment, however, he herded them towards where Ivy stood sipping ratafia by the refreshment table.

Her heart sped up a little as they came nearer. Now was the time to earn the generous compensations he had given her.

"And this is my sister, Corrine. Miss Morganstern to you fellows," he chuckled, elbowing the closest man in the ribs.

"What a pleasure, Miss Morganstern!"

"Wonderful to make your acquaintance."

"An absolute delight, Miss Morganstern."

Greetings and names were thrown at her eagerly from the men, most of them much older, but one looked almost her age with spectacles and a cherubic smile on his round face. Her hand was taken and kissed, and she tried to remember their names as they introduced themselves. She'd always been good with memorizing things on paper, as she had dealt with crests and watermarks on stationary for so long now, but hearing things was different. She hoped she wouldn't let him down and forget everyone.

Babbage and Brewster, she could remember, although she hoped she'd remember that Brewster was the Scottish one and Babbage the English. The younger one was named Chester-something. She'd ask about him later.

"Charmed to meet you all, gentlemen," she said warmly, her lessons in etiquette already coming back swiftly as the night wore on. Her father had always emphasized charm was the principle foundation of society and opened more doors than anything else.

"You can't be this one's sister!" a man named Babbage exclaimed. "You're much too attractive to be related." He winked.

Morganstern guffawed and punched the man's shoulder. "Cori, defend your favorite brother from these jackals," he rasped.

"Oh, I don't know, Reggie. I might agree with them," she said conspiratorially, causing them to break out in laughter again.

"Ho ho, the lass is sharp!" Brewster commented.

"Why do I bother with you lot?" Morganstern grumbled, tapping his cane against Chester-something's shoes.

"Because we're the only *real* scientists in the British Isles!" Babbage exclaimed. They all agreed heartily.

Ivy noted that so far, Morganstern hadn't met her eyes once. He looked at his colleagues, at his cane, his feet, but not so much as a passing glance directed at her.

Had she done something wrong? Thinking back over the interactions she'd had with him thus far, she couldn't think of anything. She had played her part carefully, at least with everyone else here.

Perhaps he didn't like her dress?

It was a bit daring with its sapphire hue and lower neckline, but she'd been assured it was the height of fashion for ladies of her age.

Maybe it was the scent after all. He was probably just being polite about it in his letter earlier.

Inwardly, she shrunk back, her stomach curling with anxiety. She didn't like not being sure of her position with her employer. After being told she wasn't fit to be in the company of God-fearing people and being turned down for so many positions, she had made sure that her work was above reproach at the paper mill. There had never been a reason for her employer to have issue with her, and she had come to rely on that confidence.

But now... She was never sure of anything with this man. She had thought that they were getting on better after having corresponded during the past two weeks, but his behavior was so erratic.

Mayhap she was reading too far into it. As the men continued to debate the merits of the BAAS over the Royal Society, she smiled and nodded, forcing herself to let go of the apprehension that had seized her. Deeps breaths in and out calmed her stomach, and she felt it unclenching.

The niggling questions in the back of her mind remained, however, as the evening continued and Morganstern remained aloof to her. In front of others, he was jovial and played the part of doting brother, but never said a word to her or looked her way otherwise. By the time Morganstern announced that they'd be departing, her nerves were frayed.

He escorted her to his carriage on his arm so her slippered feet wouldn't slide on the packed snow and handed her in. Once they were settled, silence ensued while Morganstern transformed back into Blackbourne with the removal of his disguise.

The coach had been heated with warming bricks by the driver, a comfort she hadn't even known existed. Her mother having died in childbirth, it had been just Ivy and her father throughout her childhood, and he hadn't often thought of creature comforts such as this. Even if he had, they had only employed one maid and one man-of-all-trades who managed the grounds, horses, and outside maintenance needs. They probably hadn't paid him enough to worry about things like that without requesting it. Ivette almost purred with the sensation of warmth that oozed into her feet and legs, the voluminous folds of her skirts and full-length dress coat keeping the warmth underneath.

She stole glances at Blackbourne as he performed his ritual, but it was too dark to see much of anything inside the curtained carriage. Barely a sliver of moonlight entered the conveyance as Blackbourne couldn't afford anyone seeing him taking off his disguise through the windows.

When he was finished, he sighed and leaned back against the velvet seat, positioning himself as far away from her as possible.

Just because he didn't seem inclined to talk didn't mean she wasn't going to ask him questions. "Did everything go as smoothly as you'd hoped?"

He didn't answer right away, causing her nerves to tingle. Was he going to criticize her performance?

Eventually, he cleared his throat. "For the most

part, yes," he said, a note of wryness coloring his tone.

"For the most part?" she pressed.

"Your portrayal of my fictional sister was inspiring. You should consider the stage," he informed her with an inclination of his head.

"Oh!" Ivy was glad of the darkness as she blushed easily. She shifted on the seat. "Thank you, Lord Blackbourne. I am happy to hear it, but I believe I'll stick to the one role."

He chuckled, and they fell into silence once more.

Ivy couldn't let it go. Something was wrong, she just didn't know what. "Was there ... anything I should do differently next time?"

"Erm," he struggled, loosening his cravat. "I don't think so. Everyone was quite enamored of you."

Ivy frowned. She wasn't one to beat around the bush, and she knew if she didn't ask, she would just torture herself with it later. "Then why do I have the feeling you aren't pleased with me?"

Blackbourne laughed hoarsely. "I'm quite ... that is, that's not the problem," he said shortly.

"Then what is the problem?" she twisted her hands in her lap. "Are you ... are you regretting your decision to hire me?"

"Not at all," he assured her. He seemed to hesitate, then stated, "Yet, I do regret the situation I find myself in," he mumbled.

"What's that?" she asked, fearing his answer.

"It would be inappropriate to tell you."

Ivy thought about this, then told him, "I've been out in the world on my own for quite a while, so if it's all the same to you, I think my sensibilities are probably past the ability to be offended. I promise I won't run to Almack's teary-eyed with outrage."

Blackbourne said nothing for a moment.

Ivy thought perhaps he was refusing to tell her, which just served to further irk her. Whatever issues he was having, she could probably help. She was a good problem-solver, having had to be when her life had fallen apart around her.

But then he spoke, and his words stunned her into a state of shock.

"I've thought about nothing but having you in my bed since I first saw you tonight."

Ivy's brain scattered into a thousand different directions at once.

He sat unmoving, his eyes gleaming in the dark as he watched her.

She cleared her throat, searching for something— anything—to say. Usually, she was a very direct person who had a quip for everything, but she'd never had to respond to a statement like that.

"Do you begin to see the problem?" he murmured, relaxed against the squabs like a sultan surveying a new harem girl. It was as if, by addressing the subject, he had eased into another side of himself that was completely comfortable with discussing such things with a woman in a darkened carriage.

He was dangerous like this, she realized. In his element now, she understood why he required little effort to bend women to his every whim. He was like gravity, and she wanted to go towards him, to please him. She was instantly aware of every nerve, every inch of skin that had grown sensitive and chaffed at the heat that suffused her. And yet, she felt almost numb, not in control of her own body as it wanted to do things with him that she couldn't even picture with her limited experience.

All she knew was, he created a languor in her limbs that she didn't know what to do with, and she suspected he knew it.

Licking her suddenly dry lips, she replied, "That could be a problem, yes."

He laughed quietly. "Ah, Ivette, what are we going to do?" he said curiously, leaning forward to put his hands on his knees. "If you were any other woman who'd gotten into my carriage willingly at this time of night, I'd take you right here and then twice more in my bed later without regret."

Ivy gulped and met his glowing eyes. She'd never had anyone speak like this to her before. And because she just couldn't help it, she whispered, "But not me?"

He shook his head slowly. "But not you."

She cursed herself to a thousand deaths, but couldn't stop herself as she asked, "Why not?"

He sighed and breathed out through his nose before speaking softly. "Because you're the girl who reads gothic novels in the bathtub and paints forgeries of Raphael."

Ivy blinked and sucked in a breath, her heart pounding. "And that's ... bad?"

Leaning back again, his smile twisted. "No, Ivy. That's not bad. But I could never forgive myself if I made that girl cry."

Ivy forced herself to breathe in and out when she felt as if she couldn't work her own lungs at all. Well, that explanation didn't solve anything.

He added, "And I would make you cry, because I'm very good at loving women, and also very good at leaving them when I grow bored. I grow bored very easily, you'll find. I'm sure it's a character flaw you'll dissect later, but I won't lie to you about it."

The knot in her stomach grew tighter. She wasn't sure if she appreciated his honesty or not. But the way he spoke to her as if he didn't want to hurt her. That was worth something. In fact, to Ivy, it was worth everything. He treated her like a person who had feelings and who deserved nothing less than the truth.

Her entire adult life, she had been treated as if she didn't deserve to exist, and like her very presence would taint others.

Now he believed *he* might be a threat to *her*?

What a thought.

She realized that a tear had leaked out to run down her cheek, and she wiped it away hastily, laughing. "I fear you've already made me cry, my lord. No, no," she added, as he immediately sat up straighter. "Good tears. Pay me no mind. I'm... I think the word is happy. Just happy. You don't have to worry about me going starry-eyed over your revelation. It's just nice to be treated with respect," she explained.

He looked confused. "Respecting you is definitely not what I'd like to do to you right now."

And there he went making her bloom with furious heat again.

He continued. "But as long as we understand each other, I'll attempt to be as respectful as possible while you reside under my roof."

She nodded. "That's all I could hope for."

Chapter Four

Ash sincerely hoped and dreaded she kept to her ritual tonight. It was the sweetest torture to watch her walk barefoot down the hallway after her nightly bath and sit out on the family's upper drawing room balcony, hot drink in hand. Hair unbound in masses of chocolate waves hanging down her back, he could always smell her intoxicating scent wafting to him where he stood in the shadows at the other end of the hall.

She hadn't caught him thus far, always turning away towards the drawing room and padding down the hall, sometimes humming to herself. The wrapper she wore wasn't revealing, made of plush, velour-lined fabric of a deep purple hue, but it contrasted with her skin and hair and wrapped her trim figure to make her the most tempting little package he'd ever seen.

It was odd, that thought, because he'd had many beautiful women over the years, but, somehow, they hadn't held his attention like the tiny woman who pranced around his home like she belonged there and made him think she might know exactly what she was doing to him. She couldn't walk the way she walked or ate the way she ate, languorously like she enjoyed every moment more than was allowed, without knowing she tempted him almost beyond his control.

The women he'd known in the past had carefully cultivated movements designed to draw male eyes, licking champagne off their fingers or sashaying in front of him.

But Ivy made no effort to check for his attention when she licked marmalade from her fingers at breakfast or twirled her wrapper belt as she strolled down the hall.

Which she was doing now as she rounded the corner and continued walking towards the drawing room door.

His breath caught.

She really was tiny. He would bet a hundred pounds he could pick her up and toss her on a bed without even feeling the weight of her. What he'd do to her after she was on the bed...

Ash ground his teeth while his fist clenched at his side.

What was she doing to him?

He hadn't had a woman in weeks. That's what it was. He had been focused on his plague project of late, but now that he was waiting for more source documents to be sent from a remote parish and for some clarification from Pasteur, he was at a standstill. There was no need to reside at the rented flat near the Archives for now, so he had come back to Blackbourne House with Ivette the night of the soiree and had stayed ever since.

It had nothing to do with the fact that she was here.

As she went into the drawing room, he moved forward, coming to stand in the doorway while she settled herself in the chair set just outside the glass doors on the other side of the room.

The space smelled of acrid paints, which reminded him of when his mother would go on a misguided painting binge. Ivette's paint table, easel, and stool were set up to one side where the light from the French doors would illuminate the area during the day. The rest of the room looked as it always did, his mother's decorating taste still evident in the Chippendale furniture and pale rose damask draperies.

Ivy set her mug of what he assumed was coffee or chocolate on the small round table near her and curled her legs up in the chair with her, the bundle of her form only taking up half the chair's width. He heard her sigh, and she gathered her hair and brought it around to rest over one shoulder. Two pink toes poked out from beneath her wrapper, making him smile as she took a noisy sip from her cup.

He couldn't stand it any longer.

Ash came to stand behind her on the balcony, his fingers itching to bury themselves in her hair. The night air was chilly, but it didn't seem to matter. He didn't want to frighten her, but there was something about being near her without her knowing that served to heighten his awareness of her. But he wasn't a man to stalk a woman without her permission, so he cleared his throat, making her jump.

He tried not to smile and failed. "Enjoying yourself?" he asked, moving around her chair to lean against the balcony railing facing her.

Her wide blue eyes looked up at him. "Oh, I didn't know—that is, I'll leave if you'd rather," she offered.

Ash waved a hand to stay her movement. "No, stay. It's I who has disturbed your nightly habits."

She raised a brow, hugging her wrapper tightly about her. "How do you know this is a habit?" she asked suspiciously.

He crossed his arms, keeping eye contact. "I'm very observant, Miss Wollard," he admitted. "You'd be surprised what I've observed about you over the past few days."

He watched the surprise play across her face, satisfaction at having rattled her composure coursing through him.

"Like what?" She cocked her head.

She was too curious for her own good, playing

right into his hands. "Like how you hum Beethoven's 5th when you're happy and how you never seem to be without paint stains on your arms, even after a bath," he said pointedly, nodding in the direction of her forearm where a streak of some dark color still showed.

She blushed and pulled down the cuff of her wrapper to cover it. "I suppose I need to be more thorough," she said wryly.

"If you need assistance, I'm more than happy to oblige," he said, his eyes never leaving her.

He really shouldn't have said that, based on the way her blush spread from her cheeks to—well, everywhere visible, making him that much more curious about the skin beneath her wrapper.

"I think I can manage, thank you," she replied nervously, stroking the ends of her hair with her fingers.

Ash wanted to untangle her hair for her, slowly massaging her scalp and melting her beneath his fingers. He could tell she was the type to groan at such ministrations, and it was all he could do to not cross the balcony this second and perform the deed.

"I have an idea," he told her.

It was a bad idea, there was no question about it.

"Oh?"

"I'd like to read to you," he said, pushing himself away from the railing and coming towards her.

"Wh-what do you mean?" she stuttered, her hands freezing in the strands of her sable locks.

He kept coming, putting his hands on the arms of her chair and leaning down to speak to her.

"I mean, I won't let myself touch you, Ivette, but I want to read to you while you're soaking in the tub. You enjoy that activity, yes? Give me a small concession. Please," he added softly.

She gasped. "You-We- I can't do that. That's …

no."

He grinned at her discomposure. "Yes, you can, Ivy. Who's stopping you?"

She spluttered, waving her hands. "Morals, for one thing!"

He shook his head. "I don't have to see you without your clothes. Tsk, tsk, where is your mind going?" he teased her.

"I don't understand," she said slowly. He felt her breath fan his face, the sweet aroma of chocolate begging him to delve into her mouth with his tongue and taste her.

"I won't enter your bathing chamber until you are already in the bath. You can use the sudsing lather in the cabinet, and I won't be able to see a thing," he explained, watching the way she bit her full lower lip.

He could tell she was thinking about it.

Say yes, he prompted her mentally.

It didn't matter that this was bound to end in disappointment or disaster. Ever since she had written that letter about reading novels in the tub, he had pictured it a hundred times, a thousand, maybe. It was like a compulsion, this desire to see her in that moment, to be there as she relaxed her head against the edge of the bathtub, hear her sigh as she lathed soap across her skin while steam rose from the water to wrap itself around her.

If it was her greatest indulgence, he wanted to see her in the midst of it. It would be like possessing a piece of her soul.

"Say yes," he whispered aloud.

The deep blue of her eyes sharpened on his, and he could tell she was searching his eyes for his intentions. She was going to be disappointed because even he didn't know what they were at this point. He had no idea what he was doing inviting such temptation. This kind of danger would be a first for him as well, and he was not an easy man to impress with novelty.

Finally, she breathed out, and he realized she had been holding her breath for over a minute now. Excellent. He wanted her to be affected by his nearness.

"All right," she said, holding up a finger to his slow smile. "But there has to be rules."

He grew solemn again. "Of course." She always wanted rules.

"Rule number one." She poked her finger towards him.

"Yes," he prompted.

"If I tell you to look away, you must do so immediately and not peek."

"Even if I really want to peek?" he asked seriously.

"Yes." She took a sip of her hot chocolate.

"What else?" He stood up straight, savoring his victory and the sweetness that ran through his veins.

"No touching," she declared.

He sighed and waved the statement away. "I've already said that, more's the pity."

"And…" She held up a third finger. "You have to do whatever I say, no matter the other rules."

Ash narrowed his eyes. "Are you going to make me clean your paintbrushes or some such?" he asked, crossing his arms.

"That's an idea," she said brightly. "But no."

Nodding slowly, he replied, "All right, I agree to your terms. You've twisted my arm, but," he shrugged, "if you want me to read to you in the tub, I suppose I will."

She sat up straight, almost spilling her mug. "What? I didn't ask—"

Holding up a hand, he interrupted, "Never let it be said that the Marquess of Blackbourne could refuse a lady anything."

"Why, you ingrate!" She slammed her cup on the table and stood, which Ash found intensely humorous as her stature only emphasized how much larger he was than her.

"Now is that any way to treat your employer?" he asked, stepping closer to loom over her.

She backed away a step, and growled. Actually growled.

Ash laughed. She was the most adorable little thing... "So tomorrow night then? I believe you usually do your reading around eight o'clock?"

She glared and then turned away, muttering as she stomped away. "Why I ever agree to anything you say is beyond me..." her voice faded as he watched her exit the drawing room.

Chuckling, he picked up her still-warm cup of chocolate and took a sip. He'd never much indulged in the stuff, but it wasn't half bad. The city of London shone in the moonlight as he turned to the balcony again, sipping the chocolate. For once, his mind didn't leap to calculations or diagrams. It was simply peaceful looking out over the cityscape in its myriad forms and shapes and sounds. Yes, his mind recognized the various things he could potentially figure out within his field of vision, but it didn't overwhelm like usual.

He wasn't even tupping the girl, but she stimulated him like nothing else. Even his projects and his disguises didn't keep his mind occupied like she did when she was near. Her every move, the way she sparred with him, her funny habits... He didn't know why she interested him, but she did. Other women had held his interest for a few days at a time, depending on their inventiveness in the bedroom, but it never lasted.

This probably wouldn't either. Perhaps it was because he couldn't let himself have her that she fascinated him. The proverbial forbidden fruit, as it were.

He might need to indulge himself with another woman so his hunger for Ivy didn't distract him as it had lately. That would solve the problem, he was sure.

But the thought held no appeal. He didn't want just any other woman. He wanted her.

Ash drained the cup, swirling the heavy dregs of chocolate at the bottom with his tongue.

He had just made an appointment to be in the same room while she was naked, doing the most boring thing he could think of.

Yet he wasn't allowed the touch her.

"What in blazes is wrong with me?" he muttered, and smashed the mug to the terrace below.
****

"Where in blazes is that indigo?" Ivy muttered, trying to pinpoint the right paint pot with the hovering tip of her brush from where she sat at the easel.

Having tried to concentrate on painting all morning, she was growing increasingly frustrated with herself. The Raphael was coming along nicely, but she couldn't get the shadow within the subject's cloak hem quite the right shade no matter what she did. It didn't help that she kept letting the paint dry on her brush before she even put it to the canvas, her mind wandering off for minutes at a time.

Oh, all right, she knew exactly why she kept getting distracted, but she wasn't going to admit it to herself just yet.

That man didn't deserve any more mental attention than he already received from countless other women, she was sure. From what she had gleaned from the staff and an overheard (mostly giggled) conversation between the dressmaker's assistants two weeks ago, it was clear Blackbourne had a renowned reputation where women were concerned.

As she ruminated on this troubling train of thought, the butler, Milton, entered the drawing room, salver tray in hand. She shook herself from her reverie and smiled at the elderly man. He was a dear old thing, Ivy thought, with fuzzy white hair sticking out at all angles and a familial tone when he spoke to her.

He marched towards her holding out the salver, on it an envelope. "Here you are, dearie," he gruffed.

"Thank you, Milton," she replied, taking the envelope and patting his mottled hand. "Whatever would I do without you?"

"Get into trouble, no doubt," he declared. "You young things are always up to something, especially ones like the Master."

"I don't doubt that at all, sir," she agreed wryly. Blackbourne was definitely up to something most of the time, and she probably didn't even know the half of it.

"Your painting is lovely, pet," he told her, his rheumy eyes gazing at the canvas.

She didn't bother to bring up the fact that he'd already told her so about a dozen times this week. "Thank you, kind sir! I do appreciate an admirer."

"Much better than the former Mistress's attempts, but I won't elaborate as tis bad luck to speak ill of the dead," he said, folding the tray under his arm and bowing.

"Thank you again, Milton. You are a peach," she said, kissing him on the cheek before he turned away to leave.

He blushed right down to the roots of his hair and blustered away, spine rigid as a mast.

Ivy smiled watching him leave. She then looked down at the envelope, her heart beginning to race as she anticipated what must be another note from Blackbourne.

Turning over the envelope to read the addressee, her stomach plummeted.

To Jacob Wollard, Care of Ivette Wollard
Forwarded by Chief Gaoler Ian Crick
New Bridewell Prison, Westminster, London

She swallowed and put down her brush, not bothering to clean it as she stared at the script written in precise hand on the envelope. With numb determination, she left the drawing room and went to her chambers down the hall and around the corner.

Once she had firmly shut the door behind her, she settled herself on the bed and solemnly tore open the envelope, letting two letter sheaves fall out onto the counterpane.

Ivy sighed, readying herself.

She hated this part. She hated it with all of her being. It made her feel as unclean as everyone thought she was, as if she'd never be able to wash the filth of its contents from herself.

But she had asked for this, she reminded herself. If she didn't do this, no one would.

When she had come of age, she had made sure her current address was always on file with the Gaoler for the forwarding of Jacob Wollard's correspondence. As his next of kin, she had the right to intercept his mail and deal with all legal matters by proxy. When she had come to London with Blackbourne, the first thing she had done upon waking in Blackbourne House was to send off a missive to Tothill Fields Bridewell Prison with her new address so that nothing would slip through the cracks.

Clenching her teeth, she opened the first letter

and read:

> *Mr. Jacob Wollard,*
> *I'm big admiror and like to express my sympathy that you are in gaol. They shud*
> *let you out. Plees rispond. Thank you.*
> *Adam Hurst*

Lip curling in disgust, she set that one aside and picked up the next piece of parchment, hands shaking. She recognized the handwriting by now.

> *Dear Mr. Wollard,*
> *Your methods continue to inspire those of us with the fortitude of spirit to contemplate such glorious endeavors. Be assured that your legacy of artistic execution of these deeds will live on in the minds of all who admire your work.*
>
> *I have been developing a new method of strangulation which I think you'll find is reminiscent of your technique and which builds upon it, carrying the mechanics to a new height. Your favored garrote method for many of your chosen women has made me eager to try such a visceral encounter, and so I have devoted myself to perfecting what I think you will be proud to claim was developed on the premise of your preferred practice.*
>
> *It has always been a great regret of mine that I was never able to speak to you in person about your exploits, and I often wonder what you would say to the questions I have.*
>
> *What is it like to feel the life leave someone's body as you hold her?*
>
> *Did you pursue women of low birth purely for opportunistic purposes or because they prove more spirited quarry?*
>
> *What measures did you use to ensure that your involvement was undetected by lesser minds?*

Your plight weighs on me heavily knowing that such a fundamental death artist such as yourself is not appreciated by the general public. Those who understand the subtleties of life and death as we do know that to take someone's life is to absorb their energy and channel it to a higher purpose of natural selection. The beauty that is created by that transfer of energy is something you are familiar with, and I can only hope to possess such knowledge someday soon. Such a death is as honorable as can be imagined, yet society continues to persecute us for our calling, for our appreciation of saturnine beauty. I look forward to continuing the work you so dedicatedly performed while free and will champion your cause should you ever be considered for release.

Until then,
Your devoted servant,
Claymore

Ivy gagged and dropped the parchment as if it were a hot coal. She covered her face with her hands and slumped forward.

They were getting worse.

Before, Claymore had only spoken of theoretical methods of killing, but it sounded as if he was planning on using his own sort of device to go about it in the future.

Yet what was she supposed to do with such information? She had gone to the local police in Leeds with a similar letter four years ago, but they had turned her away, stating that they couldn't prosecute someone for something they hadn't done yet, and there was no way of verifying who had written the letter with so little to indicate their identity.

Many of her father's admirer's intentionally left off a return address or identifying information, she assumed for exactly such reasons. Although writers of letters like the first one from today might not be smart enough to do so, she didn't put too much worry into them because they didn't indicate a desire to actually do anything. Plus, she doubted anyone with such a lack of communication skills had the wherewithal to plan anything truly nefarious that local authorities couldn't figure out.

But men like Claymore...

Those were the ones she spent sleepless nights over and agonized about what to do with.

She felt a tear slip from her eye to darken the silk counterpane. When she thought of the suffering her father's victims had endured...

Once the authorities had arrested him in their home that night nine years ago, they had made him state and then write a confession of every despicable deed he had done, and he had complied gladly, listing horror after horror he had performed on each and every woman before he'd ended their lives. She remembered sobbing uncontrollably in the corner of their little library as her father's voice filled the next room with his matter-of-fact recitation. It wasn't long before a detective had led her out and put her in her room down the hall while they finished the interview.

She had never been innocent after that night.

All she knew now was that, if Claymore or anyone else ever admitted they were planning to kill someone, she would have to act.

And that's why she forced herself to read every single repugnant line that was sent to her father. If one of these demented cretins ever did anything, and she had known they were going to beforehand, she would never forgive herself.

Ivy still didn't know if she forgave herself for being related to a man that had killed sixteen women over a decade's time. All those people might have been right—mayhap she was evil just like him, and when she wasn't paying attention, it would come out, and she'd do something terrible.

For that reason, she had been alone for almost ten years. She had purposefully made sure that no one was close enough to her to be in danger if she did one day follow in her father's footsteps. She didn't feel as if she were in danger of suddenly going on a violent spree, but the same blood ran in her veins, the same mind passed down to her. It wasn't worth taking any chances if her psyche did begin to twist as her father's had. It was one of the reasons she couldn't allow herself to become close to her employer or anyone here either.

But it was so hard with him.

Blackbourne had come into her life like a force of nature, upsetting the emotional independence she'd survived on for so long. He made her want to abandon her self-imposed exile and run into his very capable arms.

She knew he didn't want the kind of intimacy she fantasized about either, which was for the best. As long as he kept her at arm's length, she could do the same.

This whole business with the bath notwithstanding, of course.

Ivy groaned.

How was she to survive this job intact if he made requests like reading to her while she bathed?

Ivy instinctively knew if she'd said no to him, he would have left her be. At least she knew her position was not at stake. Somehow, she was certain he wasn't the type of man to make a woman's employment dependent on personal favors. For that, she was thankful.

Once, when she'd been desperate for a job, she'd applied as a scullery maid at a well-to-do family's home in Leeds, and the Master of the house had happened to walk by as she was being interviewed by the butler. He had interrupted and told her that he would be willing to overlook her background and lack of experience if she would agree to bed him at least twice a week. Mortified, she'd practically run from the premises and hadn't bothered to go back for her umbrella later.

No, Blackbourne wasn't that type of man. He was the type to make his women burn for him until they begged him to bed them.

She would admit she had come close to thinking about such a thing when she'd been in the carriage with him, but she wasn't one of his women that was going to fall over herself to gain his attentions.

In fact, she didn't want them at all.

Ivy threw herself back against the pillows. That just wasn't true.

Who knew that even with every luxury she could possibly want, her life could still be anguished? She had thought that not worrying constantly about becoming a beggar on the street would make everything better. Of course, that helped immensely. She had never felt as secure or happy in her life as she had the past two weeks in this house.

Yet here she was, agonizing over her employer's opinion of her and over her father's admirers. It seemed that no matter what circumstances she was in, those things wouldn't change.

Her heart skipped a beat. Such sentiments weren't likely to end soon, for in just a few hours' time, she would be bathing in the same room as the man.

Lord save her from her stupidity.

Chapter Five

Today was a bad day.

Asher's mind was a messy jumble of facts, figures, and correlations. His head ached as if hot skewers pierced his skull relentlessly, jamming more numbers and diagrams into the growing tangle until he couldn't concentrate on anything except praying the pain would cease.

Sitting at the desk in his study, he held his head in his hands, eyes closed to the world around in hopes that the lack of visual stimulation would dissipate some of the information swimming in his head. Since he had stopped working through the archival records in service to "Project Plague," as he was now calling it, his mind had been growing steadily worse. Without a specific goal or set of data to focus on, he couldn't stop the barrage of random sensory information from everywhere around him, causing the overload that now consumed him.

The only thing that had helped in the past three days since the night of the soiree had been Ivy's presence. When he saw her, spoke with her, heard her voice, even smelled her. But he couldn't simply stalk her around the house just so he wouldn't have a headache, could he? She'd think he was insane, just as everyone else would if they knew the truth.

He could picture that conversation.

Yes, Ivy, that's right. I'd just like to follow you around, watch what you do, and maybe touch your hair a bit so I don't go crazy. That won't be a problem, will it?

He grunted in disgust.

He didn't moon over women.

Ever.

There had never been a better time to find a willing woman to distract himself with, yet he couldn't make himself concentrate on the task long enough to become remotely excited about the idea. Besides not being particularly enthusiastic about the prospect, whenever he thought about bringing a woman here, he just couldn't stomach the thought of what Ivy would think of him.

Since when did he care about what anyone else thought? Even his friends knew better than to try and shame him for his libertine ways, and damn anyone else who tried.

So what was he doing obsessing over the opinion of some chit he barely knew?

Except, he felt like he did know her. Maybe that was the problem. Once he had started writing those idiotic letters back and forth with her, he had started to think of her as someone he wanted to know more about, and that was an enormous mistake. He would have to be careful not to delve any deeper into those murky waters of understanding such a creature, for it was obviously detrimental to his usual mental processes.

The whole business with the bath notwithstanding, of course.

Hearing a creak from the vicinity of the doorway, he looked up to find the subject of his dangerous thoughts standing in the doorway, rubbing one ankle against the other hesitantly.

She was dressed in an aquamarine-colored day gown made of some sort of crinkled silk that gathered under her breasts and skimmed down over her hips gently. He had to admit she was born to wear such luxury, the way her skin glowed and her loosely upswept hair gleamed in the reflection of the silk. Asher had become an expert at assessing a woman's charms based on her clothes as an indicator of breeding or her self-awareness.

And Ivy was as elegant as they came, despite her diminutive stature. He wondered how sheltered she actually was, half her life lived as a lady, the other half presumably on her own in a large city. Her deep blue eyes looked so innocent, yet seductive at the same time, framed as they were with dark lashes that whisked out from the corners like angel's wings.

Angel's wings? Really, Ash, get ahold of yourself.

He lowered his hands from his temples and sat up straight. "Hello, Miss Wollard. What can I do for you this morning?" He attempted a smile, but he was sure it looked as strained as it felt.

She frowned. "I was going to ask if you have any sheaf sachets to spare, but you don't look as if you feel well," she commented, coming into the room and lowering herself into a chair across from him.

He had told her he would be honest. "No, I'm not feeling quite up to snuff today."

"Hmm." She abruptly stood and came around the desk, putting the back of her hand to his forehead.

His lungs froze as he drank in her proximity. Her scent was the same as that first night when he hadn't realized it was her and had almost made a mess of things. Vanilla and roses. Whoever had come up with that combination was a genius.

Ratios of oils and binding agents rose in front of his eyes, and pain shot through his left temple. Gritting his teeth, he forced the calculations to dissolve into nothingness as he watched her chest rise and fall with her breathing.

Asher thought with amusement that if she were any other woman of normal height, she would have had to bend over further to reach him sitting down in his hair, but not Ivy. She was barely taller than he whilst standing and he sitting. How unfair that her bosom was at eye level, but not angled so he could see anything other than the pleasing shape of them under her dress.

"No fever," she said thoughtfully, pulling her hand away.

His hands itched to grab her hips and pull her atop him. It would be so easy to do so, and he wondered what her reaction would be. Would she gasp and pull away in outrage or would she freeze atop him, unsure of what to do? Or was she more worldly than she seemed and wouldn't hesitate to melt into him, her compact frame lithely coming into his embrace?

As she moved away back to her chair, the empty space where she'd been left a feeling of bereavement.

"I'm not sick," he told her, clearing his throat. "Or, at least, not in the usual way."

"What do you mean?" She cocked her head as she sat back down.

He wanted to tell her, which was unwise. Who knew what she would do with such information about a peer of the realm?

His cousin, who became *Guardian ad Litem* to the Marquessate if he was deemed mentally incompetent, had once planted a footman in his household to attempt to observe his "episodes," but Ash had figured out his intentions quickly. He had sent the man back to his cousin with a letter inviting him for Christmas dinner to observe him in person if he wanted the estate. Needless to say, the man hadn't shown up for Christmas.

He always had to be cautious, but with Ivy…

To Hell with it.

"I get megrims sometimes when I'm unfocused," he stated, holding still for her reaction.

She blinked. "That sounds terrible. Is there

anything I can do to help?"

He let out a strangled laugh that he turned into a cough. There were multiple ways, but almost all of them involved her naked, which he didn't think she was offering. "Thank you, but no. I just need … a distraction. Something to occupy my mind so everything else is forced out."

She puckered her lips in thought, drawing his gaze to them. "What sort of distraction?"

Ash ground his teeth. He was going to end up telling her if she kept asking so sweetly.

"I have intellectual projects that I am involved in much of the time," he told her, leaning back in his chair, "but I am at a standstill for the moment. It's nothing you'd be interested in."

She bounced on her seat and crossed her arms. "You don't know if I'd be interested or not," she said pertly.

He grinned. "Ladies don't usually enjoy discussing things like the plague," he said bluntly.

"The plague?" She thought about it, then shrugged. "I don't see why not."

Leaning forward, Ash looked at her raised brows. She was so certain of herself… Now he just wanted to shock her to see her pretty eyes widen and her lips part. "Rats. That's what's been put about as the carriers of the disease that ravaged Europe in the fourteenth century. But an associate of mine believes otherwise. He thinks there may be things inside people's bodies that crawl onto other people and make them sick." He raised a brow of his own.

To his satisfaction, her eyes did widen, but she recovered quickly, scooting to the edge of her chair. "Really? Things that crawl? What are these things?"

Asher frowned. She was supposed to be running

in horror. "Well, he doesn't really know. They are too tiny to be seen with the human eye, but they can move through the air, in water, on your skin, your breath…"

"How interesting," she breathed. "And are they inside everyone all the time, and they get sick, too, or are they the sickness themselves?"

"We aren't sure," he admitted wryly. "It's difficult to test such a theory, which is why I'm working on an algorithm that might prove the theory mathematically using the spread of the plague as a model."

The tip of her tongue darted out to curl up at the corner of her lip as she considered this. "I would imagine that's difficult with information from hundreds of years ago." She waved her hands to indicate what he assumed was the passage of time. "Were the records back then really that meticulously kept for you to be able to extrapolate a rate of infectious spread?"

Asher shook his head, smiling. Her questions showed an intelligence he hadn't expected. But as he was shaking his head, he realized—

It wasn't hurting anymore. No spikes of pain flashed from temple to temple, no figures crowded his vision.

Just speaking with her about anything was enough to cause his mind to settle into what he knew was normal for other people. Except he didn't feel as if he was numbing the insights that ran through his head. Instead, they were sharpened, focused in a way he hadn't thought possible. He enjoyed his time as Reginald Morganstern for precisely that reason—the ability to hone his mind on something and let loose his intellect on a particular subject with human interaction as the catalyst.

Yet here was this woman who embodied the best

and worst methods that he used to control his raging thoughts and combined them into a fetching little package. Which somehow made him want her with such sudden and violent hunger he almost couldn't control it.

This was not his style. He used sex for his own purposes. It did not control him.

Ash looked downward so he wouldn't meet her eyes. "You should go," he told her in a low voice, watching the pulse of her artery at the base of her throat.

Ivy leaned back. "I'm sorry, did-did I do something wrong?" she asked, her eyes clouding in confusion.

He shook his head. "No. My head..." he intentionally didn't finish.

"Oh," she said softly, coming to her feet. "Of course. I'm sorry. I'll leave you be."

"Ivy?" He met her eyes as she was turning towards the door.

"Yes?"

"Thank you," he said gently.

She paused. "For what, my lord?"

He smiled. "Nothing. I'll see you at eight o'clock."

She colored. "Yes, Lord Blackbourne." She began to walk towards the doorway.

"Oh, and Ivy?"

She turned.

"Call me Ash. It's only fair."

Ivy nodded and left the room, but Ash saw the small smile playing at the corners of her lips as she went.
****

Don't hyperventilate. Don't hyperventilate.

Ivy repeated the mantra as the seconds ticked by, and her nerves stretched to breaking point. She wondered if the sound of her pounding heartbeat was muffled or amplified by the water she sat in.

Water she wasn't sure was completely opaque.

She squinted at the steaming, milky liquid that had been thoroughly doused with the lavender sudsing lather she'd frantically searched for ten minutes ago. She hadn't been able to produce as many bubbles with the stuff as she'd hoped, but it had turned the water a milky color that she hoped masked any shape of her body beneath the surface.

Also working in her favor was the way the bath was positioned in relation to the gaslight sconces on the wall the chamber shared with the bedroom. Usually, she set an oil lamp on the table text to the tub so she could read by its added light, but tonight, she had purposefully left it unlit to provide less visibility of her person.

If he did try to touch her, she was ready. She eyed the knife that sat beside her book on the tub-side table. It had not left her side since it had been given to her by a boy who had also lived in the abandoned building in Harrogate. He had been two years younger than she, but infinitely better prepared for life on the streets. Each night as the children had gathered around their meager fire pit, he had taught her to use it. She had been a diligent pupil, learning all the motions and tricks her mentor possessed until one day, she bested him during a practice session. He had solemnly presented her with the silver-plated (most likely stolen) knife she now carried, declaring her ready for anything.

Despite that, she suspected she wasn't nearly ready to face the Marquess of Blackbourne in a different sort of game altogether.

Waiting was the worst part, surely.

She certainly wouldn't feel as if she couldn't breathe the entire time. Once he was here, it would turn out to be a perfectly civil and appropriate interaction that would end without incident once he'd satisfied his curiosity.

Who was she trying to fool?

"Perfectly appropriate, my arse," she mumbled, considering abandoning the entire thing and drying off before he arrived. Yes, that was probably best. He would just have to—

"Arses weren't part of the bargain, but if you're offering…" Blackbourne's voice echoed from the doorway, where he leaned against it till it shut behind him with a click of finality.

Ivy's heart stopped as she met his heavy-lidded gaze, which was raking over her in thorough evaluation.

He came towards the tub, running a finger along the porcelain edge, and she shrank back instinctively.

He chuckled. "Don't worry, love. I won't bite," he drawled, and then paused. "Yet."

She inhaled as his eyes flashed promises of things she knew she didn't understand.

"And your bathwater is quite thoroughly unrevealing. What a pity." He sighed, pulling the nearby chair closer to the tub and lowering himself down into it. He crossed one ankle over his opposite knee and leaned back, hands resting on his thighs.

"That's a relief," she said, hugging her knees to her chest, just in case.

Blackbourne stared at her for a long moment, and she saw his hands clench into white-knuckled fists on his legs. "You're beautiful," he said, the statement floating in the air like the steam that rose from the water around her.

Ivy shivered, despite the heat.

"I'm sure you've seen many beautiful women in more revealing states than mine," she replied, wanting to hear him deny it.

He smiled and did no such thing. "They aren't you."

She smiled wryly. "And I would bet you say that to them as well."

He shrugged, shifting his weight in the chair. "I may have a time or two."

Was she making him uncomfortable? Good. She took a breath. "Then tell me something you've never said to another woman," she challenged him, letting go of her legs to let her limbs float.

He cocked his head to the side, studying her.

"Or am I not the first to ask that either?" she inquired. She wasn't going to let him be who she was beginning to realize he was with other women. It would be too easy for him to manipulate and discard her, and there was no way she was going to let that happen, no matter the nature of their relationship.

"You are not," he said slowly. "But you may be the first woman for whom I want to answer."

"How do I know you haven't had this conversation a dozen times before?" She rolled over and came to rest her chin on the edge of the tub nearest him. Her feet stuck out on the other end, but she decided she didn't care if he saw them. They were only feet.

He smiled, watching her gambol about. "You don't."

"Then what is the point?" she asked softly.

Some expression passed over his face and was gone again, but she couldn't tell what it had been. "Now that is a better question, my sweet, but one I fear I can't tell you the answer to."

She rolled her eyes and sighed, propping her cheek on her dripping elbow. "Why is that not surprising? You haven't even answered the first question."

"It was more of a demand," he corrected in dry tones.

"Either way, I feel as if I've been much more accommodating tonight than you have," she pointed out, glancing pointedly down at the bathwater.

He grinned and leaned forward with his elbows on his knees, their faces now only a few feet apart. "I'll concede that."

"But you won't answer me?"

"Mystery is good for the soul," he rejoined, lips upturned while his ice-blue eyes held hers.

She leaned back in the tub, careful not to let anything below her shoulders rise above the water. "So is telling your employer what you really think of him, but I've controlled myself thus far." She raised a brow.

He laughed and leaned back as well. "Now I have to know. What does the Irresistible Ivy Wollard think of her boss?"

Ivy blushed at the title, which she was sure now made her bright red in combination with the heat from the water vapor. "Now why would I tell you that if you won't answer my questions?"

"Fine then," he said, tenting his fingers in his lap. "I'll you something I've never told another woman if…" he paused, and Ivy watched how the gaslight bathed his skin in light from one side. "If you wash your hair for me."

Ivy blinked. "Now?" she squeaked, reaching up to pat her hair, which she had kept in a high chignon so it wouldn't get wet.

He nodded, his posture relaxed, although Ivy knew this to be deceptive. He was waiting to hear her answer with taut focus.

She gulped. How was she to do this without showing anything of herself?

As if sensing her trepidation, Blackbourne interrupted her thoughts with a soft suggestion. "Let me help you."

The words reached out to her with tendrils that wrapped her consciousness in a sensual fog, causing the hair on her nape to rise.

This was not done, she knew. A proper lady would never allow a gentleman to touch her hair, much less while she bathed.

But what about any of their arrangement was proper in the first place? She was fairly certain proper ladies didn't masquerade as scientists' sisters or sleep in bachelor residences with no chaperone. And she could still feel the calluses on her hands that were slowly fading—something no lady would have ever had to deal with. She had lived on the streets, worked her fingers to the bone, and shared bathwater with a prostitute on a regular basis.

Why start worrying about what was done or not done now?

Who would even know? Not a soul in the world knew who she was or cared what she was doing besides the people in this room.

Besides him.

So she reached up slowly so as not to disturb the water covering her chest and drew the stickpin from her hair, letting its length fall in a heavy coil down her back.

Blackbourne's sharp inhalation echoed off the tiles in the silence.

Heart in her throat, she combed her fingers through the wavy locks as Blackbourne rose and came around the back of the tub. She wasn't sure what she was supposed to do, but her body didn't seem to be able to move regardless, so she kept facing forward without knowing what he was doing behind her.

Then his hands threaded into her hair, and she gasped at the tingling on her scalp.

"Just as I thought," he murmured. "Like braided moonbeams." His voice was close, and she could sense that he'd bent down to a knee to reach her.

The sudden urge to strike at him rose in Ivy's chest. His nearness created an instinctual impulse to incapacitate him and move to safety. Her eyes darted to where her knife lay. She could overcome him with one well-placed thrust. It would be satisfying to surprise him like that, to see his eyes as he realized the power had shifted between them.

No.

Her father's predilections would not manifest in her tonight. Not now. Not with him.

She forced herself to unclench her fists as, with gentle pressure, he guided her head back until her hair was submerged in the fragrant water.

Ivy let her body float down to a more horizontal position, her limbs beginning to relax at the kneading of his hands. Lifting her back up once more, he took the hair rinse from the stand at the head of the tub and, section by section, worked her hair into a rich lather.

Sighing, Ivy let herself enjoy the sensations, vacillating between drowsiness and an awareness of parts of her body she realized wanted his attention as well.

A bubble of hope rose in her accompanied by the ever-present fear—she had won tonight. Perhaps she could conquer her urges, unlike her father had been able to do.

"You're making me regret this," Blackbourne said as he put her hair back in the water. He dipped her head down further, smoothing water over the roots at her scalp.

"How so?" she said groggily. She opened her

eyes and looked up, seeing his face upside down above hers. His ice-blue eyes burned into her own, the hunger there obvious.

Letting her long hair flow over his palms in the bathwater, he explained in a low voice. "Touching you like this only makes me want you more. I'm afraid now that anything you give me will never be enough."

His vulnerability showed, though she also saw in his expression hope that his words were having a certain effect on her.

They were.

She wanted his hands to touch her everywhere, to skim over her skin in the same manner he was handling her hair. His lulling tone washed over her hotter than the water that encased her skin, as if he caressed her with words alone.

Trying her best to hold his permeating gaze, she replied, "Is that what you've never told another woman?"

He chuckled, his eyes crinkling at the corners. Knotting her hair around his fist, he guided her head up out of the water again so she couldn't see him behind her. Letting go of the mass of water-drenched locks, he shaped his hands over her shoulders, cupping the slick skin preciously. "No," he told her, his tone reverent. He smoothed his long fingers up the sides of her neck and gently massaged the tendons there.

Her heart beat erratically, the feeling of his hands on her skin like a brand. "You sure have said a lot of things to women, then," she said, trying to sound wry when she was about to let herself sink into the water from sheer pleasure.

"Now you're just trying to make me feel bad," he needled, but his hurt tone didn't fool her one bit.

"Have you ever felt bad for anything you've done to women?" she inquired pointedly.

"No." She heard the grin in his voice. "Usually, they're begging me not to stop, so I've taken it as a good sign," he purred, his mouth closer to her ear than she expected.

Ivy's breath caught as he slid one hand to the front of her throat and stroked the sensitive skin there before skimming down to her collarbone. One hand still around her throat, he traced the winged shape of her bone structure with a finger, the others dipping lower, almost to where the swell of her breasts began. She couldn't have moved even if she'd wanted to, every nerve ending paralyzed by the sensations his hands brought forth.

"Are you going to stop me?" he breathed, his words tickling the hairs near her ear.

His hand hesitated at the point on her chest where the valley between her mounds began, and with all her being, she wanted him to continue his path.

"In a moment," she whispered,

He laughed, and his hands stopped moving. Ivy was jarred out of her reverie as he pulled back, his hands leaving her body too quickly.

"I'm afraid another moment, and I wouldn't have been able to stop, no matter either of our pure intentions," he admitted.

Ivy sighed and sunk lower in the tub, the heat from his touch fading. "You've never had a pure intention in your life."

"You may be right about that," he said thoughtfully. "Although I thought I did when I offered you a position here."

Ivy watched him come back round the tub and sit in the chair at the other end.

She knew she was a complete heathen for wanting him to come back to her and put his hands on her again, but she hugged her arms about herself, resigned to the empty feeling. She was used to that feeling, so she sank back into it, the familiar space surrounding her once again.

"You do realize that defrauding an elite scientific organization and the *ton* itself is not pure intentioned, don't you?"

Blackbourne shrugged. "Whatever you say, Oh Paragon of all that is Proper." He crossed his legs, a smirk on his face. "Is your bath still warm enough? I'll help you dry if you'd like."

Ivy's eyes narrowed. He had made his point.

"It's perfectly warm, thank you," she said stiffly.

"Good. Now where is your book?" he asked, eyes leaving her to roam the room.

She blinked at the change of subject. "It's there on the table." She nodded her head to the round table on the other side of the tub, loathe to remove any part of her person from the warm water, which, though she'd never admit it, was cooling quickly.

He reached for it and grunted as he settled back in the chair with it, one ankle crossed over the other knee. "What page are you on?"

"Ninety-four."

"Why would you want to do this? Read to me?" she asked in puzzlement, flicking droplets of water towards him with her fingers.

He winced as the water made contact. "It's a mystery to us both, you can be sure," he said, his voice dripping in ruefulness.

Blackbourne then proceeded to read from the book whilst Ivy came to prop her head on her arms at the lip of the tub nearest him to listen.

And so began a new nightly ritual for them both, neither quite sure what it meant.

Chapter Six

Jealousy was not a feeling with which he was familiar, but it was as unpleasant as feelings could be, Asher admitted to himself, standing with his arms crossed in a corner of the Crosthwaite's ballroom.

Watching Ivy flit from dance to dance in the arms of one man after another was enough to drive a man to drink—something he'd been doing all night.

Usually, he refrained from over-indulging as he had discovered his weakness for spirits long ago. As a means of dulling his thought processes, it was quite effective, and he had allowed himself the use of it as a means of escape for a few years before realizing he had become a drunkard. Disgusted with the path he had seen himself heading down, he had put the stuff away, only permitting himself small amounts now and then.

Tonight, he had definitely had more than was advisable, the urge to wash away the bitter taste of Ivy's growing popularity too much to resist.

When he had asked her to play the part of Reginald Morganstern's sister, he hadn't intended for her role to extend as far as this. But at the last BAAS lecture, one of his colleagues' wives had invited her specifically to this gathering, so there was no help for it. It was a good way to flesh out her character, he supposed, if she was going to be a fixture in Morganstern's life, but the exposure she was now experiencing couldn't be good.

What if someone became interested in her background and discovered Corrine Morganstern didn't actually exist?

He would have to prepare for that possibility immediately. Having become acquainted with the

National Archives staff lately, it shouldn't be a problem to return some documents with the addition of some fabricated ones, just in case anyone came looking. The acquisition of a small estate in the Morganstern name might not go amiss either.

Hand clenched around his snifter of whiskey, he drained it again, shifting to keep her in sight.

Some pup he didn't even recognize was whisking Ivy about the floor, making her eyes light up and her laugh bubble out to taunt him. Ever since he'd arrived a safe ten minutes after her earlier in the night, he had had the distinct displeasure of observing her small form tempting every peer in the bloody realm to gather her in his arms for a dance or offer to fetch a drink for her.

How many glasses of lemonade could one woman possibly need anyways?

He had seen her naked, he boasted to himself. No matter what those other men thought when they touched her waist or kissed her hand, he had seen more of her than any of them. Well, he admitted, he hadn't seen all of her, per se, but the principle stood.

Thinking back to the past three nights in which he had seen her glowing shoulders and dewy cheeks hovering above the water as he read to her, he went to take another drink and realized it was empty.

Scowling into his glass, Asher didn't notice the man coming up to stand next to him until he began to speak.

"I know that look," Dominic said, leaning against the wall beside him.

Asher raised a brow and turned his frown into a grin quickly. "What look?"

"The one that prophesies church bells, my friend," the man replied with a chuckle.

Asher glared over at his friend, meeting the man's

blue-green eyes. "Not even close."

Dom sighed. "I'd wager on it, but we both know you're too smart to accept those odds since you've already calculated them."

Ash pursed his lips. Dom was one of the few people who understood him, at least to an extent. His devil-may-care façade had never worked on his friend. Dominic Tierney, the Duke of Scythemore, had always seen through to the truth of his nature. Sometimes, it was nice to have someone who knew and accepted him as he was. Dom had been the only factor that had gotten him through a childhood of hiding his mind from the world. Other times, like now, it was a great inconvenience to have someone's penetrating honesty force him from his own games.

"The odds are impossible," he stated, his eyes locking onto Ivy again as she was led back to the refreshments table by Lord Something-or-other that shouldn't have had the audacity to speak to her in the first place.

"Mmmm, yes, I see that," Dom said, snorting as he walked back towards his sister across the room.

Let him think what he wanted. Ash knew himself, and he wasn't worried. His only concern was for her identity's safety, and letting anyone get too close to her would be a disaster for them both.

Deciding it was past time to refill his glass, he made his way over to the refreshments, ignoring the targeted stare of a woman from behind her fan. He was fairly certain, based on what he saw of her face, that he had bedded that particular widow a few years ago. It was of no import now. He rarely went back for second helpings of any given dessert, and he wasn't in the mood to engage in her tilt-eyed invitation.

As he approached the gilded table with its towers

of sweetmeats, French pastries, and punch bowls, Ivy's deep purple gown twirled round as she accepted a glass of ratafia from her companion. Ash sauntered up to the two of them, pushing his way between them as he reached for the decanter of whiskey on the table.

"Oh, I'm sorry, ol' boy. Didn't see you there," he smiled at the man frowning at him from his right.

"Lord Blackbourne?" Ivy spoke up in confusion from his other side.

He turned toward her, pouring a few fingers into his glass "Yes, love?"

"I say, that's quite familiar!" Lord Something-or-other said.

"It is, isn't it?" Ash agreed, taking a sip and smiling.

The man spluttered. "This-this is Miss Morganstern, sir, and she deserves to be addressed as such!"

"I don't disagree," Ash intoned. "But "Love" just sounds so much more ... *friendly*, don't you think?"

His mouth hung open, and he turned back to Ivy. "Do you know this man?" the gentleman demanded, his eyes bulging.

Ivy's brows were raised and Asher saw her delicate throat swallow. "Erm... We have met at a recent function, yes."

"You should apologize for your disrespectful phrasing, sir," Lord So-and-so declared.

"You're absolutely right," Ash agreed, pulling Ivy's arm through his own. "Let me escort you to the terrace where I can do so."

He led Ivy away from the man, who had turned red in the face, but couldn't quite formulate anything to say, evidently. As he drifted with her through the onlookers on the outskirts of the ballroom, he took a deep breath and let it out slowly. He could breathe again, knowing she was in his presence once more.

"What was that about?" Ivy demanded, looking up at him.

"He was obviously a great bore. You're welcome," he said decidedly, leading her past the terrace doors and towards the gaming room where gentlemen lingered to play cards while their wives danced and gossiped.

Ivy scoffed. "Of all the arrogant things... I was having a grand time!"

Looking down at her, he met her flashing blue eyes. "What was his name?"

"Excuse me?" She sounded incensed.

"What was that man's name?" he repeated.

"Lord... Lord Something-or-other," she waved her hand.

He smirked. "That's what I thought."

"You're insufferable," she complained, letting him steer her past the gaming tables to a hallway near the back of the room.

"Yet here you are, allowing me to take you away from the party to an isolated part of the house for an unknown reason," he said aloofly.

"I'm letting my employer have a private conversation with me," she corrected.

"What if I weren't your employer?" he asked, looking down at the dark, shiny twists of hair piled on the top of her head. Glancing round the room to assure no one was watching their exit, he slipped them into the unlit hallway and began leading her past the doors on either side.

"If you weren't, I would still be working at the paper mill right now, unfit to wear a dress such as this." She indicated her dress, which, Ash noted, contrasted strikingly with the creamy skin of her shoulders and neck.

"At this hour?" he frowned, knowing it was well past ten o'clock. They were almost at the end of the hallway, so he tried a door to his right and, finding it unlocked, paused with her there.

She looked up at him and shook her head with a smile. "Yes, at this hour. Someone in my situation cannot afford to be choosy about their schedule. Oftentimes, it felt like I barely made it home before the sun came up, and I had to return."

Opening the door, he put his hand on the small of her back and guided her through it, following behind her and closing the door with a click.

She turned to face him, moonlight gilding her form from behind. He was reminded again of how petite she really was—how her weight would feel if he were to pick her up and wrap her legs around his waist. It would be no effort at all to carry her like that to the white chair and feel her riding against his...

"I'm enjoying my employment much more now, so thank you." She laughed, interrupting his perilous thoughts.

The room they had ended up in was clearly a sunroom, an antechamber meant to lead to the gardens in the rear of the property. With windows for walls that showed the night on the side opposite the door, it seemed larger than it was, only having the capacity to hold one wicker chair, a potted palm, and a couple baskets of gardening tools off to one side.

"You should never have to labor another minute of your life," he said softly, reaching for her hand and tracing a callus that still lingered on her palm.

"I'm working right now, aren't I?" she countered.

He felt her shiver at his fingertips on her palm,

knowing how sensitive the skin there was. Ash had touched other women's hands before, seducing them with brushes across palms and along the lengths of fingers, but everything he experienced with Ivy was new.

He understood he could have her if he employed the same tactics he had used in a multitude of past liaisons, but he didn't want to subject her to something he had done before. It was as if her demand to tell her something he'd never told another woman had taken root in his brain, and now he couldn't let it go. The thought of simply doing something he had done to a hundred others was repellent, sullying her with his past.

For the first time in his life, he regretted the times he had spent with other women, and it was a bitter pill to swallow now, when he wanted nothing more than to erase everything that had come before her and show her that she was unlike any other to him.

Ash rotated her hand until he was able to extend his fingers along hers, comparing their sizes. Chuckling at the way her tiny fingers barely reached his second knuckles, he brought her palm to his lips and placed a kiss in the center. "I hope this doesn't feel like work."

Her chest rose and fell visibly. "What is it supposed to feel like?" she whispered.

"Like this," he murmured, pulling her towards him and hearing her gasp she came up against his chest.

"I thought we agreed to no touching," she said as he wrapped his arms around her, holding her to him. Her words were breathy, revealing the effect he had on her.

Knowing he affected her thus was headier than a thousand nights with the experienced courtesans of the ton. But he wanted more. He wanted to make her breathless with pleasure, capture her moans in his mouth as she came apart beneath him, and feel her shudder with the force of it as her muscles couldn't take any more.

"All those men out there want you," he told her. "They want to touch you and hold you like this. But I want you only for myself." He put his hand at the dip in her side and gripped her tighter. "I want to take you somewhere and never let you leave until you vow you'll only accept my touch and no one else's."

She looked up at him, her lips parted and so soft he almost lost control. Eyes wide, her eyelashes quivered as she searched his face. "Whoever said I want anyone else?" she whispered.

He could hear his own breathing turn ragged at her words. A surge of pure male possessiveness coursed through him.

Now, his instincts told him. Now was the time to make her his, when she was pliable and willing in his arms. It would be the tipping point—the point at which she would sink into his embrace and let him do all the wicked things to her he had thought about since the night of the cello player.

He could tell she wouldn't resist. He had woven his net well, as he did every time.

And suddenly, he dropped his hands and stepped back, breathing hard. Waves of disgust rolled through him.

She trusted him. This woman lived in his home and knew more about him than probably anyone else did. Uprooted, abandoned, and alone, he had found her at her most vulnerable. And here he was, trying to use her like all the others.

He turned away, and he heard her say his name— his given name for once. Snatches of color, of skin on skin, different rooms, different beds flowed through his mind like water over rocks. But the rocks slashed through the images with jagged edges of pain, taking him by surprise. He put his hands to his head and turned away with a growl.

She couldn't see him like this.

"Ash? Asher, what's wrong? Are you all right?" Ivy's words were far away, yet the concern in her voice penetrated through the hammering pain that refused to leave. Numbers appeared and left just as quickly—tallies of women, of perfumes, of aggressions and games... The cold facts of his past hardened in his psyche and turned to a lump of nausea that sank to the bottom of his stomach.

He felt her lead him to the chair a few steps away. Sinking into it, head in his hands, he concentrated on forcing the throbbing to dissipate.

There was only one way he knew how to make it stop after it reached this point. But that was out of the question now. He wouldn't use her like that. She wouldn't become just another tool to fix him like the broken toy he was.

Small, cool hands slid between his, cupping his head. "Shh." She soothed, running her fingers through the hair at his temples.

Ash looked up, dazed, to find her smiling at him. He watched as if from a dream as she eased into his lap, her buttocks settling onto one of his legs while she continued to massage his scalp. Her fingernails grazed his skin, seeming to absorb all the electric energy that bombarded his head and direct it to other parts of his body.

He moaned as the aching sensation drained from his mind.

"Is that better?" she whispered, her eyes orbs of dark blue in the silvery moonlight.

"You're an angel," he mumbled, his mind still jumbled from the onslaught.

She laughed, little tinkles like stars showering

around him. "Hardly. Your head must be in more danger than it seems." Her small fingers continued to feather through his hair, and he didn't dare tell her the pain was now mostly gone.

At her ministrations, other parts of his body were beginning to take notice. He could feel himself swelling at the feel of her plump derriere positioned nicely on his thigh. Hands now lowered from his head, he put them on her hips and drew her closer up into his lap, relishing the rounded flesh that filled his palms.

She was just the right size, he thought, never having held a woman so small, yet so voluptuously endowed. Her petite bone structure allowed for all sorts of intriguing possibilities, the thought of which he struggled to banish.

What would happen if he simply grabbed her and situated her pretty little legs so that she straddled him?

Gulping, he trained his mind to let go of that line of thinking.

The strange thing was, she had now seen the ugly truth of his condition, yet he didn't feel particularly anxious that she knew. She had even teased him about it just now, but her words hadn't registered as concerning.

"It isn't my head I'm worried about just now," he told her, reaching up to tuck a loose piece of her hair behind her ear.

He saw her sense the change in atmosphere as her pupils dilated. "What is it you're worried about?"

"Treating you the way you deserve instead of the way I want to," he admitted, stroking the hairs at the base of her neck.

"I don't deserve anything," she whispered, shaking her head. Her hands dropped to her lap.

"You deserve everything," he argued, his vehemence surprising himself as his fingers tightened on her nape. "Everything I can never give you," Ash added, letting his fingers trail down her neck to rest at the place where her shoulder began.

He knew there was a large part of her that felt unworthy because of the reprehensible actions of superstitious people, but she was the opposite of evil. She was too perfect for this world altogether.

She smiled tremulously and looked into his eyes again, unshed tears showing. "Did you know you're the first person to ever touch me since I've come of age?" she said, her hands making nervous knots in her dress.

"To ever touch you like this?" he clarified, squeezing her hip.

"No." She squirmed on his lap. "I mean, at all," she corrected, swallowing visibly.

Ash froze, his eyes locking onto her anxious face. He had no idea how to process her revelation, but it might have been the most tragic thing anyone had ever told him. To not be touched by anyone in years?

He thought of his own history, using touch as a way to obliterate the pain of his megrims, of enjoying every caress and every inch of flesh he'd been presented with. Without dwelling too much on it, he knew that he hadn't gone for more than a couple of weeks without a woman's touch on his body since he was seventeen years old, much less casual interactions with family, friends, colleagues... What would it be like to not have been touched for so long?

He gathered her closer, tightening his hold on her. "You should be touched every hour of every day," he told her solemnly, letting his hands roam her figure for the sheer pleasure of feeling her feminine form. "You should be held and kissed and worshipped like the princess you are," he said, stroking her soft cheek with his fingertips.

He heard her sharp intake of breath. "I'd like to be kissed someday," she said, the words mere sighs in the air between them.

"What about now?" he asked, his stomach tightening to hear her answer. "Let me be your first everything, Princess," he whispered.

Ash's heart thudded in his chest, a tingling growing in his extremities. He was never nervous or unsure of his welcome with women. But she ... she was different. He didn't know if he was good enough to claim this from her, but he wanted it so badly that he didn't care whether it was right or not.

He watched her chest rise and fall, the shadow between her breasts curtained by the violet ruching of her gown. Her eyes fell to his cravat and then rose up to meet his again, a blind resolve showing deep within them.

"Yes."

A burgeoning joy rose in his chest, sending his stomach for loops. He was going to be the first and only man ever to have kissed this ethereal woman who had fallen into his life without warning or pretense.

She was his, in a way no other woman ever had been, giving herself up to whatever he would do. Not an abandonment of self, as other women craved, but a decision to make him a part of who she might become.

He straightened in the chair, cupping her jaw in his hand and reveling at the delicacy of her bones. Looking down at her lips, he breathed out slowly, trying to calm his reaction to their plush shape that he wanted to devour. Despite his hunger for her, this wasn't for him. It was for her, and he would make it as it should be for a woman's first kiss.

Holding her head steady, he brought his face closer and watched as her eyelashes fluttered closed. Smiling, Ash closed the distance, bringing his lips to hers and pressing a kiss firmly to them, melding them to his own. His hand reached around to the back of her neck to pull her in, massaging her lips carefully, but thoroughly.

When he felt his control waning, the hunger about the get the better of him at the feel of her petal-soft lips, he drew back, lips tingling.

Ivy opened her eyes and smiled. "That was lovely. Thank you," she said dreamily.

Ash blinked. "Lovely?" he blurted.

Cocking her head, she replied. "Yes, lovely. Did-did I do something wrong?"

"Gads, no," he told her, running his hand through his hair. "It's just ... I've never really done anything "lovely.""

"Well, it felt nice," she reassured him, patting his leg.

Ash groaned, shifting in the chair and feeling her posterior wobble to find balance again. "It shouldn't feel nice," he said grimly.

"I don't understand."

Locking her eyes with his, he explained. "It should feel like liquid fire runs through your veins and nothing else matters but that it doesn't stop. Like you can't get enough air in your lungs or contact with their skin. As if another being has taken control of your senses and forces you to acknowledge nothing but your primal urges that demand more."

Ivy's mouth dropped open. "Oh."

"Yes," he said, watching her flushed countenance.

"So you didn't kiss me like you normally kiss?" She sounded hurt.

"I ... no, of course not. You're ... you're better than all those others. You deserve better."

Ivy raised a hand and touched the tip of her

longest finger to his bottom lip, then murmured, "You don't think I deserve fire in my veins?"

Ash held still, letting her fingernail trace the outer rim of his lips. "You deserve much more," he said against her finger.

"Then why won't you give it to me?" Her eyes searched his.

At this point, he honestly didn't know. She was twisting him all up until he couldn't think straight. Her finger leaving trails of heat on his lips as she begged him didn't help his brain either, which was usually what he intended in his interactions with women, but right now...

"You don't know what you're asking," he told her, his breathing growing ragged.

Ivy wiggled her bottom atop his thigh, causing his member to swell further. "That's why I need you to show me. You did say you wanted to be my first."

He growled. "You aren't making this easy for me."

She drew closer to him, her face inches from his. "But it can be. Just kiss me." Her tiny puff of breath wafted over him while her fingers threaded through his hair.

He felt his tenuous control slipping away, replaced by the growing need to claim her in every way possible.

What in hell's name was wrong with him? A beautiful woman was begging for him to do what he wanted to her, and he was holding back.

"Ivy, you might not want this," he warned her one last time, feeling his last ounce of willpower hanging by a thread.

Ivy smiled. "You can say "I told you so" later."

With that, his control snapped, sending him into a maelstrom of desire that couldn't be stopped now if wanted.

He brought his lips down on hers roughly, forcing them apart so he could gain access to her mouth with his tongue. Growling her name, he gripped her waist and pulled her fully atop him, until she rode his hips on either side.

And Ash discovered he'd been wrong this whole time.

It didn't feel like fire in his veins. It felt coming up for air after having been under water for too long. He wanted to give her everything and hold nothing back the way his calculated maneuvers with other women had always been.

The taste of her tongue, tart lemonade and honeyed ratafia, swirled in his mouth like opium as he assaulted her lips. Claiming every inch of her mouth, showing her how to move her tongue against his, Ash dug his fingers into her corseted sides until it wasn't enough.

Reaching up, he gripped her hair and pulled, forcing her head back with a cry. His mouth trailed down her neck, taking in the beating pulse that pounded there. Giving the spot a nip, Ivy's gasp hardened him further, making him ache for her pleasure in a way he'd never experienced.

"Ash," she moaned, her hands grasping his shoulders.

"Yes?" he said between kisses, continuing his path down to her collarbone.

"This doesn't feel nice at all," she breathed, her breasts moving with the force of her lungs.

He chuckled. "Good."

He came back up to claim her mouth again, letting his hand linger near her bodice. Sucking on her ample bottom lip, she arched as the tip of his finger grazed the skin just inside the top of her dress.

He stopped kissing her to look at her face as he slipped his finger underneath her bodice. Eyes glazed with passion, Ash reveled in her dazed reaction. As he skimmed the velvety skin of her breast, he felt the shallow bursts of breath contained in her chest, indicating she was trying to hold her response back.

"Just let go, Princess," he commanded, watching her lips quiver.

"I-I can't." Strain entered her tone.

"Do you trust me?" he asked, fearing her answer. To be honest, he really hadn't given her any reason to trust him, and he knew it. He had asked other women the same question, but it meant something altogether different with Ivy.

He was asking if she felt safe giving him the piece of herself no one else had even asked for her entire life. Just then, he pitied the fools who hadn't seen the jewel that was Ivy Wollard.

He also wanted to stab them in the eye, but that was beside the point right now.

He watched her nibble on her lip, and then nod. "Yes. I trust you."

Triumph snaked its way through his veins, and he bit back a smile, tugging her dress down to expose one coral nipple.

"You're perfect," he stated, running a thumb over the puckered bud.

Her whimper met his ears like birdsong as he stroked the perfectly formed nub that topped her pale breast.

But he wasn't here for mere whimpers any longer.

Ash ducked down and took her in his mouth, flicking the swollen tissue with his tongue.

She gasped, arching her back. "Ash," she cried out, spearing her fingers in his hair as if he could anchor her to reality.

She tasted like redemption, sweet and full of light. The way she responded to the licks of his tongue on her skin flooded him with the heady sensation of conquest. As her hips naturally rolled forward, pressing against his swollen member, he felt his body readying itself for completion, something he hadn't done without being inside a woman in nearly a decade.

Ash would have loved to keep going—in fact, he had never been this aroused in his life. Her mewling sounds and soft skin called to him like a siren calls to shipwrecked sailors. Every nerve in his body screamed to possess her, to touch her in places no man ever had, to bring her to heights of pleasure she would never forget.

But her use of his name brought him back to where they were, and, more importantly, who they were.

Taking his lips from her skin was one of the hardest things he had ever done, but he gave her engorged nub one last kiss and leaned back while he pulled her dress back into position. He put his hand over her heart where it beat, watching her frown as the fog of desire cleared.

"You are the most enthralling woman I've ever met," he told her, feeling the hummingbird pace of her heart continue to beat beneath his palm. He made sure her eyes watched his lips as he said, "You even might be what can break this infernal curse over my head. God knows I wish it were so." He shook his head with a wry smile as he gazed at the moonlight playing over her cheekbones. "But I will never come close to deserving you. I am what this has made me, and I can't change that."

He swallowed, preparing himself for what he was

to say next. "So I won't be touching you again after this night. My wings in this area are broken, but yours aren't. You'll fly off to some glorious love when the time comes, but I can't follow you. And I'll be damned if I break your wings, too, just to have someone to wander this earth with until the madness finally comes for me." He cupped her cheek in his hand and let it slide down to hold her chin while he held her questioning blue eyes.

"And *that*," he whispered, "I've never said to another woman."

Ivy closed her eyes and put her forehead to his while he absorbed her heartbeats into his hand until they slowed. She sat with him for a long time after in silence, a strange new melancholy enveloping the both of them.

He wondered if he had already bent her feathers beyond repair and mourned the thought of the creature in his arms flying away from him someday, her marvelous wings unable to take her beyond the clouds his misery had formed long ago.

He needed to let her go, he knew. Yet he couldn't make himself say the words that would precipitate her flight.

Only a little longer with her, he told himself.

Just a little longer.

Chapter Seven

"Ivy," a far-off voice called, invading her peaceful world of vaporous colors and warm waves washing over her body. She didn't want to leave this place. It was nice here, with nothing to weigh her down or make demands of her.

"Ivy," it called again, and this time, a cold sensation jerked her from her lovely warmth with a vengeance.

"Ah! What?" she cried, reaching for her dagger.

From years of learning that the quickest reaction meant living to see another day, she flung the knife towards the sound of her attacker.

"What the—?" the voice yelped, a blurry form flattening against the wall.

She sat up quickly and came to her knees, scrubbing at her eyes. Water sloshed out of the tub, spilling on to the tiled floor. Heart racing, she blinked and looked around, finding herself in the bathing chamber of her rooms at Blackbourne House.

"Bloody Hell! You almost pinned me to the wall!" Ash gasped, running a shaking hand through his hair. "And I'll admit, I've fantasized about that very thing, but not like this." Her knife was sticking straight out from the papered wall a foot from his head, the handle shining in the gaslight.

"What? What's going on?" she asked, still trying to get her wits about her.

"Oh! Er... I'm just going to ... yes, I'm turning around now," Ash said.

Ivy looked over to find him spinning away from her, hand over his eyes. Her eyes registered his brown trousers and simple white shirt left open at the throat, a more relaxed look he had taken to wearing during their evenings together.

"What are you doing?" she asked curiously.

"Ahem. Well, you're naked, for one thing," Ash said wryly, still turned away.

She looked down to see that he was right. Her entire upper body was out of the water, completely uncovered and perked at the cool air surrounding it. She gasped and slid back down into the water. "Why didn't you tell me?" she scolded, scowling at his back side.

"I did!" he retorted, turning back around. "In fact, I'm very proud of the fact that I looked away from-from..." he waved his hand to indicate her person and cleared his throat.

Ivy found herself suppressing a smile. "Is the Masterful Marquess of Blackbourne embarrassed by an unclothed woman? I never would have thought..."

"What? Of course not!" he protested, but Ivy could see the ruddy hue of his cheeks darken. "I'm just off my game due to almost becoming a skewered sweetmeat!"

"You are embarrassed!" she giggled. "But I'll forget your discomposure if you forget what you saw just now. And the knife thing," she mumbled.

"I don't think that's possible," he stated, his eyes raking her form that she knew he couldn't see beneath the water. Even so, she blushed.

"You're a scoundrel," she grumbled. A yawn caught her by surprise, and she quickly covered her mouth.

He chuckled, picking up the bath towel from the side table. "And you need to be put to bed. Or my reading is just that boring, I suppose."

"The latter, I'm sure," she purred. Needling him

was too tempting when he gave her openings.

"All right, baggage, out with you," he commanded, holding up the towel.

She hugged her knees to her chest, the water having cooled significantly. "You can't possibly think I'm going to leave this tub until you're gone, do you?" She raised a brow.

"I won't look. That was one of the rules, remember?" he said reasonably. "I'm simply going to bundle you up and deposit you in bed so you don't take a chill." He shook the towel pointedly.

"That's the worst excuse I've ever heard of for being in a bed with a naked woman," she said flatly.

"Exactly how many excuses for that have you heard, Miss Wollard?" His eyes narrowed.

"You'll never know," she answered, turning her nose up.

"I promise I won't look. My only intention is to get you into bed so you don't drown like you almost did a few minutes ago."

Why did he tempt her like this? She knew his logic was all twisted, but he did an awfully good job of making it convincing. She sighed. "Close your eyes."

He immediately did so, but she could see a smile lurking at the corners of his mouth. He was too arrogant by far.

"If you look, I'm going to poison your blackberry preserves. By the end of breakfast tomorrow, you'll be toast." She chuckled at her pun and raised herself out of the tub.

"Not the blackberry preserves!" he said in mock terror. "The raspberry ones, maybe, but you'd never be so cruel as to dose the blackberry. You know how I love those."

She snorted. Ivy cautiously stepped out of the tub

and tip-toed towards him, covering her private places just in case. She watched his eyes the entire time, but, to her surprise, he really didn't peek. Shivering, she stepped into the thick, gold towel he was holding out towards her.

When he felt her come close, he immediately closed the towel around her body and scooped her up, causing her to yelp in surprise.

He laughed and opened his eyes, looking at her surprised face. "You're much too trusting, you know," he said ominously.

She couldn't wiggle at all, the towel having trapped her limbs in its folds. "I believe you may be right," she agreed, trying to keep her voice steady while being blindsided by his contagious smile.

Ash began walking with her to the door of the bathing chamber, which he opened with some expert maneuvering, and continued into her bedroom. The covers were already turned down, a nicety she secretly loved, so he was able to set her down on the sheets and pull the covers quickly up over her towel-wrapped limbs.

Although she'd insisted on it, she was a bit disappointed at his efficiency. She tried not to pout as he tucked the edges of the counterpane around her with the practice of a doting grandmother.

"There you are," he said, stepping back to survey his work.

"I'm still a bit wet," she said, trying to wriggle her arms loose from the towel, without dampening her bed any further.

"I can fix that." He came forward and began to furiously rub her form down beneath the covers.

Ivy shrieked, laughing as his hands roamed over ticklish places on her ribs. "Stop, stop!" she begged, tears coming to her eyes.

He didn't stop, and she saw his mischievous face

grinning above her as he focused on the spots that were causing her laughter.

Ivy was laughing so hard now that she couldn't stop. "Can't...breathe..." she wheezed between peals.

"Say that I win, and I'll stop," he told her, not ceasing his torturous squeezing of her torso.

Oh no. She really wished he hadn't said that. It triggered her stubborn streak—the one that had carried her through years of too little to eat and too much rejection for one person to bear. There was no way she was going to say it now.

Finally, she was able to twist her arms free of the towel. One hand making sure the covers didn't slip down, she reached for the closest hand and pinched it as hard as she could.

"Ouch!" Ash exclaimed, snatching his hands back and straightening.

Ivy's laughter didn't stop, but changed in reaction to his shocked expression.

"You little devil," he grouched, rubbing the sore spot. "I should spank you for that."

She calmed her mirth and sighed, able to breathe again. "Just you try." She lay in exhaustion under the covers, wiping her hair from her face. Thank goodness it had been dry, not needing to be washed today.

Ash shook his head and walked away.

Ivy sat up a bit. He was leaving?

But no, he came round to the other side of the bed and flopped down beside her, propping his head on his fist. Ivy's heart beat faster seeing the long length of him alongside hers.

Yet he didn't seem to be in a seductive mood. He seemed more boyish tonight, more carefree in a way she hadn't seen before.

She was startled to realize that the surge of

pleasure coursing through her was in knowing she might have had something to do with it. It was dangerous feeling things like that. She was his employee—nothing more—and she would do well to remember it. And then he broke that illusion with his next words.

"Tell me about after it happened," he said quietly, his eyes looking steadily into hers.

She swallowed, watching his lips move. Everything about him seemed designed to tempt the female sex, every curve and angle and color forming the picture of what she imagined a fallen angel to be. "What do you mean?"

"After your father was arrested, what did you do? What happened to you?"

She blinked. "That's not something you'd want to hear about," Ivy said honestly. She didn't want him to pity her or think of her as a street girl.

"But I do want to hear about it. Won't you tell me something you've never told another man?" he beseeched her, a knowing smile on his lips.

She rolled her eyes. "What do you want to know?"

He shrugged "Everything."

She sighed and laid back. "Well, after he was arrested, the local magistrate sent letters to my father's sister, apprising her of the situation and notifying her that she was in line to become my legal guardian. As far as I know, she never responded, nor did anyone else they notified. So, after it became apparent that no one was coming and she wouldn't be getting paid for her time, the cook-maid left the house with me in it. Our grounds man was nowhere to be found either. That was about a week after the arrest."

Ivy shifted positions so she lay on her side facing him, her cheek on her pillow. "I didn't know what I was supposed to do, so I stayed there for a few days more, eating what was left in the larder, until a solicitor came knocking one day. He told me I'd been relinquished to the Crown, and that I would be relocated to an orphanage the next parish over."

Ash's nostril's flared, and she felt an absurd rise of happiness at his reaction.

She smiled. "So I lied."

He frowned. "You lied? What about?"

"I said I was the maid and that Jacob Wollard's daughter had run off days ago," she told him with jaunty smile.

"That was bold of you," he murmured with raised brows.

"It was desperate, she confessed. "I had no idea what I was going to do with myself, but I knew I didn't want to go to an orphanage that could turn out to be a workhouse. The solicitor told me that the house would be in trust for dear little "Ivy" until she married, so any staff would have to leave. I did, and then after he left, came right back."

"You're insane." He shook his head.

"Yes, well, what would you have done?" she asked, genuinely curious.

His forehead wrinkled in thought. "I don't know. My parents died when I was nineteen, and I was already of age, so it didn't really matter."

"It matters," Ivy said softly, watching his amber eyelashes lower.

"Perhaps," he agreed, nodding. "But the legality was very clear. I inherited my birthright right then and there. Suddenly, I was the Marquess of Blackbourne, and everything that came with it."

"I'm sorry," Ivy said. She meant it. It didn't matter how old you were. Losing one's parents unexpectedly was a devastation she couldn't describe, and only those who had experienced it could understand.

"To be honest, I wasn't very close to my parents. They loved me, and I them, but..." He shrugged. "I don't think they understood me. I think I scared them sometimes." He was silent for a moment in which she could see memories floating behind his eyes. Then his customary grin came back, and they were gone. "Look at us. A couple of orphans," Ash commented, his eyes crinkling.

She met his light eyes. "Strangely, I don't feel like an orphan when I'm here."

His lips turned up. "I don't either, for the moment."

Ivy studied the flecks in his eyes that reminded her of ice chips, yet he was anything but icy. His warmth always reached out to her and pulled her into his gravitational field, spinning her round him like a top. She didn't know which way she was headed anymore, but something kept drawing her to him in a way that made her feel as if she might finally belong somewhere.

Yet for all that, she knew there was a strong possibility she could end his life and leave without looking back. If things went badly... Her heart skipped a beat. Perhaps it was inevitable, the violence in her veins. She had maimed people before when it came to her survival, but never anyone she cared for. Never anyone she would regret.

Perhaps she had never regretted harming someone because she was incapable of regret. She was her father's daughter, after all.

He cleared his throat. "So what happened after the solicitor left?"

Ivy took a deep breath, realizing she'd been holding it while staring at him. "It's not very pretty. The food ran out soon, so I took the only horse in the stable and went into town. I tried asking some neighboring families if they had any positions available, and I went to all the shops I used to patronize, but none would have anything to do with me. They shooed me out, crossing themselves and locking their doors. It still astounds me that people who had groveled a week before now spat at me and wouldn't even give me a scrap from their meal to eat.

"Anyways, after I realized I couldn't survive there any longer, I sold the cottage—"

"You sold it? I thought it was in trust?" Ash interrupted.

"It was. It still is. I didn't say it was a legal sale," she admitted, grimacing.

Ash laughed. "You're quite the resourceful little criminal, aren't you?"

Ivy blushed. This was what she was afraid of. Now he wouldn't trust her. "I wasn't trying to break the law, but I didn't know what else to do. I don't even know if what I sold it for was anything close to its value. The baker bought it."

"How many rooms did it have, and how much did you sell it for?" he asked quickly.

Ivy smiled. She knew he enjoyed calculating such things—he couldn't help it, although it was clear his own mental exercises overwhelmed him sometimes. "It was thirteen rooms, I think. I sold it for twelve hundred pounds."

His eyes became unfocused for the tiniest part of a moment, and then snapped back to hers. "Depending on the grounds and condition of the place, it was probably worth closer to twenty thousand."

Ivy shrugged. "C'est la vie, I suppose. No one was lining up to live there. The threat of evil spirits and madness lurking was a deterrent to most," she explained plainly.

Asher shook his head. "This is why numbers make more sense to me. What did you do after that?"

Her teeth caught her bottom lip. This was the part she didn't particularly want to talk about with him.

A smile came to Ash's lips, and as if sensing her hesitation, he said, "I'm not going to fire you if you admit to embezzlement or thievery next."

Ivy shot him a look. "You might."

He simply shook his head. "Go on."

She took a deep breath. "I traveled to Harrogate by coach and rented a flat there at a women's boardinghouse. It wasn't very nice, but the proprietress didn't ask my age, so it was good enough for me. That's when things started to become a bit unpleasant."

"So things had been pleasant up until that point? Goodness," Ash commented, quirking his lips.

"Oh, shush, Mr. I'm-a-Marquess-and-have-never-wanted-for-anything."

"There's no "Mr." It's just Marquess," he said solemnly.

Ivy swatted at him. "You are insufferable!"

He laughed, grabbing her wrist and pinning her flat against the mattress. His face loomed over her, and suddenly, there was a tension that had been missing in the past few minutes between them.

Tendrils of need wound through her abdomen and pooled into an ache between her legs. Swallowing, she struggled to control the working of her lungs as he stilled above her, his eyes moving to her lips. She saw the indecision there, his instincts warring with his oath to not touch her again.

Ivy understood his reasons for resisting the attraction between them. In fact, she appreciated his restraint. It meant he cared to keep her as an employee, even a friend, rather than just a liaison or conquest.

Yet, in moments like these, she wished he would just throw caution to the wind and do whatever he wanted to her. She had a feeling it would be wonderful, and that every second he didn't, she was missing something.

She could see the barest hint of stubble sanding his golden skin, the rough hairs catching the lamplight. Wondering what those tiny hairs would feel like against her skin, she reached up with her unpinned hand and set her fingers against his jawline, scraping her nails against the thick fibers.

But it turned out to be a mistake as the movement seemed to jolt him from the moment, and he leaned back away from her touch.

"I'm sorry." His voice was low. Clearing his throat, he scratched at the place her fingers had been on his face. "Please continue." He went back to propping his head on his fist.

Inwardly, Ivy sighed. He had more self-control than she did, and it grated to acknowledge it. Pulling the covers back up to her chin, she took a moment to think back to what she'd been saying before.

Ah, yes. Harrogate.

"I had no idea how to survive in a city, even though Harrogate wasn't very large. But compared to my village, it was an entirely different world. To make a long story short, my second day there, I had most of the money from the cottage sale stolen while I was out shopping. My room was ransacked, all my possessions gone but the clothes I was wearing and the money I had taken with me. Thankfully, I had no idea how much money things cost, so I had taken seventy-five pounds with me that morning. Anyways, it didn't last long. I know now that I was taken advantage of by the shopkeepers and vendors who sensed I would pay whatever they asked. Within a fortnight, I had nothing.

"During that time, I looked everywhere for any sort of job I could find. I was hired on for two days as an apprentice seamstress, but once my name was recognized by a patron, that was that. Word travels fast, and soon, I was unemployable anywhere, just like back home. So when I couldn't afford to pay my board for the next month, I was tossed out."

"You were only fourteen," he murmured, tugging the cover over the curve of her shoulder.

"Fifteen by then, but yes, and I was lucky for it. I quickly discovered there were many street children far younger than I with no one to look after them. The things I saw … there aren't words." She shook her head, and swallowed the lump that had formed in her throat. "I learned to survive on scraps, on begging, on sleeping in abandoned buildings with other children. But after a few years, it became impossible to stay, so I saved enough coin to pay for mail coach fare to Leeds. After a few days there, I was offered a job at the paper mill, and I worked there until I ran into you."

"Why was it impossible to stay in Harrogate?" he asked.

Ivy shrunk back. This was what she was afraid of

"Oh, you know." She looked away, evading his scrutiny. "I had grown up, and I was no longer an adorable child that people wanted to give money to."

He narrowed his eyes at her. "You're beautiful. Anyone would give money to you."

Heart racing, she attempted a smile. "Not the right kind of people, though."

"What does that matter? Money is money, is it not?"

She squirmed under the sheets, kicking the now superfluous towel away from herself. "Yes."

His nostrils flared, and she could tell he was losing his patience. "Ivy, what is it?"

She sighed, ready for his censure. "I began to get certain types of offers that I couldn't accept. They weren't offering something for nothing any longer."

His eyes widened with realization. "You— Did you...?"

"No," she sighed. "But being hungry, truly hungry, does something I can't explain. There was this one man..." She thought back to a cold night and a tall man with green eyes and expensive clothes who smelled like pipe tobacco. He had held out his hand to her, and her fingers had touched his for a brief moment in which the course of her life could have been altered forever. "I was nineteen, and I almost went with him. I hadn't eaten in almost three days, and I remember the exact moment I knew I wouldn't be able to resist that life any longer if something didn't change."

He sat up further, one hand curled into a fist in the counterpane. "You should never have been subjected to such things," he growled.

She laughed bitterly. "You're so far removed from everything that you don't even understand. You should have seen what happened to some of the women who refused. They were beaten, forced to do things. I know God saved me from that fate, but many others never had a choice in the end."

Reaching for her, Ash smoothed a hand over her dark, voluminous hair. "You're safe now. You'll always be safe. I promise you that."

Ivy lowered her eyes, looking at the stitching in the coverlet. His words both warmed and terrified her. "Thank you. But I've learned that it turns out there is very little between security and starvation. No matter how much you think you have, it can all be gone in the blink of an eye."

He tipped her chin up, shaking his head. "No. Not anymore. It might not seem so, but I've quite a knack for sums, and I can assure you, I have enough money to keep you in solid gold bathtubs and silver-plated gothic novels until the end of time," he declared with a small smile. Then he became serious again. "Tell me what you want, and it's yours."

Ivy's heart beat a tattoo inside her chest as she held his gaze. "Who are you to offer such things to someone who can give you nothing in return?"

"You truly don't see how much you are worth to me, do you?" Ash stroked his thumb across her cheek.

"Anyone can play the part of Corrine Morganstern," she pointed out ruefully.

He raised a brow. "Not anymore. It wouldn't quite have the same believability if a tall, blonde woman were to start claiming she was my sister," he chuckled.

His low laugh caused her stomach to clench. "Is that your usual type? Tall, blonde women?" Why did she do this? He scared her so much sometimes that she felt the need to drive something between them, even though she didn't want to hear his answer.

He grinned and dropped his hand from her face. "Lately, I've discovered an affinity for pretty little brunettes who are rendered incapacitated by strategic tickling."

He reached for her side, and she squeaked, burrowing away. "No, please! I can't take it!" she begged.

He groaned and rolled onto his back, covering his eyes with his hands. "I've dreamt of you saying that to me."

"That's rather concerning," she said in confusion.

"You have no idea." His deep tones were muffled by his arm now thrown across his head. "Why do I torture myself like this, hmm?" She could tell he was posing the question to both her and himself.

"I didn't know being in my presence would be categorized as torture," she sniffed, laying back on her pillow.

He rolled towards her and hovered above her, his arms caging her beneath him. "It is. Every. Single. Day." His eyes drank in her face, lingering on her lips.

She felt the tips of her breasts tingling underneath the covers. "Should I leave?" she whispered.

His breath left his lungs in a huff to fan over her face.

"Never," he growled without hesitation, his lips crashing down on hers.

Ivy moaned against his mouth, opening for his expert tongue. He wrapped it around hers and sucked, causing her entire body to tremble as if he drew forth her reserves of energy on a string towards himself.

He tasted of cranberries and chocolate, both which he had been eating as he read to her earlier. Though he claimed he didn't care for the cocoa drink she favored, he inevitably drank her teacup of it every evening, making sure to grimace as he did so.

She freed her arms from the covers and reached for the nape of his neck, needing to feel him beneath her fingers. His right hand buried itself in her hair as he continued his onslaught, the room melting away until all she could feel was his body atop hers, enveloping her in his leather-scented warmth. All that existed was the point where their lips met, melting into each other as he sought to claim her essence for his own. His lips were firm, yet velvety as they caressed hers, every point of contact a deliberate move meant to dissolve her willpower.

He dragged his lips from hers to place a kiss just under her jaw. Working his way down her neck, he nipped and licked her neck until goosebumps rose along the flesh of all her limbs and shivers climaxed along her spine.

Cool air hit her skin as he shoved the covers downward, exposing her breasts to the air. Ash continued to kiss her neck, but moved his hand down to take the weight of one globe in his palm. He kneaded it in steady circles, the motions creating a rhythm that echoed some deep need within her. Blossoms of intense desire spread from her core outward, racing into her limbs.

"Please," she mewled, not knowing what it was she wanted, just … more. "I need—"

"Don't say that you need me," he breathed, pausing to look down at her. "I can't… You don't need me," he repeated, the hunger in his eyes underscored by the worried frown on his brow.

He adjusted the sheet to lay just under her arms, covering her nakedness again. She looked at his open shirt hanging down to allow her a glimpse of his lightly haired chest, the panels of muscle clearly defined.

It was as if he begged her to take pity on him, but she didn't understand why. It was he who controlled every inch of her body, who couldn't resist his practiced kisses. Whatever power there was, he held it.

"What are you so afraid of?" she whispered, playing with the hairs on the back of his neck.

Holding himself above her with the muscles of his arms, she saw his throat work, lips pulled into a straight line. With perfect clarity, he answered:

"You."

She inhaled, breathing in the air that had thickened with discernable tautness between them. "I'm no threat to you," she stated, wanting to understand what he meant by such a thing.

He chuckled without humor. "You think that I'm the one in control here? You think this is calculated? Planned?" He shook his head. "Nothing I've done since the moment I met you has been intentional."

Ivy blinked in wonderment. "You're always three steps ahead of everyone else. I assumed—"

"—that I had an elaborate plan to lure you to my bed?" he said wryly.

Ivy flushed. "Maybe."

"Trust me, Princess. You're beyond anything I can analyze." He looked at her with a fondness that caused heat to suffuse her body in a permeating glow.

"So I scare you because you're not in control of me?" she clarified.

"No," he said grimly, his eyes skimming over her face. "You scare me because I'm not in control of myself. And I value control. I like seeing ahead and understanding the mechanics of the world as much as I hate the way my mind sees things."

"It seems as though you see everything," she admitted.

"I can't see anything past you. Everything is filtered through what you would say or do or think. It's quite annoying, to be honest." He grinned.

She squeezed his neck in retribution. His admission caused her chest to swell with a feeling she was coming to recognize as distinctly related to him. She would call it "The Ash Effect." He would probably like that. "If you want to know what I think, you can always simply ask, you know."

He lowered himself down to the side of her, trailing one hand down her sheet-covered front. He stopped at her belly button and poked the sheet into it, creating a pucker. "All right then. What do you think about going for an outing tomorrow?"

She slapped his hand away from her stomach where he was still poking her belly button in curiosity. "What sort of outing, Mr. Marquess?" she said, emphasizing the "Mr."

He squeezed her side, making her chortle. "Shopping. I want to take you shopping."

She looked at him pointedly. "I don't have very much money to do so yet."

Asher laughed, the sounds echoing out to the corners of the chamber. "You won't be paying for anything, Princess."

She snuggled down into the covers, trying not to smile and failing. "That sounds nice, then."

"It does, doesn't it?" He touched his finger to her lips. "Get used to it, because I've decided I like the feeling of spoiling you."

With that, he placed a rapid kiss on her lips and rolled off the bed, leaving her to wonder what it would have been like if the legendary Lord had stayed the whole night.

Chapter Eight

"What about these?" Ash asked, holding up a pair of lace gloves for her to inspect. "From India, I suspect. Their silk worms tend to produce a thicker strand than most, and these are approximately 2 centimeters thicker than the other pair you liked.

Ivy made a small sound of approval that he could only describe as a hoot, and came over to rub the gossamer-thin material between her fingers. "They're beautiful," she breathed.

"Correction. You would look beautiful in them," he said, enjoying the way her cheeks warmed at his comments. He was enjoying his time on Bond Street shopping for Ivy, a rarity for him as he typically couldn't often relax in public. The way his mind usually kept him wrapped up in manufacturing costs, profit margins, and the like, shopping was rather unpleasant after a certain point. Although he still calculated those things in the back of his mind, it wasn't bothering him today. He had even amused himself telling Ivy the specifications of the textiles she showed interest in, and she had listened to every word as if it was perfectly normal to want to know how many sheep had been sheared to make the deep green wool coat in front of her.

A titter from the other side of the small women's accoutrements shop made him glance up. Two women stood at the counter while the purveyor packaged their purchases, both staring at Ash and Ivy with unabashed fascination. They were of similar age to Ivy, looking to be in their early twenties and probably on the marriage mart, given their frilly pastel ensembles. One whispered something to the other, and they both fell into hushed giggles.

Anger rose in a hot tide, and he turned his body so they could no longer see Ivy as she studied the gloves. He had seen this reaction before, and it hadn't bothered him. In fact, he had gloried in it, sending winks and smirks from across the room as other women had watched him flirt. He knew he had a reputation, and he had done everything possible to deserve it. When a woman was seen with him, it meant she was his paramour, at least for the moment, and it evoked reactions ranging from outrage to envy in the ton. The women he had been seen with in the past had known what his interest entailed and had been well aware of the social repercussions, usually enjoying it.

Yet Ivy deserved no such censure. To society, it looked like he had taken an interest in Corrine Morganstern, Reginald's country-bred sister.

Reginald's innocent, unmarried sister.

It was frustrating to know that his appearance with her in public without a chaperone would hurt her reputation, especially when Corrine didn't actually exist. But he supposed false reputations still had to be kept afloat, or what was the point of this entire charade? However, it wasn't as if he could have taken both Corrine and Reginald shopping together.

This might not have been a good idea.

The realization caused him even more irritation as he normally thought of every possible outcome before taking action. His thoughts were all muddled lately, and it could cost them both their plans for her identity.

"I believe it's almost time to meet up with your brother for luncheon, Miss Morganstern," Ash said loudly, making sure the words would carry to the nosy women at the counter.

Ivy looked up quickly, her eyes questioning. He

watched it take but the beat of a moment for her to take in the situation and play along. "Yes, of course," she replied, using a polite smile. "Thank you for agreeing to accompany me during Reginald's appointment. I believe I shall just get these gloves then, and we can be off."

Through his peripheral vision as they made their way towards the counter, he saw the other women nod their heads in Ivy's direction. She engaged a shop assistant in wrapping her gloves for purchase, and watched as she dug around in her reticule for pound notes. One of the women exclaimed how lovely the gloves were from where she stood nearby.

He breathed a sigh of relief. Perhaps her reputation wouldn't be damaged by their appearance together, but he stood several steps away for good measure.

He would have to be very careful in the future. Any more public outings with her as himself were out of the question. He couldn't let Corrine's reputation suffer to the point where the BAAS would hesitate to make her a member.

If he lost his ability to engage in the scientific community, to be able to work on projects that kept his mind focused and satisfied... He felt his heart rate increase and sweat bead at his temples. If that were to happen, he truly would go insane.

As if his fear had conjured the very nightmare he had warded himself against, a singularly-hued barouche on the street outside the shop caught his eye. He immediately turned his head to look through the window, confirming his suspicion. The yellow monstrosity parked across the street couldn't be anyone else's conveyance.

He swore aloud, causing the ladies at the counter to gasp.

He rolled his eyes. Why couldn't he just have one

normal day? "Excuse me, ladies. Iv— I mean, Miss Morganstern, are you ready? I see someone I must have a word with posthaste."

Ivy nodded and tucked her arm through his, struggling to match his pace as he strode out of the boutique. "Where are we going?" she asked as he practically dragged her across the street, not caring that traffic was halting to allow their passage. The ice on the roadway didn't help her footing as she clung to his sturdy arm.

Eyes centered on the ridiculous barouche, he answered, "To catch a rat."

"What?" she asked , wobbling as she hung on to his arm for support.

"Don't say anything. Just don't engage him at all, do you hear?" he commanded sharply, his words visible puffs of angry air in the cold.

"I- all right," she agreed, but it was clear she didn't like not understanding what was happening.

He couldn't blame her, but right now, he needed to focus.

His cousin was in London, and it could be for one reason only.

To steal the title of Marquess.

Reaching the walkway on the other side of the street, he pulled his arm from Ivette's and motioned for her to stay where she was a few feet away. The buttercup barouche nearly blinded the eyes, and he cringed as he walked up to it, rapping on the door. It was clear there was no one inside, so he leaned his back against it and crossed his arms to wait. The slime would come back eventually.

Ivette had taken a seat on the bench near where he had left her, only ten feet or so away from him, her face a study in concern as she watched.

Catching her eye, he winked, customary smile firmly in place. She pursed her lips and turned her nose in the air, making him laugh. It was hard not to tease a reaction from her when he could.

"Still behaving like an adolescent, I see," a voice from behind him commented.

Ash's smile disappeared, but he quickly resurrected it and turned to face the man standing on his other side. "Hello, Max," he replied, not changing his carefully relaxed stance. "Dare I hope you've come to relinquish your pursuit of my estate and simply spend time with your favorite cousin?" His voice was low and wry.

The man's face didn't show anything perceptible, but Ash could see the fabricated disdain behind his eyes. Max was just as tall as Ash was, and built similarly, with darker hair and light brown eyes. They were clearly related and were often mistaken for brothers when in the same room. Even their mannerisms were reflected in each other, having grown up in one another's households over the years. Their fathers had been close and had remained so throughout their lives as siblings. "I'm not "pursuing" anything, Asher, and your perception of my intentions is further proof that my intervention is necessary."

He smirked. "How much have you spent on solicitors for your cause, cousin? I would imagine it's cost a small fortune by now. Surely the disappointing results of your endeavor warrant hesitation in continuing it?"

Max's lip curled, his knuckles whitening on the brief of papers he carried. "The mismanagement of the estate isn't something I will ever tolerate. Our family name deserves better than your incompetence," he spat.

Ash rolled his eyes, his nonchalant demeanor a

façade while he observed his cousin's responses. "Exactly what is it you consider negligent? That crop yields are up sixty-three percent since I inherited? That every tenant dwelling has been rebuilt using estate profits and equipped with gas lighting? Or maybe you object to the acquisition of more acreage that has expanded the family's holdings and agricultural earnings? Not to mention my railway investments, which have paid off handsomely so far. Is that what you're referring to?" he finished sweetly, eyes wide.

He could see Max's teeth grinding. "Actually, yes, I do object. Using estate funds to invest in tenant properties is disgraceful. They are earning a wage to be able to make such improvements for themselves, are they not? And every *sane* person understands that railways are a passing fancy that won't make any real money. So thank you, Asher. You've made my case that much stronger with your revelations."

Ash didn't take the bait. "Happy to be of service," he grinned, shoving away from the carriage. "When can I expect the troops to show up at my door?"

His cousin stepped forward and opened the door of the barouche. As he stepped up and in, he answered, "Around seven, I should say." With a smile, he flicked the reins and set off down the street, leaving Ash to watch his departure with narrowed eyes and a fading smile.

The wolves would be descending soon. It was time to prepare for battle.

****

Ivy had no idea what she was witnessing, but it was the strangest dinner she'd ever attended.

Ash's cousin, Maxwell Berisford, the Earl of Eydris, sat across from her at the formally-arrayed dining table, crystal china reflecting from the candlelight onto his handsome face.

A face that looked remarkably like Asher's. Aside from the Earl's hair and eyes being a dark brown, they could have been twins.

The resemblance didn't end there, however. Charm must have run in the family because the Earl of Eydris—or Max, as he'd insisted upon—was giving Ash a run for his money. Giving all manner of compliments, she had spent the entire soup course with her cheeks aflame from his attention.

She had tried to respond in a casual manner, determined not to offend Ash's family, but it soon became clear that Ash had no such concerns, treating his cousin as if he were an unwanted flea on his backside. At every opportunity, from the head of the table, Ash cut his cousin with a barbed comment, Max giving as good as he got.

"Asher tells me you are a naturalist like your brother, Miss Morganstern," Max commented. "What is it in particular that interests you about the sciences? How did you come to be involved in that sort of thing?"

Ivy swallowed the bite of stuffed pork tenderloin she had been chewing and looked to Ash for guidance. The ingrate did nothing to help her, smiling beatifically while she floundered. They had discussed what she would say to BAAS members, and he had even given her a few pamphlets and papers to study, but he hadn't given her a backstory as to how she became interested in science.

"Well," she started, thinking quickly. "As a child, I was always catching butterflies and putting them in jars." That part was actually true. "I began to take interest in which foods they liked and their behaviors. Naturally, I became curious about insects in general and began to experiment to better understand them. I've been fascinated ever since."

His brown eyes studied her face. "How charming. If you were mine, I'm afraid I'd keep you much too busy to be worried about such things."

"Keep your trousers on, Max," Ash drawled. "She's a guest here, and her brother will trounce you if you keep it up."

"He's not here now, though, is he? So there's no harm in paying the lady a compliment," Max rejoined, inclining his head towards her.

Ash leaned back in his chair and spun his fork round with the fingers of one hand. "I told you, I don't know when he'll be back tonight, but I can guarantee you he won't be happy if he walks in to find his sister being bombarded with innuendos. I'd just hate for you to be called out to a duel while here," he said, his smile conveying the opposite of his words.

Max matched his cousin's position. "Isn't he rather elderly?"

"Believe me, that won't stop him," Ash said flatly, looking daggers at Max.

Ivy barely kept herself from rolling her eyes. It was obvious their bickering had nothing to do with her and everything to do with—well, she wasn't sure what with, but their competitive demeanors bordered on detestation.

"Lord Eydris, what is it that brings you to London in this cold? I don't believe I recollect," Ivy interrupted their staring contest.

Ash snorted. "This should be good."

Max turned his attention back to Ivy, picking up his knife and fork again to cut a thin slice of meat from his breaded pork cutlet. "I am here to see to the wellbeing of our family's holdings," he answered, somehow managing to chew languidly and smile at the same time.

"Oh, so you have property here in town?" she inquired, confused. Why would Ash be amused at that?

"Not yet, but very soon," he said smoothly, keeping his closemouthed smile in place while touching his napkin to the corner of his well-rounded lips.

"Well, congratulations, then," Ivy attempted cheerfully, feeling as though she was missing something. She glanced at Asher, who groaned.

Max laughed. "Thank you, Corrine. I think you and I are destined to get along famously." He raised his glass of wine in a toast to her, eyes bright on her face.

Not knowing if she should reciprocate, she looked at Ash again, but he was glaring at Max, arms crossed. Corrine would have had no real loyalty to Lord Blackbourne other than as her host, but Ivy certainly didn't want to get in the middle of whatever was going on between the two of them.

She laughed instead and replied, "If I have any more wine, I won't be able to walk to my room tonight." She applied herself to her meal, realizing she hadn't eaten but a bite of the tender, mushroom-topped pork chop swimming in sauce before her. It was not like her to not pay attention to readily-given food, but every morsel of the conversation seemed to feed her suspicion that something was afoot.

"I'd be happy to escort you to your room, Miss Morganstern," Max offered, his eyes glittering.

"Max, you do realize the lady is under my protection while under my roof, do you not?" Ash intervened, finger drumming impatiently on his other elbow.

Max smiled lazily, never taking his eyes from her face. "I believe it's up to the lady whose protection she prefers."

Ivy had had just about enough of the two of them. She swallowed her mouthful of food. "I prefer my own company to that of swaggerts," she said pointedly, looking both of them in the eye one after the other.

She noted the hint of a smile on Ash's lips.

"Touché, Corrine," Max's brown eyes darkened. "I've often thought my cousin needed to be taken down a peg or two."

"Really, Max?" Ash feigned an injured expression, hand on his heart. "I never would have guessed. You're always so cordial when you come to call."

Max turned to Ash, a snarl on his face. "You may fool everyone else with your buffoonery and womanizing, Asher, but it's never worked on me. Your insanity will be exposed to the world sooner or later."

Ash didn't bat an eye, but grinned and spread his arms wide. "Well, then, let's hope it's later," he rejoined.

Max made a sound of disgust and turned away, motioning for a footman to clear his plate. "This course has been spoiled for me, I'm afraid. Let's skip to dessert, shall we?" He looked Ivy in the eyes. "I was never one to wait for sweet things."

"I certainly never said there would be dessert," Ash scoffed. "The sweet things in my house aren't yours to demand," he informed his cousin pertly, taking a bite of his cutlet.

And thus the meal continued until Ivy feared she really wouldn't be able to walk to her room unaided. Without realizing it, she had consumed more madeira than was advisable through taking nervous sips as insults and veiled threats were tossed back and forth between the two men. She had seen back-alley fistfights and knife-point muggings that were more amiable than the way they spoke to each other. So by the time Milton came in during dessert (it did exist, apparently) and announced that three gentlemen awaited His Lordship in the front parlor, Ivy was sluggish to react.

Ash sighed heavily and rubbed one temple while Max sat back, a smug expression on his face. "Miss Morganstern, if you will excuse me. I must attend to some business,"

Ivy struggled to process his expression. He looked weary, but grimly determined. "Oh, all right. I'll just retire then. I'm feeling a bit peaked anyways. A cool cloth and a book sound heavenly." She smiled and rose, causing both men to do the same.

Max's gaze swept her gold muslin dress embroidered in delicate tendrils of green leaves that swirled around her ribcage in intricate designs. "Asher, as you're busy, I believe I'll escort Miss Morganstern to her room after all."

She watched Ash's jaw tighten. He paused, but his eyes hardened, and he eventually nodded. "So be it. Goodnight." He gave her a short bow and exited the room in long, purposeful strides.

He was acting so strange.

Or perhaps it was just the wine playing with her senses—she wasn't sure.

"Corrine?" Max purred, sauntering around the table towards her and holding out a black-clad arm.

"I think I'll be all right on my own," Ivy insisted, unwilling to take his offer. She didn't trust him in the slightest, despite his genteel mannerisms. Maneuvering out from her chair, she took one step and felt her head expand in a rush of vertigo. She grabbed the back of the chair for support, feeling her limbs grow heavy and buoyant at the same time.

She was definitely tipsy. This wasn't good at all.

Max reached for her waist, steadying her. "Whoa

there, little peach. I believe you *could* use my assistance," he chuckled.

Inside, Ivy was furious with herself. She had put herself in the situation of having to rely on this man whose motives she didn't fully understand. She consoled herself with the fact that he was a born and bred gentleman, and with that, she could count on a certain standard of decorum from him.

She forced a smile. "I would appreciate that, my lord," she said, straightening and putting her arm on his.

He moved back a step, but kept his hand on her waist. "Not at all. I couldn't allow such a delicate lady as yourself to take a tumble down the stairs in your condition, now could I?"

"No, indeed," she agreed, cursing herself. She hadn't drunk spirits at all before meeting Asher, having been too young for them when her father was around. After that, she had been too poor to consider imbibing, even to escape the cold for just a few blissful moments. Once, a prostitute who plied her wares near Ivy's usual spot had offered her a sip of gin, and she had promptly spat the foul stuff out, to the raucous laughter of the older woman.

So why in heaven's name had she chosen now to overindulge?

She let him guide her out of the dining room, her mind following what her eyes saw a moment afterwards. It was a funny feeling, really. Waves of warmth flowed through her, and she floated on a cloud of well-being, as if nothing terrible had, or ever could, touch her.

So this was why people drank, she thought, letting a tiny giggle escape at the sight of the small, marble bum of the cherub that sat on a pedestal near the balustrade in the foyer.

"What is it, love?" Max murmured, looking down

at her in amusement.

"Oh, nothing. Just a bum," she snickered, thinking of what the word would have meant to her a couple of months ago.

Max frowned, took a breath, and opened his mouth to say something and then simply closed it, shaking his head as they began ascending the stairs to the second level. A moment later, however, he broke his silence. "What do you see in that cousin of mine, dear? You know he's a scoundrel, don't you?"

"I-I don't know what you mean," Ivy stammered, trying to summon her wits for the present turn of conversation. "He has been a good host to my brother and me these past few weeks, on behalf of the Royal Society."

They reached the second floor, and he steered her to the right, in the direction of her room. "You have something in common, keeping your secrets under lock and key. But I saw the way you deferred to him at dinner. Are you already his little bird, then?"

Knowing what the term referred to, she paused, tugging back her arm. Looking up into his golden brown eyes, she concentrated on her words carefully, knowing Ash's plans for her identity might depend on them. "Your impertinence is not appreciated, sir. And no, I am a lady. I would never enter into such a tawdry arrangement with anyone." She laced her words with disdain, hoping she came across as she intended as her mind still drifted in a haze.

Max laughed, tucking her arm back in his and continuing down the hallway. "All right, all right. I didn't mean to ruffle your feathers, only express my concern for you. He is a dangerous man, and a woman such as yourself shouldn't be subjected to his recklessness."

Ivy considered his words. She couldn't deny he was dangerous to her, but wasn't sure if Max was speaking of the same thing.

Right now, however, she didn't want to think about that. She wanted to sink into a sea of pillows and let the headiness of the wine carry her into dreams where everything and nothing made sense.

"Thank you for your concern, Lord Eydris," Ivy told him, giving his arm a squeeze. "I am sorry to see you and your cousin aren't more fond of each other."

"We were once close," Max admitted, his voice soft. "But as we grew older, Asher began to flee to another place inside himself and left the rest of the world behind. Including me." The emotion in his words was not feigned, even she in her inebriated state could tell. He spoke as if he had lost a dear friend—as if Ash had died a long time ago and left an imposter in his place.

They stopped in front of door to her room. "What do you think—"

Her words were cut short by a keen howl coming from below. The acute screech of someone clearly in agony sent shivers up her spine. Her head was still fuzzy, but she thought she recognized the source of the sound.

Ash?

She took a step back towards the stairs, but Max grasped her wrist, stopping her.

She looked at his face, the same dear shape and coloring as Ash's making her pause.

"Let go," she demanded, another piercing wail assaulting her ears.

"Corrine, no," he commanded.

She pulled at her wrist, but he didn't let go. "Something's wrong," she pleaded, her sense of urgency rising. "I have to—"

He pulled her towards himself. "No, you don't.

There's nothing you can do," he told her, shaking his head. His eyes looked haunted, but determination overshadowed it. "It will be over soon enough."

Mrs. Rushkova came out of a bedroom up ahead and nodded as she went past them. "Lord Eydris, Miss Morganstern," she acknowledged in her graveled accent. Surely she had heard the noise, yet she was acting as if nothing unusual was happening. Frowning, Ivy almost asked her about it, but couldn't formulate the right words in time, and then she was out of sight.

What was going on here?

Near to Max's chest like this, she realized more differences between them. Max had a light dusting of freckles over his cheekbones and a small scar near his jawline, as well as perfectly straight teeth, whereas Ash had one lower tooth that was slightly askew.

"How can you say it will be all right? He's obviously in pain," Ivy declared, more confused than ever.

Had Max sent those men here to hurt Asher somehow? Yet Ash had seemed to go willingly, as if he had been expecting them.

"You must calm down," he murmured, stroking her arm. "He is not in danger."

"I don't understand," she said, her eyes darting across his face.

"Don't worry yourself, little peach. Let us men do what needs to be done, and it will turn out as it should," he reassured her, tipping her chin up with one finger. "Are you ready for bed?"

"Not in the slightest," she retorted, her instinct to run to wherever Ash was still in full force. All his cryptic explanations didn't mean she shouldn't make sure Ash was all right, though she hadn't heard any more screams in the past few minutes.

Max chuckled and opened the bedroom door for her. Indicating she should enter, Ivy hesitated, but then did as he bade. From the doorway, he kissed the back of her hand. "Miss Morganstern, you're far too delightful for the likes of Blackbourne. I hope we get the chance to further our acquaintance soon. Give your brother my regards."

Letting her hand go, he promptly shut the door in her face, leaving her to wonder what was going on in this infernal house that everyone seemed to know except her.

Chapter Nine

There wasn't any getting around it.

He had to go down to breakfast eventually, but he hoped Ivy hadn't waited this long for him to show up. They had been breaking their fast together on a regular basis for the past week, but today she should have done so without him as it was nearly noon now.

Looking at his reflection in the mirror above his washstand, he raked a hand through his hair once more. The casual rakehell look he cultivated was missing today. Circles under his eyes shone in sharp relief against his unusually pale skin while his customary boyish grin had been replaced by a scowl that would frighten small animals and children to the point of tears.

The irony was, the same condition that warranted last night's proceedings also made it impossible for him to recover from them. His mind turned somersaults as he lay in bed, unable to sleep for hours afterwards due to the stabbing pain that reverberated in his skull with nowhere to go. It was the same every time—by the time morning came round, he was almost mad with the thoughts his brain chose to formulate throughout the night without the relief of sleep to interrupt them. He dreaded these nights more than anything on earth, but they came whether he wanted them to or not.

Not even a woman's company sufficed to spare him from the torture of the aftermath. Even if it did help, he wouldn't subject anyone else to his tumultuous mood on a night like that, especially at the risk of his reputation. Besides the fact that he wasn't entirely sure what he was capable of when his head was abused to that level, he couldn't afford to let anyone see him in such a state. It could mean the end of his legend as a skilled bedroom partner that he used to full advantage when approaching the fairer sex. More importantly, it could mean the beginning of a reputation as a madman, which was precisely what he was trying to avoid.

Sighing, he turned away from the offending reflection and went downstairs to the breakfast parlor situated off the main dining hall. He knew Max wouldn't be here, as he'd already had a note informing him he'd be out most of the day.

His shoulders relaxed as he saw that no one inhabited the sunny area with its octagonal table and cushioned benches creating an informal gathering place for family meals. The salvers of bacon, eggs, and crepes had been left out for him, his staff fully aware of his routine by now.

Although he still felt a bit nauseous from the pain of the night before and his head still ached, he was famished. Applying himself to eating a large portion of each offering, he soon began to feel a bit less like he had washed ashore after a shipwreck and more like his usual self.

Until he heard a small pair of slippers tiptoeing towards the parlor, their owner's visage appearing soon after.

Putting his fork down, he forced a smile to come to his lips. "Good morning."

She was clearly unsure of her welcome, hesitating in the arched entryway.

"I assure you, I haven't turned into Frankenstein's Creature during the night," he said dryly, observing as she came further into the room and sat down across from him, her eyes never leaving his face. He knew she was seeing all his wretchedness and wondered if she would bolt from the room at any moment.

"Are you all right?" she said in a hushed tone.

Asher could kiss her, she was so adorable in her concern. Hiding a smile by wiping his mouth with his napkin, he put it down and answered, "Yes, Princess, I'm just fine. No need to worry yourself over me."

He saw her posture relax somewhat, but she wasn't ready to let it go, for she said, "I heard you... That is, your meeting seemed unpleasant."

"I won't argue with that assessment," he told her.

Ash could tell she wanted an explanation, but he couldn't give one to her. Despite the way she soothed his tattered spirit with her presence, there were some things he would never share with another person. His deepest secrets were his alone, and if he had his way, they wouldn't see the light of day until he was too old to care what happened any longer. Perhaps he knew that was just wishful thinking, but he clung to that plan as if there were no other possibilities.

When she understood he wasn't going to offer anything more, she put her hands in her lap and sat back.

He couldn't stand to see her looking like a kitten who'd been put out in the garden for the night. He decided to tell her about the message he'd received from Dom yesterday, but hadn't had the chance to mention yet. "You've received an invitation from Lady Raquel Tierney," he told her, watching her eyes widen.

"I have?" she said in wonder, leaning forward once more. "Who's that? Whatever for?"

"I believe it's to an exhibit at the Royal Art Gallery. I might have let it slip to my friend you have an eye for art and a lack of social engagements here in town."

Ivy shook her head back and forth, still unbelieving. "Who is your friend?"

"Dom. Or, as he's known to most, The Duke of Scythemore. Lady Raquel's brother." The people he interacted with usually weren't impressed by titles so much because most of them were titled themselves or related to someone who was. It was amusing to see her pinked cheeks at the thought of him knowing someone like Dom.

"I'm afraid I won't be up to snuff for such an illustrious Lady," she said, twisting her hands.

Asher cocked his head as he watched her fidget. She was usually very sure of herself and more than confident in interactions with his social peers. But the thought of Ivy being afraid of Raquel was laughable.

Having known Dom's sister for years, he knew her to be the most unassuming and quirky woman he'd ever seen grace the ballrooms of London. If anything, she was probably the best person to whom he could introduce to Ivy to gain footing with the members of the ton. Well-respected and universally adored, the Duke's sister was the *ton's* darling and wouldn't dream of making someone like Ivy uncomfortable in her midst. If she decided someone or something was fashionable, it suddenly was, and that was all there was to it.

He smiled at her wrinkled nose. "I think you'll have a grand time with her. She isn't someone for whom you'll have to put on airs."

"Truly?" she perked up.

"Truly."

He watched her process the information, noting the way she bit her ripe lip in thought. What he wouldn't give to see her mouth open in ecstasy, lips parted with abandon as he overwhelmed her senses with gentle touches and rough coupling...

His hardening member beneath the table caused him to shift, his tight breeches restraining him uncomfortably. He decided a change of subject was in order—straight down to business.

No, not that kind of business, he told his erect staff.

He cleared his throat. "The exhibit is set for tomorrow afternoon, but there is a lecture series beginning tonight for the BAAS that we should attend."

"Oh? I assume you will be attending as Reginald?" she asked with a smile.

"Yes, indeed," he replied, spreading a touch more blackberry preserves on top of his crepe. "And I've had some pamphlets and other literature sent over for you to peruse before tonight. It should help you get a bearing on current research in Lepidopterology and Entomology so you can be somewhat prepared for any discussion that arises." He took a bite of crepe that melted in his mouth and finished with the sweet tartness of blackberries.

"Lepido—what?" Ivy stumbled over the words, straightening in her chair.

He swallowed and grinned. "The study of insects and butterflies. You claimed that was your field of interest at dinner last night, did you not?"

He watched her squirm, enjoying her display with raised brows. She had gotten herself into this situation and couldn't backtrack now, which struck him as inordinately amusing.

"I suppose," she said, the words strangled. She sighed and put her hands flat on the table, her lips thinned to a determined line. "You're right, of course. It's just part of my duties for the position. I'll be up to speed by tonight, you needn't worry."

His brows raised further. "There's more literature there than you can read in a month, so don't feel as if you have to scour every line. A basic understanding will be fine."

She nodded. "By the way, how much have I earned so far in my duties as Corrine, if you don't mind my asking?"

He thought for a second. Although his mind was still flayed from the night before, it wasn't a calculation that required much effort. "One hundred pounds," he told her, wanting to see her eyes light up at the amount.

They didn't.

"Shouldn't it be two hundred?" she asked, wrinkling her nose.

Ash blinked. "No. There was the BAAS soiree and the Crossthwaite ball. Fifty for each is one hundred."

"But there was also Bond street and dinner last night," she reminded him, her eyes scanning his face for his reaction.

"You're charging me for taking you shopping?" he exclaimed incredulously, leaning forward and barely catching himself before dragging his cravat through his breakfast.

"No, I'm charging you for dragging me across the street and then winking at me in public," she clarified, keeping her chin high. "Plus, you clearly called me Miss Morganstern more than once in the shop."

"You're a mercenary little thing, aren't you?" he commented, secretly liking the way her little body showed determination in every line.

Ivy shrugged. "Just practical. If you end up only needing me for a short time, I want to be prepared to be on my own when the time comes."

For some reason, the thought of Ivy needing to fend for herself again in a world that didn't deserve her made him irrationally angry. The thought of her going anywhere without his protection wasn't acceptable.

"You won't be needing to save funds, Miss Wollard," he told her decisively, sitting back. "But I will concede the two hundred pounds in wages nonetheless."

She smiled, causing his chest to swell with the pleasure of it. "Thank you. I believe I'll take myself off to study then, as it appears I have quite a bit of reading to do."

His stomach sank at the pronouncement, but knew it was better this way. He wasn't at his best today, anyhow. "As you wish. I've left the materials on the landing under my head."

Ivy paused in getting up from her chair. "Excuse me?"

"There's a marble bust of my head on the landing. The pamphlets are there," he explained.

"Oh, right. Of course there is another one." She rolled her eyes and began to walk away from the table.

"Can I help it if I want you to think of me while you're reading?" he asked innocently.

A look came into Ivy's eyes, and she paused at the entrance to the breakfast room. "You know, I think that might be appropriate after all," she mused. "— considering I'm reading about insects one usually avoids."

Ash laughed as she exited. "What if I'm a butterfly?"

She didn't answer.

"Ivy?" he called. "I'm more of a butterfly!"

****

Ivy didn't know what one usually wore to a scientific society lecture, but she'd chosen a day dress of green and white striped poplin, which she thought struck a balance between femininity and intellectual refinement. Not that the two were opposites, but it was distressingly true that there was a lack of female presence in the scientific community, so she didn't want to appear as if she didn't belong.

As she sat next to "Reginald" during the first part of the lecture, she realized that these people were actually going to change the world. The man speaking from the podium in the small meeting area was presenting his research and patents on experiments involving transmitting electrical currents across great distances. William Cooke, a rather dashing 34-year-old inventor, had explained how his device, the telegraph, was even now being put to use between railway stations in England to transmit messages via electronic signals across wires. As a demonstration, he had set up two of the devices across the room from each other and proved that any message could be instantly sent across the wire connecting them, with the simple touch of a finger.

"It's amazing," Ivy breathed, clapping along with everyone else at the conclusion of the display.

Ash turned to her. "Yes. Now I can call you down to dinner without having to take my old knees up the stairs, Cori," he chuckled loudly, others around him doing so as well.

The crowd retired to the adjoining room, which had been set up for socializing and refreshments. As she walked on Reginald's arm, she nodded to several people whom she had met before, finding their acknowledgement reassuring. Nearing the refreshment table, Ash spoke up in his roughened voice. "Well, would you look at that! Blackberry tartlets!" he exclaimed, taking two in one hand, his cane in the other.

"I'm a strawberry man myself, but I certainly won't complain," a voice to their left chimed. The man took a tartlet from the table as well.

Ivy's eyes widened, recognizing the man. It was Cooke himself, smiling crookedly at the two of them while he munched on the sugar-topped pastry.

"Cooke, my good man!" Ash unhooked his arm

from Ivy's and held it out, leaning his cane against his leg. "Capital demonstration! I foresee you going far, my boy. Reginald Morganstern, if you please."

"Thank you, sir," he said, taking Ash's hand and shaking it. "I'm honored you think so."

"So has the Royal Society gotten to you yet?" Reginald asked Cooke conspiratorially.

Cooke chuckled. "Not I, but I'm afraid my partner, Wheatsone, has presented to them in the past. I personally favor the BAAS over the Society, but I can't convince him. He's dazzled by the peerage and such."

"Smug bastards," Ash grumbled. "Useless, the lot of them."

Ivy raised her brow and saw Ash smile under his gray beard.

"I don't believe I've made your acquaintance," Cooke said, angling himself towards Ivy.

"Miss Corrine Morganstern, sir. A pleasure." She held out her hand, which he took and kissed briefly.

"And you are Mr. Morganstern's...?"

"Wife."

"Sister."

Ash and Ivy looked at each other.

Ash's eyes were wide as he realized his mistake. He laughed and turned back to Cooke. "I mean, is it wrong to tell everyone she's my wife? The boys will think I'm quite the rascal."

Cooke's face froze in an expression akin to having stepped in dog poo. "Er..."

Ivy realized she was looking at Ash with the same look and gulped. Recovering, she laughed brightly. "Oh, he's only teasing, Mr. Cooke."

A new voice chimed in from a few feet away. "The pretty thing's married to him? I thought they were brother and sister. Damn it."

Ivy fought the urge to smack her forehead.

"She's always been my sister, Freemont!" Ash called out to the man.

"Well, that's just wrong," the man mumbled, tottering off with a glass of madeira.

Ivy grit her teeth. Wonderful.

As they continued to converse with other lecture attendees, she started to have an idea of how large a knowledge base Asher's intellect truly allowed for. For every subject brought up by someone, he seemed to know a vast amount about it. During some of the conversations, she wasn't even able to follow the subject matter as it became more in-depth and technical. Reginald was a large player in these circles, and his insight was greatly sought-after by his colleagues and casual enthusiasts alike. It was obvious now why he wanted so desperately to maintain his identity as Morganstern.

Then, during a spirited, but good-natured debate between Charles Babbage and another member to whom she hadn't been introduced, the subject swung around to her.

"Perhaps Miss Morganstern could enlighten us," Babbage turned to her. "What say you, Lady? Has there been a definitive preference measured for the use of a specific species of spider's webs versus others in wound dressing?"

Ivy smiled, grateful she'd always been a fast reader. "As a matter of fact, there have been some attempts to cultivate a steady supply of medical webs from a base of the specimens in Greece. After testing three different species, they opted for the imported black widow, which has been a dangerous enterprise due to their particularly poisonous venom. I believe the factors they based their decision on, however, were rate of production and longevity. So I'm not certain if additional medicinal properties of the webs were included in the study, but as black widows produce superb cobwebs of the tangle variety, I would imagine their webs are ideal for the intended structural purpose of packing wounds."

She looked around the group to discover nodding heads and choruses of affirmation, but Ash's jaw was simply hanging open.

She winked at him, which caused him to shut his mouth abruptly and blink several times.

Reginald didn't have much to say after that, adding comments here and there, but staying in the background of their interactions with others.

The evening wore on until, at last, they were on their way back to Blackbourne House, Ash's disguise put away for the night. Ironically, he was just as pensive as the last time they had ridden back from a BAAS function, but she knew it wasn't an inadequacy on her part this time. She felt she had done well.

"Why so quiet?" she asked from across the carriage.

"Would you believe it's the same reason as the last time?" he murmured, his arm resting on the window frame beside him.

Ivy swallowed, and her heart sped. "You're thinking about taking me to bed?"

Ash nodded, his relaxed pose somehow more threatening to her than if he'd been leaning towards her. "But it's strange. I want you to the core of my being, yet I can't decide whether to be fascinated or frightened by you."

Ivy laughed. "I can't imagine you being either," she confessed.

Ash smiled, his eyes glittering in the moonlight coming through the windows. "Oh, but I am. And tonight, you proved just how intelligent you are. Most of my life has been spent muffling my own thoughts, so it's incredibly erotic to see a woman employ her knowledge to its potential."

Goosebumps rose everywhere on Ivy's thighs and arms. "And why is that frightening?" she asked, hoping he couldn't see the way she held her hands in her lap to keep them from shaking.

The squabs squeaked as he shifted his hips and crossed one ankle over his knee. "It's frightening, my dear, because I fear I can't manipulate you as easily as I do others. I can't see myself outmaneuvering you or leaving you in my intellectual dust, so to speak."

Ivy pursed her lips. "You're quite arrogant. You know that, don't you?"

"Yes," he agreed readily.

"Everything just comes to you so easily. Sums, money, women…"

"Not you."

Her fingers curled around her reticule strings. "I have given more of myself to you than anyone, despite all the reasons not to. Does that not fit the definition?"

He chuckled and leaned forward to rest his forearms on his knees. This only served to put him at eye level with her. "What you and I have done is not nearly enough to be considered worth counting on your list of things I have attained."

The words stung and gave rise to a rush of indignation. Her stomach knotting, she pressed herself into the cushions at her back. "I apologize if my feeble ventures into the sort of passion you're used to was lacking."

Ash swiftly moved to the squabs beside her and took her face in his hand. "You misunderstand me. What I mean is that all that you have given me is but a thimbleful in the ocean of things I want to do with you."

Her heart pounded. Surely he could hear it in the heavy silence in which their breaths mingled. His eyes glimmered in the dark, a blue fire lit deep within them. Did he see the same reflected in her own? He must know how he affected her, regardless of his admissions of uncertainty.

"I want to kiss every inch of your body and count the speckles scattered over it." He touched one of the freckles on her neck with his fingertip.

He touched another of the freckles further down on her collarbone, his eyes caressing her skin as he smoothed his fingers over it. "I want to number them and mention that number to you in public to make you blush at the memory of what I did to you there."

Ivy shivered at the contact and let her eyes shutter closed as he grazed her skin.

His hand slid over her chest and up to the nape of her neck. "I want you to say my name over and over and let me into every part of you until you can't think of anything except begging me to be inside you again."

Her breath arrested inside her chest as he fisted his hand in her hair. Scalp tingling, she moaned softly at the flash of desire washing through her.

"I want you shamelessly addicted to my hands so that you'll let me do anything I desire to you without resistance."

"What if I already am?" Ivy whispered, opening her eyes to watch the intensity of the expressions pass over his face.

"Soon," he promised, coming closer to let his lips hover above hers.

"When is soon?" She was already shameless, wanting to know the things of which he spoke.

"When I—" He stopped, his bottom lip touching

hers. Then his pulled back, and his hands dropped from her. "When I am worthy of you. And that will never happen."

Ivy swallowed. "There's no such thing as worthiness." She had learned the hard way that everyone was but one step away from desperation. No one was above doing whatever they had to in order to survive, and she had long ago abandoned her judgement of such things.

"No?" he countered, hands clenched on his thighs. "So your father was worthy of your mother, then?"

Ivy reared back as if slapped.

He quickly reacted. "I'm sorry. I shouldn't have—"

"No, you should not have," she said stiffly.

"Ivy, I'm sorry. Forgive me." He reached his hand out, palm up. "You know that I hold no condemnation over you or your family."

Ivy hesitated. Though she had believed herself immune to the sweetness that dripped from men's lips, but her anger slowly dissipated. She cautiously put her hand in his large palm, and he enveloped the whole of it in his warm fingers.

"As I said, you frighten me," he repeated his earlier admission. "And I attack when I feel threatened."

"That's ridiculous," she scoffed, pulling her hand back. She couldn't frighten such a man.

He shrugged. "I did not expect you to be what you are—a worthy opponent."

She shook her head. "Why is it that everyone is an opponent to you? Clearly, you and Max have some sort of sibling-esque rivalry, but no one is playing some grand chess game with you, least of all me."

"Aren't they, though?" he leaned forward. "Every

single person has their own agenda and will use whomever comes their way to accomplish their ends. Their motivations, the likely outcome of actions perpetrated by one person on another … it's all a game that one can win if one sees all the pieces. There are consequences to remaining in the dark about such things. If you don't see that, you're a fool."

She knew exactly what he meant, but she scooted backwards, arms crossed. "So is that what I am to you, then? A piece to be sacrificed on the board of your imaginary games?"

She could tell he wanted to give her a quick and decisive answer, but he hesitated. He looked at her face, his features inscrutable. "I don't know."

She sighed through her nose. "At least you're honest, I suppose."

"I would never hurt you," he said, reaching out to cup her cheek. "When I first met you, I admit I only thought of your usefulness to my alter ego. But you have to know that's changed."

"Do I?" Ivy asked softly.

He dropped his hand, and his eyes grew shuttered as he looked away. "It doesn't matter. All you need to know is I won't let anything happen to you, no matter Corrine's standing in society."

"That's not what I'm worried about," Ivy replied.

He looked up sharply.

She smiled briefly, enjoying catching him off guard. "All you need to know is I won't let anything happen that will cause you to lose your game, whatever it may be."

The carriage continued along its route home, its passengers staid in a silence that neither understood the reason for until it was over, and any further conversation was lost to them.

Chapter Ten

"You let him *what*?" Lilah exclaimed, violet eyes blinking wide

Raquel, Lady Tierney, choked on her caramel ice cream.

Ivy reddened. "He asked, and he's so ... persuasive."

"To be honest, I might not have said no." Raquel smiled, forcefully pushing a pin back into her hair knot. The Duke's sister was pale with freckles across the bridge of her pert nose and a wealth of soft waving hair the color of apricots that seemed constantly determined to escape her coiffure. When Lilah raised her brow at her, she shrugged unrepentantly. "What? I think someone reading to me is incredibly romantic."

"Whilst naked," Lilah Hayworth added. Then she chortled. "It is rather wonderfully salacious. I wish men wanted to do those sorts of things with me."

Raquel snorted. "Oh, they do. It's just that most men don't dare even speak about that sort of thing to a lady. Blackbourne, however..."

Ivy looked around the ice cream shop where they had decided to go before the art exhibit. They sat at a small table in the corner, one governess with her young charge the only other people in the creamery. Shaking her head, she looked at her companions. "I fear I'm in over my head with him."

"You definitely are," Lilah agreed. "He's considered the greatest lover in London, you know." Lilah looked the sort of woman who would know such things with her starkly beautiful face and black tresses, but as an Earl's daughter, she was raised to be as pure as her creamy complexion suggested.

Ivy gulped. "I'm not even sure why he would be interested in me, if that's the case. It's not as though I'm experienced or exotically beautiful." She hurriedly brought her spoonful of frozen dessert to her mouth before it dripped, the nutty flavor filling her taste buds. She had never had ice cream before, and it might have been the most delicious thing she'd ever eaten.

Raquel rolled her deep green eyes. "You're as lovely as anything out there, darling."

Lilah nodded sagely. "It's true. I don't know why we've decided to be friends with you, to be honest. You'll make us look bad."

Ivy burst out laughing. "You can't be serious."

Both women stared back at her, completely solemn.

Clearing her throat, Ivy sobered. "I've never really thought about it, I suppose."

Lilah raised a dark brow. "You've never thought about your own appearance?" She spooned a lump of ice cream between her plump lips.

"When you're working day and night—" Ivy started, then caught herself. "W-working day and night to take care of an ailing father in the country, appearance is the last thing on one's mind."

Raquel nodded and Lilah "Mmmm'd."

"You father passed recently?" Raquel asked, compassion in the lines of her small face

"Erm..." Ivy struggled to remember what Ash had told her about her fictional parents. "It was a year ago last month, which is why I'm out of mourning now and able to come to town with my brother." She hated lying to these people, especially since they had welcomed her with open arms. She had felt an instant kinship with the both of them, despite their difference in station.

As Lady Delilah Hayworth was the daughter of an Earl, and Lady Tierney the sister of a Duke, the two of them represented the highest social circles in the entire country. If Ivy's life had gone the way it should have, she might have briefly crossed paths with them at one time or another, but a squire's daughter wouldn't have had much reason to become closely acquainted with someone of their standing. Even her identity of Corrine Morganstern, the sister of a Knight, wasn't near their social equal.

As someone sponsored by the Marquess of Blackbourne, however…

If nothing else came of this charade, being in the company of these ladies was worth the uncertainty. Being an only child had been lonely during her upbringing, and after her father's arrest, even lonelier. Simply being in their presence was like drinking water after years in a desert wasteland of solitude.

After ice cream, they met up with Lilah's cousin, Grant Hayworth, who was a bonefide Viscount with aristocratic bone structure and flaming red hair. Ivy immediately liked him and his country mannerisms. He wasn't stodgy or staid and even referred to them all by their Christian names, which was not at all proper. And best of all, he loved art as much as she did. Ivy listened to his explanations of the artwork exhibited long after Lilah and Raquel had grown disinterested.

"Grant, you're boring us to tears," Lilah tugged on his jacket. "Miss Morganstern is never going to want to come out with us again."

"No, I'm not—" Ivy tried to interject.

Raquel bustled up to them. "If *one* more flighty debutante asks me if my "brother" is a bachelor, I'm going to set this place on fire."

Lilah snickered and explained to Ivy, "Everyone

who doesn't know them thinks Grant and Raquel are related—because of their hair, of course. And they thought me and her brother—" She paused, and the light left her eyes. "Well, it's just a funny coincidence is all."

Grant laughed and patted the fuming Raquel on the back. "Now, now, "Sis," don't be upset that the ladies love my hair."

"You look like a baboon's backside," she replied, shooting daggers with her bright eyes. "My hair isn't even red. It's blonde."

Grant shrugged, grinning. "If you say so."

"I think it's lovely, like the beginning of a sunset," Ivy said firmly.

Raquel smiled beatifically at Grant and turned away from him. "Why, thank you, Corrine."

Lilah simply sighed and rolled her eyes.

By the end of the outing, Ivy was exhausted from so much interaction, but happy as a clam. Even if the Marquess was proving vexing, she now had friends.

Friends. What a wonderful word.

****

Having managed to avoid Max for the past twenty-four hours, bolster Ivy's identity as Corrine, and not toss his accounts after the cranial examination, he should have counted his blessings.

But Ash was not in the mood to count his blessings today.

Ivy was out with Lady Tierney at the Royal Gallery, and her absence was rendering him a complete dullard, it appeared.

He was The Marquess of Blackbourne, and he had never been considered dull. Wild, yes. A rake most definitely.

But never dull.

Pondering his unexpected dotage, he sat at the

desk in his study and twirled his quill with nimble fingers. He had begun to keep a ledger specifically for Ivy's wages, drawing it up this morning after their conversation in the carriage the night before. Having annotated it with each event's requisite earnings and records of wardrobe costs since he had met her, he was now caught up with financial matters. He hadn't been to visit some of his holdings in a couple of months, but that wasn't unusual, so there wasn't really an excuse to leave town for now. The next BAAS lecture wasn't scheduled to happen for another month, and there wasn't enough data yet to continue with his plague research.

He hated boredom.

It terrified him more than anything on earth. Feeling his mind begin to whir at the lack of stimulation, he abruptly stood, shoving his chair back. A faint ache had started near the base of his skull, and he knew where that would leave him in a few minutes if he didn't do something to alleviate his mind's wandering.

Not knowing exactly where he was going, he left his office and trotted up the stairs. Perhaps sitting on the balcony in the crisp winter air with his eyes closed would soften the sharp edges he felt encroaching in his head. If he concentrated on other sensory inputs besides sight, it often helped with impending megrims. Passing the door to Ivy's room, he paused. It was obviously in the midst of being reset for the evening, a chamber maid re-laying the fire for later use.

When the girl saw him stop in the doorway, she paused. "Oh, I'm sorry, my lord. Did ye need sumfin from me?"

He smiled and waved a hand. "No, Sarena, do continue. Pay me no mind," he reassured her.

She nodded and blushed, turning back to the fireplace

Most of his maids did that, he noticed, but he was very careful to give no indication of interest in his staff. Taking advantage of women in his employ had never appealed to him, although he knew men who had no compunctions about it.

Ivy was another matter altogether that he didn't care to examine.

Stepping into the room, he smelled the faint aroma of vanilla and roses. He would never again smell those two scents without thinking of Ivy. As the maid finished and hurried from the room, a sheet of foolscap sticking out from the drawer of her bed table caught his eye.

He told himself he had every right to know if Ivy was corresponding with someone, due to the need for her position with him to be kept secret, but that was a lie.

Opening the drawer, he saw that there was a whole sheaf of papers with various amounts of writing on them, looking to be letters. Ash sat on the bed and drew them out, setting them carefully on the bed next to him.

At first he was confused, but the nature of the correspondence soon became clear. They weren't Ivy's correspondences at all, but her father's. Some were written to Jacob Wollard from men whose minds were clearly warped beyond redemption. There was one letter from a woman wanting to know why he hadn't chosen her to be the subject of his morbid desires as she had thought he fancied her. Another was a response from the ward of Tothill Fields Bridewell Prison informing Ivy of his inability to pursue the concerns she had raised regarding her father's admirers.

And there were two letters from Jacob to his daughter, letters that were soft and wrinkled with wear. In them, Wollard expressed how sorry he was that he was not able to be there for her, to watch her grow up and

MAYHEM AND THE MARQUESS

take care of her. He spoke of his time in prison, and, from what Ash knew of gaol conditions, the man had obviously made it seem much more palatable for the imagination of his little girl than it could be in reality. He asked her questions about her life—how she spent her time, if she had married, if she needed anything...

By the time he had read all the way through them, his teeth were grinding painfully against each other, and there was a tightness in his chest that his deep breaths could do nothing to ease.

The man who'd written these letters had singlehandedly ruined the life of his daughter and caused untold suffering to others. He was the reason for every moment of Ivy's pain, every cold, sleepless night, every missed meal, every sneer she had endured for years...

Yet he still thought he had a right to ask her these things, as if he was simply away on an extended business trip and would return to claim the child he had unwillingly abandoned?

He flung the last letter aside in disgust.

How could a man be so self-centered? So completely oblivious to his own deeds that he believed he deserved a woman like Ivy's love after everything?

Ash rubbed at his eyes and sighed heavily. He didn't know what to do with the information he had stumbled upon. There was no question it helped him understand Ivy in a new light, but there was more to it than that.

Some of those letters were murders waiting to happen.

From the looks of it, she had tried to do something about it and hadn't gotten very far.

But that was before she had the Marquess of Blackbourne on her side.

He painstakingly gathered the letters back up, put

them in the correct order, and laid them back in the drawer.

All he had to do was wait for her to trust him enough to tell him.

****

By the time Ivy came back from the exhibit, dinner was being laid out, and Max was back as well. Thankfully, the conversation had revolved around Ivy's experiences at the gallery and the people she had met.

He would have to check into someone named Grant Hayworth, whom Ivy had mentioned several times during her retelling of the events of the day.

"And then Mr. Hayworth told the funniest jest. Let's see if I can get it right." She wiggled in her chair, thinking. "There was an artist, and he asked the gallery owner if anyone had wanted to purchase his paintings recently. The gallery owner said, 'I have good news and bad news. The good news is that a gentleman enquired about your work and asked if it would appreciate in value after your death. When I told him it would, he bought all 23 of your paintings.' 'That's wonderful,' said the artist. 'What's the bad news?' Then the gallery owner said, 'The man was your doctor.'" Ivy paused and then hooted. "Isn't that just terrible?" she exclaimed delightedly, spearing another bite of poached salmon.

Max laughed heartily while Ash raised a brow. "Yes, terrible," he murmured. It was wonderful to see Ivy lit up with excitement as she was, yet he hadn't caused it, and so there seemed to be a niggling burr sticking him as she spoke of her outing. He knew full well it was childish and unfair, but that didn't mean his logic could will the feeling away.

After two more courses taking all he could of Max's obvious attempts at flirtation with Ivy and her oblivious responses, he decided he'd had enough. "Miss

Morganstern, would you like to accompany me to the roof? I'd like to show you something."

"The roof?" both Max and Ivy repeated.

He smiled. "Yes. Max, if you'll excuse us." He stood and held out a hand to Ivy, who set down her custard spoon and followed suit.

Leaving Max sulking at the dinner table as he took Ivy from the room was immensely satisfying. Anything he did to thwart his cousin's enjoyment was.

"Why do you hate Max so?" Ivy asked, looking up at him as they climbed the back stairwell.

Ash sighed. He supposed he'd have to tell her sometime, but he didn't want it to be now. "You don't need to be worrying about that, Princess."

"So you *do* hate him," she pressed.

Ash raked a hand through his hair. "It's complicated. I didn't start the animosity between us."

"Did you … love the same woman or something like that?" she guessed.

She surprised a laugh from him. "Gads, no. I've never had a feud over a woman. That's ridiculous."

Something in her tone changed, and he sensed a turn into dangerous waters. "Why is that ridiculous? You've never had your heart broken or cared enough about someone to fight for them?"

Ash scoffed, pulling at his cravat, which had suddenly become too tight. He opened the door to the roof and led her out into the cold night air. It was a crisp and clear night, perfect for what he wanted to show her. "I don't … allow emotional entanglements of that nature," he said carefully.

Ivy's breath puffed into the air in a cloud. "So you're content to be a rake of the first order for the rest of your life without ever finding anyone for whom you actually care?"

Well, when she put it that way, it sounded depressing. Fortunately, he had an answer for that question that should satisfy her infernal curiosity. "No, I intend to marry an empty-headed lass eventually who will bear me some average heirs and who won't mind if I fulfill my needs with others."

Ivy shook her head. "That sounds terrible. I pity the woman who would agree to that, no matter how convincing you are."

"I told you I wouldn't lie about my intentions," he reminded her. "And I can be very convincing," he added slyly, looking down at her pert nose, the tip growing pink with cold.

"Don't I know it," she grumbled, shivering.

"Come over here," he said, tugging her towards the edge of the structure.

"Is this how you get rid of unwanted employees? Toss them off your roof?" she quipped, hugging herself.

Seeing her teeth chattering, Ash shrugged out of his evening jacket and threw it around her shoulders. Her immediate sigh warmed him enough to withstand the chill sinking into his bones. "Meddling cousins, maybe," he replied in all seriousness. Approaching the tri-legged device, he asked, "Do you know what this is?"

"No. Should I?" Ivy walked around it, looking at the cylindrical shape tilted off-center.

"It's an achromatic refracting telescope," Ash told her, trying to keep the pride from his voice. It had taken quite a bit of time to track one down that the owner hadn't minded parting with for a price.

"And what does it do?" Ivy asked, running a hand over its length.

The motion did odd things to him, despite the cold.

"It can show you the stars." He watched her

reaction as she pulled her hand back.

"What do you mean? I can see them already," she said, waving at the bright night sky.

The hairs in his nose bristled with cold as he bent to adjust the angle of the instrument. Once he had gotten it positioned just right, he stepped back. "Not like this," he declared, grasping her by the shoulders and guiding her to where the eyepiece was. "Look," he commanded softly, standing close behind her.

For him, the eyepiece was about Adam's apple height, but she had to stand on her tip-toes to put her face up to it. Still holding onto her shoulders, he blinked as a stray lock of her hair wafted across his cheek.

A gasp.

He chuckled.

She took her eye away from the eyepiece to look at him. "Are those really the stars?" she breathed. "It's not a picture inside?"

He shook his head, smiling at her impossibly wide eyes. She immediately put her eye back up to it and grabbed ahold of it with one hand.

"How?" she asked.

"There are a series of lenses curved to make objects appear closer," he explained.

"Why doesn't everyone have one of these? How is it I've never heard of this telescope?"

"Some people do. Wealthy people and scientists. I happen to be both."

"They're incredible, like a dream," she remarked, finally taking her face away from the lens and turning to face him.

"I thought the same thing when I first saw you," he said softly.

Ivy's lashes went down. "No, you didn't."

He frowned. "I can assure you, it's true, though it

might sound trite," he said defensively. She really didn't let him get away with the usual lines, did she? And that had been a pretty good one. In fact, he didn't think he'd ever compared a woman to stars before.

"No, I mean ... you first saw a filthy, rag-wearing woman with nothing to her name. You felt sorry for me, perhaps, but you didn't think I was anything other than a problem to be dealt with."

He cocked his head. "You're right," he admitted. "But I have never been so happy to be proven wrong."

She looked up at him. "So I'm no longer a problem?" she smiled tentatively.

"Oh, you're definitely a problem," he corrected her.

She narrowed her eyes.

"But one I'm having so much fun solving," he murmured, wrapping his hand around the back of her neck and bringing his lips down to hers.

Her warm, wet mouth was more pleasurable than the majesty of any star-studded sky. Cold fingers touched his neck as she sighed into the kiss. He brought her closer, feeling the nip of her waist and how it flared into her hips.

He had been drunk many times, but the way she accepted him past her lips and into the recesses of her mouth felt like the most potent of liquors going to his head. She made him want things he knew he couldn't have from her—things he suddenly found erotic. To teach her how to make love, how to feel her own pleasure, would be the pinnacle of his own exploits, unlike anything he'd ever desired before.

Growling into her mouth, he slipped his leg between hers and pushed her feet wider.

Ivy inhaled sharply at the unexpected movement causing her to shift her balance.

Ash gripped the small of her back firmly while his other hand gathered her skirts up. He made quick work of it, and she didn't seem to mind the cold on her silk-stockinged legs, but her breathing quickened as his lips hovered on hers.

"Do you still want me to be the first to touch you, Princess?" he whispered, his breath smoking over her face. The heavy trails of her dress flowed over his wrist as he made sure they were still positioned to cover her as much as possible.

His lips were so close, he felt her bite her lower one. "Will it hurt?" she asked, her trepidation clear.

He chuckled. "No, darling, not at all. This will feel good, I promise."

"All right," she breathed, digging her fingers into the fabric of his lawn shirt. "Touch me."

Those two words hardened him like nothing else ever had. He closed his eyes, feeling her jerk as he skimmed his hand up the inner thigh of her left leg. The skin there was delicate and soft, like fine powdered sugar.

When he reached the apex of her legs, he ran his thumb over the cotton of her drawers, feeling her swollen sex underneath.

Her breathing was ragged now, and he smiled at her untutored reaction. There was so much more to show her.

Using his pointer finger, he traced the crease through her panties, reveling in the way her breath fanned his ear in uncontrolled waves. She was already wet, he could feel, the soft fabric dampening under his ministrations.

He wanted more than anything to press himself against her, to let her feel his steel-hard member against that wetness. Groaning, he let his forehead lower to touch hers, holding out against the onslaught of throbbing need pushing its way through him.

Moving his hand up, he slid his fingers down the front of her garment, the nest of curls brushing his fingers. He went lower, cupping the folds of her in his large palm before slipping his longest middle finger inside her.

Her breath rushed out, and the grip she had on the shoulders of his lawn shirt tightened as he felt the trembling of her unsteady legs. Ivy's brief moan caused his cock to twitch and harden further.

Lips against her forehead, he gulped. "You're so tight and wet."

"Is th-that good?" she quivered.

"It's glorious," he replied, beginning to pump the length of his finger in and out of her snug heat.

Ivy cried out, and he caught the sound in his mouth, muffling it as he continued to work the inside of her passage. Forcing his tongue into her mouth, he mimicked the motion of his hand, her moans vibrating against his lips.

He could tell she was close to coming, her slick muscles constricting around his knuckles.

"Yes, that's it. Come for me, Princess," he told her, needing more than anything to feel her climax against his fingers.

"Ash, I'm ... don't stop," she whispered, her heated cheeks visible in the night.

"Never," he vowed, thrusting his finger deeper with each stroke.

Behind him, a creak and the click of a door reverberated.

He froze, his heart beat sounding in his ears as he listened.

"Asher, are you up here?" Max's voice called

from the other side of the roof.

Ash cursed and Ivy gasped, rearing back.

Shielding her with his body, he hastily withdrew his hand from under her skirts and made sure she had them rearranged properly before stepping back.

As he turned towards the hutch that housed the door, Max came around the corner of it, hands in his pockets.

"It's deucedly cold up here, cousin," he remarked, strolling towards them. "Miss Morganstern shouldn't be out in this, wearing your clothes or not." He raised a brow.

Ivy quickly shrugged out of his jacket and handed it back to him, the heat in her cheeks blossoming even further. Ash noticed she was still affected by his touch, her fingers trembling as he took his evening coat from her.

"No need to disparage chivalry just because you're lacking it," Ash rejoined, leaning back into a deceptively lazy pose against the wall around the roof.

"Oh, stop it, you two," Ivy intervened, crossing her arms over her front. "Lord Blackbourne was showing me his telescope. Have you an interest in such things, Lord Eydris?" she asked, indicating the astronomer's device to her right.

Max came further towards them, looking it over. "Can't say that I do. I'm surprised Ash does, to be honest. You haven't been particularly scholarly for the past decade, have you? More interested in things within arm's reach," he commented pointedly, looking daggers at Ash.

Ash grinned, although his teeth ground together painfully. "Jealous, coz?"

"Not in the slightest," Max growled, his mouth twisted in a snarl.

"It *is* cold up here," Ivy said, rubbing her arms. "I think it's time I retire for the night."

Ash straightened. "Capital idea." He held out his arm to her. "Max? The door?"

Max's jaw ticked, but he held the door for them as they left the roof, muttering about not being a "bloody servant" the whole way.

As the door closed behind Max, Ash looked back at the telescope standing by its lonesome at the corner of the roof, the bright sky illuminated with thousands of stars behind it.

He would certainly never be able to look through its lens again without becoming hard as a rock, thanks to Ivy.

Perfect. She was now getting in the way of his scientific pursuits. And it was his own fault, to boot.

Bloody hell.

Chapter Eleven

Ivy didn't want to open the letter that had arrived for her that morning.

She wanted to lie about in bed all day thinking about what Ash had done to her the night before. The way he'd kissed her, held her, whispered things that made her want to float away and sink through the floor in embarrassment at the same time.

And his hands…

She pressed her face into her pillow to hold in the sound that was equal parts bemoaning and celebration.

It shouldn't have been allowed. With a few flicks of his talented fingers, he had formed her into a state in which she would have let him do anything at all to her.

It didn't take a genius to figure out why women wanted the man like cats after cream. He was positively gifted at manipulating the female form, at least from what she could tell in her limited experience.

A thought occurred to her. Maybe he was terrible at it, and she just didn't know it because she had nothing to compare him to.

She snorted, pushing her hair from her eyes and resituating the covers around her shoulders.

Not likely. Every time they had been in public, she had noticed women trying to gain his attention, and the things that were said about him in the clusters of women along ballroom edges was confirmation of his abilities.

Who was she to think she could resist such a man when he wanted her?

And he did seem to want her. It wasn't fathomable that he would desire her, of all people. She wasn't alluring or knowledgeable or even just respectable. But every time they were near one another, a fire seemed to build till it burst into flames that neither of them could control.

Yet she had to resist him. There was no future with someone like him. He had explained that to her clearly on more than one occasion. She didn't understand his reasons, but he seemed adamant about them, nonetheless.

That was what she couldn't figure out. One moment, he was carefree and excited with her, and the next, a heaviness came over him, and he shut down to everyone around him. Something he had said repeated in her mind.

"...until the madness finally comes for me," he'd said.

What did that mean? His mind was sharp as a tack, and she'd never seen him act like a candidate for Bedlam. He did say he got megrims, but that was a common enough ailment and didn't signify a mental illness.

No matter what it was that troubled him so deeply, he had convinced himself that he needed to bear the burden alone. If he was determined to go through life having superficial interactions with women, she wouldn't allow her heart to be a casualty of that decision. She knew herself too well to think she could continue to play with fire and not be burned. Every kiss, every caress that meant nothing to him would singe her soul until it was black with bitterness.

Besides that, she had her own demons to contend with. Not a day went by that she didn't mentally examine herself for signs of her father's predilections. It was an informal bedtime ritual—go over every interaction and every thought she'd had, making sure no violence had entered her thoughts or actions.

Jacob Wollard's tendencies hadn't awoken in him until after he had gotten married, after he'd loved someone and been with them physically. Her mother had been his first killing, she had realized years later, after a series of in-depth periodical articles had been written about the string of murders. His brief explanations of her death in childbirth had been nothing but a fabrication meant to placate his daughter, the only person he had left.

Who knew what would awaken in her if she allowed herself to be with someone that way? She would never let anyone wake beside her someday to find her taking their life just as her father had done to his spouse.

So it seemed neither of them was willing to chance the complications of that sort of relationship.

Heat flashed through her as the memory of his finger sliding into her kaleidoscoped behind her eyes.

It was so blasted difficult to resist him! And she couldn't deny that she simply enjoyed his company. Every conversation with him was interesting, every experience something new. Even just eating breakfast with him was somehow wonderful.

"No," she said aloud, clenching the bedcovers and sitting up.

She would guard her heart and body carefully, be a model employee, and continue to monitor her father's correspondence. No one else would, and she might be the only person that could prevent something terrible from happening to some poor soul in the future. That was her burden, and she wouldn't shirk it just because some handsome, intelligent, charming, rich, fascinating…

All right, that wasn't helping anything.

Sighing, she reached over to the salver on her bedside table and plucked the letter from its gleaming silver face.

She opened the outer envelope quickly, which was the forwarding packaging from Tothill Fields. When she saw the handwriting on the inside envelope, she clenched her jaw.

Claymore.

With nervous fingers, she ripped it open and unfolded the foolscap.

Dear Mr. Wollard,

I believe I've found her—the one. The one who will fulfill my destiny and lead me to a greater understanding of this plane of existence and the next. Her name is Charlotte, and she is the sweetest thing to walk this earth. Her lovely neck will be a spectacular debut for my device, which I have now perfected. She is the daughter of a local dairy farmer and has the most charming blush you've ever seen. I am growing impatient to see what her skin looks like after the blood no longer flows in her veins, but I still have a few details to arrange so that suspicion is not cast on me when the time comes.

By the time the snow melts, I will be able to consider myself among your ranks, among those whose comprehension supersedes all earthly laws and authority. I have you to thank for helping me realize my true calling. I hope you'll be pleased when you hear of my deed, for I will make sure it is worthy to reach the ears of England far and wide. Your methods continue to inspire and guide me throughout this splendid process, and I can only hope that you eventually come to think of me as your equal.

Ever Your Enthusiast,
Claymore

Ivy's hands shook.

This was what she'd always feared.

Claymore was going to kill a woman named Charlotte, and she hadn't the faintest idea what to do. It wasn't a hypothetical any longer. In fact, she didn't know how much time there was to do anything. There wasn't a set timeframe, except winter, she supposed. "By the time the snow melts" could mean all sorts of deadlines, depending on where in England one lived. Considering it was now February, it could be as soon as a month from now, or any time before that.

It may have already happened.

She growled and pulled hard on her braided hair in frustration. What if, since he'd sent the letter, he had already carried out his plan? Letters sometimes took weeks to reach their destination. It was entirely possible that she was already dead.

There hadn't been anything in London's papers about a murder like the one Claymore described, but reports might not have reached the capital city yet.

No, she wouldn't think about that now. There was a good chance she was still alive, and she would do everything in her power to see that this young woman— Charlotte—stayed that way.

But how?

Was it even possible to determine who this Claymore was without more information?

Not according to the prison warden and the authorities in Leeds, whom she had presented with the letters more than once. They had told her that they were sorry, but there was nothing more that could be done without more evidence.

Frustration gnawed at her as she rubbed her temples. She needed to think about this from another angle if she had any chance of impacting Claymore's plans. She needed to see the problem from outside of it and use whatever resources she could to find him.

Another angle...

Her employer just happened to be the most intelligent person she'd ever met, and had more resources than she probably knew of. She had hoped that he would never come to know of the sordid letters or the problems she bore. Her employability was next to nothing, and if he decided she was more trouble or danger than she was worth...

She would be back on the streets faster than Ash was able to lift a woman's skirts on a rooftop.

And that was quite fast.

Yet she had to do something. She couldn't sit around and wait for news of a grisly murder that might have been prevented. When it came to it, there wasn't any choice, at least not for her. A woman's life was more important than anything else.

But perhaps there was another way to gain more information without involving Blackbourne.

The thought she was contemplating caused her heart to race and cold sweat to congeal on her skin. She would have to dredge up nerves of steel for it, but it was the only avenue she could think of that might yield results.

She was going to have to visit her father in one of the most notoriously violent prisons in England.

She gulped. It was definitely not a good idea, but Charlotte's life depended on it.

If there was one thing Ivy was good at, it was surviving in any circumstances in which she found herself.

She began to pray her instinct for it still lived within her, for she was going into the belly of the beast as soon as she found a way to do so without alerting Blackbourne.

Ivy had a feeling if Ash found out her plans,

Charlotte truly would be doomed.

****

It turned out to be much easier than she'd thought to arrange a visit to her father. All she'd said to Asher was that she was going to Westminster with Lady Delilah Hayworth and her cousin, Grant. And while this was true, she didn't tell him she'd be making a stop beforehand at New Bridewell Prison, as she'd found out it was now called after being moved to a new location several years ago. Only minutes from where she was supposed to meet Grant and Lilah, Ivy hoped to be in and out before anyone of her acquaintance was the wiser.

It was an unfamiliar feeling, having to worry that people who knew her would care where she was. She both resented and cherished it.

After stating her identity and request for visitation to the guard at the front fate, she was ushered into a small waiting area to wait for the Warden's permission. It was a drab room without adornment or color, just stone walls like everything else she had seen of the prison so far. There were only two chairs, one of which she took so her knees wouldn't knock together or fall out from under her.

Smoothing her sky blue walking dress she hadn't had occasion to wear until today, Ivy tried to control her breathing. A thousand thoughts and emotions warred for prevalence in her mind, causing her hands to shake where they sat in her lap.

She had imagined seeing her father again countless times, playing out scenario after scenario in her mind. Sometimes, the scenarios were fantasies ending in tear-filled confessions that they had arrested the wrong man, and they were going to live happily ever after. Other times, she imagined slapping him across the face and telling him every hardship she had endured while he begged her forgiveness.

Until now, she had never thought such an interaction would ever actually occur. Her private imaginings had stayed safely in her mind where they couldn't hurt her. Now that the reality of all her fears and hopes was fast approaching, she wanted to run straight back to Blackbourne House and forget the entire thing.

She clamped her mouth shut to stay the chattering of her teeth.

Just stay calm. Be completely detached. Don't engage in anything besides the questions you have about Claymore.

Forcing herself to regulate her breathing, she closed her eyes. Ironically, the fact that she was in a heavily fortified prison with hundreds of criminals around her wasn't contributing to her state of anxiety. She had lived amongst criminals and vagabonds long enough to not fear their nature the way most law-abiding citizens did. The thought of speaking to her father whom she hadn't seen in almost a decade, however, shook her to her core.

It had been quite a while since she'd been left with her own thoughts, the better part of an hour. Lilah might be waiting for her by now, but there was no help for it. She continued to scrunch her eyes tightly shut until she heard footsteps approaching the metal door of the waiting room.

Warden Crick himself stepped into the room, followed by a guard. A behemoth of a man, he towered over her as she stood to greet him, his broad shoulders emphasized by the lines of the dark gray uniform he wore. His hazel eyes were kind, but contained a hardness that she could only assume he had cultivated in the course of his difficult duties.

"Miss Wollard," he nodded to her. "I'm sorry for the wait. Precautions had to be taken. You're here to see your father, Jacob Wollard."

It wasn't a question, but she nodded, her heart in her throat.

"I can let you have a five-minute visitation, but no longer," he said gently. "Today is already one of upheaval for many of the inmates due to renovations in that wing, so I can't be having anyone upsetting their schedules or stirring up trouble. I'm sure you understand."

"Of course," she assured him with a tremulous smile. She could tell he didn't like being unnecessarily rude, a quality that was surely unusual in a prison warden who needed to control violent lawbreakers on a daily basis. But what did she know? Perhaps all prison wardens were large, gruff teddy bears like Crick. "I just need to ask him a few questions, and I'll be more than happy to leave."

He nodded. "Follow Masterson," he indicated the guard who had followed him into the room, "and stay close to him. The commons has been cleared for your passage. Your father has a private cell at the end of the East Wing, and Masterson will take you there. You'll have to stay in the corridor, but you'll be able to see each other through the door. For security, Masterson will be present the entire time. You cannot touch the door or window bars. Do you understand?"

"Yes, sir. Thank you," she said earnestly.

"I would have said no if your father wasn't a model prisoner, and if he didn't talk about you all the time," Crick stated, his eyes steady on her face.

Ivy blinked, processing this information. But she quickly realized she couldn't at the moment, and shoved the information to the back of her mind for later examination. Right now, she had to focus on what she needed to do.

She smiled briefly at him as he turned to go, leaving Masterson with her.

"Shall we, miss? Just stay right behind me, and everything will be fine," he said, his cockney accent coming through.

"Lead the way, sir," she said stoutly, taking a deep breath.

He led her out of the room, down a corridor, and then out a gate into a large open area that was circular in shape. A tower rose in the middle with windows on all sides at the top, presumably to be able to watch prisoners as they congregated in the common area she was walking through. She had to admit, it was an intelligent set-up, the guards having a secure way to observe everything going on around them from a bird's eye view.

She followed Masterson across the space to a wide open corridor on the other side of it. The air cooled as they entered the stone passageway that was lined with metal doors on both sides. Each cell had a window in the door with bars across it, as well as a lower slot where food or other items could be passed back and forth to prisoners.

Clutching her reticule to her stomach to keep the hovering nausea at bay, Ivy tried to keep her eyes everywhere at once. The first few cells they passed didn't give any indication of life within, but by the third door down, faces began to appear at the bars.

"Wot's a cove like 'er doin 'ere?" one called, his dirt-encrusted fingers wrapped around the short bars across his window.

Ivy's heart sped up, and she glanced over to see a bald man smiling at her with exactly one tooth sticking out of his gummy jaw.

"Don't answer them. It only riles them up," Masterson turned his head to tell her without breaking stride.

Ivy looked away from the man quickly and sped up close to her escort.

"Give me five minutes wiv 'er!" another inmate called out as they passed. "I'll show 'er what a real man is!"

Laughter from several cells around followed this pronouncement as Ivy turned red as a beetroot. She kept her head high though, having endured much worse ribbing when she lived on the streets. The difference here was, these men couldn't get to her, which was a world better than what she had had to worry about in the past.

Hoots, whistles, and more vulgar demands flew out of the prison doors as more prisoners became aware of her presence in the corridor. Before long, the noise became a grating din that she had to grit her teeth to block out as she walked silently behind Masterson, who didn't seem at all fazed by the cacophony.

They turned a corner and went to the right. This hallway was quieter than the last, but some inmates still watched her pass with hungry, glowering eyes as if they both hated and craved the sight of her.

One man called out to her to save him, proclaiming his innocence in a desperate cry.

This one, she turned to look at, meeting his frantic eyes while he reached his arm out between the bars seeking her response.

"Please," he rasped, his hand palm up in supplication.

She swallowed, both wanting to stop for some reason and look away from the sight of him. But Masterson did not slow, and so she broke eye contact and hurried after. When she did so, the prisoner wailed as if his very life were being ripped from him.

Tears pricked at her eyes, and she blinked them

back resolutely. She could not think of anyone's plight today but a woman named Charlotte who lived somewhere on English shores and whose life might be snuffed out at any moment if Ivy did not do this.

A new sound assaulted her ears—the sound of hammers and the cracking of rock up ahead. They rounded another corner, and the atmosphere changed. Four men in dusty, serviceable clothing were demolishing the wall of several cells on the right side of this hallway. They were taking picks and mallets to the mortared rock, splitting large chunks off of the existing architecture. Two were on a single ladder, working to remove the upper hinges from a massive door that was in the way of their progress.

Three more men, these ones in prison garb, were all chained together and were helping to clear the debris from the work area, moving rocks and sweeping chunks from underneath the other men's feet. A guard armed with a pistol and a saber watched them like a hawk from a few feet away.

The prisoners on the other side of the corridor were all at their doors, watching the work being done. She supposed, as far as entertainment went, it was as good as they were likely to get in here.

"Your father is just down here at the end," Masterson informed her, pointing to the last cell at the end of the hall on the left.

Attempting to control the wild beating of her heart as the cell door drew closer, she carefully picked her way past the work site to her right, nodding at the workmen who stopped to watch her passage. The prisoners stopped what they were doing as well, but made no attempt to communicate or touch her, for which she was grateful. It was hard enough concentrating on not casting up her breakfast without worrying about other inmates.

"Get back to your task," the guard with the saber growled, giving her a smile and a wink as she went by.

Ivy smiled at the cheeky man in return, the simple gesture bolstering her confidence for what was to come. The bashing of stone resumed, its jarring noise somehow reassuring. If it was silent, she would hear the pounding of her blood in her ears.

And all of a sudden, she was at the door of her father's cell, but she hung back out of sight of the window.

She still wasn't ready for this.

"Wollard," Masterson grunted. "You have a visitor." He rapped on the door, looking through the barred window, and moved aside.

"A visitor?" a puzzled male from within inquired.

That voice.

She hadn't heard it in so long, but there was no mistake it was her father's deep, cultured baritone.

Every bone in her body shook as she approached the window and faced the man who had ruined her life and taken so many others.

****

Ash looked over the rim of his glass at the Duke of Scythemore as he took a sip of bourbon. The two reposed in Ash's study where armchairs sat comfortably in front of the fireplace. It was customary for them to have a single glass every time they met. The liquor burned a path down his throat, reminding him of a time when he had used that familiar heat to obliterate all thought night after night.

The Duke, on the other hand, had never had a problem with overindulging in anything. Ash had never seen him lose control, not once in all the years of their friendship that had begun as boys. Dominic was all that everyone expected a Duke to be. Tall with black hair and sea-green eyes, his presence captured a room's attention instantly—if Ash wasn't nearby, that was. Dignified, reserved, and honest to a fault, he intimidated people at best and, at worst, alienated them when they did not live up to his standards.

Except Asher.

There was no way Ash had ever been upstanding enough to earn Dom's approval, but he hadn't needed to be. Dom had always accepted him as he was for some unknown reason, no matter how debauched Ash had become over the years. His friend had observed in silence as Ash's predilections became more evident, never once condemning him, but not joining him either.

"I forgot how good your liquor cabinet was stocked," Dom commented from where he sat, holding the glass of amber liquid up to the light.

"Not as good as it used to be," Ash chuckled. "Back in the days when I wouldn't have been able to tell you what I'd done the night before."

"Yes, what is your vice now? Still women?" Dom inquired, a small smile on his face.

"They don't leave me with cottonmouth and a headache." Ash grinned.

"They can leave you with far worse," he murmured.

"Are you speaking from experience?" Ash raised his brow. To his knowledge, Dom had only ever been involved with one woman.

Dom grinned, but didn't answer. "I prefer the company of my hounds to women."

Ash rolled his eyes.

"They're more loyal in my experience," he added pointedly.

"That may be true."

"How fares our investment?" Dom asked.

Ash leaned forward and set his glass on the stand between them. This, he always enjoyed discussing with his friend. Dom was an intelligent man and had trusted Ash to find him ventures that would keep his Dukedom prosperous. Ash had risen to the task eagerly, making them both a lot of money over the past several years. Taking a poker and nudging a log in the grate to a better position, he answered. "Quite well. The railway will be finished the end of June, all on schedule. If the Leeds and Selby Railway's success is anything to judge by, the profits from this finished connecting line with Great Western Railway will be substantial. I was impressed with the numbers I came away with from Leeds last I was there, and their profits could be considered a comparable model for the GWR."

Dom nodded, sitting up straighter in his chair. "Excellent. But that's not the only thing you came away with from Leeds, is it?" His friend's sharp eyes assessed his reaction.

Ash's heart skipped a beat. "I don't know what you mean."

Dom laughed, something he did rarely. "Don't play games with me, mate. I know you're playing host to some scientist named Morganstern and his sister since your trip to Leeds. Yet there's only one guest room being used, and it's for a woman."

Ash blinked. "How in blazes do you possibly know which of my guest rooms are being used?" he asked incredulously.

"I have my ways," Dom sipped his bourbon.

Ash raised a brow and waited.

Dom sighed. "All right, I overheard your housekeeper telling one of the maids to change the sheets, and thanking Heaven it was only the one guestroom. She also remarked that the "lady's room" was always tidier than yours."

Ash slumped. "She only speaks Russian with the maids," he mused.

"That's true," Dom smiled knowingly.

With narrowed eyes, Ash acknowledged his friend had beat him. "Would you believe me if I said she was my mistress?" he tried.

"No." The Duke stretched out his long legs and crossed them at the ankle. "You've never kept a mistress in your own home, and certainly never amused yourself with one woman for this long."

"What's your theory, then?" Ash was curious.

Dom looked into the fire and scratched at the dark stubble that was already appearing on his face. "My guess is there is no Morganstern. It's this woman who's the scientist, and she hides behind the guise of having a brother to gain entry into the right circles."

It was too close to the truth for Ash's comfort, but his shoulders lowered in relief. Morganstern's identity was yet a secret. It was hard to fool the Duke of Scythemore, but Ash had been acting for a very long time now. "That would be rather scandalous. A woman in the BAAS while they all think it's her brother who's the brains." Ash didn't bother telling his friend he was misguided in the assumption that the society didn't desire women amongst their ranks.

Dom looked over at his friend. "It sounds like exactly the type of thing you'd get yourself neck deep in."

Ash grinned, shrugging. "What can I say? I get bored being good all the time."

Dom scoffed.

At that moment, Milton entered carrying a missive on his usual salver. "A lady has just arrived, my lord. She's been seated in the front parlor," he intoned, his face somber. The calling card could have been a dinner invitation from the King himself, and Milton would have looked as if he'd found weevils in his porridge.

"Thank you, Milton," Ash said happily, smiling widely at the dour man as he snatched the card from the tray. Ash knew the man was cheerful as a hedgehog in a breadbox around Ivy, the traitor.

Milton's expression didn't change. "Of course, my lord. Your Grace," he acknowledged, bowing first to Dominic as the higher ranking peer and then to Asher.

As he left, Dom commented, "I like him."

Opening the note, Ash replied, "Yes, your dispositions are distressingly similar." He frowned reading the feminine script. Holding up the card, he read, "Lady Delilah Hayworth."

Dom froze in his chair and cleared his throat. "What was that?"

Ash looked up to find his friend's stormy eyes fixated on him. "Lady Hayworth. That's who Iv- Miss Morganstern was supposed to be meeting this afternoon."

"She's here?" he choked. The Duke looked around the study quickly, as if the lady would materialize out of thin air like a reaper come to collect his soul.

Ash struggled not to smile. "I believe that's the situation, yes."

He watched his friend loosen his cravat, his mouth a tight line as if preparing for battle.

"Ahem. Well, I'd better go see what's afoot," Ash declared, amused at his friend's overwrought demeanor that was so far removed from his normal stoicism.

"Yes, I'll-I'll stay here," Dom stuttered, shifting in his chair.

"You do that," Ash said wryly, rising from the

chair.

He left his friend sweating bullets in the study and went to the parlor. As he entered, a woman with jet-black hair rose from the settee. She was stunning and statuesque, her coiled raven tresses creating a striking contrast with the violet of her eyes. Ash had never seen eyes that hue and knew that, if circumstances were different, he wouldn't have hesitated to attempt a seduction of this woman.

But this one was off-limits and had been for as long as he could remember. If Ash had even thought of making her his paramour, Dom would have killed him slowly in a thousand different ways while denying any connection to the lady.

The particulars of that history Ash would give his right earlobe to hear.

"Lady Hayworth," Ash smiled warmly. "A pleasure to finally meet you." He took her proffered hand and pressed a kiss to the knuckles.

She cocked her head, the fine bones of her face luminescent in the light from the bay window. "You're taller than I expected up close," she said finally.

Ash chuckled. "Interesting. What makes you think I'd be shorter?"

"Corrine," she said simply.

Ash's stomach tightened. "And what does Corrine say about me?"

She smiled, her white teeth momentarily dazzling him. And he wasn't easily dazzled, preferring to be the other party in such interactions. "That you're quite adept at kissing."

His breath froze in his lungs. This woman didn't pull any punches. He could see why his friend had almost bolted from the premises at the mention of her name. Swallowing the sensation, he replied in a much lower tone. "Is that so?"

She laughed. "But let's keep that between you and me, Lord Blackbourne."

"I promise nothing." He winked.

"You're as big a rascal as they say," she admonished him, stepping back. "Where is Corrine anyways? I thought we were going to meet at Westminster Square, but when she didn't show up after half an hour, I thought perhaps I had misunderstood and we were riding together."

A sinking feeling entered his chest. "You were to meet at Westminster."

"Yes," she replied, looking at him in confusion. "My cousin, Lord Bastion, was to escort us from there. I sent him on without me."

Westminster Square was a stone's throw away from New Bridewell Prison. Ivy's father was there. It was too much of a coincidence, and he wasn't going to take the chance that she was somewhere else at this very moment.

"I don't know her well enough yet to know if she's late often," Lady Hayworth continued, "but I thought I might as well head this way in case she was waiting for me."

"She's not the type to be tardy," he said, the portent in his voice causing Lady Hayworth to narrow her eyes.

She put her hands on her hips. "So I was correct? We were supposed to meet there?"

Ash nodded slowly, his mind working to predict the possible outcomes of interfering in Ivy's personal business. After a brief pause, he had decided there was nothing for it. She might not like it, but it he wasn't going to let her face her father without him. Not to mention, New Bridewell prison was no place for a lady, even a street-savvy one.

"I believe it's time to extract Corrine from prison," he murmured.

Delilah's eyes widened. "She's in prison?" she screeched, taking a step back.

Ash's smile turned wry as he met the lady's lilac-ringed eyes. "She's not incarcerated, but Corrine might have a few secrets she hasn't told you yet."

"Clearly," Delilah said, blinking.

He watched her shocked face. "Does this alter your friendship?"

She paused, thinking. Then a slow grin lit her features. "I think Corrine might be just the breath of fresh air Raquel and I need this stuffy season."

Ash winked. "I knew you were a woman of good taste."

Her smile widened. "It's been ages since I've been connected to a good scandal. Seems high time I muddied the waters again."

"If you could make sure the waters stay clear for the time being, I would greatly appreciate it," he told her.

"Of course. Just how grateful are we talking, Lord Blackbourne? I believe I heard Corrine mentioned she likes classic artwork, and Bath has plenty of exhibits this time of year." She crossed her arms in front of her.

Ash didn't hesitate to play the ace up his sleeve. He wasn't above using the circumstances to his advantage. "How about you keep Corrine out of the broadsheets, and I won't tell the man sitting in my study that you're still madly in love with him?"

Delilah froze, but recovered quickly. "Excuse me? Whoever this man is, you're absurdly mistaken," she laughed.

"It's the Duke of Scythemore," he stated. "Although I believe you were once on a first name basis with my friend Dominic."

He waited for her reaction, which didn't take long. In fact, it was remarkably similar to his friend's. Her breathing stopped, and then restarted again much faster than before. Eyes that had been filled with deviltry a moment before were now wide with panic. She backed away from him, bumping into the arm of the sofa.

"You can't— I'm not..." she stuttered, gulping like a fish out of water.

Ash chuckled. "Yes, clearly your feelings for him are non-existent."

"He's here now?" she whispered, putting a hand to her stomach.

"He is," Ash nodded. "And he knows of your presence as well."

"I have to go," she breathed. She began to walk quickly towards the door.

As she tried to pass him, he grabbed her waist, stopping her. "Do we have a deal?" he pressed.

She looked up at him, although she was tall enough that she didn't have to tilt her face overly much. "I don't require anything in return for loyalty to my friends. You can tell him whatever the hell you wish."

Ash smiled. "I thought that might be the case." He let his hand fall from her side. After a moment, he added, "Dom is a lucky man."

Her lips tightened, and she swallowed visibly. "Yes, he is—that I didn't blow his kneecaps off as he deserved three years ago."

Ash laughed as she swept from the room. He was beginning to see why his friend had never recovered from that woman.

Now he had to go see about the woman he might never recover from if something were to happen to her.

Chapter Twelve

Jacob Wollard's face gazed back at her, still recognizable in its distinguished lines, but aged significantly. His stare immediately affixed itself on her face, and his blue eyes, so like her own, widened in recognition.

"Ivy?" he choked. "My little flower vine, is it you?"

She couldn't speak. Seeing his familiar features brought forth both love and revulsion in equal measures, neither of which she could or wanted to express to this man. She took in the weathered lines and loose skin that hadn't been there the last time she'd seen him, and the hardship of prison written there almost made her soften towards him for a brief moment.

But she wasn't here to reconcile.

"Hello, Jacob," she said carefully, relieved that her voice did not reveal her fear.

"You've come for me. I knew you would come. I've missed you so much," he confessed, tears swimming in the whites of his eyes. He reached out through the bars, aiming for her cheek.

Ivy stepped back quickly, her breath coming rapidly. She wasn't sure she could handle being touched by him, although part of her ached to let him do so. But if she let him, her composure, her purpose, might shatter into a million pieces that she couldn't rebuild quickly enough to accomplish what she needed to do.

"I'm not here for you," she stated, watching him pull his hand back.

Some of the excited light left his eyes. His shoulders slumped, but he nodded. "I understand. What can I do for you, daughter? Anything that is in my power to do, I will."

Trying to ignore the effect his words had on her, she took a deep breath. "You can help me save a woman who is going to become a victim of someone like you."

Jacob blinked, acknowledging the reference to his crimes. "I don't understand how I can help."

"A man writes to you. His name is Claymore. I need to know who he is," she told him.

"Claymore," he contemplated the syllables. "Yes, the name is familiar. But I am not allowed to receive mail any longer. I believe that was your doing," he said gently, no accusation in his tone, just acceptance. "I haven't heard from him in a long time now."

Ivy kept her expression neutral. "I have."

He processed this information. "I'm sorry," he finally said.

Ivy pushed his sympathy aside, but it rent a hole in her heart that she knew would ache painfully later. "Do you know who he is? Do you know anything at all about him?" she demanded, coming closer to the bars.

Frowning, his eyes left hers as he thought. Ivy let him take his time.

"I'll tell you if you answer my questions," he countered.

Ivy had already anticipated this response and had decided it was worth playing his game. "Fine. Ask."

Her father had always been a charismatic man, able to give a compliment or a diplomatic response in any situation. He had charmed little girls, women, and men alike, and Ivy hadn't realized until many years after he had been taken from her that he was better at it than most. Yet now, she watched his Adam's apple bob trying to form questions he had probably asked her a thousand times in his mind.

"Are you … are you faring well? Are you being taken care of?" he rasped, his eyes on her face.

A particularly loud piece of rock crumbling to the ground made her jump and look to the side for a moment. When she met his eyes again, they were searching her face for every minutia of expression.

At least now that she had met Blackbourne, the answer to this question was an easy one. "Yes. My employer provides well for me. I lack for nothing." Here in this place, she realized how very lucky she was that this was true.

"Good," he said, smiling with teeth that were straight and, unlike other prisoners, still present. "Are you not married then? I cannot imagine that a woman as beautiful as you have turned into has not been pursued by eligible gentlemen. You-you look like your mother," he added softly.

At this, she felt a rising of resentment that burned its way up her throat. "It was difficult to be available for courting when I lived on the streets, begging for food," she said without inflection. "And I wouldn't know if I look like her, as I do not even have a picture of her left to keep."

He reared back, shock opening his mouth. "What do you mean? Your aunt would never—"

"She didn't want the daughter of a murderer," she spat, her chest heaving. "No one did." Ivy hated that she was letting her emotions get the better of her, but if he truly wanted to know what her life had been like, then he would hear exactly how he had crippled her existence.

"No," he whispered. "I'm sorry. I'm so sorry. I never meant—"

Her hands balled into fists. "You never meant?" Ivy cried, interrupting him. She closed the distance between herself and the window, making sure he saw every bit of fiery pain in her eyes. "You never meant what? You never meant to hurt all those women? To destroy entire families? You never meant to abandon your only child to the mercy of those who thought she was just as evil as her kin?" she snarled, wrapping one hand around the bars on the door. "What didn't you mean, father of mine?"

Tears streamed from Jacob Wollard's eyes, and he squeezed them shut against her tirade. Putting his hands over his face, he sobbed into them, hunching as her words washed over him.

"I'm broken," his voice cracked from where he crouched on the floor of his small cell. "I was always broken. I thought ... I thought your mother could fix me—that she would be my salvation, that should could cleanse me from these demons," he moaned.

Ivy struggled to maintain any façade of coolness. "At least you killed her before I had a chance to find out what having a mother was like," Ivy stated, her chest a maelstrom of every emotion she had experienced at the hands of this man over the past nine years. "I don't even miss her."

"I do," he breathed, so quietly she might have imagined it.

"You don't deserve to be a father." She swallowed. "I wish I'd never known you," she threw the words at him, knowing she would regret them later.

His shoulders racked with sobs, Jacob Wollard finally looked like the defeated man he was. And though satisfaction coursed through her veins at finally having said what she had needed to for so long, another man's face swam in her mind—one who had once said she might be the cure from his own demons.

She closed her eyes, a single tear escaping her lashes to trail down her cheek. Taking a deep breath, she collected herself again. Whatever this man in front of her had done, he would always be her father. He would always own a piece of her that could belong to no one else.

Clearly, Jacob Wollard was a man tortured by the mistakes he had made. It was difficult to see the things he had done as mere mistakes, but the truth of it was, his urges controlled him as surely as Ash's controlled his own mind. The only difference was in the result of whatever thoughts afflicted them. Ash refused to let himself hurt anyone.

Ivy opened her eyes and watched as her father tired himself out, his sobs becoming sniffs. He wiped his face on his worn, brown sleeve and stood again, eyes red-rimmed, but lucid once more.

"I am sorry for what you have endured for my sake," he stated, his voice low and still shaking.

Words she had wanted to hear for what seemed like millennia. Yet she couldn't afford to bask in them now. "That's past. What matters now is Claymore. Perhaps you can find some redemption in helping to prevent another innocent from dying."

He shook his head. "There is no redemption for me, especially now that I know what I have done to you." He sighed. "The only thing I can recall is that he mentioned time quite a bit in his letters," he shrugged.

By the time the snow melts...

Jacob continued. "He mentioned fixing time once. He compared taking someone's life to stopping a pocket watch, and then giving the time to someone else."

It was Ivy's turn to frown. Claymore liked his metaphors, but she didn't remember anything about stopping time. Not that that even helped. Perhaps the man was a watchmaker?

"Did he say anything about where he lived or did

he ever use a different name?" Ivy asked, growing more desperate.

Her father shook his head. "No, darling. I'm sorry."

Ivy sighed, slumping her shoulders. That was it then. There was nothing else to be gained here. "Thank you. I..." She tried to think of what she should say. It might be the last thing she ever said to him. She had already condemned him and forced him to face what he had done, at least to her. Was forgiveness what she wanted to leave him with?

He didn't deserve absolution. There was nothing he could do or say to make up for the things he'd done. Yet she didn't believe in leaving someone without hope. She had felt that herself at various times, and it was soul-crushing. It was stabbing pain and vast emptiness at once, and she wasn't sure anyone deserved to have their loved one sentence them to that forever. She believed God would be his judge. He was her father, and perhaps her words were the only ones that could lead him to his right mind. So, even if she didn't feel it all the time, she would give him this.

"I forgive you, Papa," she said softly, the hammering of the nearby picks almost blotting out the words.

At this, Jacob Wollard leaned his forehead against the bars of his door, lips trembling. "I love you. That has never changed."

Ivy gulped. "I kno-"

A shout from behind her caused her to flinch. She turned as movement caught her eye and gasped, watching as a large piece of the ceiling across the corridor began to crumble above the wall they were demolishing. The meter-wide block of stone gave way, falling towards the ground and clipping the side of the ladder still holding a laborer. Echoing from the walls, the massive block crashed to the ground, trapping one of the other workers' legs beneath it. The man screamed, pulling at his leg futilely. The ladder fell sideways, its occupant yelling as he toppled over. Unfortunately, the cheeky guard was directly in the path of the falling ladder and didn't quite move fast enough to clear its path. He was knocked off his feet, the worker falling on top of him.

Dust clouded the corridor as Masterson pulled her backwards. "Get behind me!" he ordered.

"Ivy?!" her father called frantically.

She couldn't see what was going on, coughing on chalky dust particles as she moved behind her escort. There was movement and shouting, Masterson taking out his club while changing his stance to a defensive one. More screaming, and then, suddenly, nothing but shuffling noises in the smoky hall.

When the dust dissipated a few seconds later, the situation was clear. In the space of the few seconds, three things had happened.

Both workers' and the guard's throats had been slit, their blood pooling around them, while the other two workers had apparently bolted. The prisoners on work duty were no longer chained together, their manacles laying uselessly on the ground, a guard's key sticking out of the last pair. And the prisoners now had a saber, a pistol, and a pickaxe, focused on the two people left in the hallway that could hinder their escape.

Ivy's airways constricted in fear as she felt for the wall at her back.

"Lay down your weapons immediately," Masterson said. "You won't get far."

One of the prisoners, a wiry man with the guard's pistol pointed straight at Masterson's chest, licked his cracked lips and smiled. "We ain't stupid. It won't be just the three of us. We're clearin' the place out," he informed them.

At this, hoots and hollers of celebration came from cells all down both sides of the corridor. The doors began to rattle as prisoners shook the bars on their doors.

One of the other prisoners went and removed the keys from the shackles on the floor.

"No!" Jacob Wollard pleaded from the other side of his door. She could see a sliver of his panicked face from the angle at which she stood.

Ivy watched, trying to think of anything that would save them as the situation worsened by the second. She cursed herself for not bringing her dagger. She would never make that mistake again. The man with the keys went to the door of the cell next to Wollard's and opened it. The man inside came out laughing, patting his savior on the back.

"Whatever sentence you have will be doubled if you leave your cells," Masterson called, voice holding steady. His pronouncement was barely heard over the din of excited inmates.

Ivy had to admire his fortitude, although she could see his hands shaking as he clutched the club, knowing it was no good against a gun.

An alarm bell sounded from a tower somewhere on the premises, clanging fiercely in the suddenly silent hall. Perhaps the laborers had alerted the guard. Someone knew there was trouble, and Ivy prayed help would come quickly enough to save them from whatever fate these men would choose for her and her guard.

One by one, the prisoners were set loose, and they began to congregate, moving towards the end of the hall where Ivy and Masterson stood frozen. There were about a dozen altogether, a couple of them wizened old men, but most looking capable of anything at all.

Ivy had been set upon by two thieves one night while she lived in Harrogate, the men chasing and cornering her in an alley from which she couldn't escape. They had taken her meager earnings from the day's begging, but decided she was too much trouble to do anything else with after she sliced open one's hand and nicked the other's jaw. She had survived with a bruising to her ribs and a cut on her thigh that night.

As she took in the manic eyes and ravenous looks on the men's gaunt faces, she realized that this was worse than mere street thieves. Much worse.

"What is your name, sir? We can negotiate," Masterson tried, holding out his hand palm-up towards the man with the pistol.

"My name is Franco, but that's none of your business. We ain't trying to negotiate. Wee's is gettin' out of this piss-pot, we is."

Cheers from the other prisoners gathered echoed around them.

"I know people that will pay you handsomely for our release," Ivy said, hoping it was true. Though she was only his employee, she knew Blackbourne wouldn't leave her to these men if money could save her.

"Oh, don't worry, luv. I'll get my use out of you," he assured her. "Whatever rich cove is tupping you might pay up in the end, if you're still alive."

Prickles of fear climbed up her spine.

"Wot's the plan?" one called out.

Franco answered him. "These two is going to be our tickets outta here," he said gleefully.

More cheers went up, but one shouted over them. "Why can't we have some fun with the wench? She's only a little thing, but I'm bettin' she could take a few of us before we get our arses out of this place!" he guffawed. The other inmates made sounds of affirmation and drew closer, jostling for what they could see of her behind Masterson.

"Come out from behind him," Franco commanded.

She didn't want to refuse and get Masterson killed for her pride, so she did as he asked, stepping out from behind him with her chin tipped up defiantly. One hand clutching her reticule and the other balled into a fist, she hoped they couldn't tell her legs were trembling uncontrollably underneath her skirts.

She was going to die here, and she was going to die horribly, used and degraded before being sent to her Maker.

The thought flitted through her mind, but then stayed, sitting heavily in the center of her disjointed thoughts.

Another followed it She had never been loved by Asher Blackbourne.

And absurdly, that thought saddened her more than the former, which she knew made her codswallop crazy.

"You will not touch her," Jacob Wollard growled.

Ivy fought tears at the vehemence in her father's tone. At least she had one person in this world who would mourn her, no matter the caliber of his soul.

"Agreed," a low voice from behind the group of prisoners rang out. Turning as one, the gaggle of inmates stared in confusion at the source of the voice.

Through a parting in the men's bodies, she glimpsed two sets of boots and the edge of a greatcoat. Definitely not guards' uniforms.

"And just who are you?" Franco called.

The prisoners parted to reveal two men standing with dueling pistols aimed directly at Franco.

One of them was Blackbourne, blue eyes

shooting icy daggers at the inmates as he held his pistol trained on their leader. His face was a mask of fury, and Ivy wouldn't have wanted to be on the other end of that glare for the world. It was a look that promised death to anyone stupid enough to test him.

Ivy sagged in relief. They were saved.

"We're your reckoning if you're not back in your cells before I count to three," the one in the billowing black greatcoat declared.

Ivy didn't recognize this black-haired man, but Ash stood shoulder to shoulder with him in complete solidarity.

"You only have one shot in those, guvnors, and they ain't gonna stop all of us," Franco replied, still keeping his own gun trained on Masterson while he spread his other arm to indicate the group.

"If you harm one hair on her head," Ash growled. "I will tear you apart with my bare hands. So gun or not, do not think you will survive my wrath should you touch her."

Franco wiped his forehead, which had begun to bead with sweat.

"Who are they?" Masterson whispered in puzzled awe.

"One," counted Ash's companion, his gaze unwavering.

At this, some of the other inmates began to shift nervously.

"You're not the one making threats here!" Franco called out, but his voice had a note of concern in it now.

His words had no effect on the man in black.

"Two."

"Now wait a minute!" Franco screeched.

He looked around him to find the other prisoners begin to shuffle away back to towards the cells.

One shrugged in apology as he went. "I'm not looking to die today," he said.

Even the other two inmates that had been on work duty with him went into the cell next to Wollard's and shut the door solemnly.

"We outnumber them!" Franco screamed, but no one answered. Doors began to clunk shut and silence reigned. Even the clang of the alarm in the distance stopped, as if on cue.

Franco was fuming, his nostrils flaring and chest working to keep up with his panicked breathing.

"It's just you now. Stop this foolishness before someone is hurt," Ash said calmly.

"I aint goin' back in," Franco declared, standing up straighter.

"Three." The man in black cocked his gun, the click of the gesture unmistakable.

Eyes widening, Franco looked back at Ivy, and a gleam came into his eye. Just as the man in black pulled the trigger, Franco moved towards Ivy, shoving Masterson away and pulling her around in front of himself. The shot blasted into the stone behind where Franco had been milliseconds before.

She gasped and lost her footing as he swung her slight frame unexpectedly. He dragged her upright, pressing the tip of the pistol to her head. His other arm went to her neck and she grasped it for purchase as she struggled to gain her footing back.

Masterson fell into the corner, but froze when he saw that Franco's gun was now pointed at Ivy's temple.

Ash took a step forward. "Wait!" he bellowed.

"Please, no!" Wollard cried from his cell, his knuckles white on the bars.

Ivy's heart raced. She hadn't thought Franco would be insane enough to continue his escape attempt once his comrades had abandoned him, but it seemed the man had nothing to lose. She was is only leverage now, and might be the only leverage he needed to get out of here without anyone attempting to stop him.

Franco smiled, his breath foul as he leaned his head on the side of hers. "You 'er lover?" he nodded at Ash. "Nob like yerself don't want to see yer mistress get 'er 'ead blown off, now do ye?"

She hated touching his filthy skin, but he was taller than she and already she stood on her toes to be able to keep her balance. So she kept her grip on his scabby arm, trying not to choke as he squeezed it tighter around her neck.

"What she is is *mine*," Ash stated. He still held the gun pointed at Franco, but there was no way to take a shot without possibly hitting her. His friend stayed silent, his now useless pistol at his side. "And I will do whatever is necessary to keep her safe, so tell me what it is you want."

"I want out of 'ere," Franco told them. "I want to walk out of 'ere wiv 'er, and no one will stop me."

Ivy could see Ash's eyes flaming in the gloom, his frustration at his impotence in the situation clear. "I can make that happen, as long as you promise to let her go once you are safely away," Ash assured him.

"Or," Ivy interjected, clearing her throat and pulling on his arm until he released her windpipe a bit. She was not going to go quietly with this ruffian. Now that his mob had deserted him, he was no more menacing than the street thugs who had accosted her before.

She met eyes with Ash and smiled. If this didn't work, she wanted the last thing she saw to be him. He cared for her in some odd way, and if nothing else, he was bloody lovely to look at.

"You could trade clothes with this guard," she

pointed at Masterson, "and walk out of here without anyone the wiser. No fuss, no one chasing after you. You could lock us up in a cell and walk away freely."

She held her breath as he thought about it and Ash's lips turned up slightly at the corners.

"You know, that ain't a bad idea, luv. Got a brain up there, eh?" he said, tapping her temple with the gun.

"What a surprise," she mumbled.

Ash's companion raised his brows in admiration. His voice rumbled out in the corridor. "You won't find a better option than that."

"You're right," Franco agreed. "I like this plan."

"You can put them with me," Wollard spoke up, his face pressed to the bars of his window.

Franco turned to Wollard, studying him. "Yer a murderer, ain't ye? Killed a bunch of folks for the fun of it?" he asked him.

Wollard swallowed, looking Franco in the eyes. "Yes."

Franco smiled. "I'm all right with that situation then."
****

Thus, a Marquess, a Duke, and a tiny woman helped an inmate escape New Bridewell Prison rather successfully, if you asked Ash.

Franco must have been convincing, because it wasn't five minutes later that prison guards rushed into the corridor, and they were set free from the cell. It was an awkward five minutes with Wollard, to be sure, Ivy introducing Ash to her father. When Ash then introduced Dom as the Duke of Scythemore, Ivy blinked and Wollard's eyes widened to the size of teacup saucers. This often happened around Dukes, Ash had found, and this one in particular.

Her father was a gracious host for the duration

and made no attempt to come near Ivy with him and Dom positioned protectively on either side of her. In fact, he seemed awed at Ivy's connections, which suited Ash just fine. The man needed to be intimidated, lest he tried to interject himself into Ivy's life once more.

The guard, Masterson, was busy attempting to cover himself with a blanket from Wollard's bed after having had to undress down to his skivvies, muttering about improving the quality of prisoners' bed coverings.

He didn't relax until they were all bundled into Dom's carriage on the way home. They had been questioned exhaustively by Warden Crick and helped to identify all of the prisoners involved in the escape attempt. By the time they left New Bridewell, the sun had set and streaks of magenta rent the sky.

Ivy still didn't understand why they had showed up in that corridor instead of a phalanx of prison guards, and Ash was happy to explain, stroking her hair as she leaned against his shoulder in the carriage. He was coming down from the high of the prison confrontation and was so relieved that Ivy was safe in his arms that he wanted to shout from the rooftops and fall asleep in exhaustion with her by his side all at once.

That was an excellent idea. He would just never let her leave his bed after tonight, and that would prevent anything like this from happening again.

"How did you know my father was located at New Bridewell?" Ivy asked after he had explained about Delilah's visit.

He snorted. "I knew the day I hired you. I make it a point to take a look at the local prison registers at least once a month. It just makes sense."

"It makes no sense whatsoever," Ivy told him. "I suppose you remember all the names?" she looked up at him with a small smile.

He shrugged. "Of course."

Dom, sat in silence, but grinned at this. Ash winked at him.

He continued. "I didn't know anything about the riot until we got there, but I didn't want you to be alone in there. It turned out to be a good instinct. We had already been shown the way to your father's cell and were halfway there when the alarm sounded." He cleared his throat, admitting, "We might have ignored orders to wait for the hostage negotiations."

"This is one time I'm glad you're a complete reprobate," Ivy said with a tired smile, yawning into her hand.

"So you know him well, then," Dom murmured, affixing her in a blue-green stare that both transfixed and scared the average person, in Ash's experience.

His inscrutable friend had the unique talent of charming and unnerving everyone whom he came into contact with, while Ash preferred to seem as shallow as a tide pool to the casual observer. Dom simply didn't care either way what his impression was, although Ash knew him to be one of the most conscientious people he knew.

Only one woman had been able to breach Dom's defenses, and she was the reason he had come along today.

"She doesn't know me as well as I'd like," Ash said wryly, saving Ivy from having to reply.

Ivy shoved at him, apparently too tired to do anything more. "Don't say such things," she chastised, but there was no heat to her words.

Dom cocked his head to the side, and Ash didn't like the rare light in his companion's eyes as he said, "I didn't think there was a woman alive who had thus far resisted my friend's charms. You must have better sense than most."

Ash watched Ivy's cheeks color. She was pale enough that, even in the darkness of the carriage, it was obvious.

"I'm staying in the same house with the man, as I'm sure you know, so clearly not good enough sense," she replied, eliciting a chuckle from Dom.

There was way too much amusement going on at his expense, and he could no longer tell if his character was being lauded or assassinated. "I'm an excellent host, thank you very much," Ash defended himself.

"Rants about the plague notwithstanding," Dom interjected.

Ivy laughed. "He's not wrong."

"You wanted me to!" Ash exclaimed. How had this turned into the two of them in league against him?

"True," Ivy admitted, laying her head back down on his shoulder. "But I'll never say I know anything about it in front of company."

Ash could tell she was fading fast, her eyelids fluttering closed and then popping open trying to stay awake. The slight pressure of her head on his shoulder radiated contentment through his bones. She was safe, here with him, and he would keep her that way. He watched as her lips finally parted, her features slackening as sleep claimed her.

"I fear I am to lose a friend soon," Dom commented after a few moments in silence.

Ash noted Dom's eyes taking in their positions. "Not like that," he assured him. "She understands what I am, and that it won't change."

Dom nodded slowly. "I know you think you cannot overcome the side of yourself that carries the weight of your mind, but you're stronger than you think, friend."

Ash shook his head. "You know nothing," he said

softly, careful not to wake Ivy.

Dom didn't react to his friend's statement. "I know you think you're cursed, and that you will never be able to live a normal life with a woman such as the one beside you. But you're wrong."

"And how do you know that? Are Dukes fortune tellers now?" he said acerbically.

His friend shifted his weight, one hand tapping on his knee. "I have watched you battle your demons for a long time. You don't need to control your mind, Ash. You need to set it free."

Ash's nostrils flared. His friend had observed more than he had wanted him to, but part of him had suspected his friends had had him pegged all along. But he wouldn't argue with Dominic about this. He didn't know the half of what his mind had cost him and what lengths he had gone to do just as his friend was suggesting. That was the entire point behind the creation of Reginald Morganstern—to let his mind do what it needed to without the scrutiny of his title.

Little did Dom know even that wasn't enough to slake his mind's lust. The useless equations still overpowered his faculties with little provocation and the blinding headaches occurred with increasing frequency unless he found ways to distract himself.

"If you think you've stumbled onto something I hadn't thought of, you're wrong," Ash stated.

"Perhaps I am wrong. Yet I've never seen you as true to yourself as you have been in the last few minutes with this girl, who is obviously not who you say she is, scientist or not."

Ash swallowed, but wasn't going to concede the point. "You realize this is coming from the man who almost hyperventilated at the knowledge of a certain woman's presence a few hours ago."

"I did not hyperventilate. Dukes don't do that sort of thing," Dom informed him immediately.

Ash snorted. "And Marquesses aren't bested by prettily-packaged little bluestockings."

Dom grinned. "Now we're both lying."

Ash took in his friend's features, which Ash knew were a careful mask he'd worn ever since Delilah Hayworth had 'not shot him in the kneecaps.' Ash's smile slowly grew to match his friend's, who was one of the most powerful men in England. "God save us both."

Chapter Thirteen

The next BAAS gathering was when things became more complicated. Ash should have known that there was a danger of Dom's sister, Raquel, coming to an event such as this. It wasn't a lecture series tonight, but an experiment at a member's home, and if Raquel Tierney was known for anything, it was being where she most definitely shouldn't have been. She was usually to be found fleecing young pups out of their inheritances in the billiards room, but tonight, it was obvious her interest had been piqued by the nature of the experiment being set in motion by some of the BAAS members.

Some fellow from Russia, Nobel, was setting off explosives in the garden, blowing up bushes and pottery pots for the amusement of the patrons. Truth be told, it was quite fascinating, and Ash had been itching to ask the man questions ever since he'd heard of him.

It was just that Ivy looked like a living flame of Prometheus' fire dressed in her deep red gown that trailed on the ground behind her like a descent into the inferno itself. He'd had to have her. He'd had to whisper in her ear to meet him around the back of the hedges where there was a secluded bench amongst the dormant foxgloves.

She had come and succumbed to his ravenous kisses just as he'd hoped.

And now his hand was sliding up her leg as she reclined on the stone bench, her breath coming in little gasps on his neck. The night around them was warmer than usual, the stars out in their blazing brilliance. Still, goosebumps rose on her thigh, and he smoothed them away with the warm palm of his hand.

He had to admit, it was more difficult to kiss her without dislodging his beard, and he wondered if the scratchy thing was bothering her as much as it was him. Reginald Morganstern certainly needed some lessons in finesse. Yet he couldn't stop himself. She was all he thought about, and her eagerness to accept him in all his convoluted flaws was like opium, addictive and hazy.

Was that why he hadn't heard the crunch of woodchips nearby? By the time he did come up from the fog her lips created, it was too late.

"Corrine?!" Lady Tierney's voice squeaked.

Ash froze, and then let his forehead thunk onto Ivy's.

"Let me up," Ivy whispered frantically, trying to pull her dress back over her legs.

Ash gulped and tried to make his mind play out the scenarios of how this could turn out.

It didn't work. His mind was a completely blank sheet without anything helpful whatsoever. Fine time to finally be free of the stupid thing. He levered himself up and brushed off, avoiding eye contact with Lady Tierney.

"Erm…" Ivy attempted. "It's not what it looks like."

Raquel just blinked and crossed her arms.

Ash stood there, looking like an old fool who had been caught molesting a beautiful young woman, he was sure.

"He's not—"

"Your brother?" Raquel's eyes narrowed.

"No, he's not my brother," Ivy rushed, rising to her feet and feeling her coiffure.

"It's Blackbourne, isn't it?" she said flatly. It wasn't even a question. "Why am I not even surprised?"

"Er…" Ash really didn't know what to say, but this was very bad. Why was it that he couldn't seem to think straight, even for a normal person, when Ivy was involved?

"You reprobate!" Raquel walked up to him and punched him in the arm. "You're an idiot, and I should tell Dom this very night unless you can give me a good reason not to."

That kicked his brain into gear. "Darling Raquel, you know I've always been fond of you." He put his arm around her shoulders. "You're like a sister to me."

She shrugged him off and pointed a finger in his face. "Don't you give me that, Asher. I know you too well to let you butter me up. You think you can keep this charade up forever? Why in heaven's name are you dressed up as an old man anyways?"

"It's for me," Ivy blurted, coming between them. "It's so I can be accepted in society. I don't have a brother, and I know no one here. I just thought if I had connections to a Marquess through a family member, I would have better prospects than in the country."

Raquel's shoulders slumped, and she sighed. "You're not going to have better prospects if people think you're taking up with your brother, an old man, or even Blackbourne himself."

Ivy took Raquel's hands. "I know. I'm so sorry to have put you in this position. It's—"

"Stop." Ash couldn't let her do it. Ivy deserved to have someone she didn't have to lie to. "It's not for her marriage prospects, Raquel. It's she who is doing me a favor."

Ivy whirled around and met his eyes. "What are you doing?" she whispered furiously.

Ash smiled. "She's your friend," he said, pushing her to the side. "She is indeed from a genteel family in the country, but I suggested an arrangement in which she can stay with me while in London posing as a BAAS member's sister so I can keep my false identity's place in the organization."

Raquel thought about this in silence. Then, "You know what? I don't want to know why you're doing it. I only care that Corrine—"

"Ivy," she interrupted softly. "My name is Ivy."

Raquel blinked and then nodded. "Ivy's reputation doesn't suffer because you can't keep your hands to yourself. Your reputation is well-earned, Asher. Don't make me have to set Dominic's dogs on you."

Asher nodded. "Understood. You won't tell him?"

She snorted. "Please. I've been keeping secrets from Dom since the perambulator. The high and mighty Duke doesn't need to know everything."

"Thank you." He told her. "I am—"

"What's this, now?" A man came around the corner of the hedge. Ash recognized Brewster, his Scottish accent giving him away. "Are the ladies fearful of the explosions?" he asked, coming closer.

Ivy and Raquel shared a look, and Ash saw Raquel roll her eyes.

"Oh, yes," Raquel turned to him and took his arm. "I'm quite frightened. Would you mind letting me lean on you for support? My poor constitution. I'm sure my brother, the Duke of Scythemore, would greatly appreciate it if you'd walk me to the house for some rest."

Brewster loosened his necktie as he gazed into Raquel's liquid aquamarine eyes. "Of-of course, my lady. T'would be me honor to escort a lovely lass such as yourself."

Raquel turned back to them and winked as Brewster led her away.

Ash sighed in relief. That was much too close.

They were extremely lucky that Raquel had a rebellious streak and didn't mind keeping secrets.

"I've changed my mind, sir." Raquel announced a ways off. "Back to the explosions, if you please."

"But-but—" Brewster spluttered.

"No dilly-dallying. The Scottish aren't a cowardly lot, are they?" Raquel firmly led him in the direction of Nobel's experiments, leaving Ash and Ivy in the dark as booms sounded in the distance.

"Perhaps—" Ivy started.

"No more kissing," Ash stated.

"Absolutely." Ivy ran her hands down her dress, smoothing the wrinkles.

"Gotten out of hand, really." He rubbed his neck, not making eye contact.

"Couldn't agree more."

"Maybe just once again?" He raised his bushy gray brow.

Ivy huffed and walked away. "Men."

Splendid.

****

"There's something I need to tell you," Ivy stated, standing in front of Ash's desk the morning after the Nobel experiment.

Ash looked up from his correspondence. "Oh?"

She took a deep breath, the smoldering of his eyes still like a punch to the gut when she met them. It was now or never.

She'd only worked up the courage to come to him after a long sleep and copious amounts of strawberry preserves nervously spread on her biscuits at breakfast. He needed to know, especially after the New Bridewell incident.

Ivy balled her fists. "The reason I went to visit my father was because I've been receiving letters from one of his admirers. I believe he is dangerous."

Ash didn't look shocked. "Go on."

His nonchalance wasn't reassuring. Was he going to write off her concerns?

"I think he's going to kill someone—soon," she said bluntly. "And we have to do something about it."

He watched her silently, hands tented under his chin.

She knew it. He thought her a complete ninny. How dare he—

"I couldn't agree more," he quipped, straightening the stack of papers before him.

"I'm sorry ... what?"

"We need to examine that letter more closely," He twirled his pen.

Her eyes narrowed. Now she understood.

"You went through my letters, didn't you?" she accused him.

He made no attempt to deny it. "Yes."

"Those were private!" she raged. When he didn't react at her outburst, she growled. He was so sure that she hadn't the wherewithal to make him sorry. He wasn't regretful in the least. She could see it in the way a hint of a dimple played at the corner of his lips.

Looking for something on his desk, she eventually chose his recently shuffled stack of papers and shoved them off the desk completely. The papers cascaded to the floor, several swooshing out in awkward directions.

He raised a brow. "Did that make you feel better? Are you done?"

Ivy gritted her teeth. Maintaining eye contact, she put her index finger on his inkwell and deliberately tipped it over, watching the ink spread over his desk in her peripheral vision.

He didn't look away either, seemingly unconcerned at the mess she was making. If anything, his eyes burned brighter into hers as he said, "Anything else?"

She was going to murder him herself. But instead, Ivy came around to his side of the desk and grabbed what she knew was his favorite quill from betwixt his long fingers. He leaned back in the chair, a small smile on his face as she snapped it in two.

Ivy was rather proud of herself for that, thanking her lucky stars his quill had been made from hollowed wood rather than solid metal. He was so arrogant! He thought of nothing but what he wanted, regardless of others.

"That was my favorite pen," he remarked in a low tone.

"I know." She stood ramrod straight, unwilling to act even the littlest bit ashamed. He was the one that should feel guilty for his transgressions.

Ash rose suddenly from his chair, forcing Ivy to back away a step until her derriere came up against the edge of the desk.

Ivy gasped as his full height loomed over her. His face was a combination of harsh lines as his eyes turned to melted chips of burning ice. He didn't stop as she leaned away from him, his legs pressing into her skirts. Her hands grabbed the edge of the desk as his face came closer to hers.

Perhaps she had gone a bit too far.

"I liked that pen," he purred, his hand coming up to stroke her face.

She gulped. "I like my privacy."

"Are you going to replace my pen?"

"Are you going to un-read my letters?" she replied, trying not to stare at the way his lips moved as he spoke in the smoky voice that strummed along her nerves like a cello's bow.

He smiled, his breath fanning over her face as he let out a bark of laughter. "Perhaps it's too late to stop for either one of us," he said, and Ivy knew he spoke of things other than pen and paper.

"It's been too late for a long time," she breathed, the fabric of her dress chafing the puckered tips of her breasts as his chest came up against hers. Her rapid breathing only made the sensation worse, causing her breasts to rub against him with every intake of breath.

His eyes flashed as he pressed her further backwards, his hands positioned flat on the desk on either side of where he had her trapped. "I'm going to ruin your dress now."

Ivy didn't have time to process his words as his lips came down on hers with forceful precision. He grabbed her thighs and lifted her onto the desk. A sound of both encouragement and protest escaped her lips.

While his tongue dueled with hers, he pulled her closer to the edge, against the pressure of his hips. The intimacy of their position drew tendrils of sharp desire down to the apex of her legs, settling into a throbbing pulse.

She brought her hand up to his cheek, feeling the movement of his jaw as he ravaged her mouth.

"Ivy," he whispered, pulling back to nuzzle the hair at her temple. "You'll be the ruination of me." His fingers kneaded her just below the edge of her corset where the indentation inside her hips was most sensitive.

Need curled downward from his touch. She looked into his eyes, white flecks crystallizing the blue of them. Something on his face caught her eye, and she burst into an undignified giggle.

He frowned. "What is it?"

Ivy quickly ran her eyes over the black smudge of ink on his jawline, and shook her head. "Nothing. Kiss me."

He obliged, putting such force behind it that she had to lean back onto the desk. His body followed hers, and she came to rest on her elbows, Ash's unyielding chest atop her own.

She knew he wanted to demand things she couldn't give.

But the way he kissed made her forget every reason why she shouldn't give into the heights of desire he brought forth in her. She wanted all his passions, all his vast knowledge of how to make her body thrum like a plucked string.

He pulled her hips closer, a distinct bulge in his trousers coming up against her. Hiking her skirts up her legs, his hands skimmed the outside of her thighs thoroughly as he went. He left burning paths of sensation on every inch of skin he touched above her stockings. She was thankful she'd chosen the knee-high ones today which left much more exposed to his roaming hands.

Ivy sighed as his mouth left hers and moved to her shoulder, placing kisses like wet freckles along the ridge.

The peachy hairs on her legs rose as he exposed them. He shoved her skirts the rest of the way up to above her waist and stepped closer, slowly pressing his insistent member against the silk of her drawers.

Ivy inhaled sharply at the pressure, and she knew Ash was watching the expressions play across her face.

She vaguely understood the mechanics of sexual intercourse, Priscilla having given her plenty of description over time. She knew his staff became hard and would enter her, but the way Priscilla had told it, it didn't seem very pleasant.

Yet Ash's relentless physicality was the most exhilarating thing she'd ever experienced. His member prodding against the entrance to her most private place was like holding a hot coal in her hands and hoping it wouldn't burn her.

As his eyes begged the question, her heart stuttered with the knowledge of what he was asking.

She couldn't let this continue. It was too dangerous. "Maybe we should stop."

He inhaled, the motion pressing his chest more firmly against her breasts. "I thought you said it was too late."

"It's not my fault you make me forget myself," she complained, trying to scoot away from him. He didn't let her. "You're the greatest rake in London, after all."

At this, something in his eyes died, and he stepped back, dropping his hands from her hips. "Yes, you never let me forget."

The note in his voice brought her up short. "I didn't mean—"

He waved her protest away. "I know you didn't. You're too pure hearted to throw my own nature in my face."

She pushed herself up on her elbows and cocked her head.

He sighed, running a hand through his golden locks. "You wouldn't understand."

Ivy blinked slowly. "Try me."

"You're just an innocent girl!" he burst, turning away. One hand came to rest on his slim hip. "You have no idea what it's like to be forced into an existence you never wanted." He turned back around, meeting her eyes. "To have a burden you can never be rid of and then have the results of that become something you can never wash from your skin."

Ivy laughed, throwing her head back. "Don't I?" She adjusted her skirts so she wasn't exposed to him.

"You're not your father," he stated, pointing a long finger at her. "Other people may see a blemish upon you, but it's not there. For me, it is all my own doing." Ash came back towards her, reaching up to stroke her face. "Then you come along, and, suddenly, I can see the marks on my own body, on my soul. Ugly stains borne of actresses' nails and willing widows' lips—stains I have ignored and covered up with more for as long as I can remember." His forehead dropped to hers. "Why did you have to show them to me? I'll never be clean again."

The anguish in his words brought tears to her eyes. Part of her understood what he meant. He had built a life on the pleasure of woman after woman, and he finally saw his house of cards for what it was. But that didn't mean she accepted his assessment of himself.

"You can't change the past, Asher." She put a hand to his chest, over the beat of his heart. "But your life can be whatever you wish it. You just have to make it so. You have no marks. They're only in your mind," she said, willing him to believe it.

Instead, he scoffed and pulled away. "That's always what it comes down to, isn't it?"

"What do you mean?"

His thumb stroked the downy curve of her cheek. "Nothing. You're perfect, and I'm unwilling to be the catalyst in changing that. So don't tempt me, Princess."

Ivy raised a brow. "I believe it was you who kissed me."

"Mmmm," he rumbled. "But it was you who tempted me to kiss you."

Ivy laughed. "With that logic, you can get away with anything."

"Exactly." His crooked smile was back.

"What if I want you to keep kissing me?" For some reason, every time he told her it was a bad idea, she wanted to counter it. She even agreed with him, yet she was loathe to let their interaction end this way.

The light came back into his eyes. "You're playing with fire, love."

Her heart rate increased, the heat in his gaze made her bold. "Perhaps I want to be burned by you. Perhaps I want you to leave a mark on me."

Ash groaned, his hand almost unwillingly trailing down her neck to skim across the top of her breast. "I want to make you go up in flames."

"Then make it so," she encouraged, pushing her breast into his palm. The heady elixir of his desire for her pooled in her core. She craved the danger his touch elicited, though she knew she'd regret it later. But she wanted to regret doing something with this man rather than regret not knowing what would have happened.

He shoved his hands under her skirts once more and claimed her lips roughly. Growling into her mouth, his hands squeezed the flesh of her hips. "Wrap your legs around me," he commanded, his breaths coming fast.

She did as he bade, pulling him closer with her slippered ankles crossed behind the small of his back. Feeling him pressed against her again was intensely satisfying. The power of having this man under her thrall was more potent that anything she'd ever felt.

He was even harder than before, his erection thrusting against her most intimate area as he braced his hands on either side of her. Ivy could feel her drawers becoming damp with her own need for him.

"Lay back," he said.

As she did so, he ran his hand down the front of her dress, stroking between her breasts, over her stomach, and then down further. She jumped as his hand flicked the edge of her drawers and then kept moving down. He chuckled.

"What?" she gasped, her nerves tingling.

"Just leaving a mark."

She looked down at herself to see a streak of shining black ink running from the V of her collarbone to the valley between her breasts. Eyes widening, she began to object, but the stroke of his finger over the cleft of her folds shot lightning through her limbs, making her gasp instead. All other thought was obliterated.

"You have a little pearl here," he said, rolling the tip of a finger over the nub at the beginning of her nether lips. "I'm going to play with it and make you writhe until you beg. Then you'll catch fire. Understand?"

Ivy already felt she was on fire, her fingers scraping at the desk just to keep her sanity as he touched her. The wood of his sturdy furniture was more impressionable than she would have assumed, and she felt her nails create curls of indentation in its surface. "Yes," she said, her breath hitching.

Ash began to stroke the tiny mound that felt as if it contained the secrets to her every desire, sending waves of pleasure from her core outward to her limbs. She gasped as her very fingertips vibrated with warm rays of sunshine that reverberated from his one finger against her most intimate place. He slowly moved his finger in circles over her pearl, eliciting uncontrollable jerks of her legs against his hips.

Letting her head fall back, she gave herself over to his masterful touch. It was almost too much to bear, the sensation overwhelming her every thought until all she could think of was bringing him closer, needing him inside her being with a force she couldn't explain.

She swallowed as he pushed her legs yet wider

and pulled her drawers to the side.

He exhaled, the sound not one of control. "I want you so badly," he rasped.

She knew he was looking at her exposed parts, but didn't feel embarrassed. He made her feel perfect. Beautiful. Like treasure he wanted to sift through with his hands and keep forever.

Tension like a wind-up doll built inside her while he increased the speed of his repetitious circles on her nub.

"Ash," she begged, unsure of what she was asking for.

Without breaking his pattern, he used his other hand to part the folds of her cleft and plunge a finger inside her passage. She cried out, the feeling of both hands working in tandem causing dark tendrils of pleasure to spiral from place of need.

"Is this what you want?" he demanded, allowing another finger to slide into her alongside the first.

"Please," she pleaded. "I can't..." she trailed off, now knowing how to say what she was experiencing in words. Sweat misted at her temples, and she curled her fingers into balls on the shining wood to either side of her.

"Yes, you can," he told her, upping his rhythmic pumping until she was so frenzied, she couldn't think, much less speak.

Something was coming. She could feel it looming closer, an inescapable tidal wave rolling towards her senses brought on by the expert movements of his hands.

Her eyes came open briefly, and suddenly, all she could see was light as wave upon wave of glorious pleasure washed through her. She opened her mouth to cry out, and his mouth came over her lips, muffling the sound as he continued to invade her with his fingers. Her legs shuddered, and she squeezed them tighter around his torso as she rode out the vibrations that wracked her body. Every pulse of sensation was intensified by the force of his fingers entering her over and over while his other hand didn't cease its cyclic pattern of pressure on her pearl.

His heartbeat was next to hers, the sounds mingling as the ringing in her ears slowly dissipated, and she returned from the place of pure brightness he had sent her to. She unclenched her legs and tried to slow her labored breath as he drew his lips from hers.

He breathed quickly as well, studying her face in the aftermath of the devastation he had wrought. He slowly drew his fingers from the slick petals of her womanhood and carefully positioned her drawers over the throbbing area.

Gently, he wrapped an arm around her back and brought her up with him till she was sitting close against him on the edge of the desk.

"Are you all right?" he asked hoarsely, cupping her face.

She didn't know what to say. "It was…"

Ivy looked into his eyes, searching for what she was trying convey. His brows grew furrowed, and he gulped, pulling away from her.

She clutched him tighter. "No, please."

He paused. "Did you… That is, was it not … pleasurable?"

She had never heard him so unsure of himself. The reigning king of London's bedrooms didn't know if he had pleased her?

She laughed.

His frowned deepened.

She dug her fingers into his arms. "It was like seeing stars through a telescope for the first time.

Entirely new worlds of light brought close enough to touch."

He blinked, and then exhaled slowly, closing his eyes.

"I wish I could have ... brought you with me," she said, not knowing what he needed.

He shook his head and opened his eyes once more, smiling. "Knowing you were there is its own world of light, one I didn't know existed."

"I don't understand."

He kissed her forehead. "I don't either." Ash pulled away from her embrace, and his tone changed to one of resolve. "But I cannot touch you again. I told you I'd never make you cry. And you deserve better than to be debased without the sanctity of marriage. You deserve someone who will dedicate their life to you." Swiftly untangling himself from the circle of her arms, he took purposeful strides and left her alone in the room.

Still dazed from every word and touch, she knew it didn't matter what he had said in the past. He would make her cry one way or the other.

And she would go willingly into that fate until the shadows enveloped them both. She only hoped it wouldn't be the end she feared awaited anyone who dared breach her defenses to find out the proverbial apple didn't fall far from the bloody family tree.

For if anything ever did happen to Ash, perhaps her father had been right after all, and there was no going back from that kind of brokenness.

Yet she had a feeling losing her heart to the seductive Marquess was just as dangerous.

She feared it had already happened.

****

Asher's head was so awash with names, dates, births, death, and marriage records that he might very well have reached the limits of his formidable memory. He had been looking at records gathered from the width and breadth of England for days without ceasing except to attend to his basic needs. His flat near the Archives looked as if a crazed paper collector had amassed a thousand years' worth of historical chronicles on a whim, tall stacks of folders and papers covering every available surface.

Normally, his mind basked in the challenge of retaining information, of sorting and mentally organizing a vast amount of data. But time was of the essence, and a woman's life very likely depended on finding the one man in England who, unbeknownst to her, wanted to kill her. He had developed an algorithm of sorts to quickly sort through the infinite records using the clues he and Ivy had discussed. There wasn't much to go on, but the right combination of factors could provide the key to who this man was and where he lived.

Claymore was highly educated, based on the vocabulary and syntax in his letters. That most likely meant either rich merchant class, landed gentry, or aristocracy. He might have a profession involving something with clocks or timepieces. Ash didn't think the man was in the later stages of life if he was just now exploring his penchant for murder, yet his writing suggested a sophisticated maturity. There wasn't a good way to assume an age range, but Ash figured he could eliminate those younger than twenty and older than sixty.

They also had Charlotte as a piece of the puzzle. She was the daughter of a dairy farmer, so that narrowed the locales somewhat. If she still lived with her family, the woman could be of young, but near marriageable age.

So he was looking for a man possibly named Claymore, age unknown, who lived in the same area as a dairy farm where there lived a young woman named

Charlotte.

The information certainly wasn't narrowing things down quickly enough.

This is what normal people must feel like, he thought, rubbing a hand over his tired eyes as he sat at the desk underneath the solitary window in the room.

Unable to comprehend a solution to the problem at hand, he was growing frustrated even as he continued slogging through the mountains of papers. He couldn't wrap his mind around how he was going to examine every document and determine its pertinence before it was too late.

There were thousands of records, and each parish had its own way of collecting information, even though it was supposed to be somewhat standardized. Some were simply lists of names in a book with dates of births and deaths. Some were marriage and betrothal contracts, death reports, baptisms, birth certificates, burials, and property titles. They were all written copies sent to the National Archives to be housed there for the Crown's knowledge.

Most of the records were for the purpose of determining legalities of inheritance and pedigrees, so he was aware that many poor folk did not even bother to register the birth of their babies with the parish. Then there was the corruption that was rampant in parishes where it was a simple matter to pay off the clergymen to alter documents cutting someone out of their birthright or marital property entitlements. Combine that with the abysmal handwriting on many of the records, and Ash feared he would never be able to sort through the mess he was mired in.

A knock sounded at the door, jarring him from his pessimistic wonderings.

He rose and went to the door. Opening it, one of

his footmen bowed.

"Sir, Miss Morganstern sent this," the man said, holding forth a folded note.

"Thank you." He turned away and unfolded the piece of foolscap.

I believe I have some information that will aid in your endeavor. I have narrowed down the production of the paper on which the letters were written to a paper mill located in Worcester. Based on the dyes used, it can only be Midas Touch Mills. I believe they distribute solely to the southeastern section of the country, so it would be wise to focus on areas southeast of Swindon. Thank you.

-Ivy

Finally. That certainly helped matters.

Ash exhaled, not realizing he'd been holding his breath while he read her words. A small part of him had hoped she'd say something … else. Something unrelated to Claymore that would have him longing to see her at the end of this mess.

But no. He crumpled the note.

That way lay disaster. Thinking about Ivy and hoping for things with her that could not be would only torture his already strained mind. Thoughts of her delectable little body wrapped around him taunted his desire like no other woman ever had.

But he acknowledged that it was more than that now. He wanted to hear what she had to say about anything and everything that floated around in his head. He wanted to shelter her and protect her from any possible moment of pain or worry. He wanted to watch her paint just to see the way she captured the light on a tress of hair that he wouldn't have seen otherwise.

She was infinitely fascinating in a thousand

different ways, more than any matrices or pattern he became obsessed with. He had never met a woman so resourceful, yet so innocent in all the ways that mattered. Understanding he would never be able to put her in a box like he did with the rest of humanity was equal parts maddening and exhilarating. Every individual he interacted with fit into a vast configuration of traits, a web wherein their characteristics and motivations intersected to pinpoint exactly where they fit and into what categories he could place them for later examination or use.

Ivy, on the other hand...

Just when he thought he knew her well enough to manipulate her into what he wanted, she caught him off-guard, forcing him to rethink every preconceived notion he had of her. Yet she was always quintessentially herself.

Giving into the feelings that he had developed for her would be like sinking into a steaming tub of water after a long, cold day, bone melting and scalding all at once.

Yet, they would both drown eventually.

Even if his mind would let him be content with only one woman, there was the tiny matter of Ivy's identity in society being a complete sham. If she were to become his Marchioness, there would be much more scrutiny of her past than a mere well-to-do scholar's daughter incited.

He could not let himself have her.

Yet for all these things, he did. He burned for her with a passion that defied logic or control. Even when he wasn't thinking of burying himself inside her, he couldn't help but just watch her innate ... Ivy-ness.

He wondered if she'd ever noticed his flagrant stares, the way his eyes followed the movement of her fingers or wrinkling of her nose.

What he needed was to get himself out of her snare.

He knew the way to do it. Bedding another woman would allow him to gain perspective on this infernal cycle of desire for the diminutive brunette.

Did the idea of seducing some chit he barely knew appeal to him? Not exactly, not when the woman he truly wanted was sitting right in his own home a few minutes away. But in times like these when his head wouldn't let him concentrate on anything else, a willing bed partner who required nothing other than his momentary engagement relieved him of the deafening noise inside.

So that's what he would do.

As soon as he had re-organized the room into a manageable state of affairs he could sort through given the information Ivy had revealed, he would go out for the night.

And he wouldn't come back until his head was filled with another woman's curvaceous form—anyone's but the scrap of a girl who made him grit his teeth in frustration every waking moment.

Chapter Fourteen

Asher hadn't come back for dinner or anytime afterwards.

Ivy cupped a handful of water from her bath and splashed it onto her face. She had been in the bath for over an hour now, waiting just in case he made an appearance, but it was time to accept that he was probably staying the night at his flat.

Perhaps he had been making headway on the Claymore case and didn't want to interrupt the flow of things. Or maybe he wasn't making any progress and felt the need to dedicate more time to it. Either way, she was grateful that he had taken it upon himself to give them a fighting a chance at cornering the twisted man before he did anything irrevocable.

Toweling off quickly, she put a robe on and stood in the middle of her room, wondering what to do next. Normally, she went down to the kitchens and said hello to the cook while her cup of chocolate was being poured. Then she would go out to the cold balcony and sip her chocolate as her hair dried.

However, Max had come back to Blackbourne House, and dinner had been awkward enough without Ash as a line of reason for his cousin to hesitate in crossing. Not to mention, it was now a bit more suspicious that "Reginald" hadn't shown his face at all, though he was supposedly staying at the residence. She had laughed his questions about her brother away, citing his penchant for playing games of chance late into the night as an explanation for his absence.

The Earl's questions about Corrine, though, were growing more personal than she would have liked. She couldn't exactly blame him for attempting to flirt with her as she was a single woman who, as far as he knew, would benefit greatly from as association with an Earl.

"So what is the most scandalous thing you've done here in London so far, Miss Morganstern?" Max had asked, leaning away from his plate as a footman cleared it in preparation for the dessert course. "I assume having grown up in the country, our heathen city has tempted you to behave naughtily in some way." He had raised his brow and looked at her with a half-smile so reminiscent of Ash that her heart stuttered momentarily.

Swallowing, she considered her answer carefully. The most scandalous thing she'd done was let a Marquess debauch her over an office desk, but she would have snuck into the Louvre and painted a mustache on the Mona Lisa before admitting that to Max. She hated lying, but she supposed that was what she had signed up for. "Oh, I'm not too fond of scandal." She had smiled. "Although I did sneak a sip of bourbon from the Marquess's sideboard one evening, just to see what it tasted like."

He laughed. "Come now, that's all? A pretty little thing like you must have snuck a kiss or two behind a potted plant or perhaps dampened your dress one night for a ball?"

Ivy laughed nervously as a ramekin of pumpkin custard was set before her. "Nothing like that, I'm afraid."

"Well, just say the word, and I can provide a bit of excitement whenever you'd like," he drawled.

Ivy had eaten her custard with extraordinary speed and excused herself from the table quickly, leaving Max to a glass of port. Now, she didn't know whether it was wise to traipse about in her wrapper while he was about. It wasn't likely that he would choose the feminine sitting room to repose in at this hour, but she didn't feel quite safe in such informal dress knowing he was in the house.

Grumbling, she resigned herself to staying in her room the rest of the night. Heading towards the bed, she looked around the room for the novel she had taken to reading when Ash wasn't there to read to her. It didn't feel right to read ahead without him, so she had started another book about a woman pursued across three continents by a madman bent on forcing her to be his consort. She knew it was a bit ridiculous, but it was a pleasant way to pass the time while she waited to hear from Ash.

It seemed everything revolved around him these days. Every thought, every choice. Her every mood was dictated by their interactions.

It wasn't a good thing.

He had told her before he wouldn't allow himself to be emotionally entangled with anyone. Even his idea of marriage was detached, a solid plan for producing an heir while still continuing to bed whomever he pleased.

Why did she have to fall in love with a man like that?

She could admit it now. She loved him. She loved everything about him—the way he ate his toast in the morning, his forever inky hands, the magnificent mind which wrapped itself around a piece of information and teased it to its full potential before anyone else even knew what it meant.

He had seen her as a person when everyone else had seen a plague. The last two months had been the most wonderful of her life, every day an adventure of figuring out the riddle that was Asher Blackbourne.

If he wasn't so determined to be alone, she would...

She would what? Continue to play Reginald Morganstern's sister forever? Be his mistress? Hope that someday, he would make her his Marchioness, and they would live happily ever after?

Ivy laughed aloud, her stomach roiling with nerves just thinking about how stupid she was being.

Men like Asher weren't meant for people like her. He was right. He would break her heart into a thousand pieces, and she would have to watch as he moved onto woman after woman. That was what awaited her if she let herself succumb to loving him.

She cleared her throat.

Dwelling on that wasn't going to serve her well if she intended to keep her employment with him. Emotions didn't matter when survival was on the line. Ivy had learned that lesson long ago.

Giving herself a mental shake, she spotted the book. As she scooped up the leather-bound novel from the little table near the fireplace, a knock sounded at the door.

Immediately, her heart began to race.

Was he back?

She trotted to the door, too excited to make him wait for her to put on her chemise. Opening it, she blurted, "Did you find—?"

But it wasn't Ash.

It was Max, his breath smelling heavily of port as he grinned down at her. Eyes lingering on the V created by the edges of her wrapper, he swayed a bit as she stepped back.

"Oh, I'm sorry. May I help you with something, Lord Eydris?"

"You know I'd prefer if you called me Max when it's just the two of us," he told her, reaching out to stroke a lock of her damp hair.

Ivy stepped back further, her heart now pounding for another reason. "I think you're a bit tap hackled, my lord. Perhaps we can discuss it in the morning?"

His features were tinted with the firelight coming from her room, sensual lips turning down in a pout. "Now why would I want to do that when we're both already here?"

Ivy tugged the sides of her wrapper tighter across her chest. "I'm actually ready to retire for the night, so if you would—"

"What a coincidence!" He spread his arms wide. "I was hoping to be in bed soon as well."

Ivy began to shut the door, but he caught it more quickly than she expected given his inebriation.

"No, no, no," he protested, his words just barely fuzzy around the edges. "My cousin and I don't share the same predilections, my dear. There's no need to be afraid."

"Yes, clearly." She didn't think her sarcasm reached him.

"His madness isn't curable, more's the pity," he said, leaning one hand against the doorjamb while the other kept pressure on the door lest she attempt to close it again. "—but I am the sort of man that you could count on to treat you as you deserve."

She narrowed her eyes. "What do you mean, 'madness?'" Why does everyone keep alluding to that? The Marquess isn't mad," she said incredulously.

Max's face was solemn. "Oh, but he is. Has been ever since that day. He hides it well, doesn't he? I think I've said too much." He frowned.

"I don't think you've said nearly enough."

"Let's talk inside, love." He stepped through the doorframe. "You seem distressed. I can comfort you."

If she wasn't getting any more information out of

him about his cousin, then she had had enough. She summoned the attitude she had heard Priscilla take on numerous occasions with her more forceful customers. Drawing herself up to her full height, she announced, "I'm not distressed, and if you take one more step forward, you're going to find out what it's like to live without the ability to sire children."

Max came up short and blinked. "Blast, what a wench you are," he said, his glazed eyes wide on her face.

"And don't you forget it." She slammed the door in his surprised face, his slack jaw making her snort.

Asher had better come home soon or she feared she was going to end up irreparably maiming his cousin without a single regret.

****

At this rate, Asher was never going to get home.

He had gone out later than he had planned, the files at his flat weighing on him until he'd reached a point he felt comfortable leaving them for the moment. Thanks to Ivy's deduction with the stationary, a skill he had never valued until today, he had been able to narrow the prospects down to a few stacks of parish records in the areas she had suggested which also were known to have dairy farms. He was proud of those stacks that now seemed much friendlier than the massively unruly piles he had been wading through earlier.

The gentlemen's club he was at currently did not lack for female company to choose from. The ball he was at before hadn't either. After an hour of dancing and meaningless conversations laced with innuendoes which did nothing to whet his interest, he had decided that paid companionship was what he needed instead.

So he had gone to Delecto's, one of the more disreputable, but upscale hells that offered light-o-loves for discerning gentlemen. He didn't often indulge in ladies of the evening, as he preferred to hunt his pray before the kill, but tonight, his heart just wasn't in the chase. With these women, though, that didn't matter. They didn't question one or make one work for scraps of attention. If he was looking to get lost in a haze of lust, they would lead him there without his having to lift a finger.

And it was always their choice—he had done extensive research into the practices of Delecto's to make sure these women were not being forced into taking men to their beds. The agreement was a mutual decision by both parties.

He sat smoking a cigar in a room off the main gaming hall, the settee he sat upon bright red satin. All the furnishings and décor were crimson, the better to set off the jewels cushioned therein. Women of all kinds lounged about or sauntered past, letting their charms tempt the men who wandered in. There were five other men in the room at the moment, all engaged with a girl on their laps or with arms draped around them in preparation to either take them home or up to a room on the upper level.

It was clear there was immense interest in him from the way the women looked at him from their poses on nearby furniture, giggled behind fans, or asked him if he needed anything from them. One by one, they swayed by, a blonde with tilted blue eyes, a brunette with enormous ... assets, an exotic dark-skinned woman with black hair and eyes...

They were all beautiful, the way the lamplight played off their powdered skin and reflected in their eyes. Yet it was more of a detached observance rather than an interest in their intimacies. He had experienced this detachment before when he hadn't felt the need for distraction, but never because another woman held his interest.

They were all either too something or not enough something. Too tall, too blonde, too dark-complected, too plump, too revealing.

Too revealing? That was just ridiculous. That was the entire point.

He rubbed a hand over his face, wondering if he shouldn't just take himself off to a cold, empty bed after all. As he glanced towards the clock that stood against a nearby wall (another sign he wasn't up to his usual standards), a woman walked through his line of vision.

He froze. Her hair was dark, and she was more petite than most of the women in the room. As if his gaze willed it, she turned around and met his eyes. From where he was, he couldn't tell what color they were, but her face was oval with a cupid's bow mouth that was almost as wide as...

She came towards him, sensing his keen interest. Her instincts were well-honed because she didn't make any overt movements other than to sit down next to him at a distance that would have been proper at any aristocratic gathering.

She smiled, her face turning heart-shaped. "My name is Fleur. Are you looking for someone to talk to?"

Her eyes are green, not blue. Pity, was his first thought.

But he realized he was judging her unfairly on her appearance for no other reason than she wasn't Ivy.

He smiled back, continuing his languid pose. "I might. What sort of conversation do you enjoy providing?"

She blinked. "That is usually not of import."

He watched her cross her legs at the ankle. Ivy would have worn heels to appear taller. "It is to me."

The woman smiled again, this time with genuine warmth. "I think we might have a lot to discuss. Would you like to accompany me upstairs?"

Ash knew he wasn't going to find a better opportunity to indulge than this.

He nodded, put out his cigar, and let her lead him up the stairs to another floor where opulent bedrooms lay behind the doors on either side of the hallway. As she opened the door to one and waited for him to follow, he knew a moment of hesitation, but he pushed it aside and went in after her.

She meandered to a sideboard table across from the large, green satin bed that held the center of attention in the room. There were various pieces of furniture tastefully littered about, the better to be inventive with. No gaslight here, only soft lighting from candelabras placed around the space.

"Would you like a drink?" she asked, pouring a finger of some type of liqueur into a glass.

"No," he answered, coming up behind her. He put his hands on her waist, the tight nip of her curves almost familiar. She was a little taller than Ivy, the top of her head coming up to his lips.

She set the glass down and curved back into the embrace, arching her back like a cat. "I like a man who doesn't waste time," she purred.

He turned her around to face him, his heart beat erratically pumping in his chest as if it didn't know quite what to do. She smelled of orange blossoms, a scent he knew was popular this year with women both high and low-born.

Looking down at her face, he knew she was lovely. It was the same loveliness he would assign to a hothouse bloom or an intricately painted vase. He had no desire to touch it, but he forced himself to pull her towards himself. Hoping her proximity would elicit a response in his uninspired loins, Ash cupped her derriere firmly.

His heart was pounding, and a ringing in his ears left his brain fuzzy.

It felt wrong. The entire situation was wrong. Wrong feel, wrong scent, wrong face looking back at him. Bedding this woman would constitute a breach of something he couldn't name, and it frightened him.

Suddenly, his trepidation turned to frustration.

Who was *she* to dictate the way he lived his life? Who was she to make him feel like a naughty school-boy caught with the governess' knickers? She had no claim on him. He had specifically told her more than once that he would not change his habits. They were necessary to who he was.

He was going to enjoy this moment, and damn any misguided feelings for a woman that wasn't here.

Ash brought his lips down on hers and meshed them with her softness. She brought her arms around him and opened her mouth to his kiss, her expert tongue snaking around his own. He began to back her towards the bed, wanting to entangle himself with her as soon as possible. He just needed this idiotic bit of conscience to cease tormenting him.

Her kiss was not like Ivy's. When Ivy kissed, her full lips trembled and sought his with a hunger that matched his own. When Ivy kissed, it was as if the entire world had narrowed to the mingling of their mouths, and he felt the soul of her rise up to meet him with blatant and unapologetic enthusiasm. There was always hesitance and curiosity in equal parts with her, the combination a beautiful and unsolvable equation.

No matter. This woman—Fleur—kissed well enough. He kneaded her lips, closing his eyes in order to feel the sensation as he stopped at the edge of the bed.

But the sensation didn't leave his mouth. The nerves there felt what was happening, but nowhere else in his body did he feel the kiss. Even his heartbeat was slowing instead of pumping harder at what was to come. Most importantly, the interaction was not eliciting so much as a twitch from his lower regions, his own flesh betraying him.

When he realized it, an icy chill swept through him. He let go of her immediately and stepped back.

She gasped at the sudden movement and fell back onto the bed, leaning on her elbows. "Is something wrong?"

Ash breathed heavily, unsure of what to do in this situation. He had never before been at this point in a liaison only to have his own body not respond to the woman in front of him. "I'm-I'm sorry. It's not you."

He turned away and paced the rug in front of the bed, pulling at his hair. His insides roiled with shame.

She sat up fully, hands in her lap looking at him. "So you really *do* need to talk," she said wisely. She patted the bed beside her.

Oh, no. He was disgusted with himself for more reasons than he could count at the moment, and this woman was pitying him for it.

As if sensing his thoughts exactly, she said, "I'm not in the habit of judging people for the situations in which they find themselves, Lord Blackbourne." She smiled at his look of surprise. "Yes, I know who you are. One of the other girls pointed you out the minute you walked in. Come, sit. I promise I won't try to steal your virtue." She winked. Her position on the bed wasn't meant for seduction, but was as prim and proper as could be.

It wasn't often he didn't have the upper hand in

an intimate setting with a woman, but Fleur certainly knew what she was doing. He did as she bade and sat beside her, uncertain what he should be feeling at the moment. What he really felt like doing was throwing himself off the nearest five-story building (which he knew to be 732 meters from there, according to previous calculations), never to be seen or heard from again. Sighing, he ran a hand through his hair.

"It's a woman, is it not?" Fleur asked, watching his profile.

"Of course it is. Why do they have to be so blasted complicated?" he grumbled.

She laughed. "If we weren't, it wouldn't be worth it, would it?"

"None of it is worth it. I could lose everything," he admitted. Why he was telling her any of this was beyond him.

"But perhaps you have everything to gain as well," she said softly.

Ash didn't respond. He didn't want to acknowledge her words because they might be true. Yet, she didn't understand the ramifications of what could happen if he allowed his guard to drop. Even if he did let Ivy into his life, what if, later on, the megrims won? What if he did go mad one day and she was stuck with a blithering idiot for a husband? Or what if his cousin succeeded in stealing the Marquessate from under him someday and she was stuck with a penniless failure who couldn't give her anything?

Even worse, what if he continued to need the diversion of other women to keep his mind from crumbling under the weight of its own ponderings? He could never let Ivy sit at home and wonder whose arms he was in or if he was spending their money on time with other women. He couldn't bear the thought of her thinking he would rather be in some lightskirt's company than hers.

Wasn't that what he was doing at this very moment?

He shifted uncomfortably.

"I can't be with her. It's out of the question," he declared. "Yet it seems I can't be without her either." Ash chuckled without humor, hanging his head.

"So perhaps she is more mistress material?" Fleur suggested.

Ash turned to her. "I'd sooner attempt to poke a sleeping tiger than ask that of her. And besides, it's not her that's the problem. It's me."

She considered him, pursing her lips. "It's none of my business, but if you care about her, and you believe she feels the same, then you should go to her. Don't let fear or anyone else keep you from being with the person you want."

Ash shook his head. "You know, for someone in your line of work, you're awfully romantic about these things."

Fleur tossed her supple hair. "Perhaps I speak from experience. Perhaps I made the same mistake you're making, and now it's too late."

Something in her tone made him ask, "Is that the case?"

She smiled. "No. But a girl can dream, can't she? I do know if there was ever one man I wanted above all others, I wouldn't hesitate to make sure he never left my side."

Ash chucked her chin. "I don't doubt it. Thank you for the conversation, Fleur." He stood and pulled out a neat clip of bank notes from his jacket pocket. Laying the entire clip on the bed where she still sat, he said, "I would appreciate it if it stayed between us."

"Of course, my lord." She stayed seated, but wasn't vulgar enough to reach for the money yet as he headed for the door. "I hope you decide to poke a sleeping tiger. Or marry it," she called, laughing as he shut the door behind him.

Chapter Fifteen

Ivy was already in a bad mood when she began to paint that morning after two days of waiting for Blackbourne to come back, and it got worse from then on.

"Bloody hell," she muttered, attempting to wipe a hasty brushstroke from the canvas.

She had awoken with a headache that hadn't gone away with breakfast or the large glass of orange juice she'd drunk. After dressing and praying Max wasn't around, she decided it was time to finish the Raphael. The previous layers she'd been working on over the past few weeks had cured fully, and she wanted to be able to present it soon. Painting usually calmed and satisfied her.

Not today.

There was a niggling feeling in the back of her mind that trouble was brewing, and dread had her stomach in knots. She had no idea what it was that made her feel such, but it was there, nonetheless. Perhaps it was the interaction with Max last night or the fact that she hadn't heard from Blackbourne since his curt, "Thank you," note in response to hers yesterday afternoon.

Either way, she did not react well when Mrs. Rushkova announced she had a visitor waiting downstairs. She was in no mood for company today, and she really couldn't see who it would be anyways, as she hadn't made any plans with Raquel or Lilah. Dunking her brush and wiping her fingertips on her apron, she shrugged it off carefully.

She had wanted to look her best if Blackbourne returned, so she had risked painting in a day dress of delicate peach silk. The gown hugged her shoulders and tapered to accentuate her corseted waist before flowing out in a bell shape with scalloped lace edging at the hem.

She went downstairs to the main salon, grumbling. But when she saw who it was, her dispositioned brightened.

"Lord Bastion !" She came towards him, hands outstretched.

Viscount Bastion, Grant Hayworth, stood smiling in the middle of the drawing room, his red hair contrasting terribly with the yellow tones in the room.

"Miss Morganstern, you're looking lovely today," he said, taking her hand in his.

She was certain proper etiquette said he should bow or kiss her knuckles, but she liked that he never seemed to do the proper thing. It was clear that, despite his aristocratic upbringing, he didn't heed all of the social etiquette that someone of his station should practice.

"Thank you, sir. You're looking quite well yourself." She smiled. "To what do I owe the pleasure of your company this morning?"

"I was wondering if you'd fancy a visit to my townhouse here as Lilah is already there. I have a gallery of classic works that I thought you might like to see."

"That sounds wonderful! I was actually just working on something upstairs, if you'd like to see it," she told him.

"I most certainly would!"

His good-natured energy was contagious, and Ivy found herself in a better mood as she showed him the Raphael imitation.

"Miss Morganstern, this is quite good. I would never be able to tell the difference between it and the real thing."

"That's the idea," she said, a bit proudly.

They continued to discuss art, ranging from the technique to the style of various well-known works. It was wonderful to be able to speak of these sorts of things with someone who enjoyed it as much as she did, but she couldn't be completely honest with him either. Her father had loved art and had taught her the conventional knowledge of art history now at her disposal. She had always had a knack for painting, which her father had encouraged throughout her childhood.

However, it was her time at the paper mill that had honed her technique to what it was today. Once her skill had been established, she had been charged with designing and producing the high-end stationary watermarks that now graced the mill's more expensive paper. Even more refined artistry had been required for the custom work the mill had offered to clients for special events, family crest imprints, and the like. Ivy had dived into projects at the mill with enthusiasm, and the more she did, the more people had wanted her artistry.

Of course, they never knew it was her, or even a female, behind the exquisite designs the mill produced for them, but she had been all right with that. She couldn't afford attention, and hiding behind the miller's ambition was fine with her. She had enjoyed the challenge and had taken pride in her growing repertoire, not to mention it gave her time away from the grueling printing duties she'd done most of the time.

Her true passion had been painting, and so when the mill threw away paint pots that she knew she could squeeze a little more life from, she had seized her chance. Whenever she wasn't too exhausted from the mill, Ivy had been up late or up early painting anything and everything, from stills to people to landscapes. She had rarely showed them to anyone, but her paintings graced Priscilla's room down the hall and one was hung in the miller's home, which is where Fabrice had first seen her work.

Ivy knew she couldn't tell Grant Hayworth any of that, but at least she could share a little piece of her soul with a kindred spirit. She had tea brought up for them, thinking it was pleasant to feel for a brief moment what it would be like to be the lady of a home like this, to play hostess to her friends and enjoy the simple comradery she hadn't had the opportunity to develop in a very long time.

Grant was testing the limits of her ladylike manners telling her about a terrible sculpture he'd seen the week before as they took their tea.

"And I just couldn't fathom why everyone else was so titillated by the thing. I am telling you, it was truly hideous, like Medusa had a child with a potato and decided to dress it up as King George," Grant described, making vigorous motions with his hands as he did so.

Ivy couldn't catch her breath she was laughing so hard, trying to set her sloshing teacup down on the table before she dropped it.

"Sounds fascinating," Ash's deep voice interrupted from the doorway. He leaned against the frame, arms crossed with a deceptively lazy smile.

Ivy choked on the rest of her laughter and straightened. "You're back. Did you— Were you successful in your endeavors?" she asked carefully with a glance at Grant.

Ash's lips quirked. "Depends on your definition, I suppose. But yes. If you're quite finished behaving like children, I need to speak with you. Mr. Hayworth, is it? I'm afraid Miss Morganstern's brother has requested her presence."

Grant didn't lose an ounce of his cheer or correct Ash's obvious slight of not using his title. "Of course. It's been a pleasure, Miss Morganstern. I'll give Lilah your regards."

She saw him out to the foyer and then turned to face Ash, who had watched him leave in silence. "How dare you!" she fumed, her hands balling in to fists. "You were rude to him! He has done nothing but treat me with respect, and you made him out to be an errant puppy."

Ash didn't back away in the face of her ire, but stepped closer. "That's exactly what he is. He's a dog after a bone, and I don't share my bones with anyone."

Ivy's eyes widened, and she stepped back, shaking her head slowly. "Of all the arrogant, idiotic things you've said, that tops the turret on the imaginary castle you've built in your head, Oh, King of all you Survey."

Ash's eyes narrowed.

The rage built inside her, and there was no stopping now. "I am not a possession of yours to toss over a desk when you please and then leave, only to come back and claim when it suits you." She could tell she'd struck a nerve, but his stubborn expression didn't change. "The audacity of your assumptions is staggering, and I refuse to stand here and be played with as the toy you seem to think I am."

She turned on her heel to leave, but he grabbed her wrist and used her momentum to swing her into him. "Not so fast, sweetheart," he said darkly, capturing her arms against his chest. "We aren't through here."

"Yes, we are."

He didn't relent or let her go, eyes blazing into hers. "Perhaps you'd like to stop throwing a tantrum and hear what I've found out about Claymore," he stated.

This brought her up short. She was furious with

him, and her instincts warred with the knowledge that she couldn't afford to let her feelings get in the way of their investigation. But that didn't mean she had to like him.

"What?" she ground out.

His eyes flashed. She could tell he thought he'd won something, and it grated on her like a pumice stone against a wound.

"I narrowed our search down to two candidates that match our criteria and have sent inquiries to the local authorities of both villages. They went out the day before yesterday."

Being close to him was doing things to her senses without her permission, and she struggled to focus. She tugged herself free and took a step back. "How did you do it?" she asked, impressed in spite of herself.

After relinquishing her, he put his hands in his pockets and shrugged. "Once you narrowed down the geographic imprint, I was able to use the rest of the parameters to thoroughly examine records for possibilities. One man is a fine watchmaker in Horsham by the name of Claymore Rodding, and the other owns a railroad switch manufacturing factory in Aylesford, name of Thomas Claymore. Both live within six leagues of a dairy farm associated with a woman named Charlotte."

"Thank the Lord," she said in relief. Perhaps they would be able to stop him in time. "When do we leave?"

"Leave?" he frowned. "You're not going anywhere. Neither of us are." He came closer, putting his hands on her shoulders so she couldn't move. "As soon as I hear back from the authorities confirming whose handwriting it is, I—not you—am going to the authorities and we'll bring the bastard in."

She made a sound of disgust and threw his hands from her. "I'm the one who brought you into this. This is my responsibility. It always has been." She stuck a finger into his chest. "You have nothing to do with it."

Ash laughed and grabbed her finger and backed her up. "Nothing to do with it? You're under a delusion if you think you could have figured out anything without me."

Oh, that was it. He thought because he was so smart and so good with his hands she would just turn to mush and leave things to the men? "You are so arrogant," she spat, unwrapping his fingers from around hers. "So unbelievably—"

Ash jerked her against him and took her mouth, and she felt his tongue dart inside to swirl around like wine in a glass. She meant to make a sound of protest, but it came out as a moan of surrender. The scent of him surrounded her, tangy and dark like a deep copse of wood at night.

He tore his lips away to whisper, "You're mine. And God help me, I can't seem to want anyone else. You're in my blood, my mind, my soul…"

As he ran his hands over her bodice to squeeze her hips that jutted from beneath her corset, she said, "I don't want you to think of anyone but me," The words surprised her. She knew it was foolish to try to lay claim to him.

He chuckled. "Even when I try to amuse myself otherwise, being with you is all I can think about."

His words created a heady blossom of desire in her, but as she processed them, the haze retreated. She came off her toes and let her heels touch the floor again. His lips on her neck were making her drowsy and languid, but she blinked hard and asked, "What do you mean, try otherwise?"

He froze, his teeth gently scraping across her skin as he leaned back, looking into her eyes.

A feeling of dread crept into her stomach.

Her hands fell from his neck. "Ash?"

"Ivy. I—" He ran a hand through his hair, causing the locks to become disheveled. "You must understand. I have needs that … that can't just be ignored or put away like some men's."

She shrank away, feeling a numbness come over her. Knowing it was covering a pain that would soon overcome everything else, she stared slackly as he continued to speak.

"I wanted to prove I didn't need you. That anyone could satisfy this craving like I've always been able to in the past. I didn't mean—"

Holding up a hand, she stopped him abruptly.

"You didn't mean." She let out a half-laugh that was devoid of humor. "You know, that's what my father told me just a few days ago. He didn't mean to hurt me. He didn't mean to hurt anyone. Do you think he was telling the truth? Do you think I should have run into his arms and forgotten all the horrible things he's done?" Tears began to fall, and she couldn't stop them this time.

Ash shook his head, eyes bright. "I'm not your father. You're comparing me with him?"

She could hear the ache in his voice, but didn't care. Hugging herself, she spoke to the blurriness of his too-familiar face. "You're not him, no. But you're not far from one another either. All that matters to you is this-this sexual energy. You're so wrapped up in what you want, what you think you need. Did you know that's what he said as well?" Her lips trembled as she forced the words out. "A doctor interviewed him once a few years ago, and foolish me read the article hoping for I don't know what."

Ivy paused to wipe her nose on her sleeve, unconcerned with what she looked like. "But he said he had needs that ordinary men couldn't understand. That his head wouldn't let him rest until he had done those things, and that it felt like a marvelous release until the need came back again. As if it wasn't within his control to stop himself. But do you know what I think?"

Ash closed his eyes and whispered, "What?"

"I think it's a load of rubbish. I think you're both perfectly capable of controlling yourselves, and yet you choose to let that darkness into your minds until it corrupts your very souls." She waved her hand to indicate his person. "Maybe you do have marks all over you that will never go away. You chose every single thing you've done and excused it all with a tale of keeping some mysterious madness at bay." She came a step closer and put a hand over his heart that she could feel pounded with terrified precision. He opened his eyes, and there was an anguish in them she both wanted to soothe and to rip to shreds at the same time.

Her voice shook, but she did not stop. "You think you are cursed, but what you really are is a weak wastrel wallowing in your shallow depravity."

Ash didn't say anything at first, his chest heaving with the obvious effort it was taking him to not unleash his fury on her. But then his lip curled, and he spoke in tones more disdainful and hopeless than she'd ever heard. "You think you understand, but you have no idea what lies beyond your world of sanity. Your every waking moment isn't a battle for control."

He began to force her backwards across the room using his utterly merciless visage to tower over her. "I have to labor every hour just to create the impression that I think as you do, without a thought but the most obvious coming to mind at any given moment. The world is so much more than you see, but you'll never know."

The condescension dripping from his words

stung, and she bit the inside of her cheek until an acrid taste filled her mouth.

He shoved her hand away as if he couldn't stand her touch. "I didn't ask for this. I didn't ask for these infernal thoughts or for my parents to die before their time, or for you to demand more of me than I can give. Yet you think you have the right to tell me I'm weak?"

He backed her against the wall of the foyer, next to the stupid marble bust of his perfect face. "You would be nothing but a street girl without me. No one wanted you until I pulled you from your small life and gave you everything."

Ivy choked, his words piercing a part of her she had fought to encase behind years of self-sufficiency and survival.

Pinning her shoulders with his large hands— hands that had given her such pleasure the last time they'd seen each other, Ash threw more words that were meant to strike back with the same callousness she'd shown him. "How can you possibly maintain moral superiority when, with a single touch, you dissolve into clay in my hands? You think you're better than me? You don't understand anything of control."

His fingers dug into the flesh of her shoulders. "I could have had you any time I wished, but I didn't. You're just as wanton as every woman I've ever bedded and never thought of again, but you think you're somehow special because I chose not to."

He ran the side of his pointer finger down her cheek, and she could see desire and fury warring in his eyes. "It's not me who is weak, little girl. You have more of your father in you than you think. The only difference between you is you're too dull to want anything I haven't shown you."

Bile rose in her throat. This was what he truly

thought of her all along. She had always been only a piece in a game. He had even told her so many times, but she hadn't listened.

Well, two could play at that.

Mustering the strength to stand straight and as tall as she could ever hope to be, she looked daggers into his crystalline eyes. "Perhaps that's true. But I'd rather be on the streets than whore myself out to someone who doesn't have the ability to appreciate anything but a woman's bed play. I hope you are happy with your manipulations, Asher, because that's all you'll ever have," she spat. "You'll certainly never have me. Your touch might be practiced and pleasurable, but it is empty. Perhaps that's why you are never satisfied. Your soul can't be filled because it's a sieve, always empty with nothing to give in return."

A moment of pure shock showed in his eyes as if she'd physically struck him, and she used it to shove him backwards. His foot caught on the edge of the Savonnerie rug behind him, and he stumbled. Falling back, he slammed into one of the columns that lined the foyer behind him, but he didn't seem to sense any pain.

Without taking his eyes from her, he slowly smiled. It was the most terrible and beautiful smile she'd ever seen, a silent roar of desolate resignation. Ivy couldn't take her eyes from him, her heart stopped somewhere between her vitriolic words and the devastated quirk of his lips. It was like watching those vases tumble out of her cart one by one, her future lost to her forever in lovely shards of broken grins and shattered souls.

He didn't try to stop her when she finally tore her eyes away and bolted, arms slack at his sides.

Not bothering to look back, she ran up the stairs to her room.

She allowed herself one moment of terrified paralysis before going to her bedside table and stuffing the bank notes she had been saving from her wages into her reticule. She didn't waste time bringing anything else with her except her letters. Clothes and toilette items could be bought later.

What she couldn't buy was the courage to be in this house one more moment for fear of seeing his face again—a face she knew would haunt her more painfully than anything her father had ever done.

She had survived having her heart ripped out and her identity destroyed once before. She could do it again.

Corrine Morganstern was gone, and Ivy Wollard had never been very good at living life. It was time to become someone else altogether. It was time to disappear.

****

The sound of the front door to Blackbourne House closing behind her was when he remembered it beginning. Burning tentacles brushed against his cranial nerves to wrap themselves around his every betraying thought.

When he was in such a state, his staff knew not to disturb his rituals and attempts to avert disaster. Knowing they wanted to help him always showed, however, in the form of a fresh basin of cold water and cloth set out in his chambers or the drawing of all the curtains in case someone were to look in and see him engaged in odd behavior. But they did not dare approach or speak to him after years of seeing their Master battle his mind for control.

He tried everything to halt what he knew would be an episode such as he hadn't experienced in years. He went to the roof and stood shivering in the wintery air, hoping the cold would block out other sensory input.

When that failed, he dragged himself to his quarters and had a bath drawn, but it only made it worse when thoughts of seeing Ivy naked and wet rushed in to torment him.

The pain grew until he could barely see, white dots flashing across his vision. When he exited the bathing room, he couldn't concentrate on drying off, but yanked on his trousers and strode from the room to try one last thing as incapacitation loomed.

Clutching his temples, he stumbled down the hall to the family drawing room. The smell of paints hung in the space, adding to the pounding in his head. Clutching the doorframe for support, he didn't know if it was wise to enter given the fumes that were making things worse.

Ash knew he was losing control quickly. Panic began to well up, his heart rate increasing until he knew he had no other choice but to move forward. Rivulets of water from his hair streamed over his face as he staggered into the room, moving towards his goal.

When he stood in front of the Raphael painting and focused his blurry vision on the image, he suddenly knew a moment of blessed peace.

Everything simply stopped.

The white-hot poker sensation in his head ceased, and the room fell away as he took in the deft brushstrokes Ivy's talented hand had wrought. It was a scene wherein a woman stood in front of a window looking down at her two children who were clinging to her cloak. The bright, messianic colors, the way the expression in the woman's face serenely beheld her children...

Ivy had created something exquisite, and somehow, the beauty of her own soul was there on the canvas as well. It was in every stroke, the way she had lovingly recreated a piece of art purely from a passion to do so without thought of recognition or acknowledgement. She truly enjoyed every moment of it, and hadn't been able to express her talent until given a simple set of paint pots and canvas.

Until a chance meeting had allowed him to be the one to see her transform into the vivacious woman she was always meant to be.

He had let himself become fascinated with her. Every word, every hair on her head, every expression to pass over her face. Her very toes, wrinkled and peeking out from the tub as she listened to him read, were precious to him.

She had been right. He had gone after pleasure for pleasure's sake instead of finding a way out. Every woman he had ever sought after had been nothing but a selfish indulgence that he had let eat away at his ability to care about anyone.

Yet he loved Ivy with an uncontrollable ferocity that had nothing to do with bedsport. He would love her until the end of time, even if he never kissed her lips again.

And now she was gone.

He fell to his knees, his breath rushing out as sharp jabs of pain ate into his mind once again. Curling into himself, he grabbed at his head, trying to pluck the daggers from his skull.

As darkness closed around the edges of his vision, only one thought remained. He groaned out into the silence with a hushed cry.

"What have I done?"

Then it took him.

Chapter Sixteen

The Sparrow Inn on the western outskirts of London wasn't Blackstone House, that was for certain. Her tiny room had only a lumpy bed and chest of drawers with a basin on top. That was all. The room's flowered wallpaper might have served to brighten the room at some point, but it was so faded and torn that it was only a depressing reminder of how far in the world she had fallen.

Again.

But there was no point in being choosy any longer, not when she only had two hundred pounds with which to reinvent herself and survive on until she could find employment again. That employment needed to be somewhere far away from London and the reach of Asher Blackbourne.

Not that he was going to come looking for her. That possibility had been doused rather efficiently upon her departure.

Once the hack she had hailed had deposited her at the inn and she had been shown to her room, the rush of energy she'd been running on immediately abandoned her. Apparently, the numbness that had sustained her until that point was not to be trusted because it left her faster than a man leaving Priscilla's flat when the sun came up.

The things she'd said... The things he'd said...

No sooner had she set her reticule on the bed than her stomach rebelled. She rushed to the basin on the chest of drawers and vomited. There wasn't anything in her stomach since she hadn't eaten since the scones she'd had with Grant that morning. But she continued to retch, her nerves jerking until her stomach settled down.

After that, the tears came. And came and came and came.

She cried for the awful things she'd said to someone she loved more than anything in the world. She cried for the things he'd said back, things she had feared were true and that she had mistakenly hoped he could somehow erase inside her.

But most of all, she cried for a future she had let herself foolishly fantasize about. A future with Ash that could never have been, no matter what she felt for him.

With that came the realization that she truly belonged nowhere now. She had no one and nothing to call home. Anyone she had met during her time as Corrine Morganstern was forever out of reach to Ivy Wollard, daughter of a murderer. She could not go back to living the way she had, not knowing if she could afford to eat or if she would be tossed from her own bed one day. Not a lady, not a street girl, not a mill worker, and not loved by anyone. She was nothing.

When she had cried all she could, an emptiness enveloped her that quickly turned to exhaustion.

Yet if she were to help Charlotte before it was too late, time was of the essence. She knew she had to rise early in the morning to catch the stagecoach to Aylesford, but she needed to plan her journey carefully with the funds she had at her disposal.

Ivy wiped her nose with a kerchief and opened her reticule to reassure herself with the pound notes inside it. Rummaging around trying to separate the mess she'd made when stuffing everything inside it earlier, she finally dumped everything on the bed. As she shifted through the papers, a sealed envelope caught her eye. She didn't recognize it, but Milton must have put it with her correspondence that morning, and she'd gathered it up with everything else. In the growing dark, she had trouble reading the words, so she held it up to the almost-empty oil lamp resting on the headboard of the bed.

When the handwriting came into focus and she was able to read the inscription, she gasped.

To: Corrine Morganstern
Blackbourne House
Grosvenor Square, London

It was Claymore's hand. She would recognize it anywhere. With trembling hands, she tore it open and read its contents.

Dear Corrine:

We haven't been formally introduced yet, but I am writing to congratulate you on being chosen to represent my first great demonstration of a project I've been working on for some time. I believe you'll be perfect for the role, although your host, the Marquess of Blackbourne, is really to thank for pointing me in your direction. He has recently attempted to become involved in the project, and so I have accorded you, his mistress, the honor of being displayed at the first exhibit. It was presumptuous of him to assume he could invade my privacy, but I believe in repaying in kind—and that's where you come in.

Fret not, for I have altered my plans so as not to cause you the need for travel. I am in London now and will be making your acquaintance very shortly. I must say, when I first saw you through the window of your paramour's home, I was almost giddy at the prospect of our meeting. Your beauty will serve me well and will be even more spectacular than what I had originally planned for my debut experiment. It will not be long until I come for you, so please do try to look your best. I look forward to our time together creating what is sure to become the talk of the town and await your company with bated breath.

Your Newest Admirer,
Claymore

Ivy's lungs tried and failed to keep up with the welling terror coursing its way through her body. As if the paper were scalding her hands, she dropped it and spun around. She scrambled from the bed and backed herself into the farthest corner of the room while reaching into the back of her bodice.

The warmed metal of her slim dagger slid out from between the placards of her corset to rest familiarly in her hand. She flipped it through the air and caught it deftly before making a slashing motion, testing too-long unused skills.

He was here in London. He had been watching.

And he was coming for her.

The light from the oil lamp sputtered into darkness as her eyes fixed themselves on the doorknob.

It would be a long night before morning came.

****

"Asher? Asher, are you home? Your blasted butler isn't even answering the door."

Max's voice registered on the peripherals of his mind, but he made no attempt to respond. All he was capable of was concentrating on the pain that burrowed inside the tunnels of his brain, as he had been doing for the past several hours. He was aware Max's presence was dooming, but couldn't muster any strength to prevent the inevitable.

"Asher? What—?" Max's voice was clearer now, only a few feet away. "Bollocks, what happened?"

Ash knew what his cousin was seeing. Lying on the floor of the drawing room, the mighty Marquess looked as enfeebled as a child with his head in his hands and sweat dewing on his face. He knew he had vomited at some point, but didn't know where he lay in relation to it. His eyes were closed, but Ash clenched his teeth and opened them to see Max's boots approaching.

His cousin leaned down, but didn't try to touch him. "So this is what happens when the insanity comes over you, is it?"

Ash focused on his own breathing, in and out, in and out. His naked torso was cold now, but he didn't dare move to try to cover himself.

"I admit, it doesn't give me pleasure to see you this way. I wish—" Max stopped himself, drawing back the hand he had been reaching out. Clearing his throat, he rose. "I know you don't understand why I am determined to see you fall. You think it's because I want to steal the Marquessate from you. That I'm jealous or I need more power or money." He let out a laugh which turned into a groan. "Oh, how I wish that were true," he whispered.

Ash was confused. What in blazes was his cousin blabbering about? It was over. Max had won. There was no going back now.

This time, Max's voice held a note of sorrow that Ash hadn't thought was possible for his scheming relative. "You were my best friend," he said, throwing himself into a nearby chair. Through dimmed eyes, he saw Max rub the bridge of his nose. "I thought we always would be. And then—" He waved a hand heavenward. "Then you had to fall out of that stupid tree."

Ash blinked the sweat from his eyes and tried to speak. "What?" he gasped. He had no idea what Max was referring to. He'd never fallen from a tree.

"Ironically, I believe it was an ash tree. "He snorted. "We were only eleven, but I remember it like it was yesterday. I thought you were dead when I climbed down and saw the rock you'd hit your head on. It was a mess, blood everywhere. I thought I'd be blamed for it, but our parents knew it wasn't anyone's fault." Max opened the drawer of the table next to his chair and removed a humidor.

Ash thought he'd rid himself of the filthy cigars years ago, but apparently, his father had stashed some around the house while he'd been alive. Asher couldn't stand the smell of smoke. Not since he had walked through the remains of his family's manor in the lake country. It was the one vice he had never been able to indulge in.

Max snipped the end from a cigar and lit it.

Immediately, Ash's stomached roiled at the noxious fumes, and the pain worsened.

Max continued. "Two months. You were unconscious for two months, and I stayed with you. I tried to make sure you were entertained, just in case you were bored being asleep for that long. I told you stories, played with tin soldiers on your bed. I kept thinking if I made it exciting enough, you would wake up to play with me again.

"When it finally happened, I was forbidden to ever speak of it to you. You didn't remember anything, and your parents thought it would do more harm than good to remind you of it. Everyone pretended it had never happened, and I was glad to do so, too. I had my friend back."

Ash took shallow breaths as he tried to process Max's words, the carpet beneath his face scratching his cheek and jaw.

"But you weren't the same. All of a sudden, you weren't interested in playing outside. Every time we tried to go anywhere, you withdrew. You wouldn't speak, wouldn't move. You never really came back. I was alone after that."

Ash was reeling. He had hit his head? And no one

had told him? The cigar smoke curled around his senses, clouding his thoughts further.

"Sounds selfish, doesn't it?" Max remarked, blowing out a stream of sweet smoke. "I suppose it is. But all I knew was my best friend didn't want me around any longer. When we went to school, you got top marks in everything, and I think my parents couldn't help but compare me to you. Even after school when you were carousing about town with every lightskirt you could find, you didn't think to include me in your new world."

Ash felt salty wetness drip onto his lips. He hadn't tried to shut Max out. He had felt more alone than his cousin could possibly understand.

Yet his isolation had happened exactly how Max had described it. Now he knew. He hadn't always been the crumbling mess he was. He had injured his head.

No one had told him. It was like a missing puzzle piece that suddenly snapped into place. He truly was broken, and there was no fixing him.

Max's next words pulled him from his thoughts. "It doesn't matter now. I must do what needs to be done." He put out his cigarette on the surface of the table. "For what it's worth... I'm sorry, cousin," he said softly.

Max rang the service bell, and dashed a note off for a footman to deliver posthaste. Just after the footman left to complete his errand, Milton came into the room.

To Ash's pleasure, Milton spoke directly to him regardless of the awkward situation. "I regret having to disturb you, my lord, but a letter has come for you. You had said to inform you if such a missive arrived in relation to certain matters. As soon as you are recovered, it will be waiting for you in your office."

"That won't be necessary, Milton," Max interjected, taking the envelope from his tray. "I'll be taking care of estate business from now on."

"But-but—" Milton floundered, clearly unsure of his authority in this situation.

Ash ground his teeth. "Just go," he breathed, the pounding in his head overpowering his attempt to rise from the floor. The muscles in his biceps bulged and shook, but it wasn't enough. Every second was excruciating, and he couldn't even defend his own staff or privacy because of it. His life was slipping through his fingers, and he couldn't move a muscle.

Max's voice was pleasant. He was clearly enjoying every moment of this. "You are dismissed for the moment, Milton. Thank you."

Milton blustered for a moment more before bowing. "I believe I need to accidentally misplace some documents," he said archly, and left the room.

"What have we here? Urgent, is it?" Max sat back down in the chair, and Ash was forced to look at his shiny Hessians as he tore open the letter. "Let's see. From someone named Claymore. Never heard of him."
Ash's eyes flew open, and Max read aloud in a bored tone, oblivious to his cousin's reaction.

Dear Lord Blackbourne,

Did you really think you could interfere in my endeavors without repercussions? Everything was going swimmingly until an acquaintance informed me of your inquiry with the local authorities. Now I must adjust my previous plans, all because you couldn't stay out of someone else's business.

So I have decided to take away something of yours that I hope will cause you as much inconvenience as you have caused me. Once I was in London, it wasn't hard to find out that your houseguest, a Miss Corrine Morganstern, means more to you than simply being the sister of a fellow scientist. I believe taking someone of value to you will create more suffering than anything else

I could do in revenge upon you.

Please know that everything I will do to her is solely because of you. Yet I must also thank you for providing me with a canvas that is so delicate and lovely. I can see why she has entranced you, but she will soon entrance the entire city with the importance of my work. Don't worry— You'll see her again after I have created her into something worthy of spectacle. I am excited at the thought of having her pretty little neck all to myself.

Yours,

Claymore

Max chuckled. "I knew you were tupping the girl. Seems you have some competition now."

The blood pumped in Ash's ears as he lay prostrate on the floor.

Claymore was coming after Ivy.

"Please," he ground out, stretching a hand towards Max's boots. "I need—" He paused to catch his breath.

Max didn't make a move to help. "There's no point in trying to keep your mistress now, cousin. You have bigger problems to worry about. The doctors should be here soon to escort you to Middlesex Asylum in Hanwell. I've heard it's quite nice, as far as these places go."

"No," Ash whispered. He began to rise to his knees, head spinning.

His fate didn't matter. He didn't care where he went afterward, but he wouldn't let Ivy be taken by that madman. He fought to push back the pain in his head as razor-edges sliced through his skull. Sweat beaded on his forehead as he tried to speak.

"Claymore will kill her... I have to go... Have to save her."

"You really are mad, aren't you?" Max pondered,

leaning forward to watch Ash's face as he struggled. "I suppose it does make this easier. You'll be better there. They'll help you."

"Max," Ash pleaded, his head feeling as if it was about to explode. Lights danced in front of his eyes, and he felt himself slipping.

"Don't worry. I'll make sure you're taken care of, Ash. I'll be with you the whole way." Max put a hand on Ash's shoulder.

The sensory awareness of being touched was too much. Ash fell back as he cupped his head, letting out a roar. He closed his eyes, knowing he couldn't overcome the blinding pain causing him to shake with nausea.

As shadows encroached on his consciousness, he prayed for forgiveness. He couldn't save her. She was going to die.

And it was all his fault.

****

A knock on the door startled Ivy awake.

Her eyes flew open, and she frantically held up her blade in preparation for attack.

"Miss? Miss? I have your breakfast!" a feminine voice with a heavy French accent called from the other side of the door.

Ivy slowly let the knife down and groaned as she pushed herself up from where she was crouched against the wall. Her legs felt like jelly as she moved towards the door.

This could be a ruse by Claymore, but she doubted it. If he hadn't tried to catch her unawares during the night, she highly doubted he would risk exposure now without the cover of darkness to aid him.

"What's your name?" she called to the person on the other side of the door.

"It is Alouette. I am the cook's assistant,

Mademoiselle," she said cheerfully.

"Please set the food down in front of the door. Thank you."

"Are you sure, Mademoiselle? I can pour your tea and refresh your bed for you as well."

"Yes, I'm sure. I'm ... naked," Ivy blurted. She sighed and rolled her eyes. Why?

"Oh! Of course. Very well," the girl replied. She heard the tray being set down and retreating footsteps.

Dagger still in hand, Ivy opened the door and peeked out into the hallway. It was empty and quiet. Looking down, she saw the wooden tray of food sitting on the floorboard and quickly drew it inside, shutting the door behind her. She took it to the bed and sat down, looking at the food.

There was a bowl of oatmeal with a pat of butter and brown sugar melting into it, as well as a plate of sausages and a hard-boiled egg. Her stomach was in knots, but it growled in hunger, nonetheless. She devoured the sausages, egg, and half of the oatmeal while keeping her eyes on the door the entire time. Feeling more satiated afterwards, Ivy let herself slump on the bed, holding her blade.

There was nothing for it. She had to go back to Blackbourne House. Asher would know what to do. He had power and sway with London's high authorities and would be able to alert them to the presence of Claymore. If Claymore was watching Blackbourne House, she couldn't take the chance that he would go after Ash if he couldn't find her.

She would rather die a thousand deaths than see Ash hurt because of her. She should never have brought him into this mess in the first place.

Ivy rapidly gathered up her things and left the inn, hailing a hackney back to Blackbourne House. Her eyes scanned everything around her for potential threats, and she kept the knife in her hand inside her reticule just in case. He probably hadn't followed her here if he hadn't made contact by now, but there was no telling the logic of such a person.

When she arrived at Blackbourne House almost two hours later without issue, she made the driver walk with her to the front steps and wait until she'd entered. No one had caught her eye as she took note of her surroundings, but the people of Mayfair were out and about in full force on this sunny morning. Ladies with parasols strolled down the street, some on the arms of men. Gentlemen in relaxed morning attire tipped their hats to ladies and as they walked or flicked the reigns of their landaus.

He could be anyone, and she wouldn't know it.

After giving the hackney driver a generous tip, she shut the door behind her. Nothing looked out of place in the foyer, but the pain of what had last happened here rose to make a lump in her throat.

She couldn't think about that now. Finding Asher was all that mattered.

The click of her slippers as she walked across the foyer brought Mrs. Rushkova rushing into the room.

"Thank the Heaven, you have come back!" she burst, bustling up to Ivy and enveloping her in a great bear hug.

"Oh," Ivy exclaimed, unprepared for the large woman's unusual greeting.

Milton followed on her heels as Mrs. Rushkova set her down. "Madame, you must help His Lordship!"

"What's going on?" Her stomach curled in on itself. Had Claymore made a move to seek Asher out?

"It's Maxwell, miss." Milton explained.

Ivy let out her breath in relief.

Milton continued, taking her hands in his. "After you left, His Lordship's head was paining him awfully, and then the Earl came. Miss," his voice dropped. "He has had the Master committed to a lunatic asylum. They took him in the middle of the night. I have never seen him in such a bad way."

Ivy's heart stuttered.

"What?" she whispered. "That can't be." Asher wasn't crazy. His mind worked differently, yes, but he was the most logical man she knew. They couldn't have just carted him away.

"Yes, Lady. They carried him out on a stretcher, muzzled like a dog," Mrs. Rushkova said, her voice breaking.

"No," she said, tears pricking her eyes. She couldn't stand the thought of Asher being treated like an animal that needed to be caged.

"What should we do?" Milton demanded, his hair fluffed out and eyes bright.

"I'll think of something," she said, stepping back.

But the more she thought, the less she knew what to do. Should she go after him? Write to someone? Who would believe her over what surely had to be the opinions of professionals?

Max had begun to establish his cousin's questionable sanity a long time ago. She understood now what he had been playing at the entire time. He had always been looking for an excuse to get his cousin out of the way, and he had finally succeeded.

Suddenly, a thought occurred to her.

The Duke.

Lord Scythemore would know what to do, and she knew Ash's friend would never allow him to be taken like this without a fight.

"How far is it to the Duke of Scythemore's

residence?" she asked Milton.

"Oh, only a few minutes ride, I should think. His London residence is in Mayfair."

Ivy smiled. It was time to rescue the Marquess with a little assistance from the person who had helped rescue her only a short time ago.

Chapter Seventeen

It was past social calling hours in the afternoon, but she luckily found the Duke at home. She had quickly explained the situation, and he had growled, "The only one allowed to call Blackbourne insane is me." He immediately began to formulate a plan.

Unfortunately, Scythemore suspected the only way to have a chance of freeing Asher was to have genuine scientists declare him sane and give testimony to that fact.

Which was where it became troublesome. There was a whole organization of people with the credentials to be able to do such a thing, but none of them knew the Marquess of Blackbourne. They knew someone named Reginald Morganstern, which didn't help in the slightest.

That's when she knew the truth had to come out.

The Duke had listened without interruption as Ivy had explained everything—from Ash's secret identity to her role in his charade. When she had finished, she waited for his reaction.

No expression showed on his face as he raised a brow. Ivy held her breath.

"That certainly clears a lot of things up."

She had breathed once more.

Though Scythemore wasn't easy to read, it was clear he was prepared to move heaven and earth if that's what it took to get his friend out. He quickly rallied an army of servants to do his bidding, which involved summoning as many people from the BAAS as could be found in a matter of hours. With Ivy's help, a list of personages she remembered from the BAAS gatherings was compiled. He sent every conveyance he owned out to bring back anyone willing to do the Duke of

Scythemore a personal favor.

After five hours, the last carriage returned. As it turned out, everyone who had been reached was quite enthusiastic about meeting the elusive Duke of Scythemore. Of the seven men who were escorted to Scythemore Manor, three were determined to be qualified to testify on Ash's behalf. One was a doctor of both psychiatry and medicine, Dr. Freemont, while another was a doctor of internal medicine, a Dr. Prodging. The last was an astronomer named Owenby who had used "Morganstern's" calculations to design a more advanced telescope he was developing.

Once they had narrowed down their candidates, the Duke sent the rest of the men home that evening with an invitation to an exclusive house party at his estate outside London for a later date.

Then came the hard part. There was no help for it. Ash's identity had to be revealed.

The Duke carefully explained that Ash had been spying for the Royal Society, but had found the BAAS more to his liking. All three men had immediately congratulated each other and forgiven the Marquess of Blackbourne, who they were quite pleased to have amongst their ranks. Freemont was especially gratified to know that Corrine was not in an incestuous relationship with Blackbourne, but was simply his employee.

"Are you ready?" Scythemore asked the others riding in the carriage.

Ivy looked around at the group she and Scythemore had rounded up. It wasn't the most intimidating posse of rescuers, but that part would be left up to the Duke.

"Absolutely."

"Can't wait."

"Haven't had this much excitement in years,"

Owenby remarked, an elderly man who was a bit hard of hearing. "The field of astronomy can be a bit slow." He winked at Ivy, thumping his cane on the floor of the carriage.

Scythemore nodded with a grim smile while Ivy grinned.

The carriage, the official Ducal Conveyance, lurched to a stop in front of the asylum. The Duke's outriders opened the doors and helped them to alight. Scythemore had wanted every ceremony and pompous ritual observed during their visit, though it was well past normal visiting hours. His influence as one of the highest ranking men in the realm was crucial to their endeavor.

Ivy prayed it would be enough.

****

Ash prayed to die.

Every moment was an agony he no longer had any wish to fight. The slashes of pain in his head would never stop, and without Ivy, he had no reason to keep them at bay. What was the point of attempting to best this curse if she wasn't there to enjoy it with?

His title, his lands, his projects—they could all go hang. There was nothing left for him here. If God had any mercy at all, He would allow the pain to finally overwhelm his fragile brain until every pathway was scorched beyond redemption and blessed nothingness descended. He could not—should not—live if he couldn't protect Ivy from the fate that awaited her at the hands of Claymore.

After having been poked and prodded by several people, he had been deposited without ceremony in a small room, the muzzle being removed after it was clear he was in no state to resist. All the same, the confining strait jacket had been left on. The small cot in the gray room would have been unpalatable under the best of circumstances, but Ash had no perception of its comfort one way or the other.

After several hours, the pain lessened enough for him to briefly become aware of his surroundings. Ironically, the blank slate of the walls and door served to deprive his mind of stimuli, which helped somewhat. Yet every time he thought he could become cognizant enough to rise or speak, the thought of Ivy alone and afraid sent him spiraling back into the abyss. Even now, she might be suffering, and he couldn't sound the alarm.

It wouldn't have mattered anyways. No one would hear him here, and his screams of protest would only be one among all the others. He was the Mad Marquess now, and there was no hope for justly condemned men such as him. He had been doomed from the moment he had fallen from that ash tree all those years ago.

There was no evading the truth. She would be gone soon.

They both would.

****

One didn't have to wait long when a Duke was around, Ivy noted, as she and Scythemore were ushered into the asylum director's chambers. The BAAS members were left in the antechamber to wait.

The director, a man named Cassius Flemming, was a small, but round balding man with an obsequious manner towards Scythemore. "Your Grace, what an honor. What can I do for you? Would you like tea? Biscuits?" He smiled, indicating a seat in front of him. He didn't bother to address Ivy at all, which was fine with her.

The Duke did not take the seat, but remained standing, which caused the director to awkwardly bounce back up from the chair he'd been about to sit in.

Ivy stood to Scythemore's right, taking in the predatory stance of the Duke as he addressed the director.

"There has been a grievous mistake, I'm afraid," Scythemore said in ominous tones, resting the tips of his fingers on the man's desk as he leaned over it. "A very close friend of mine was erroneously incarcerated here last night, and I am here to collect him. His immediate release is non-negotiable."

The director's eyes grew wide, and he patted his shiny forehead with a handkerchief. He looked as if he didn't know whether to feign cordiality or cry. "This wouldn't be the Marquess of Blackbourne, but any chance, would it?" He laughed nervously.

Scythemore only smiled.

"Right. Of course," the director said, searching through a pile of papers on his overcrowded desk. "I have personally seen to His Lordship's case, and I regret—" He swallowed visibly, although how his Adam's apple was visible under his neck rolls, she couldn't quite figure out. "I re-regret to inform you that the man is undoubtedly suffering from-from lunacy."

He waited for the Duke's reaction as if waiting to be sentenced to the gallows.

Scythemore sighed through his nose and straightened. "I believe you are aware of the repercussions of displeasing a man such as myself, Director. I would so hate to have to involve my friends in this matter."

The man wrung his hands. "Wh-who are your friends?"

Scythemore collapsed into one of the chairs and spoke softly, as if the trouble of explaining was almost too much to bother with. "I can have the Prime Minister here by nightfall. If that's not enough for you, our young

Queen Victoria is quite fond of me and won't hesitate to sever your career should I mention your distasteful governance practices. She would be very interested to know how a peer of the realm is being unlawfully detained under your supervision."

Flemming sat quickly and mopped his brow again. "That's… That won't be necessary, I'm sure. The board will meet again Thursday next, and his case can be re-examined to determine release. I'm confident they will find the Marquess irrefutably sound of mind."

A smile that was not a smile formed on the Duke's lips. "I will be leaving with him today. As I said, it is not open for debate."

The small man began to breathe heavily and wiggled his disproportionately large behind in his chair. "I cannot act without the board's approv—"

Scythemore rose again, his stormy eyes burning. "I don't give a damn about the board. Whatever paperwork needs to happen can go to hell, for all I care." He came around the desk and leaned over the director. "Blackbourne leaves with me. Is that understood?"

The man's chair creaked as its occupant squirmed. "Th-the only way to-to do such a thing would be if a qualified individual testified on h-his behalf in person in front of the board."

"Even if we have people who can testify today?" Ivy interrupted.

The director acted as if she hadn't spoken. "If Your Grace would wait until next—"

Scythemore held up a hand. "I was hoping to avoid this, but apparently, less refined techniques will have to do."

"Your grace?" the man whimpered, cowering in his chair.

The Duke turned to Ivy. "Miss Morganstern, I

believe it's time for Plan B."

Ivy took a deep breath and then nodded once.

She and the Duke left Director Flemming spluttering in his chair.

"What's Plan B?" he squawked "Your Grace? Your Grace?"

Ivy strode toward the men waiting in the reception area. "Gentlemen, I'm afraid we will have to employ other means to free Lord Blackbourne," she told them quietly. "Are you in or out?"

Owenby grinned. "Count me in, Madame."

Nodding, Freemont removed his pristine white gloves. "I've been itching for some action ever since Waterloo ended too soon."

Prodging shrugged. "Why not? It's not as if they're going to prosecute a Duke."

The astronomer frowned. "I don't know if that sort of immunity extends to the rest of us..."

There was a silence in which everyone looked at the rest of the assemblage.

Scythemore grabbed two of the doctors and shoved them forward. "Too late now."

As the group began to exit the room towards the hallway leading to the patients' quarters, the director's secretary raised protest. "You cannot go in there!"

She was subsequently ignored, and Ivy followed the men into the hallway.

"This reminds me of prison," Ivy said in the sudden silence glancing at the barred windows on the doors lining the long corridor.

"Yes, well, let's hope this goes better than last time," Scythemore remarked, looking into the window of the first room. "Spread out and find Blackbourne."

They did so and began to check each cell.

As she looked at the people behind the doors, she

knew—this was worse than prison.

She had to get Ash out of here.

After a few seconds, Prodging paused. "Erm... What exactly does Blackbourne look like? I haven't met the Marquess in person. Well, except as Morganstern."

Ivy froze, then sighed. Of course. "Blonde hair, blue eyes. Tall. Fit. Rather like a fallen angel who—"

"Ahem."

She looked at Scythemore. "Right. Moving along."

Just then, two male orderlies came rushing through the reception door, outfitted in dark green uniforms. "You must all leave immediately," one ordered, brandishing a club.

"Oh good," Prodging exclaimed. "I was starting to think no one was going to try to stop us."

"If you will not leave voluntarily, I am authorized to use force against the lot of you. "Er, except for you, Your Grace," he added, giving the tiniest of bows to the Duke.

"I suppose that makes this easy then," Scythemore replied. Walking up the one of the orderlies, he promptly punched him in the face, sending the man crumpling to the floor.

The other orderly shrieked and dropped his club.

"Go find him," Scythemore called, striding after the green-clad man as he tried to dodge the Duke's blows. Another uniform entered the corridor, but Ivy didn't stop. The Duke could handle himself.

Ivy and the others split up into two parties, each taking one side of the hallway. When they didn't find the Marquess, they agreed to go to different floors, Ivy and Owenby going up while Freemont and Prodging took the stairs downwards.

News of their renegade intentions must have

spread, however, because as soon as Ivy opened the door to the hallway a floor up, three orderlies came towards them from the other end.

"Hello, boys," Ivy said, sliding her dagger from its position in her corset back. Owenby breathed heavily behind her, leaning on his cane. "Who's first?" She nimbly maneuvered the knife between the knuckles of her fingers.

At the sight of a well-dressed woman eagerly wielding a wicked-looking blade, they stopped short. "Now, miss, we don't want to hurt you. We just—"

She stepped forward, causing them to retreat. "Let's dispense with the formalities, gentlemen."

"You look much too comfortable with that." Owenby wheezed, looking at her sideways.

"I enjoy being comfortable as opposed to the alternative in these sorts of situations." Ivy winked.

"How many times have you attempted to break someone out of a lunatic asylum?" he asked incredulously.

"This would be the first."

One of the orderlies came towards her, and she used his momentum against him, turning sideways and flicking her blade against the man's arm. She didn't want to hurt him, but if it was between injuring him and having to leave Ash in this place...

A shallow cut appeared on his arm, and he gave a shout of surprise. While the man ogled his forearm in shock, Owenby pushed him into the stairwell and pulled the door closed, sticking his cane through the metal handle.

Another of the guards growled and unhooked his club from the belt at his waist. "That's enough. It's time to go."

"I haven't had nearly enough," Ivy told him. She

pointedly wiped her knife on the folds of her dress.

Owenby grunted behind her as the first orderly banged on the door from the other side, and she looked back to make sure he was all right.

While she was distracted, the club-brandishing orderly reached for her and shoved her against the door. He slammed her arm against the wall beside her, and the knife clattered to the floor several feet away.

Ivy grimaced and quickly used her other hand to poke him in the eye, earning an enraged yelp.

"Now, see here, you tosspot" Owenby exclaimed to her right.

Ivy glanced over to see the gray-haired man attempting to kick the other orderly in the shins as the man tried to get to the door. She hiked her skirts, grabbed the orderly's shoulders who had one hand over his eye, and kneed him squarely in the baubles. The man groaned and fell to the floor. She didn't feel good about leaving Owenby on his own, but there was no help for it. She used her opening to lean down, grab the set of keys from the man's belt, and run down the hallway, picking up her dagger again as she went.

"Ash! Ash! Are you here?" she shouted, bolting from one door to another.

Nothing except the angry tones of Owenby giving the orderly a piece of his mind as they squabbled.

She continued her search, frantically checking each room for the man who should not have been there in the first place.

Finally, in the last room on the left-hand side of the corridor, she looked in to see a golden-haired man lying on the narrow cot. It was dark in the room, the only light coming from the fading light through the tiny, barred window opposite the door. His torso was encased in a black straitjacket that prevented movement from the waist up, but he didn't look as if he would have moved if he could. His eyes were shut, and he was trembling uncontrollably.

Ivy's breathed rushed out. "Ash."

The man opened his eyes, and their familiar glacier blue stared back at her through a mist of pain.

"I'm here," she said, trying to give him a reassuring smile. She slipped her knife back into her corset.

He closed his eyes again and lowered his head to the cot, defeat in every line of his restrained bones.

Seeing him thus made her fumble as she looked away and began to try different keys in the lock. After finding the right one, she hurriedly unlocked the door and went in, kneeling at the edge of the cot. Gingerly, she touched his cheek, noting the feverish heat coming from his skin.

Ash opened his eyes again to murmur, "You came for me. Are you real?"

Ivy nodded, stroking his hair. "I'm real."

Shouts outside the room caused her to turn around. She saw the Duke standing in the doorway, his face sheened with sweat and flecks of blood. Prodging and Freemont appeared behind him. "Is he—?"

"He's all right."

Scythemore nodded, but turned around as he saw Ivy's eyes widen on something behind him.

More guards had come, including the director himself.

"Get him out of there. Leave them to us," Scythemore told her, rolling up his sleeves once more and diving back into the fray.

Ivy didn't waste any time and began to undo the series of buckles on Ash's restraint garment.

Seeing Ash's eyes focused on her, she asked,

"Are you all right?"

"Depends on your definition, I suppose," he answered, giving her a weak grin. He shook his head as if to clear it.

"Don't worry. You'll be out of this place soon." She continued to work her way down the straitjacket.

"Could we stay until tomorrow?" His voice was growing stronger, and his eyes were now clear.

Ivy stopped and frowned. "What?"

"It's just, I've got a card game going with King Louis, who happens to be staying right next door, if you can believe it."

Ivy shoved at his shoulder and got back to work setting his loose. "Can you ever be serious?"

"Would you want me to be?"

Ivy smiled. "No."

One of the orderlies fell through the doorway, having been tripped by Owenby's cane. The old man chuckled and blew on the tip of his cane. "That was a good one."

"Time to hurry this up," Ash stated.

Ivy reared back as Ash rose up on the bed and shrugged out of the restraining jacket, sliding it over his head, though half the buckles were still in place.

Ivy's mouth dropped open. "You-You—"

"Oh, yes, I figured out how to get out of this thing hours ago," he admitted. "You just looked so damned adorable when you were determined to save me by undoing all of those buckles."

She stood, hands on her hips. "Why, you conniving wretch!"

Ash grabbed her shoulders and moved her to the side, punching the orderly behind her in the jaw. The man was almost as tall as Ash and burly, but he went down all the same.

"Stop this madness at once!" the director's shrill voice commanded, his obvious terror at the situation undermining his words.

Everyone in the vicinity froze, some mid-swing.

After a second, Prodging quipped, "That's a bit ironic, don't you think?"

The director's shoulders heaved, and he mopped his head with his kerchief. "Obviously, we are at an impasse. I cannot allow the injurious laying of hands on Ducal personage, and the Ducal personage will not stop laying hands on my staff!" He threw his arms up.

Scythemore shrugged and grinned back at Ash.

"If you will agree to the story that the Marquess had resided here until the board's formal release approval next Thursday, then you can all leave. Please leave," he added, slumping.

Scythemore crossed his arms. "We accept those terms, as long as the official public story is that he never resided here at all."

Ivy could tell Flemming was grinding his teeth. He must have thought it quite a feather in his cap to claim they housed members of the peerage.

"Fine," he finally mumbled, his handkerchief waving limply at his side.

"Too soon. Just like Waterloo," Prodging mourned, taking his gloves out of his pocket and wiping his bloodied nose with one.

"I, for one, had a splendid time," Owenby declared, waving his cane in a great arc.

"I can't say the same." Ash took Ivy's hand. "Let's get out of here."

Ivy looked up at him. "Are we … are we going home?" Not knowing what their relationship was now, she didn't want to assume anything.

He pressed a kiss to her forehead. "I certainly

hope so."

Ivy felt a balloon of hope expand inside her chest. He wanted her at Blackbourne House.

Their odd party left the asylum in decidedly good spirits, the BAAS members ribbing each other over their lively altercations. They even had the Duke of Scythemore laughing on the way back to Mayfair. Ash was quiet, but smiling, so Ivy took it as a sign that his head wasn't troubling him overly much.

Once everyone had been taken back to their respective residences with promises to meet for tea and a rousing discussion of the ergonomics of cane fighting, they arrived at the Duke's residence. Ash's carriage still sat parked in the front of the manor, driver asleep on his seat. They said their goodbyes to Scythemore, Ivy kissing him on the cheek.

Ash wanted to say a few words to his friend, so she bundled herself into the carriage before him. She could hear them murmuring a little ways off, but didn't want to eavesdrop. Some things were meant to be said only between friends.

Not that she was an expert on the matter. Until recently, the only friend she had was Priscilla, and that had been a rather need-based relationship.

Ivy sighed happily. She now had friends. Lady Tierney and Lady Hayworth were her friends. Though she had only been in their company a handful of times, she felt a certain bond with them already that she hoped would grow over time. As long as she was able to keep her position with Asher—

The carriage lurched forward, interrupting her thoughts.

She stubbed her toe on the opposite seat's heating block as she tumbled backwards. Stifling an oath, she right herself as quickly as possible. The coach continued to gain speed.

Shouts from Asher and the Duke rang out, but soon faded away as the carriage flew down the street.

What in blazes was going on?

None of Ash's drivers would leave him in such a manner. Perhaps the horses had been spooked?

Ivy cautiously poked her head out of the window to look up at the driver's seat. "Hello?" she called, squinting against the icy wind. "Hello? Sir?" She could see the man's boots in the carriage lantern light from her position, but naught else. He flicked the reigns, not attempting to slow.

Then realization dawned. It was too much of a coincidence. There could be no other explanation.

Claymore had finally come for her.

Chapter Eighteen

Ash roared and crumpled the note in his hand. He stood in the entry hall of Scythemore Manor, struggling to keep his fear-induced rage from boiling over. According to Scythemore's butler, while the Blackbourne driver had been waiting with the carriage, a man in Blackbourne livery had approached him on horseback to inform him that his wife had had an accident. He had offered his horse to get home speedily and taken his place with the carriage. No one in the Scythemore household had thought it anything other than what it seemed at the time, for such things happen.

There had also been a note delivered for the Marquess, which Dom was informed of immediately. The Duke's staff had been about to give it to the Marquess' driver when they had returned from the Asylum. The note read:

Thank you for making this so easy. I will make sure she suffers while you flounder about, wondering what you could have done differently.

-Claymore

The truth of it nearly undid him.

He wracked his formidable brain for a solution. He couldn't just sit here while that lunatic took her from him. To have her back only to lose her again…

He felt the pain begin to gnaw at the edges of his mind.

No.

Not this time. He would not let himself succumb to it if it meant Ivy's anguish at Claymore's hands.

"What is it?" Dom asked, his eyes skimming over his friend's foreboding face.

"It's a long story."

Dom crossed his arms. "I have time."

"But Ivy doesn't," Ash replied, shaking his head.

"Tell me."

Ash looked at Scythemore. He trusted the man more than anything, but he had already done enough for him this night. Perhaps one more favor though... "Your hunting hounds. Are they as good as you say?"

Dom smirked. "Better."

Scythemore collected one of his hounds from the back of the house. The dog's tail swished back and forth as he waggled right up to Ash, straining at his leash.

"This is Jasper," Dom introduced him. The dog's deeply wrinkled brow didn't stop him from looking up at his master expectantly at the sound of his name. "He can track just about anything. He once tracked a little girl over seven kilometers who had been lost in the woods for three days. But a person on a moving carriage is going to be trickier. I don't know how long he'll be able to track him for, but the more time that passes, the harder it will be."

Asher frowned as he crouched down to the dog's eye level. "You've used them to track people?"

Dom nodded. "I don't hunt, Ash. Never have. I've let others use them for hunting on my estates, but that's not what they're meant for."

Ash rubbed the dog's velvety ears that flopped down around his face. "You use them to find people," he said in wonderment.

"Yes. Jasper has found six people so far. After storms, in the snow... The local magistrate even requested him last year to find a child who had been taken by his relative. Jasper found the child and culprit in under an hour."

"Remarkable." Ash smiled at Jasper, whose jowls

trembled as his tongue lapped out towards Asher's face. He whispered to the dog, knowing this was the only way he could save Ivy. "Will you help me find her, boy? I can't live without her."

Jasper licked Ash's face in response. That would do.

Dom let Jasper catch the scent of Claymore's note, and then led him out to the street. Gas lampposts emitted light from either side of the roadway, catching reflecting fragments of tiny snowflakes in the light. However, the inky blackness of night still prevailed, threatening the comfort of anyone who found themselves out of doors at this hour. Their breaths puffed out in clouds of white as Jasper immediately bayed and began to pull ferociously at his leash. The Duke loosened his tight reign, letting the dog have his heading. "That's it. Good boy," he urged him on.

Ash and Dom followed the dog, sometimes running, walking, or waiting for Jasper to pick up the scent again at an intersection. The streets of Mayfair at this time of night were almost empty, save for the occasional carriage or people going to and from the entrances of homes lining the street. If someone happened to glance their way, Ash tipped his head to them and moved along quickly without a word, past caring about the oddity of their situation.

Jasper kept his nose to the ground for the most part, slobbering on the cobblestones and wood blockers as he sniffed the ground with avid concentration. It was fortunate the street sweepers had had little to do for the past few days, as only a dusting of snow layered the ground.

Ash wondered if Jasper's nose felt the cold, and if it affected his sense of smell. It was obvious after a little while that both of them felt the bitter cold settling into their bones, but neither man complained. There were bigger things to worry about. At one point, Dom traded his black greatcoat and gloves to Ash to wear for a bit, and he didn't refuse the gesture dressed as he was in only the thin gray shirt the asylum has issued him.

While they followed Jasper out of Mayfair and into the more populated area of Covent Garden, Ash told Dom about Claymore. Dom listened with his usual unruffled silence, waiting until Ash was done before speaking.

A carriage clopped towards them, and Dom pulled Jasper out of the road for it to pass before they continued along the middle of the street. "How long has this man been writing letters to Jacob Wollard?" he asked.

Ash blew on his hands to warm them as they walked briskly. "I don't know." Images of Ivy's letters flashed in his mind. "The first letter I saw was dated October 1838. But based on what Ivy has told me, her father has received letters from him for quite some time before that."

"I only wonder what manner of man we are dealing with. How long has he been planning this? How old is he?"

"We have run into the same problem. With so little information, it has been nearly impossible to know anything about him. However, he is either twenty-eight or forty-one years old."

Dom grunted. "Either way, he is most likely fit and able to defend himself."

"Agreed. Hopefully, your pistol should be a deterrent to any physical combat." Ash nodded to Dom's waist where his flintlock rested at his hip.

"It's a handy thing, I'll admit. Made in America."

"You trust a foreign weapon?" Ash asked him.

"The Americans may be brash, but their weapons are the finest you can buy."

Ash certainly hoped so because Ivy had now been in Claymore's company for over two hours. Who knew what the man could have done to her in that time?

His terror at the thought of what might have already happened to her overwhelmed him for a brief second before he forced it down to a place where it couldn't reach him. He couldn't afford to let his fear paralyze him now.

They continued to talk of weapons, crossing over the Thames and beyond as Jasper led them onward. The streets here were empty, no late-night entertainments to be had near this industrial area. The cold ate into their energy and numbed their exposed skin as they trudged on until Jasper stopped dead in his tracks and brought his head up, ears perked.

Ash stopped, too. "What is it?"

Dom frowned. "I don't know." He tried giving the dog a sniff of the letter again, but the dog simply sat down on the spot, looking up at them. "He must have lost the scent."

Ash sighed and looked around them for anything that might lead them onward. "We can't stop now."

"I would never suggest it," Dom said, giving Jasper a pat on the head and a small piece of dried meat from his pocket. Jasper's tail thumped on the ground as he chewed noisily on the treat.

Ahead of them, London Bridge Station loomed, its twin iron gates beckoning. "Thomas Claymore," he murmured. "He's in the railway business. I wonder…"

"You think he would bring her here?" Dom asked, looking up at the gates and the columns beyond.

The station was open to the air, a complicated pantheon-style train depot in the heart of London.

Despite its design, however, Ash couldn't see anything of the inside as no street lamps had yet been erected to illuminate the structure. Trains did not stop at this station after dark, so there was no need to light the area for pedestrians.

"Perhaps. There's only one way to find out," he said, approaching the gates. They were locked with a large ironworks key bolt system, and Ash knew it wasn't one that could be picked. "Bollocks."

"If Claymore does have her in there, there must be another way in," Dom said.

They skirted the wall separating the station from the street. The iron bars could have been climbed, but they both agreed that Jasper should stay with them in case the dog picked up Claymore's scent again.

As they rounded a corner, exactly that happened. Jasper woofed and lunged forward, putting his nose to the ground once more.

Ash breathed a sigh of relief. They were close. He could feel it.

He only hoped he wasn't too late.

****

Cold water trickled down her cheek, and Ivy spluttered. Blinking, she looked up to see Claymore's face above her, an awful smile on his face.

"Time to wake up, little one," he told her, wiping at the water on her cheek with his thumb.

Heart pounding, she looked around, struggling to remember where she was. Her wrists throbbed, and she straightened, taking the weight of her body from them. Her mind was fuzzy and slow as if her thoughts moved underwater.

Claymore stood in front of her, looking more relaxed than he should have as he watched her eyes dart.

When she tried to move, it became clear her

limbs were all tightly secured to something behind her. She was standing against a hard surface, her wrists and ankles bound to it. Her feet stood apart while her wrists were bound close together above her head. Aching from the strain, her shoulders felt as if they would dislodge from their sockets at any moment. The restraints seemed to have been made for a taller person as she struggled to not put strain on her wrists.

Nothing looked familiar. In the dark, she could barely see a set of train tracks to her right, and she seemed to be under the shelter of some sort of building with columns lining the length of what she assumed was a railway platform. A lantern sat emitting light from a few feet away, casting dancing shadows over her filthy dress.

Yes, it had to be a train depot. Which one, she had no idea.

How did she get here? Her breaths came fast as a wave of panic swept through her.

Then she remembered.

She had been in the carriage and had jumped out, hitting the ground roughly and rolling over the cobblestones. Then Claymore had come after her. Before she could even rise, he had yanked her up by her hair and chastised her for trying to escape. Crying out, she had tried to reach for her knife, but couldn't manage it. The last thing she remembered was a sweet-smelling cloth smothering her mouth and sending her into a swirl of black.

He had drugged her, which explained her sluggishness.

Ivy looked at Claymore, her lips curling into a snarl. He was a tall man of good proportions, and his clothes were expensive. Not Asher Blackbourne expensive, yet it was clear he was a man of means. He would have been handsome, but his face was pockmarked with scars and tiny divots, possibly from a previous illness. Eyes of indiscernible color possessed a manic light that drew in the darkness around them like a maelstrom.

He watched her process her surroundings with a small smile. "You're like a little bird on a branch," he said softly. "I could watch you all day."

Ivy swallowed, her mouth full of cotton. "So…" she cleared her throat. "I'm to be tied to the tracks, is it? A little cliché, don't you think?" She looked to the left where a round metal cog-wheel was attached to the boards to which she was bound. She knew whatever it was didn't bode well for herself.

"You read too many novels, Miss Morganstern." He chuckled. "And no, I would never do anything so inelegant." Claymore reached out and stroked a hand down her neck, his fingers lingering on the skin beneath her earlobe.

She strained her neck away from his warm fingers, but the straps holding her to the wall didn't leave much room for movement.

Staring at her throat, he said, "Specimens such as yourself deserve ceremony. The subtleties of releasing someone's soul from their body is an art." He met her eyes with his dark ones and smiled. "I don't want to watch your body fly into a million pieces. I want to observe the light leave your eyes second by second. Do you see the difference?"

Ivy's breath hitched. "Not even a little bit."

Claymore just smiled and folded his arms. "You don't seem surprised by your situation."

"Should I be?" She took a deep breath, willing the white blur at the edge of her mind to clear. Ivy let out words she had kept from herself all this time. "I think I always knew it would come to this."

"Really?" He shifted his weight. "That's quite interesting. Why would you think that, I wonder? Do you feel destiny's hand upon you, as I do?"

Ivy snorted and twitched her nose as a stray snowflake alighted upon the tip of it. "What I feel is that insane people do insane things, and I have known you're insane for a long time. It was always my responsibility."

He frowned. "Why should you feel responsibility?" Waving, he didn't wait for her to respond. "It's of no matter. I don't particularly care. I think I'm too excited for what comes next to quibble with you any longer."

Ivy watched him smile, his teeth a flash in his pitted face. Her breaths were shallow and fast. She knew what came next.

Claymore came closer, and she held her breath. She felt his hands slide around her neck, the touch both panicking and reminding her of another night in which Ash had caressed her neck so carefully.

Where are you, Ash? I need you.

"I thought you would struggle more, to be honest," Claymore admitted, fitting something cold around her throat. He buckled it with a practiced hand, the metal seeming to burn her skin.

"I know men like you," she said. "It won't matter if I struggle."

"You keep saying things that intrigue me, but it won't work." He stepped back again, his hand resting on something to the left of her head. "Are you not afraid at all?" he asked her, looking into her eyes.

She looked straight back, saying, "If there is only the one thing I can do to lessen your pleasure, I will do it. So if you want to see me cower and grovel, you will leave here unsatisfied."

His nostrils flared. "I doubt you will feel the same soon."

Ivy shrugged as much as she could and deliberately looked away.

A creaking sound of metal on metal rang out. Suddenly, the strap around her throat tightened.

Her airway constricted, and she choked, her fingers curling.

He made a sound of satisfaction. "Lovely." His breathing became heavier.

Ivy tried to suck in air, but couldn't quite get enough to satisfy her starved lungs.

Claymore turned the crank again, the rhythmic clanks quick in her ears.

Water streamed from her wide eyes, and she arched her back as terror at the lack of air blazed through her body.

"Yes, that's it," Claymore whispered. His mouth hung slack as he watched.

Ivy squirmed, darkness impinging on the edges of her vision as she struggled to free her limbs.

"Please," she gasped.

The strap abruptly loosened with a turn of the wheel in the opposite direction.

Ivy drew in lungfuls of air, her breaths ragged. She coughed as Claymore took a deep breath and ran a shaking hand over his lips.

He licked his lips and put a hand to her neck, running a finger along the edge of the strap. "I've heard there's a euphoria that happens when one's air is restricted. Is it true?"

"No," she rasped. She was dizzy, and she had felt a slight rush as air came back into her lungs, but she wouldn't give him the satisfaction.

"I'm glad I decided to put the hand restraints

above you. The way you toss about is quite becoming."

"You're sick." She continued to take deep breaths, dreading the inevitability of her air being cut off again. Tingling needles shot through her wrists as she twisted them, fearful of the numbness that had crept into her hands from their position.

"I've come to understand that people will never see the potential of things the way I do. But someday, when my work is more fully developed, there will be no denying the contribution I have made to humanity."

Ivy laughed weakly. "Contribution to humanity?" She shook her head, wincing as the leather strap chaffed her neck. "You're hardly giving out food to the poor or taking in lost puppies, you imbecile."

He came forward with a smile, wiping a stray tendril of hair from her forehead. "Ah, there is the fight in you."

She turned her head, the tears on her cheeks cold in the night air. "Don't touch me."

"Or what? What will you do?" he said softly. His breath fanned her face, smelling of black licorice.

She hated black licorice.

"It's brilliant, isn't it?" he asked, his eyes moving over the contraption that held her captive. "Perfect control over human life. It makes everything slow enough to savor. One should enjoy their work, don't you agree?"

She tried not to gag at the sickly sweet vapor from his lips. "Quite, yes. Why wouldn't anyone get their jollies choking someone to death? Oh, that's right— because it's deranged."

His teeth made a squeaking sound as he ground them together. "What a silly little girl you are. Quaking in your ignorance, trying to prove you are not afraid of what will happen to you."

"I know what will happen. It doesn't matter. Because Blackbourne will find you, and when he does, your suffering will far outweigh anything you can do to me." She smiled seeing his eyes widen and then narrow for a brief moment.

Finally, he grinned back, his straight teeth reflecting the lantern light. "Well, then, I had better let myself give into temptation while I can." He reached his hand up to the cog wheel and pulled the handle towards himself.

Ivy took in a breath halfway just as the bruising pressure pinched off her air supply. Her mouth opened of its own accord, the instinct to take in air overwhelming her knowledge that she couldn't. It was as if she had no control over her own faculties as her body arched outward, struggling towards anything that would allow her lungs to expand again. Her limbs twisted in their restraints, desperate to find a way out.

Claymore put a hand to her waist, his eyes riveted on her face.

She bucked against his hand, past caring about his fingers sliding over her stomach as she writhed. Inky blackness darted into her field of vision, scattering her thoughts.

He drew back on the crank so that the strap loosened ever so slightly.

Ivy gulped, drawing in a trickle of air. Yet it was barely enough to stave off the darkness that threatened her consciousness.

"So beautiful," he breathed, his hand smoothing over the front of her dress to cup her breast.

A wave of nausea swept through her, sending chills along the tiny hairs of her arms and legs. "No one will know. Maybe just this once..." he whispered, stepping closer until his hips brushed against hers.

Ivy flattened herself against the boards behind her as much as possible, unable to voice a protest. Her throat burned from trying to suck in air as she choked. She felt his hardness push against her belly, and panic flashed through her in a hot burst.

Please no, she prayed. Not like this. She closed her eyes against the sensation of his leg sliding between hers.

"Don't pretend as if you don't enjoy my attentions," he murmured, wetting his lips and lowering them to hers.

What little air she had been surviving on was muted as he fit his slimy mouth over her own. She tried to twist away, but the cuff digging into her neck wouldn't let her move.

Just as she opened her mouth to chomp down on his lower lip, the strap loosened with a movement of his hand.

She breathed in air scented with his noxious breath, the cold mingling with his heat.

"Kiss me," he told her, shoving his knee between hers and pinning her to the rough wood. She tried to close her legs to his invasion, but her ankles were cuffed too far apart, exposing her to his effortless access. His lips mashed against hers, and she shrieked into his mouth.

He pressed harder, forcing his tongue past her teeth.

The cuffs of her restraints rattled as she fought to free her limbs.

She bit down hard on his tongue, and salty warmth flowed into her mouth.

He roared, stumbling backwards.

Ivy spat his blood out, breathing hard. Satisfaction and relief coursed through her.

Claymore wiped his mouth, growling. "You must think you're above the honor I'm giving you. You were nothing, just a rich man's whore, before I chose you."

Ivy laughed, the sound trickling from her body in a wheeze. "And you're just another common bastard who thinks his sick fantasies are special."

Claymore growled and strode up to her again. He took her throat in his hand and squeezed until she gasped. "You have no idea what I'm capable of."

"Yes, I do," she panted. "You're just like him, and you're both idiots for thinking you're something superior."

"Like whom? I am like no one," he scoffed. His eyes cut into hers like daggers daring her to say anything else he wouldn't tolerate.

She let out a puff of breath that turned to vapor in the air in front of her. "You're all the same. You, my father…"

"Was your father cruel to you, little girl? That means nothing to me."

Ivy blinked and then began to laugh, the sound manic to her ears. Tears leaked out from her eyes, a product of her terror and hysteria. She let her torso sag for a moment as her peels of laughter rang out, then cringed as the pressure caused the straps at her wrists to slice further into them. "You don't know who I am."

"What are you talking about?" he snarled, putting more pressure on her windpipe.

Ivy coughed and spluttered. "My father … is…"

He unclenched his fingers from her throat, but kept them there.

Once she had caught her breath, she said in a ragged voice, "Your precious hero." She watched his brows contract as he narrowed his eyes. "I am the only daughter of Jacob Wollard."

Claymore's eyes widened in horror, and he mouth went slack. He stepped back, dropping his hands. His boots crunched in the smattering of snow beneath them.

Ivy smiled, his reaction like a balm to her exhausted body.

"No," he whispered. "It can't be."

She smirked. "Why do you think the Marquess was looking for you? I asked him to do so."

"You ... you're Jacob Wollard's—?"

"I know. I'm not happy about it either, so we have that in common."

His chest heaved. She could see he was at war with himself, the look in his eyes different now as they swept her person. "I cannot— Please forgive me. I did not know." He stepped towards her and held out a hand almost reverently. She half expected him to drop to his knees before her.

"Your contrition comes a bit late, wouldn't you agree?"

He took quick, long strides until he was behind her, and she could no longer see him. After a moment, the cuff at her neck slackened, then the ones at her wrists as well. Her arms dropped, and she cried out, pain jolting through them at the sudden lack of support. She fell forward, hugging herself as her ankles were then freed.

Ivy's teeth chattered as throbbing pain entered her previously numb extremities. As she crouched there, arms around her knees, Claymore bent down beside her.

"Are you all right, Miss Wollard?"

Recoiling, she looked him in the eye. "How could I possibly be all right?"

He rose and turned his back to her, running a hand over his face. "If I had known, I would never have ... that is, I could never hurt the child of my greatest mentor. I would never dishonor Jacob Wollard by harming someone of his own flesh and blood."

She craned her neck to look up at his backside. "Yet you would hurt someone else's loved one?"

His words could become meaningless any second, and so she forced her aching arm to reach around to slide her knife from her corset. She grimaced as she quickly drew her arm in again, hiding the knife between her crossed forearms in front of her.

He did not turn around. "That's different."

"No, it's not." She attempted to clear her rasping throat, but the pain remained. "And eventually, it wouldn't matter whose daughter I was. You would kill me without thought if you felt your need grow. My father did the same to his own wife, no matter what he felt for her."

Claymore turned back to her. "You do not think I can control myself?" He bent down and cupped her cheek in his hand. Stroking his thumb across the bridge of her nose, he smiled wistfully. "I admit, it is difficult with you. You're far too lovely to leave alone."

Ivy's heart beat erratically. She did not know what he would do next.

"I wonder..." he muttered. He brought his face closer to hers and hesitated, his damp breath ticking her face.

She fingered the knife and clenched it at the ready in her palm.

"Perhaps I was meant to find you." He cupped his hand around the back of her neck and drew her forward, closing the distance between them.

Ivy drew her arm out from between them, the warmed metal familiar in her stiff hand. As he touched his lips to hers, she grit her teeth and rammed the knife into his belly with all the force she could muster. It went in more smoothly then she would have guessed, like cutting through raw meat.

Claymore gasped in surprise, his hand dropping from her neck.

Ivy wrenched the knife out and scrambled backwards, ready for a retaliatory attack. Memories of learning to use the blade she carried flooded in, and she drew her legs under her to a crouched position.

Claymore clutched his stomach and looked down, his face a mask of shock as his hand came away with blood on it. He began to rise, but fell back onto his knees with a groan. "You-you—" He grimaced, scrunching his eyes shut.

Her heart pounded in her ears, and the energy flowing through her veins contrasted garishly with the peaceful snowflakes wandering through the air to rest on the ground. When it became clear Claymore wasn't able to steady himself, she rose cautiously.

Standing over him, her hands began to tremble. A feeling of terrible power came over her as she realized the control she held over him. Eyes fixed on his hunched form, Ivy squeezed the handle of the knife harder, as if doing so would wring the answer she sought from its gleaming surface.

She could kill him.

Right now, she could rid the world of his presence and any fear of him would be gone. It would be quick. All she had to do was pull his head back and slice his throat… Ivy saw the action play out, bright spatters of blood landing on the tussled snow where she had been only a moment ago. He would fall forward, gurgling as his own blood choked him to death.

It wasn't as if he didn't deserve it. In fact, it might very well be the right thing to do. If she didn't, and he left here with the ability to carry out his tendencies on someone else again…

The part of her she feared most knew she wasn't just quibbling about right and wrong. Ivy understood it was the instinctual violence begotten of her father that would now determine Claymore's fate.

What would it feel like?

Would the blood be warm against her chilled hands as she sliced through his stubbled skin? Would she feel satisfaction at the sight of his life slipping out of him second by second? The motion would be easy, a practiced movement of the hand she had done again and again while sparring with her friend years ago.

Tipton would have been proud of her for incapacitating her adversary as she had done. Would he approve of ending this man's life if she could?

Would her father?

She swallowed, trying not to think about it and failing. She had never been sure if her father had considered his actions wrong or not. He hadn't indicated so either way, even in newspaper interviews. For certain, he would approve of her defending her life. Even in prison, he had been protective of his only child.

But this wouldn't be defending herself.

The roaring in her ears drowned out the sound of Claymore's grunts. He lay on his side now, hands over his stomach. Blood had seeped through his shirt, his hands now soaked in it.

She didn't know if the wound she had dealt was a fatal one. Perhaps she had killed him already.

Panic at the thought seized her. Her feet were rooted to the ground, and her chest tightened until she felt as though she were still being strangled by that infernal device.

Had she just become a murderer without even making the decision?

"Please," Claymore croaked, reaching out a hand

across the ground. "Help me."

She stepped back out of his reach. She didn't want to help him.

If she stood here and watched him die, was that the same as killing him?

And if she did kill him, what did that make her?

What if taking someone's life created an irrevocable desire in her for killing, as it had her father? If this was a test, she feared she would fail. She would become just like him, taking human life without conscience or regret, needing that feeling of power over and over.

Holding his life in her hands was heady, she could admit to herself.

Was it simply an instinct for survival that created this potent feeling? Was it besting an opponent? Pride?

Or was this what her father had felt every time he took life from someone fighting to live?

Despite the cold, she was perspiring, the knife growing slippery in her fumbling hand. Glancing down at it, Ivy then turned her eyes back to Claymore.

He was pitiful now, not the towering figure from her nightmares any longer. Deep furrows marred his brow and he trembled, whether from blood loss or the cold, she didn't know.

No one was coming. No one would take the situation from her hands.

Ivy closed her eyes and sighed. She couldn't leave him there.

The decision immediately cast a blanket of heaviness over her, for there was only one choice left. She couldn't live with herself if he went away from this place to inflict pain on someone else. Yet neither could she take the risk of helping him enough to turn him in to Scotland Yard.

If she were anyone else—if she were actually Corrine Morganstern—she could hobble away from this place with her life, and not a single person would blame her. She would be lauded for escaping such a horrific fate, and not one would ever think a lady would attempt to control this situation against such a man.

Yet she was not who or what anyone thought her to be.

She had to kill him.

Forgive me, she prayed, tears running in hot rivulets down her face and then quickly turning cold.

She blinked, reaching up to touch the wetness on her cheek. Then she laughed in relief.

Tears. Not of triumph, but of sadness. She could not have the same inherited viciousness as her father if the thought of taking this wretched man's life caused her sorrow.

Ivy put her hands on her face, feeling her skin as if for the first time. She had not betrayed herself, nor the morals she tried to live by. The authority she held over Claymore and the actions she would take here tonight did not define the recesses of her heart. Ivy dropped her hands to her sides, the knife firm in her grip again. *I am not my father.*

Smiling tremulously, she forced herself to step forward. If this was what must happen, she was thankful for the callousness granted to her from years of caring for naught but survival. She took another step until her creaking limbs unhinged themselves and obeyed, taking her towards where Claymore lay prostrate.

She skirted him cautiously, aware of his every movement. It would have to be quick if she wanted to mitigate the chance of him fighting her. Even deathly injured men would fight for their life if they knew what was happening.

She swallowed, a sour taste in her mouth at the thought.

As she made her way behind him, he didn't make any movements except for the shivers that wracked his large frame. The dampness at the hem of her skirts weighed heavily and caused swishing sounds on the paving stones as she positioned herself over him.

The thick thatch of hair on Claymore's head boded well for her purposes.

Everything was muted as she listened to her own heartbeat thudding inside her like an animal in a cage.

You must do it, she told herself, fighting the nausea that was bubbling up. The handle of her dagger pressed an imprint into her palm as she gripped it tightly.

One deep breath.

With a swift motion, she crouched down, grabbed a hank of dark hair, and pulled his head up back towards herself. Her dagger came to his throat in a flash, and she pressed it to the taut flesh, preparing to slice from under one earlobe to the other.

As her thumb pressed the knife into his skin, Claymore let out a roar. He reached for the dagger as Ivy gasped and tried to wrench herself away from his reach.

It was no use.

He pried the weapon from her grip and pulled her over his shoulder to slam her into the hard ground. She landed with a bone-jarring thud that knocked the wind from her and scraped the skin from her shoulder blades. She gasped, scrunching her eyes in pain.

Knowing she could not afford to lay idly before him, she forced herself to turn over so she could use her hands and knees to rise.

Claymore didn't let her, putting a large hand on her shoulder and yanking her onto her back once more.

She blindly clawed at him, crying out as he

grabbed her hair in one fist. Her legs tried to kick, but they were mired in her dense skirts as he rose over her.

"Be still," he commanded. His chest rose and fell rapidly as he held her own knife to her throat.

Ivy froze and looked into his pale face, shrinking at the rage in his eyes that were too bright. He had lost a lot of blood, which she was now lying in.

"You're mine now," he said hoarsely. His right knee pinned her hips to the ground while his other hand pulled her hair back as she had been doing to him not a moment before.

He would kill her now.

This was how her life ended. In bloodshed, without anyone who cared about her to see. It was probably fitting, for her life had been steeped in carnage since before she could remember.

I'm sorry, Ash, she called out silently. She hoped he would find peace in this life. Perhaps he would find her in the next one.

Ivy breathed out a sigh and closed her eyes as the blade hovered over her throat. It was time.

Chapter Nineteen

Ash and Dom followed Jasper through the gap in the brick wall where two railway platforms met. The dog was ferociously following Claymore's scent again, his jowls quivering with excitement.

Once they were fully inside the station, everything was slated into shades of gray and black as the street lamps' light faded behind them. They passed a ticket booth that was closed up for the night, its glass-front window giving an eerie reflection of the two men in the pale moonlight. All was quiet, and then…

Ash heard voices from up around the corner of the platform. Dom pulled his gun from his holster and cocked the action lever. Ash ran towards the faint sounds, striding ahead of Dom and Jasper, whose ears were now pointed towards the sound.

"How could I possibly be all right?" the muffled voice echoed.

He paused. It was Ivy's voice, cold and furious.

Thank God. She was still alive.

Jasper whined from behind him, his tail thumping on Dom's leg. The hound knew he had found his quarry.

Ash took another step towards her voice, ready to round the corner of the platform towards where he could see another row of columns began, separating the two waiting areas.

"I'll take that, Guvnor," a voice from behind them said cheerfully.

Ash turned back towards Dom, who was holding his hands up. A man stood behind him, pressing a pistol into his back.

Dom un-cocked his gun, and the man grabbed it

from his hand. Ash could see the fury in Dom's face as his jaw ticked.

"Thank you, Sirrah. You two are always a boon to me, ye are."

Dom turned to face the man, giving Ash a better view of him. He narrowed his eyes. That voice was familiar, as was the bald head shining in the moon's rays. "Franco?"

The escaped prisoner took a step back and bowed. "At your service, Milords."

"Some hound you are," Dom said to Jasper, who was sitting with legs splayed beside him, not the least concerned for his master's safety.

"Franco, we don't have time for this," Ash warned, his heartrate rising. She was so close and yet the universe conspired to thwart his attempts to get to her. "We need that weapon now."

"That's not gunna happen, now is it? This'll fetch a pretty price in Seven Dials, it will," he said, turning the pistol this way and that.

"Why are you even here?" Dom asked, his deep voice rife with aggravation.

He twirled Dom's pistol round his forefinger. "Saw you two strollin' along. Oy've been following you since Tavistock Street. Seemed like a strange thing, two Coves and a dog running about in the middle of the night. Decided I'd see wot's afoot since I hadn't anyfing else on me schedule. Turned out right beneficial, if I may say so." He grinned.

Ash rubbed his face. "Fine. Take the damn thing. Now shut up and get out of here."

"But you haven't told me wot it is you're up to." He sounded like a child denied a sweetmeat.

"Why do you care?" Dom ground out.

"I feel invested, I do."

"Franco, if you don't leave immediately, I swear I will bring Scotland Yard down around your ears, and they will not stop searching for you until you're back in New Bridewell."

Franco's shoulders slumped. "Fine. If that's how it's to be. I thought we were getting along right fine just now."

"Give me back that gun, and I'll show you how well we're getting along," Dom growled.

The fugitive stood up straight. "I rightfully stole this now, didn't I? No need to be getting angry. You can buy another one," he reasoned.

"Goodbye, Franco," Ash said pointedly.

"No appreciation for honest thieving," Franco grumbled, turning away and slipping back into the darkness.

Ash looked at Dom. Dom shrugged. They were now weaponless against Claymore.

Why fate had forced them to help that rodent Franco was a mystery he would never solve.

Ash didn't bother to ruminate on it now. He moved forward, Dom and Jasper following behind. When he came around the corner onto the next platform, his heart stopped.

Ivy was on the ground, Claymore on top of her with a knife to her throat. He could see blood in the light from the lantern nearby soiling the white snow in clumps.

Was it Ivy's blood? He couldn't tell.

"You're mine now," Claymore said to her. He leaned over her, adjusting his grip on the knife.

"Stop!" Ash called out. The element of surprise was useless if he could not get there in time.

Claymore looked up, his eyes wide in surprise. He was a muscular man with bold features that cast hulking shadows on the ground in front of where he knelt. It was Thomas Claymore, all right, the maturity of his face showing him to have lost the roundness a younger man night have had.

There was some sort of wooden wall with ominous-looking straps protruding from it set up in the middle of the platform near them, looking out of place. Ash didn't spare it attention for the moment. All that mattered was Ivy and that Claymore didn't move the knife he held precariously against her neck.

Claymore growled and sat back on his haunches, keeping his knife hand where it was. "Lord Blackbourne, I presume?"

"Yes," Ash answered as calmly as he could. He took steps towards them slowly, not wanting to alarm him.

As Claymore shifted his weight, he held a hand to his stomach, wincing almost imperceptibly.

Ash's eyes were drawn to the man's abdomen, and he realized Claymore was injured and bleeding steadily. He didn't doubt Ivy had done that to him, her talents extending beyond what the average lady would have had at her disposal.

Claymore nodded towards Jasper and Dom standing a few feet away. "You used a dog to track me?" Claymore chuckled, shaking his head. "I applaud your resourcefulness, Blackbourne, and whoever the hell you are," he said to Dom. "But this doesn't concern you. If you turn around and leave, I will not spill her blood while you watch." To make his point, Claymore pressed his hand more closely against Ivy's throat, eliciting a cry from her.

Ash stepped forward again. "If you hurt her, you are a dead man," he assured him. "I am not going to leave, and threats against her are not in your benefit because there will be nothing standing between you and I if she is gone."

"You think I fear you and your lackey?" Claymore sneered.

Dom snorted, stepping up alongside Ash. "I don't think anyone's ever called me that before."

Claymore answered. "There's a first time for everyth—"

Before he could finish, Jasper suddenly lunged forward with a baying call.

"Jasper, no!" The leash slipped from Dom's hand, and the dog took bounding leaps towards Claymore and Ivy.

Upon seeing the great hound barreling towards him, Claymore leapt up, preparing for attack. Ivy rose up on her elbows, and Ash gave thanks she looked relatively unharmed.

"He won't hurt you," Dom yelled, and Ash could hear the panic in his friend's voice.

Jasper rushed up to Claymore in clumsy bounces, his tail wagging frantically. It was clear he was beside himself with joy to find the person he had been tasked with searching for. As Jasper reached Claymore and attempted to put his paws on the man's thigh in celebration, Claymore drew back the knife. Ash watched as he grabbed the dog by one ear and jerked him sideways. Jasper yelped, but the gesture didn't deter him, determined as he was to check on his target. The dog jumped back up on his hind legs again, and this time, Claymore didn't hesitate, thrusting the knife into Jasper's torso.

"NO!" Dom roared, running forward.

Jasper howled, falling onto his back before trying to rise again.

Ivy stood to her feet.

Calculations burst like fireworks in Ash's mind. Force and velocity of the blade, blood loss in an animal of Jasper's size, the odds of the knife having missed the creature's lungs or heart... They were not good.

Ash ran after Dom, who was sprinting straight for Jasper.

Claymore lunged towards Ivy, trying to regain his hostage.

He would not let him touch her again.

Upon seeing Claymore's direction, Ivy turned and began to run, her skirts tripping her as she went.

Dom reached Jasper and slid onto his knees, cradling the dog's head on his thighs.

Claymore caught Ivy by the wrist just as Ash reached him.

With a roar, he tackled Claymore, heedless of the knife the man still held. He knocked Claymore off his feet, but the man rolled away before Ash could stop him. Rising, they faced each other, both understanding that only one of them left this place with their life or their freedom.

Circling, Claymore eventually darted forward, attempting a slash at Ash's midriff.

"No!" Ivy screamed from where she stood against one of the columns on the platform.

Ash nimbly dodged the motion and back away. He knew he was at a disadvantage without a weapon, but there was nothing...

The lantern. Ash's gaze slid to the right where the lantern sat on the ground.

Claymore followed the direction of Ash's eyes and sprung towards it at the same time as Ash.

Getting there a hairsbreadth ahead of Claymore, Ash made a dive for it. Claymore raised his arm to stab downwards at Ash's chest, but Ash scrambled back out of reach just in time, the knife hurling through empty air.

Feeling the platform of Claymore's strangulation device at his back, he used the structure to push himself to his feet, lantern in hand.

"You should run from here," Ash told him, watching for any sudden movements. Claymore's chest was heaving from exertion, and he was pale from blood loss, but he looked ready to fight an army. "You cannot best all of us, and someone will go to Scotland Yard. At the word of a Marquess and a Duke, they will descend upon this place and not rest until you are captured. Go while you still can."

Claymore's jaw clenched as he put a hand over the wound in his abdomen. "I understand the mechanics of time, Lord Blackbourne, and even you cannot manipulate it to suit your ends. If you had not rushed in here tonight, I would have been a step closer to governing the time a man has left to live. But you have no idea the ramifications of anything I'm saying, do you? You don't realize what was lost by your bumbling interruption." He stepped closer to Ash. "It's no matter. After I dispatch you and your friend, I will drag your little whore back and do with her as I had intended, regardless of her bloodlines."

"She will never suffer at your hands again," Ash vowed.

"We will see." Claymore came at Ash with the knife poised to strike at his ribcage. As Claymore thrust the knife forward, Ash saw his intention and dodged to the side of it. He wasn't quite fast enough, the knife ripping through the material of his shirt and scraping the barest sliver of skin from his side. Catching the man's arm, Ash used it as a fulcrum to swing the lantern around to collide with the side of Claymore's head.

The glass walls of the lantern shattered, and lit oil spilled onto the wooden platform as the lantern was jarred from his grasp. Flames began to link at the planks of the device, growing larger every second.

Claymore went down hard, falling onto his back with Ash atop him. They grappled for the knife, Ash holding the man's wrist as Claymore tried to wield it against him.

"Ash, no!" Ivy cried.

"Get away from here," Ash told her, grunting as his opponent kicked him in the pelvis area.

"I'm not leaving," she replied, coming towards them.

"Ivy, get away!" Ash yelled, panicking as she approached.

She didn't listen, but came up to Claymore and began to pry his fingers loose from around the knife as Ash held his wrist to the ground.

Ash met Ivy's eyes for a brief second, orange flames reflected in them.

Claymore bellowed and thrashed more forcefully, bucking Ash off of him. Ash continued to control the man's arms while Ivy accomplished her task. Frenzy boiled in Claymore's eyes as he saw his control circling the drain.

Finally, Ivy wrenched the knife away from him and jumped back out of reach.

Ash let go of Claymore's arm to punch him squarely in the jaw with all the strength he had left. The man went limp immediately, eyes closed and mouth slack.

Ash breathed out heavily, rising. He kept an eye on the man as he went to Ivy and enveloped her in his arms.

She clung to him, letting tears soak into his shirt

as the fire's warmth emanated around them.

"I'll never let anything happen to you ever again," he promised, kissing the top of her damp hair.

"I believe you," she replied, her voice muffled in the folds of Dom's greatcoat.

Dom....

Ash released Ivy and looked over at his friend, who still knelt on the ground. Jasper was still in his lap, the dog's paws twitching feebly.

Approaching his friend, he put a hand on his shoulder. "I'm sorry, old friend. Is he...?"

Ivy knelt down beside Dom and began to stroke Jasper's head. Dom held his cravat pressed against the wound, which was bleeding through the white material. The knife had punctured the dog's armpit, but it was unclear the direction of the thrust. Jasper's eyes were wide and rolling while his muzzle blew out little puffs of air that set his jowls to wobbling.

"He is breathing," Dom said, looking up at Ash. "But I fear he won't last long."

Ash didn't vacillate for a moment. This dog was responsible for saving Ivy's life. "Then we mustn't delay. I have a friend who is a professor at the Royal Veterinary College. He will help."

Ivy smiled at Dom as he gathered Jasper in his arms. "Thank you for everything."

Dom nodded, rising.

Ivy rose as well. "He is a hero," she said firmly, rubbing one of the pup's ears between her fingers.

A noise behind him made Ash turn. Claymore had regained consciousness and was rising to his feet. "Stay down if you know what's good for you," Ash told him, pushing Ivy behind himself.

But it was clear Claymore was beyond reason, the madness in his eyes gleaming from under the sweat on his forehead. He took a step forward, clutching his stomach with one hand.

"You cannot win this," Ash said, holding forth the knife in his hand.

The man didn't listen, grimacing as he began to charge forward. Claymore roared as he gained speed, his manic appearance far removed from the status his elegant clothes implied.

Ash braced himself, stepping forward to meet him. One way or another, he would end this.

Boom.

Just as Claymore raised his arms to attack, he jerked back as if an invisible hand had halted his progression.

The echo of a gunshot reverberated off the platform's many columns.

Ash blinked in confusion, watching as Claymore fell to the ground. A bloom of red appeared on his chest, growing with every second. The man's eyes remained open, but there was no life in them any longer.

Turning to look behind him, Ash saw a pleased Franco standing several feet away, rubbing a gun's still-smoking muzzle on the edge of his shirt.

"You're welcome, Guvnors, Madam," he said, tipping back and forth on the heels of his feet.

"Franco?" Ivy said incredulously.

"Tis I, miss." He bowed. "Figured I'd repay the favor you done me a spell ago."

"Er ... all right."

Franco approached her, Ash ready if the convict tried anything. It was remarkable that she didn't flinch at his nearness, given their history.

"Twas no trouble at'all. Wanted to test me new weapon, I did. And I wanted to ... um ... apologize for wot happened in New Bridewell. I truly didn't want to hurt ye," he confessed, his entire head turning red as an onion.

Ivy raised a brow. "I appreciate the apology, sir. May I ask what it is you were in gaol for? It wouldn't be shooting someone, would it? You have awfully good aim," she commented, looking at the sight of the fallen Claymore.

Franco puffed out his chest. "I was in Her Majesty's Royal Navy, Ma'am."

"Really?" Ash frowned. "How did you come to be in your ... situation?"

Franco stuffed Dom's gun into his waistband. "I was imprisoned for defying my commandin' officer, Milord. Tis a long story, and not a pleasant one, but I don't regret me actions none. Twas the right thing to do."

Ivy took the man's hands. "Franco, we have to go now. But I can truly say you are one of a kind. Take care of yourself, please—for me."

Franco blushed again. "Aye, Miss. That I will." He turned and meandered off into the night, seeming to lack the furtive purpose he usually possessed.

"What about him?" Dom asked, nodding at Claymore's still body.

"I'll report it to Scotland Yard in the morning. The fire won't spread over these stones and snow. Right now, we must get your hound to Dr. Delmere."

Jasper whimpered as Dom readjusted the dog's weight in his grasp.

Ash took one more look at Claymore and then at the device which he had constructed. Its leather straps no longer posed any threat, flames roaring up the vertical portion of it. Still, it sent chills down his spine.

They exited the platform and located Ash's carriage, which had been left on the other side of the train station by Claymore. Ash drove it himself, drudging up racing skills he hadn't used since his wilder days. Ivy and Dom were inside the carriage binding Jasper's wound as best they could. Urging the horses faster, he navigated through the empty maze of London's streets, signs of the city waking starting to appear. The sky was beginning to take on a pale light, and Ash pushed the horses, knowing he needed to get to his destination before the morning's traffic became obtrusive.

Ash remembered where Dr. Delmere lived, having visited the man once before to gain his expertise on rat anatomy for Project Plague. He had been a wealth of information and an animal lover, his cozy home awash with dogs, cats, and even a pet raccoon. Ash knew if there was anyone willing to be disturbed at this hour for the sake of an animal's life, it was Dr. Delmere.

Although he hoped more than anything the hound survived the night, he knew a sense of profound relief that Ivy was now safe. No matter how this venture ended after this point, he could rest assured that Claymore was no longer a threat and she was back in his care again.

He intended to never let her go. Whatever else happened, whatever tricks his mind played on him, it didn't matter. He wouldn't let anything stand in the way of being with her, and he would make certain every day of the rest of her life was happier than the last. She deserved it.

And, he thought, perhaps he did as well.

When they arrived at Dr. Delmere's residence, the man himself opened the door, looking bleary eyed from sleep. Seeing three decidedly disheveled people, one with an injured dog in his arms, his eyes widened. "Oh!" he exclaimed, his gaze drawn to Jasper. "I'll get my supplies. Tea, anyone?"

They went inside, introductions made on the way, following the man to his kitchen where he pulled out a large medicine bag from under the central kneading table. As Ivy explained the injury, Delmere laid down a blanket over the surface of the table, indicating the dog be placed there. Dom carefully laid Jasper down, the dog whining at the movement.

"Shh, you'll be all right," Ivy crooned, petting the beast's head.

The doctor directed Ash to bring two bowls of warm water and some dish cloths, which he did promptly.

Ash watched his friend as Delmere prepared his tools across the table's top. Dom stood a few feet away, jaw clenched, as if coming any closer would cause the doctor's process to fail. He knew the Duke was not one who tolerated the loss of control well, especially when it concerned someone he cared for. Jasper was not just a dog to Dom. The dog was a member of his family, and so Ash went to him and put a hand on his shoulder.

Dom did not react, but kept watching as the doctor began to unwrap the makeshift bandage.

"Hm, yes," Delmere murmured to himself, examining the wound. "No paradoxical chest movements. That is a good sign." He stuck his forefinger into the wound and Jasper rose up off the table with a yelp.

"Hold him, please," Delmere ordered.

Dom came forward and silently held Jasper's head and body down while Ivy held his back legs.

Ash felt helpless watching and began to pray that God would take pity on the poor beast. Such things should not happen to creatures like Jasper, whose only crime was wanting to please his master.

Jasper's cries intensified as Delmere opened up the wound and dug into it with his fingers. After delving around in it for what seemed like a lifetime, he held the dog's leg up and poked it with a wicked-looking scalpel down the length of it. Jasper did not react.

Once he had pressed a compress to the wound to slow the bleeding, Delmere sighed. "There is good news and bad news, I'm afraid," he announced.

"Will he live?" Dom asked, his low tones causing Jasper's ears to perk at the sound.

"I cannot say," he admitted. "Although the blow missed his lungs, there is internal bleeding due to a nick of the liver, which could pollute his other humors. Canine livers are situated higher than humans.' And I am afraid his leg…" He shook his head. "The connections have been severed. His leg will have to be amputated either way. It is now a matter of whether he can survive the procedure."

Dom swallowed visibly. "And if we do nothing?"

"If we do nothing, he will bleed to death within an hour, perhaps less."

With shaking hands, Dom softly stroked his hound's neck.

Ivy sniffed, tears falling from her red eyes. Ash pulled her to him, and she leaned her head on his shoulder.

Dom cleared his throat. "Then we have no time to waste. Do whatever it takes, and I will make you the richest veterinarian this side of the Atlantic."

Delmere's eyes widened. "I will do what I can, Your Grace, but not for your money. I would like nothing more than to see him live through the night."

Dom did not waver. "You will get it either way."

"It will not be pleasant to watch for those with delicate constitutions." Delmere looked at Ivy.

"I am staying," she declared, wiping her eyes. "I have seen worse than this."

Delmere nodded, his eyes lingering on the ring of

angry red around her neck. "It seems you have. Let's begin."
****

It was close to four hours later when Ivy finally fell into bed beside Ash. She had elected for the quickest bath in the history of mankind when they'd arrived home, her exhaustion catching up to her in dizzying waves. Her bones felt weighted, every muscle screaming at her movements.

Ash had evidently been waiting for her, his damp blond locks curling over his brow as he lounged on the counterpane. Her breath hitched as she took in his long limbs and open-throated shirt. "I hope you're not expecting a rousing welcome into my bed tonight," she told him, keeping her distance from his heat beside her. "I fear my response would wound your pride."

He frowned, his eyes moving to her neck, which was bruised all the way around from Claymore's contraption. With visible effort, he forced his eyes to her face and unclenched his jaw. "Although I'd like to, I'm not so cold-hearted as to make you bend to my lascivious whims after the night you've had." He held out an arm to her, and she cautiously scooted nearer, laying her wet head carefully on his chest.

Sighing, she settled into his warmth, her nightgown bunched around her thighs. Ash casually traced circles with his fingertips on her bare shoulder, making the hairs on her arms raise. His large frame surrounding hers had to be the best feeling in all the world.

"You were right," Ash said softly, using his other arm to draw her closer into himself.

"I know," Ivy replied. "About what, exactly?"

"Me. About everything. I have been a fool, and I didn't see it until you came along with your pottery cart and upset everything I'd been doing."

Ivy's heart warmed, a kernel of hope erupting inside it. "Excuse me, but it was you who crashed into me." She poked his firm stomach.

"And I'm grateful that I've been paying for it ever since," he told her, squeezing her hip. .

"Er, about that." Ivy flushed. "Those vases, they weren't… Well, they weren't real Wedgwoods, so you never owed me anything, really."

Ash looked down at her, eyes narrowed. "You painted them, didn't you, you little forger?"

Ivy squirmed. "Maybe. But the vases were valuable to me," she stated, explaining about her opportunity with the merchant.

"I'm sorry I ruined your life."

Ivy raised her head to meet his eyes. "I'm not. You gave me a life—a life with you. That is worth far more than a few thousand pounds."

"I should hope so. As a Marchioness, you'll be worth quite a bit more."

Ivy's eyes grew round, and she stuttered, "What-what do you mean?"

Ash took her cheek in his hand and pressed a chaste kiss to her lips. "I mean, marry me, Ivette Wollard, smartest and most wonderfully frustrating woman I've ever met," he said, his eyes searching hers.

Ivy's lungs seized up. "I can't marry you," she said, the words forced past a lump in her throat.

"Why not?" he said with the arrogance only a peer of the realm would use in such a situation.

"I'm not … I'm no one. I'm not Corrine Morganstern, Ash. I'm Ivette Wollard, and no one will acknowledge me once they know."

"I've been thinking about that," Ash said.

"That's not good."

"Shush. I believe it's time for Reginald Morganstern to die and pass along his legacy to his favorite protégé, the Marquess of Blackbourne."

"My poor brother."

"Indeed. Don't worry. Twill be a peaceful death."

"And how does that help my situation?"

"Well, when dear old Reginald died, he made me promise to take care of his beloved orphaned sister, whom, consequently, I have come to care for as well."

"Have you, now?" she said, holding back a smile.

"Quite. In fact, I may be deeply," he kissed her jawline, "madly," he moved to her neck, "in love with her."

Ivy's breath left her. "You love me?" she whispered, trying not to dissolve from the way his skilled lips brushed kiss after kiss on her still-tender throat.

"Silly girl, can't you tell?" he asked, skimming his fingers down her arm.

"No. I can never tell anything with you," she admitted.

He chuckled. "And here I thought you had me pegged, for all your insights into my soul."

Ivy looked down, her stomach tightening. "I'm sorry for the things I said."

He shook his head. "It is I who am sorry. I didn't mean any of them."

Her lips twisted. "I think we both meant them, but..." She looked up into the fiery blue eyes that had become so familiar. Her heart was pounding, yet the warmth she saw in his gaze bolstered her. "Perhaps we can work on those things together. Perhaps we can help each other to be better."

He smiled wryly. "You've already made me into someone I don't recognize, and I think we can both agree that's a good thing. "But does that mean you'll say yes?"

he pressed.

Ivy fidgeted. She wanted to say yes with all her heart, but it was too good to be true. There must be a catch. "So, I'll be Corrine Morganstern forever? It doesn't seem right."

"Absolutely not. You'll be Lady Corrine Ivette Blackbourne, who prefers using her middle name amongst friends. I have made certain no one can ever find fault with your background. You can be exactly who you are, and everyone will love you."

She gulped. "It cannot be that simple," she insisted. "I can't just marry you."

"Don't you trust me, Princess?" he implored.

His face melted her resolve to find fault in his reasoning. "Yes?"

"I'm going to turn that question into an exclamation of pleasure if you don't answer me," he warned.

Ivy laughed. "Your threats leave something to be desired."

"It was not a threat. It was a promise."

"What if I give you an answer, but I still want the consequences?" she asked him.

He smiled a last smile. "I can make that happen."

Ivy took a deep breath. "Then, yes. Yes, Mr. Marquess, I'll marry you."

Ash grinned. "That's more like it."

Then he kept his promise.

Epilogue

Exactly one year later

"Ash, you're getting my book wet!" Ivy exclaimed, holding her novel above the steaming water.

From behind her, Ash continued his finger's path over her nipple. "That book is ridiculous anyways. Have you ever heard of someone named Krakentoot? I mean, really?"

Ivy arched her back, pressing her arse into his front. "I didn't ask for your opinion."

"I'm more interesting than him anyways," he told her, nibbling on her earlobe.

She groaned, surrendering and putting the book down on the floor next to the tub. She turned around to face him. "You might not want to insult people's names too awfully much."

"Why is that?" he asked, pulling her closer until her legs were wrapped around his hips. The water sloshed around them, spilling onto the floor.

"Well, we're going to have to name our child after plant life, you know. Ash, Ivy…"

He laughed. "I'll be sure to pity the poor thing should it ever come into being."

Ivy bit her lip. "That might be sooner than you think."

The smile left his face, and his mouth hung open. "What do you mean?"

"For a scientist, your powers of deduction are notoriously absent."

"Are you—? Are we—?" he breathed.

Ivy nodded. "Lilah's doctor confirmed it this morning. I went to see him after I suspected."

Ash gathered her to him. "I can't believe it."

"Again, it's science."

He leaned back and tucked her hair behind her ear. "It's not science. It's magic."

Ivy giggled. "I think so, too."

"I'm going to be a father," he said in wonderment.

Ivy let him process the phenomenon in silence as he touched her imperceptibly pooching stomach.

"Are you going to tell your father?" Ash asked, taking one of her hands and kissing the wrinkled fingertips.

"I don't know. Visiting him these last few months has been good for me, but I don't want our children exposed to him, especially in such a place."

Ash nodded.

"Are you going to tell Dom? I don't mind," Ivy smiled.

"He's still off in Andorra, training his dogs. Do Raquel and Delilah know?" He didn't wait for an answer, but rolled his eyes. "Of course, they do."

Ivy kissed him. "They only know before you because they noticed the signs and suggested I go to see the doctor."

"What signs?" Ash waved his hand incredulously. "I haven't noticed any signs!"

"That's because you're a man, dear, but it's all right. I know you've been busy with your projects of late."

"That's no excuse. I believe a thorough inspection of every part of your body is in order."

Ivy squeaked as his hands grasped her rump. "I won't say no to that, especially if you do that thing you did…"

Ash traced the cleft of her bum and murmured,

"Oh, you liked that, did you?"

He still had the power to make her blush. "Yes, you very well know I did."

"What if I do that thing right now?" he asked, his finger dipping lower.

She slid backwards out of his reach. "You have to meet with Maxwell early tomorrow, remember? We had better go to sleep. It's ghastly late already."

Ash groaned and ran a hand through his wet locks. "I fear it's pointless. If even the bank doesn't know what he took from the deposit box, Maxwell isn't going to tell me."

"It must have been important if that was his sole purpose in having you declared insane."

"I agree. All of that just to gain control of the Marquessate for a single day. I'd like to murder my solicitors for granting him Guardian Ad Litem privileges so quickly, but it appears Maxwell had prepared everything carefully beforehand."

"What do you think his true aim was?"

"I honestly don't know. I hadn't even looked in that deposit box since I first inherited, and there didn't seem anything of terrible value. It was mostly sentimental things from when my family was first granted the Marquessate in 1538."

Ivy frowned. "Well, I suppose if you haven't missed it by now, you don't have need for it. Perhaps we ought to let it go."

"Do you even know me, Lady Blackbourne?" he smiled wryly. "When have I ever forgotten anything?"

She rolled her eyes. "You'd better go to bed then, or you'll be rubbish in the morning."

"I can't leave you. Not now that I know..." He put his hand on her stomach carefully.

"The lemon-sized baby and I will be fine here in

the tub, and tomorrow, too," she told him, kissing his forehead.

He stroked her belly softly under the water. "So... Petunia?" He grinned.

She pursed her lips. "No."

"Spruce? Sort of sounds like Bruce."

"Not even close."

Ash reached for her ribcage and tickled her. "Why are you being difficult?"

Ivy laughed, attempting to stay his hands. "I like making things hard for you."

He growled. "You don't have to try at all. Aren't you afraid you'll cause me a megrim with your stubbornness?"

Ivy rolled her eyes. "Good try, but you haven't had one since last year."

He leaned forward and whispered in her ear. "I could let you sit on my lap and run your fingers through my hair, just in case."

Hearing his tone, her resolve melted. "Maybe you could just stay a few more minutes."

"This is going to take longer than that," he informed her.

"Maxwell doesn't want to see you anyways," she reasoned, feeling the familiar heat suffuse her at his touch.

"Exactly," Ash agreed, taking her in his arms. "And you know how I love to frustrate him."

Ivy laughed. "As long as you keep me satisfied, I don't care how frustrated he is with you."

"Twill be my pleasure, Princess."

By the time Ash was done thoroughly satisfying his wife and showing her how pleased he was with her news, the night was gone.

It was his favorite time of day, when the sky

blushed a surreal cast of tangerine over the face of all things. He enjoyed looking out over the city's skyline knowing the day would only bring more wonder. His head hummed with calculations, and it was a pleasant accompaniment to his thoughts. He would have to tell Ivy his theory about the stability of the new building being erected in the distance.

"Come back to bed, Ash," Ivy mumbled from where she lay bundled beneath the covers.

He looked back at her tousled hair and smiled, glad to obey her command.

Jasper beat him to it, getting up from his rug near the hearth to hop over to her side of the bed. His flopping ears perked as he checked to make sure she was where she should be and then plopped down next to the bed with a blustering sigh.

The hound had adapted well to the loss of his front leg, but the high-piled carpet tripped him up once in a while, causing him to stumble a bit as he galloped around Blackbourne House after them. His rescue days were behind him, but he was quite content being spoiled by the Marquess and his Marchioness on a daily basis. Ash had to admit he was Ivy's dog, really, as there wasn't a moment in the day when one wouldn't find him sprawled in all sorts of undignified positions near wherever Ivy happened to be.

Slipping beneath the sheets and gathering her to him, Ash held her as she sighed. This was all he needed, he thought, sinking into the heat flooding him with love for the woman twined around him.

And then he rested, his body and mind in perfect accord as the next glorious day dawned over them. Only one of many more he knew they would share.

The End

www.winhollows.com

EVERNIGHT PUBLISHING ®

www.evernightpublishing.com

www.ingramcontent.com/pod-product-compliance
Lightning Source LLC
Chambersburg PA
CBHW052006240626
47153CB00012B/256